PRAISE FOR

*In the Hope of Risi...*

"At first blush, Helen Scully's exquisite debut—a stirring melodrama about the Riant family of Mobile, Alabama—is like one of those long-forgotten ladies' novels of a bygone age, generally written by a Mrs. This or a Miss That: the kind of deliciously moldering relic you might find on the shelves of a gracious, if slightly reduced, old Southern home. Yet *In the Hope of Rising Again* is by no means merely a deftly executed genre exercise. Yes, the defenseless reader may swoon with each perfect sentence, as if felled by a blushing dose of Southern charm. But, as Scully traces the Catholic Riants from Reconstruction to the Great Depression, we come to realize that her rightful fictional forebears belong to a more rarefied Southern pantheon: Flannery O'Connor and James Agee, Tennessee Williams and Margaret Mitchell. . . . This is Southern Gothic writ both large and small, with historic sweep and drawing-room intimacy; the delicate story of one Southern family forced by indelicate circumstance to rise anew."
　　　　　　　　　　　　　　　　　　　　　—*Los Angeles Times*

"A spiritually rich yet unassuming book, replete with well-observed details of its characters' becalmed Southern lives . . . an astute, gracefully wrought book about the art of endurance in everyday life . . . surprising and captivating."　　　—*The New York Times*

"[A] remarkable first novel . . . Helen Scully's hypnotic style works its magic, provoking a dreamy surrender on the part of the reader. The details are perfect, from the food . . . to the sasanquas in bloom . . . a clear-eyed love letter—to family and to the South, with all their strengths and frailties, comforts and heartbreaks, beauty and sadness. 'Dazzled with grief' it is, and dazzling too."
　　　　　　　　　　　　　　　　　—*The New Orleans Times-Picayune*

*continued . . .*

"The Southern family saga is a staple of American fiction, but Helen Scully's *In the Hope of Rising Again* stands out because of the intimate way in which it brings to life its indomitable heroine, Regina Morrow. . . . In the end, this is a novel about the unmaking of a belle and her emergence as a modern woman. As such, it is an engrossing portrait of a dying society on the verge of rebirth."

—*The Baltimore Sun*

"[A] gently ambitious debut . . . Scully's light touch, even when tackling the heaviest subjects, paints a sweeping yet subtle saga; her message of resilience is inspiring while eschewing melodrama. . . . An impressive historical novel by an author to watch."

—*Publishers Weekly*

"Imaginative and enchanting, incisive and engaging, Scully's debut novel is reminiscent of works by the giants of Southern fiction."

—*Booklist*

"Though not yet thirty, Helen Scully spins an authentic tale across a twenty-year spectrum of experiences that encompasses young love, motherhood, domestic disappointment, and senility. She effortlessly renders the details of life in a Catholic household in Mobile, Alabama—hair tonic, dress patterns, the flowers lining the driveway—after World War I. The Riants' dreams and disappointments are conveyed with grace, humor, and a lushness verging on the febrile. . . . Scully has mastered the art of building narrative momentum, and her wit enlivens every page. . . . She knows how to tell a story, however, and she will surely have many more to tell."

—*The New Leader*

"Tis the best Mobile novel in fifty years . . . a thoughtful, beautifully written exploration of family, faith, and community remarkable from the pen of one so young. . . . Helen Scully has done a marvelous thing. She has captured old Mobile like a firefly in a bottle, in all its exotic complexity and grace."

—*Mobile Register*

# In the Hope of Rising Again

## HELEN SCULLY

RIVERHEAD BOOKS

NEW YORK

**THE BERKLEY PUBLISHING GROUP**
**Published by the Penguin Group**
**Penguin Group (USA) Inc.**
**375 Hudson Street, New York, New York 10014, USA**
Penguin Group (Canada), 90 Eglinton Avenue East, Suite 700, Toronto, Ontario M4P 2Y3, Canada
(a division of Pearson Penguin Canada Inc.)
Penguin Books Ltd., 80 Strand, London WC2R 0RL, England
Penguin Group Ireland, 25 St. Stephen's Green, Dublin 2, Ireland
(a division of Penguin Books Ltd.)
Penguin Group (Australia), 250 Camberwell Road, Camberwell, Victoria 3124, Australia
(a division of Pearson Australia Group Pty. Ltd.)
Penguin Books India Pvt. Ltd., 11 Community Centre, Panchsheel Park, New Delhi—110 017, India
Penguin Group (NZ), Cnr. Airborne and Rosedale Roads, Albany, Auckland 1310, New Zealand
(a division of Pearson New Zealand Ltd.)
Penguin Books (South Africa) (Pty.) Ltd., 24 Sturdee Avenue, Rosebank, Johannesburg 2196,
South Africa

Penguin Books Ltd., Registered Offices: 80 Strand, London WC2R 0RL, England

This is a work of fiction. Names, characters, places, and incidents either are the product of the author's
imagination or are used fictitiously, and any resemblance to actual persons, living or dead, business es-
tablishments, events, or locales is entirely coincidental.

Copyright © 2004 by Helen Scully
Cover art and design by Royce Becker
Book design by Stephanie Huntwork

All rights reserved.
No part of this book may be reproduced, scanned, or distributed in any printed or electronic form with-
out permission. Please do not participate in or encourage piracy of copyrighted materials in violation of
the author's rights. Purchase only authorized editions.
RIVERHEAD is a registered trademark of Penguin Group (USA) Inc.
The RIVERHEAD logo is a trademark of Penguin Group (USA) Inc.

First Penguin Press hardcover edition: August 2004
First Riverhead trade paperback edition: August 2005
Riverhead trade paperback ISBN: 1-59448-103-2

The Library of Congress has catalogued the Penguin Press hardcover edition as follows:

Scully, Helen, date.
    In the hope of rising again / Helen Scully.
        p. cm.
    ISBN 1-59420-025-4
    1. Southern States—Fiction.  I. Title.
PS3619.C79I5 2004
813'.6—dc22              2003070747

PRINTED IN THE UNITED STATES OF AMERICA

10  9  8  7  6  5  4  3  2  1

FOR MARY TRIGG SCULLY

# Part One

## THE FATHER

## Epithalamium

THEY WERE LED TO THE CAR by a raucous crowd. After waving from the window and exchanging shy smiles—*my going-away suit is beautiful*—they were alone on the road. Adjusting themselves on the bench. The Chevrolet, a touring car, reached the toll road and picked up speed. He wondered how many feet it would take to come to a complete stop at thirty-five miles an hour. She envisioned the car's trunk, filled with a set of light brown leather suitcases with French blue trim, and ran rapidly through the important items in her luggage. They would arrive at Choctaw Bluff, a good eighty miles from Mobile, by nightfall.

"What time will we get there?" she asked with a smile.

"Nightfall," he said, taking her left hand in his right. She felt far from everything she had known and it was a good feeling, she decided. They went forward, letting the car go forward, not letting the car go forward, next to each other on the seat. It was May 1919. "What will we do tomorrow?"

"You'll rest," he said, releasing her hand. "I've got to go to the lumberyards."

"All right."

The smell of manure penetrated the automobile as it went deeper into the country. "It was a strange day getting married, don't you think?"

"Yes," she answered and turned toward the window.

They were cutting north with the late sun on the left side of their faces, the roads becoming bumpy and kicking up clouds of pale brown dust. A crepe de chine veil over her smart black hat and black gloves protected her face and hands, but her duster gradually turned reddish brown on the arms and shoulders and lap, and Charles's face was caked with red dust, sparing the white circles under his driving goggles. Ahlong crossed her mind but she didn't bother with it. Fields of cotton shot past her eyes. The light reddened as the reeds on the side of the road became thicker.

At dusk they stopped for she-crab soup and Lime Cola, and back on the road they began sorting out the relatives, laughing and discussing their gifts. It grew chilly as the evening advanced, but raising the roof and fastening the side curtains did little to warm them. They hit patches of mud. Three times Charles had to use a piece of wood to jack a back tire out of a pit of wet clay. Their pace slowed to a crawl, as it was impossible to go quickly over such uneven roads. Falling silent, they held hands. She thought of Ahlong, turned to Charles.

"How do you think it will be?"

He stiffened. "What?"

"It will be good with us—marriage—don't you think?"

"Yes," he said.

By the time they arrived at the clapboard cabin Regina was sound asleep across the front seat, and Charles carried her barely awake across the threshold. They sat by light from a kerosene lamp at the small wooden table in the kitchen having cold fried chicken and warm beer from their picnic basket. She felt her energy return, and Charles began to tell her in low tones about a recurrent dream he had—of a black dog and a white dog fighting each other on a green lawn—and how sometimes, when lying in bed just before falling asleep, he felt a boulder of dust rolling toward him down a hall and rolling over him, crushing him, he, nothing but vastness.

"Don't you recognize anything?" she asked gently.

"I recognize the confrontation in it, of course. But no."

"Do I ever appear?"

"Sometimes in another type of dream." He shot her an intimate look, which she ignored by clearing the dishes. "Do I?"

"Sometimes," she said.

A strained silence reigned in their little bedroom at the back of the house.

"Should I prepare for bed?" Regina asked.

"Yes."

"Are you tired?"

"Yes. Are you?"

"Yes," she said, and began to take down her hair. He opened the windows and let in the late-spring air and a faint smell of the river. The idea of bed was delicious to them both. Walking up and down the room, he removed his coat and vest. He took off his shoes and socks and embraced her.

"Beautiful," he whispered, and she believed him. They tired themselves of their mouths. He was amazed there were so many layers of cloth between himself and her skin. They compared tongues, thumbs and knees, argued briefly over whose skin was softer. *This is the beginning,* she thought, and let her breasts be just as they were. She counted up his ribs while he kissed them—seven. When it was over he noticed her cheeks were wet. Then they talked and then they didn't talk while memorizing the flecks in each other's eyes.

She slept deeply, clutching his arm. It wasn't until morning that she saw her new life in full light. She was charmed by such simplicity at first. The plank floors were carpetless, the ceilings low and the windows, one to each room, were shutterless and curtainless. All the walls were white, all the furniture unvarnished pine. Charles had designed the house himself, she knew, one large box divided into four equal-size rooms, parlor and dining room at the front, bedroom and kitchen at the back, with a central hallway between front and back doors, a stone pantry and maid's room shooting off the kitchen. It was all relatively clean.

Outside she realized her isolation. There was no front porch. A couple of yards of land, splotched with tufts of neatly trimmed weeds, separated the house from a dirt road. No doubt Charles had gotten a yardman to try to make it presentable. Walking around the side, she encountered an underground storehouse which was locked. A low, plain porch extended across the back of the house. Here the land, broken occasionally by swampy patches where reeds, cane and mosquitoes grew up, extended flat forward in pale brown grass, hitting impenetrable woods just before the eyes' limit.

Looking to the ground, she laughed to herself, because she was sure she was nowhere, laughed because the thought was hilarious: that marriage is a wilderness. She had chosen this and now she must love it; now she must make it comfortable. Mathilde's last words to her, trailing across the silent landscape of her mind, could not make her feel regret. To the right of the porch was a small herb garden beside a water pump; at some distance was a chicken coop. A stone path leading to a cluster of hollyhocks suggested the route to the privy, an oak box barely scented by honeysuckle. Well, she would get used to it. "Last night was wonderful," Charles had said that morning before he left for the lumberyards.

"Yes," she said, studying her plate. The last mystery was over and she felt proud to be on the other side of it. Yet she was embarrassed that the motions of sex had come to her so effortlessly. "I love you," she said, pouring him another cup of coffee to hide her loss of composure.

"I love you, too," he said as he stood and kissed the top of her head, "but I have to go."

Within a week Regina established a system to protect her from idleness while Charles was at the lumberyards. Before dawn she was up, dressing herself, making coffee and frying bacon all at the same time, the biscuits browning in the oven below, the eggs lined up on the counter. She sat next to him on the wooden plank bench while he ate. It was too early for talk. When he drove off, she opened all the windows, ate her own breakfast and returned to bed, where she lay, imagining how he would touch her when he got home. She dozed and read in bed until ten. Sweeping, mopping, dusting and dishes were followed by a light lunch.

In the remaining hours before his return, she scoured the roadside for wildflowers to place around the house in the wedding-present vases. Or she sewed curtains for the parlor, crocheted lace for the trim of a second nightgown and rehearsed the things she would tell him when he returned. With repetition, the motivation behind such tasks dulled, but fortunately she was not averse to physical labor. Hour upon hour she decapitated the dandelions that popped up ceaselessly from the edge of the porch to the woods, an expanse three times that of her father's property on Government Street.

Her maid, Camilla, traveled up from Mobile at the end of June to help with the pregnancy. By then a flower garden of violets, brilliant scarlet geraniums and a clump of white daylilies was thriving opposite the herb garden. Next she had the Negro yardman Jack build a stone walkway to the storehouse. Her garden laid out, she began experimenting with poultry powder, which promised to double a hen's production rate, and cultivating several types of late-harvesting tomatoes.

Long after the sun had ripened and poured its reds through the window of the room where she sat resting, after the temperature had dropped so that she pulled a light blanket over her knees, after the crickets, locusts and fireflies had gotten to their noise, and after she heard the passing of several horses that weren't his, she heard her husband's footsteps in the sand by the front door. Rapidly she lit the lamps. Camilla prepared supper while Regina watched over him having his drink, remarking to herself on his growing handsomeness. She was not yet sick of the smell of wet pine that came off him. "How was your day?" she asked, taking his hand and sliding close to him on the couch.

"Oh fine, just fine," he said with a smile.

"How can it be fine when I'm not there to keep you company?"

He chuckled. "That's what I meant to say, darling. I can't wait until this whole business is over and I can spend my days following you around the house. As it is, things might take longer than I thought."

"Oh?"

"The demand for lumber has fallen off since the end of the war, you know."

"I don't mind, Charles. Look at this," she said, thrusting the daily evidence of her wifely industry under his nose, today a pillow embroidered with a large *M*. "If you stayed home, we'd have to teach you to sew, wouldn't we? And I don't know if you'd ever catch on. Then your confidence would plummet, and you'd suffer, I'm sure, from purposelessness."

He was laughing. "No, I was planning just to sit around and watch you work. I'll be your biggest decoration. Surely that's a purpose!" The dinner bell rang; he stood and looked down at her. "But you'll have to pay for my services—in kisses."

"Well, I'm not sure if I can afford it," she said as she took his hand and he pulled her to her feet. "They're selling Father's newspaper, you know, and I get a portion." She positioned her face in the air close to his, "but I don't think I'll make any kisses off of it."

"You'll have to pay me back with the ones I give you, then," he said, pressing his mouth to hers until Camilla appeared in the doorway.

Overexcited by the china and Charles, both of which were flattered by the candlelight, Regina forgot how tired he was and tended to chatter or excessively critique the menu. When he was reading the newspaper in the parlor afterward she still had things she wanted to discuss. "The smoked ham isn't a problem, but with it getting warmer, the beef has rotted twice this week. Sometimes I can't stand the thought of the coming heat. But I also love summer."

He looked up. "All right," and returned to the paper.

"So we'll have to eat it the day we buy it," she said a moment later.

His eyes scanned the newspaper before flicking up at her. "Right," he said. "You know, I've had about enough of Europe. I don't see why we have to teach them anything. They can all go to the devil as far as I'm concerned."

"Well, I've always wanted to go to Vienna for the opera. But I think it would be wonderful to have an international government. The League of Nations—it sounds, I don't know, mighty, don't you think?" His eyes had dropped to the paper but he was listening. She continued, "They should let everyone belong to it and everyone have an equal vote: every individual in the world."

"It doesn't work that way," he said, his eyes glimmering.

"Well, that Cabot Lodge is awful."

"I know." He chuckled quietly as he turned the page.

She rose and spent some time closing the curtains. "Don't you like these curtains, Charles?"

"I love them," he said without lifting his head.

She moved to his side of the sofa, sitting very close. "Maybe we should be less affectionate in front of Camilla."

"I don't care, but if you do we can stop."

"I don't care either," she said, her hand on his thigh. He continued to read.

She crossed the room and began rummaging through a small box on the bookcase—she had already read all the books—returned to the couch and thumbed through her sewing notes. Camilla had stacked the letters from her brothers on the side table, but she read them only when she wanted to remind herself not to return to Mobile. "We tried rubbing corn oil into the floor to make it shine," she said after a moment, "but it didn't work. It did work, but we realized it would take too much." He didn't answer. "I guess you've read enough of the paper for one night, don't you think?"

Soon she had moved to his lap, draped her arm around his shoulder and had him reciting to her the reasons he loved her, that she was sweet and beautiful and smart, things she knew. He expanded on his plans for the house he would build for them on his land at Spring Hill, describing the gardens, porches, baths, nursery, promising her every appliance under the sun, though she, smiling and playing with his buttons, shook her head at such ostentations. "Don't banana trees have such nice leaves? You can do a lot with them, actually, in terms of flavoring."

He tipped her chin back and kissed her neck. "Flavoring what?"

"Pork," she whispered, bringing her head up and pressing her lips to his eyelids. "I've been hungry for you all day."

"We'll have two hundred banana trees then."

In bed beside him was more luxuriously comfortable than she had thought possible from life. They began making love with Camilla in mind, trying to be quiet so that she wouldn't hear them. Midway they'd forgotten that anyone existed but the two of them. They fell asleep, entwined in each other's arms, love palpable in the air over their bed. They had innumerable positions for sleeping: he on his back, she on her stomach with her forehead against his shoulder; he on his side, she on her side pressed up to his back; she on her stomach facing away from him, he on his side facing her with one arm on her back and one leg over the back of her legs, but his leg was too heavy and she had to slip out from under it after he had fallen asleep. Throughout the night they maintained some physical contact, a hand on a thigh or chest or stomach.

Sleeping was heaven; being awake with him at times annoyed her. If she went to bed earlier than he did, he might come into the room with whiskey breath and whiskers and try to kiss her or grab at her breasts. He failed to comb his hair. He didn't realize when little pieces of bread were stuck to his lips and she found herself wiping his face for him. When she was reading before sleep, her favorite quiet time of the day, if he tried to lie next to her, he sniffled at the wrong times and too often he was unaware of his body. He bit his nails and spit the chips onto the bedspread, scratched the inside of his ears at length, readjusted his genitals.

On receiving Regina's letter, Camilla had agreed to leave Mobile and help with the pregnancy. She had some distant relatives among the Chickasaws and, she replied, Mobile was no fun with the Colonel no more and Regina gone, too. Regina was grateful to have company during the long hours without Charles, but the two women could thoroughly clean the cabin in less than an hour. Tired of inventing tasks, they sat on the back porch watching the landscape burn out. Occasionally one or both of them strolled to the edge of the woods and even sat there in the pale, dry grass, looking back at the house. Or they set off to an indeterminate spot along the sceneryless road—the river was too far for Regina—before stopping out of sheer boredom and returning the way they had come, covered in dust. Returned to the back porch. Talked about hairstyles. "That's how they is" was what Camilla said when Regina ventured a complaint about Charles.

"Maybe so," she said as she followed a mosquito near her elbow. "I suppose so."

Camilla slapped at her ankle. "They bad," she said. "But as far as the mens, it's God's way and they ain't nothing wrong with God."

"He says he wants to do everything for me," Regina said, flicking at her knuckle and waving the air near her ear. "I don't understand what the 'everything' is," she went on with a nervous laugh, "because when he's home he reads the paper."

"That's liable to wear on a marriage." Camilla made it to her feet and went indoors to gather the laundry. While the sheets boiled, they hummed "I'm Always Chasing Rainbows" over their sewing until it became too hot to sew or sing. Then Regina took up *Tess of the D'Urbervilles*, but no amount of iced tea could prevent her mouth from becoming parched after reading half a chapter aloud, and Camilla kept calling Tess a fool. Soon they stared off over the grass at the signs of a scorching summer to come. "It's on the way," Camilla intoned, and Regina shuddered.

Already she didn't feel well. So constantly was she nauseated that the slightest disturbance caused her to vomit. The presence of flies in the kitchen, the slimy water at the bottom of her vases and the smell of ham conspired to send her gagging to the side yard to spit up the little she had eaten. She could not bear to be without Charles for so long during the day, and though she endeavored to hide it, her uncontrollable crying one morning at the beginning of July delayed him from the lumberyards for several hours. Stroking her face, he pleaded with her to bear up. "Things might take longer than I originally thought," he said, "especially if I stay home every morning."

She had heard him say this so many mornings, her worry evolved into a silent panic she tried to ignore, though not always with success. "What things, Charles?" she asked now with a tight smile. She would never get her mind around the things that would take so long. "What exactly are you trying to do? Maybe I can help."

But he scowled, she noticed, whenever she offered to help. "I'm trying to fix up the property for sale, so we can use the money to build our house at Spring Hill. I've told you this a hundred times, Regina."

"I know. What do you need to do to get it ready for sale?" But he didn't answer. Later she would admit to having never understood what Charles accomplished during their time at Choctaw Bluff. The lumber business wasn't sold until many years later, and when they left town at last, in the middle of December, whatever his goals had been were not reached. For now she concentrated on stopping crying. "It's going to be fine, Charles."

"That's what I keep telling you, darling," he said.

When he was gone, she fell instantly to sleep. It was late afternoon when she woke; the kitchen was empty. She went out to the porch and found Camilla there.

"It's on its way," Camilla said, and Regina looked off toward the distant trees with a new blankness, imagining that the heat was a material thing, and an enemy, advancing on their little house. "We'll make it, babe," Camilla said softly. Moments later the frogs, beginning a song, gave them their cue to go in and see about the dinner. At ten o'clock she was back in bed staring at the ceiling; Charles was still not home.

## Pax Mobilia

COLONEL RIANT WASN'T REALLY a colonel. At the end of the war he had been just a lieutenant. Though the *Mobile Chronicle* would make a great deal of the twenty-six bullet holes in his uniform and the small poniard he owned, the handle of which was a Yankee bone, he was unable to boast about the number of Yankees he had killed.

Clear in his mind as to the righteousness of the cause, he had joined up with the Louisiana Chasseurs, a band of foot soldiers collected in New Orleans, even before Fort Sumter. He was prepared to die, but the Chasseurs waited around Fort Pickens through May and June 1861. After advancing on East Pass, they were recalled to Bayou Dreux, which the seventeen-year-old Riant found an excellent spot for fishing. At last called out to Virginia for what would be the First Battle of Manassas, the Chasseurs made it only as far as an oil factory in Pensacola before the order was rescinded. Much to his dismay, Private Riant was forced to remain there through the summer months, playing euchre with the local ladies, lending money to friends and making it to Confession as often as he could.

The middle of September, it seemed he'd gotten his wish: the

Chasseurs, after stopping for several weeks in Montgomery, were to march into Virginia to win the war. But after a brief advance toward Manassas under the great General Beauregard, his regiment retreated to the hills. There through the month of October, he found time to go hiking and eat a large number of grapes, walnuts and chestnuts. Already the excitement of war had worn off. He missed his family terribly—their letters, he wrote back, were "balm to a bleeding heart." While on duty he had waking dreams of sitting next to his mother at High Mass on All Saints' Day in New Orleans and bringing flower arrangements to the family graves. A series of Confederate blunders put him near Centreville for the holidays, when his homesickness reached its height. In March of '62 the Chasseurs were involved with some friendly fire against the Washington Artillery in what he called "one of the coldest battles of the war"—a snowball fight.

He prayed. And kept up his spirits, though two of his dear sisters died of scarlet fever while he was gone. Perversely, he came to value his intelligence as often as he was frustrated by the incompetence of his officers. And came to loathe inactivity so much that he took to writing poetry:

*AN ODE TO THE OCCASION*

*We have left our homes in the Sunny South,*
*To sustain our rights at the cannon's mouth;*
*And drive back the foe who so insolently*
*Proclaims that the South shall no longer be free:*
*And the yoke of the Tyrant in Washington,*
*Shall adorn the neck of each true Southron';*
*And the homes where we sported in childhood's days*
*Shall light the morn with their lurid blaze.*

*But let the Yankees beware of the day*
*When the Chasseurs shall meet them in battle array.*
*For each one has registered an oath, to imbrue*
*His hands in the blood of that hireling crew,*
*And make the proud North resound with the cry*
*Which is borne on the air when loved ones die.*

*May the wrath of Heaven fall on and blight*
*The first who shows symptoms of cowardly flight;*
*May the earth offer no spot on its broad face*
*To shelter him in his deep disgrace.*
*But those who fearlessly bear their part*
*Shall have a place in each Southern heart—*
*Though ages may pass their names will still be*
*Linked with the Southern Confederacy.*

In battle near Sharpsburg in June, he earned the nickname "Achilles." The Chasseurs charged. Private Riant didn't notice his comrades retreating and marched proudly uphill through direct fire. Behind enemy lines, he captured thirteen Yankees single-handedly, after which he was made lieutenant. Twenty-six other brave Chasseurs were dead, however, and Riant was trapped through the winter outside of Richmond, waiting for his battalion to be reformed. He instigated some night skirmishes near Black Water but got news of Chancellorsville while wallowing in a trench in Suffolk. Malaria struck him prior to Gettysburg, which he spent in the Louisiana hospital in Richmond, being looked after by the Sisters of Charity and continuing his letters.

Reading *Life of Mrs. Elizabeth Ann Seton, Afterwards Mother E. A. Seton*, he wrote to his cousin Thérèse, "has made me wish more to be a woman so I could be a Sister of Charity. How I did envy the inhab-

itants of St. Joseph's Valley whilst I was reading it. I have also read another book called *Lionello;* it is a Catholic novel, something like *Florentine.* This one, however, treats of Secret Societies led by Garibaldi,
Massini and other Red Republican leaders, who have bathed Italy in
blood since the time of the first Napoleon. Poor Sister Mary Vincent
has no easy task in supplying me with books, for I read one of 350
to 400 pages in twenty-four hours; she has even been so good as to
send to her friends in town to get some for me. Ain't she a Sister of
Charity!"

At the hospital he received the transfer he had sought under the
assumption that he would see more action as a Marine. But when he
reached Fort Gaines he was commanded to remain with his sights
on Farragut's blockader, listening to the fall of Mobile from across
the water. On August 5, 1864, he was captured in a combined attack
by the federal fleet and army and moved to the Union prison at
New Orleans. By this time everyone was past exhausted with the
war. His family and friends loitered daily outside the prison window, bribing the Union guards with bananas to see him. After visiting with his family, he drank coffee with the same guards and
discussed the merits of Stonewall Jackson.

Already the generals were making deals. Chosen to be traded for
a Union soldier of equal rank, Lieutenant Riant was moved from the
federal prison to an office building on Common Street and held under special guard.

"That exchange being delayed," the *Times Picayune* would de-
clare in a story about the Colonel that they ran at the turn of the
century,

he soon made preparations to escape, which were for a time foiled
by a traitor. Securing his removal among them, more rapid progress
was made, and on the night of October 13, 1864, with twelve other

men, Riant escaped through a hole they had made in the brick wall. Leaving Paymaster Richardson within the prison walls, who, being disabled by a wound, remained to amuse the guard by discoursing sweet music on the flute, Riant climbed over the balconies to the street and found temporary refuge with friends in the city. He was furnished with funds from the Prisoner's Relief Committee and driven outside the city in a carriage by his friends. Plunging into the swamps, Riant evaded a party of pickets he encountered, stole a frail pirogue from a German Yankee sympathizer and set to navigating the tortuous bayous.

After seven days and nights of desperate struggle he reached Ponchatoula, about fifty miles distant. He returned to Mobile by walking, and met along the road Captain Fry, the famous Confederate naval officer, who lost his life years after at the hands of the Spaniards at Santiago, Cuba. Riant was given command of two thirty-two-pound guns on Captain Fry's gunboat *Morgan*. In this capacity he served until the boat surrendered on the Tombigbee Waterway on April 21, 1865.

If, as Lieutenant Riant claimed, guardian angels protected him during the war, then they never left his side. War had shown him how easy it is to break the column of life. His heart had been devastated too many times to name—the deaths of his sisters, his boyhood friends, two of his cousins and countless comrades beside him—enough to know that there is nothing to do in this life on earth but help others progress as far as they can and to take as much pleasure in it as possible.

After Appomattox he obtained parole and moved to Mobile to propose to the love of his life, Regina St. Peter, daughter of his dear friend and superior Major St. Peter. Fueled by the stories that her father had told him during the war, Lieutenant Riant had used her image, however vague, to give him strength in many of his hours of misery during the war. When passing through Mobile with Captain Fry, he made it a point to call on her. Her gentle face and manners confirmed for him his peacetime destiny. Mutually desperate for union, they were married within a year, after which he moved into the St. Peter mansion on Government Street with his bride and her father and there enjoyed what he would remember as the two most blissful years of his life. Yellow fever struck her down in the summer of '67. He nursed her around the clock, prayed with her, begged her to communicate with him beyond the grave, promised never to re-marry, vowed to unite with her in the afterlife. Her father died of the same affliction two weeks later.

Though his beloved had gone, Riant could not leave Mobile. In-stead, in his grief, he made it a business to love the city, a business that for him was lucrative. Suddenly he was rich, charming, single, faithful and prematurely gray, and before long he became known as "the Colonel" out of affection and respect. It was custom in the years following the war to call all Confederate veterans by a high rank. In Mobile there were two Generals and countless Majors but there was only one Colonel—Colonel Riant. For one thing, the death of the St. Peters left him majority owner of the *Mobile Chronicle*, the only newspaper in town.

And then there was the dairy. When a herd of cattle was deliv-ered to the docks with no one there to claim them, he was on the spot to sign the receipt. Before long every household in town put out bottles for the Colonel's morning milk. The sons of a friend had bi-cycles but no place to ride, so he built a bicycle track on his land, charged a small entry fee and gave half of the proceeds to his unhinged uncle Edwin in exchange for running the place. Soon everyone in Mobile had a bicycle and was riding around Colonel Riant's track. By the time he had made himself sole publisher of the

*Chronicle,* he was a member of the United Confederate Veterans, the Knights of Columbus and the Mardi Gras secret society, the Order of Myths. Knowing he would never return to New Orleans, he had twenty graves of loved ones moved from there to the Magnolia Cemetery in Mobile.

Colonel Riant knew things had been easy financially for him since the war, and while thanking God daily for his good fortune, he never supposed he deserved it. Even before he took control of the newspaper, he was sending flowers to if not attending every funeral written up in the local section. He sent hams to all Baptisms. He picked up any ill-used person in his path and invented a career at the paper for him or her. Drunks and street urchins became paperboys. Negro boys became proprietors of corner newsstands. Widow Sabatier was made book reviewer, and the spinster Battiste sisters were made gossip co-columnists, a position they held until their deaths less than two hours apart some thirty years later. The Colonel put the money down for Lou Fontaine's photography studio and funded part of the electric streetcar line.

He bought winter coats for the many characters who roamed the streets and hired vagabonds to work in his dairy. A town council member, prize giver at livestock fairs, a ubiquitous figure at historical society meetings, benefactor to Providence Hospital, host to visiting opera singers, namesake to streets, lector at Mass and auctioneer for ladies' benefits, he was all the time buying meals for the prostitutes along the docks, helping old Negro women across the street, giving candy to children and flattering ladies' hats.

Elected to play King Felix in the Mardi Gras celebrations of 1873, Colonel Riant was instrumental in establishing the local fairy tale: that Mobile is capital of a vast empire and is ruled by a potentate named Felix. The extent of his empire is so great that Felix can visit only once a year. At high noon on Shrove Monday, citizens see his ship sashaying over the waters of Mobile Bay. Entering the city, he gallops down Government Street and stops at Bienville Square under the balcony of the Battle House Hotel, where sits his queen. He salutes her and rides on through the streets, bringing his message of revelry and basking in the glory showered on him as he clatters past. He returns to the side of his queen to hold court and feast in earnest until midnight on Shrove Tuesday, when he disappears across the ocean for another year.

Colonel Riant didn't stop there. He helped Bishop O'Sullivan formulate a plan for the support of Catholic orphans, and when the citizens of Mobile were quarantined during the last great yellow fever epidemics of 1878 and 1897, Colonel Riant threw himself behind the Can't Get Away Club, which raised money for, hired, organized and distributed paid nurses and medical supplies to the suffering, white and Negro alike. He himself worked tirelessly in the places not yet infected, tacking up cheesecloth to the windows and bringing formaldehyde and sulfur candles to each household. He was everywhere at once, praying with the living, draining ditches, answering questions at the club office, delivering food to the bereft, running to the bank to cash checks.

Fifteen years had passed in this flurry of activity, and at last Father Lusch gently suggested that he find a new wife. At the age of thirty-eight, the Colonel remarried, remarkably, a second Regina, this one Regina Dumaine. From the beginning, he was conscious that he was marrying her out of esteem rather than love. Her family had suffered financially since the war, yet she was so proud! It made him smile. She was pious, handsome, quiet, and possessed an air of sadness about her that he took for depth. Though she had been only three at the start of the war, her two older brothers perished—one at Vicksburg, one in the Battle of New Orleans—and she enjoyed fame for many years after surrender for being the little girl who spit at a Yankee officer.

Until the end of her life, she crossed the street to avoid passing a

Yankee on the sidewalk, and could tell anyone who asked which Mobilians had Yankee blood. Though he possessed a more forgiving nature, the Colonel appreciated this rebellious quality in his new wife; he took it for bravery. He couldn't help being disappointed, however, in the way this second Regina performed her wifely duties—with frosty equanimity—but he told himself that their burgeoning family made up for it. She bore him four sons—Peter, Louis, Felix and George—and one daughter, the third Regina.

The second Regina, hence Mother Riant, had also entertained hopes of loving the Colonel but decided early on that genuine intimacy would not be possible. She thought the Colonel was selfish, pompous and sentimental, and the fourteen-year age difference did nothing to endear him to her. She saw him as a slave to the populace, a victim of the city's demands on him, though she pretended to be proud of his civic involvement. She thought it tasteless how he threw his money around, and grew sick and tired of hearing him tell the story of his oh-so-gallant escape from the New Orleans prison, a story that got longer and longer with each telling.

She had no one to complain to—all the men in town were his friends and none of the women had any sympathy for her. In 1889 hers was the first house in Mobile to have electric lighting. She had no reins on her personal expenses. If she required fashion or furniture, china or silver or gold, art or travel or turquoise, she could simply request it in her always accurate manner. If it occurred to her that a room needed rewallpapering, she had only to pick up the new telephone. The mansion on Government Street had belonged to the first Regina, however, and in every cornice, every floorboard, every doorframe she could find traces of her influence. No matter how much of the Colonel's money she spent, she couldn't change the fact that his first wife had lived and died in this house.

It was noon on August 4, 1898, when the third Regina was born.

The Angelus was playing on the church bells, so Mother Riant chose to name her daughter Angela Mary. She was bedridden, however, and could not attend the Baptism—when the Colonel went against her wishes and officially registered the baby as Regina Angela instead of Angela Mary.

Mother Riant was furious when she heard: a third Regina! Who could bear it? She felt betrayed. As mother of the child, she had final rights to decide the name, and she thought it sly that the Colonel would take advantage of the very process that had delivered the child to go against her wishes. Why did he love the name so much? She was sick of it! Its heaviness, the sound of it put a thickness in her throat. It sounded medical and made her think red. She felt, without knowing why, that the Colonel had named their daughter after the first Regina instead of after her. She didn't want to compete with another Regina—a third!—for her husband's attention. What nerve!

Any trace of fondness she held for the Colonel evaporated after this Baptism, and behind the screens of prosperity, life became increasingly difficult for Mother Riant, as is often the case for wives of popular men. Such a wife either complements her husband with a feminine version of the same sociability or, if prone to jealousy, she sets out to define his opposite, accentuating his lacks by filling them so consciously. With her insistence on the economical, Mother Riant made her husband appear excessively generous, and next to her reserve, his geniality seemed garish. He bought an automobile but she refused to ride in it. Since he liked his bourbon, she drank lemonade, and as he divided himself among the town's charities, she made an only cause out of her sons. She imagined she needed to take everything seriously that he did not, lest something important fall through the cracks, and her unwavering focus on "the good" made him look careless. But no one likes to be so sober, and Mother Riant felt forced into it by a law of reaction that she had done nothing to create. Meanwhile she was dimly aware that she would rather be her husband than herself.

What she achieved in positioning herself against the Colonel was her own isolation. All she had were her four sons, who, under her auspices, grew up in splendid attire with the best of schooling, the latest of toys and, later, more expensive fancies, such as mohair-lined coats from St. Petersburg, collections of rifles from the Revolution, horses, sandalwood soap, hair oils, four enormous rolltop desks and, eventually, a red felt billiard table. It was expected that the sons would take over the running of the newspaper at the Colonel's retirement, but they were ill equipped when the time came. Colonel Riant was a presence indomitable; they figured that preparing for his absence was useless, while Mother Riant insisted they were too precious for hard work.

# The Third Regina

PERSONALITY IS A TRAIT that makes for rare bursts of color in the long, thin branches of the family tree. There are those, like the four sons, that look bad on paper, that seem to have been inept and incapable of personal success, but among their contemporaries they were well loved, at least by Mother Riant and the third Regina. All the Riant children were spoiled, but what Colonel Riant had in the way of guardian angels, in the way of charm, in the way of a love for God and the gift of life, he passed to his daughter, the third Regina, Regina Angela, heroine.

Dedicated to the Virgin Mary at birth, the third Regina wore the Virgin's colors of blue and white every day for the first seven years of her life. From the day of her Baptism, she was a point of contention between her mother and father. As an infant suffering with colic, Regina tested her mother's and nurse's patience. They could do nothing for her. She would cry all night long unless the Colonel held her in his arms, back and forth and back and forth in the rocking chair, humming a song that, as the night advanced, evolved into a sad and slow *uhhn, uhhn, uhhn*. Then the two drifted off to sleep in each other's arms.

On the grounds that Regina was being treated too much like a baby, which of course she was, Mother Riant launched her initial complaints. "If she doesn't get used to her nurse, she'll be whining for you day and night and you'll never get a moment's rest." But Colonel Riant hoped she would whine for him. By now he had a way with his daughter, could tell that their personalities were suited to each other, and he knew more than anyone how to get her to sleep. When called away from his guests by her shrieks, he saw proudly that his very presence brought her peace. Later, after she had recounted all her brothers had told her, he assured her that there weren't ghosts under her bed by whispering, "Don't believe anything your brothers say, child," and soon he could simply ask her to please go to sleep.

During the day he took her around town with him, introducing her to all his friends—gentleman farmers, sharecroppers and shopkeepers, servants, society ladies and women of ill repute, white and Negro children her age and older, priests and aged aunts. He would often leave her to entertain the copy editors for the few minutes it took him to handle business in the *Chronicle*'s inner office, then the two continued their pleasure tour, with excursions to Fort Conde, to Monroe Park, to Dauphin Island, never ending without a series of treats, usually chocolates, cherries and fresh cream, but also toys and clothes and useless things that attracted her eye.

Regina never wanted the days to end, and stretched out the treat-finding portion of their excursions for as long as possible. Mother Riant was of course livid for one reason or another when they returned. She noticed the patches of sticky dirt on each side of her daughter's face and would yank her to the sink and rub at her cheeks and hands with a rough, wet towel. "You're spoiling her dinner, rotting her teeth and setting a dissolute example for her soul," her mother would say to her father. "I'm scared to see what will become of this child."

Colonel Riant looked uncomfortable but rolled his eyes at his daughter, who giggled. He was surprised that he didn't care what his wife thought on this subject. He was sure he was doing nothing wrong. He taught Regina to ride a horse, then a bike. He taught her to read, and by the time she was six had her reading the Sunday edition of his newspaper, cover to cover, giving her a silver dollar for every typo she found. In the evenings he drilled her on her addition and multiplication tables, telling her, "It's better to give away money than to have it stolen from you. Always double-check your figures, and always overpay the people who work for you."

When Regina was older, they spent the evenings reading aloud from *A Tale of Two Cities,* commenting on the Christ-like sacrifice of Sydney Carton. She even learned to recite his last lines before the guillotine—"I am the Resurrection and the Life, saith the Lord: he that believeth in me, though he were dead, yet shall he live: and whosoever liveth and believeth in me shall never die"—but Mother Riant often found an excuse to enter and call her away. "Men and women have different minds, you know," she said to the Colonel. "It's not healthy for a girl to be so precocious." Then she pushed Regina up the stairs to the dressing table and used a comb to rip the tangles out of her hair, her anger and disapproval unmistakable as she combed and combed, while Regina's eyes filled with tears.

On the morning of her First Communion, before they left for the ceremony, her father took her to a remote corner of the back garden and crouched down so that they were eye to eye as he presented her with a heavy golden cross, flecked with rubies, with her initials, RAR, and the date, MAY 12, 1910, engraved on the back. "Today you have reached the age of reason, and you are expected to know that only Christ is responsible for your salvation," he told her sternly as she stared at the gleaming object against its black velvet box. "You are expected to conduct yourself as an angel from here on and beg Christ to forgive you for your weaknesses. It is a great privilege. Do you understand?"

"Yes," she said, looking earnestly into his eyes.

He turned her by the shoulders, hooked the clasp at the back of her neck, adjusting her white lace collar around the chain, turning her back around and positioning the cross on the center of her dress. He put both hands on her shoulders and looked at the cross. "Every Sunday, after you take Communion, kneel down, say a Hail Mary, and ask God for the salvation of your soul—that's all it takes to be saved. Do you understand what I mean?"

"Yes, Papa," she said. "I'm going to be a Sister of Charity."

"We'll see," he said kindly, standing with his hand on the back of her neck. "I'm very proud of you," and he led her back to the house.

As soon as she saw the cross, Mother Riant protested that it was "far too nice an object for a twelve-year-old to wear," but Regina and her father promised, with the special understanding they shared after his recent speech now thick around them, that she would wear it only on Sundays.

When it became time for her to enter all-day school, both she and the Colonel were unbearably sad, but the Colonel felt no compunction in taking her out early to join him for lunch at the Belmont, to shop with him for birthday presents for her brothers, to eat fresh oysters along the docks. She did well in school, and in the afternoons her father helped her with her schoolwork and constantly gave her real-life examples, had her handle the money for any purchases and instructed her in how to treat others from all walks of life with respect. When Mother Riant put an end to these adventures by instructing the nuns not to let the Colonel take her out of school, both of them were disheartened.

They knew their day trips could not stop. To work around Mother Riant's dictates, the Colonel spent the time while Regina was in school on the lookout for presents for her. Then he picked her up after school, and they would begin their rambles from there, returning home later and later. "Do you think there's a hell?" she asked him one afternoon as they drove home. That afternoon they had shopped for a winter coat. She hadn't been able to decide if she wanted a coat or a cape, so he bought her both. She was thirteen.

"They say there is, but I can't believe many people actually get sent there. God must be too loving to send people there for all eternity."

"What about killers?"

"I don't know, child." He pulled into the driveway and turned off the Cadillac. It was dark and both of them were regretting having to enter the house. "I can't believe anyone actually kills on purpose; it's more like a horrible accident, and they're sorry for it afterward. Even in war . . ." He trailed off. In the sparse light from the carriage house his face was deeply lined. "Wars are accidents, too, on an enormous scale. In war, men are just instruments; that's the horror of it." Again he paused. "I have no idea how many Yankees I killed, but then I was willing to die myself."

"That's all right, Papa," she said, resting her cheek against his arm. "You're not going to hell."

"I hope not," he mused. "Now, killing yourself is another story. That's one thing God can't forgive. Well, maybe he can. None of us would have much of a chance if God weren't merciful."

"What about robbers?" she whispered.

"If there is a hell, robbers don't go there. We have everything, but not everyone does. Having everything is therefore a great responsibility. We have to show God how grateful we are by sharing what we have, otherwise God or the robbers will take it away." He opened the door and put one foot on the running board. "Plus, everything is nothing. This family has been rich and poor ten times since they arrived with Lord Baltimore in 1680. Fortunes change overnight, and people die in their sleep."

"What about people who are mean?"

He swiveled to look at her in the seat. He smiled, put his hand on her head and pressed fondly. "Let's go inside," he said. "I'm hungry."

## Along Comes the Savior

ALL NIGHT SHE TANGLED in the hot bedsheet, turning on her back, on her side, staring at the canopy, adjusting the mosquito net. She struggled not to think about bad things but they came nonetheless. That her mother had made her iron a pile of her brothers' bow ties that day, how she had found her rouge and thrown it away. Regina agreed with her girlfriends that the ideal woman had a child every eighteen months, but her mother never spoke of such things. So she exchanged with her girlfriends very practical information about men: weaknesses, finances, brow. Speculated in whispers about the nature of sex; they had suspected it anyway, and the more horrible it was the better. At the same time, they mimicked the older ladies' headaches, delicacies and white lies. They were not animals but they wanted to be mothers. So was the awful mystery of the body to them.

Lying on her back, Regina listed old loves: Frank Conti, dead of yellow fever—she said a quick prayer—Pierce Circumbers, she hadn't been fast enough for him she supposed. Charles Morrow, lacked confidence. And poor Archibald Treme, not as bright as she.

She prayed for them all, if distractedly, before launching into regular nightly prayers, which consisted mainly of her naming every friend and family member and asking God to bless them. Sometimes the rhythm of it put her to sleep; tonight she got distracted in the middle of listing the Senac cousins.

Her brother's friend Ahlong was coming to Easter dinner. She had heard about him for years and was curious to meet him. Now she was itching to wander the grounds under the already purpling dawn. She didn't have too much longer to choose a man. She remembered with irritation that her mother had told her that a year ago. But when finishing school was over, Regina, then seventeen, had joined the suffragettes. The Mobile chapter did little more than drink tea. They had marched here and there. The citizens, sure that Alabama would never ratify the amendment, were seemingly supportive. The newspaper had remarked on how handsome they were as they marched.

She was hungry. At last she heard Esperanza on the rear stairs, gathering wood from the back porch and lighting the stove. She rinsed her face in water from the basin and threw on the spring finery she had been waiting for so long to wear, her dress of dusty blue georgette silk, tapering toward the hem, with a fitted, beaded bodice and long flowing arms, her lightweight blue serge cape, her white shoes with the little curved heels and her close-fitting picture hat, trimmed with cherries.

As she dressed, she thought of the skin cancer on the side of her father's nose and part of a prayer for a good death ran through her mind: *When relatives and friends compassing me round about, melt into tears at my sad state, and invoke you in my behalf, merciful Jesus have pity on me.* . . . But it annoyed her that she was thinking this way.

She turned into the darkened hallway and unlocked the back door. The freshly cut lawn gleamed this Easter morning 1915. As she stood at the top of the porch, the early light filtering through her hair created a halo behind her small head, which seemed to set her shoulders on fire. She stepped out into the morning. Dewdrops clung to the monkey grass lining the drive. Fuchsia azaleas blushed; bed after bed of purple, yellow and white tulips, irises, African lilies and jonquils crisped and colored up as she passed. She stopped beside the rose arbor, where a group of red amaryllis gave her a view of their burgundy stripes in a cup. Next to them was a trishaded violet bush, Yesterday, Today and Tomorrow. Against the chirping of birds, Regina heard the horses snorting their strength in the far-off stables and saw the chickens, disturbed by the ascent of changing air, running loose in the side yard. She rushed on, past her brothers' old tree house—tromping over the beds of scarlet pansies, the bamboo grazing her neck, the scent of magnolia thick in the air—toward the back gate, where she stopped again, looking through the cast-iron curls.

She felt a surge of power as she focused on the empty road, and its vision on this particular morning made a print in her mind. Soon she would strike out; great things awaited her, travel and love—the courageous search. Where would it take her in this life? It occurred to her to say a prayer, but she didn't know for what. The empty road, so familiar to her, gave little inspiration and the feeling of power dulled. As she turned and stalked back through the sweet stirrings of the garden, she felt an urge to expose herself alongside the flowers, but knew she could not, not yet. Suddenly violent, she lashed with her new parasol against the elephant ears in her path. Then, sap on her shoes and in the webs of her fingers, moth wings in her hair, she returned by the same routes through the dark and chilly downstairs, sipping cold black coffee until sick and unable to sit still, waiting for the house to wake.

She was tired, sat on the couch in the library with poor posture and watched the festive morning pass slowly. Her father's cousin Thérèse and her daughter Josie arrived at ten, bearing boxes of Heavenly Hash, which could not be touched until after Mass. Her brothers stood in a semicircle in front of the bay window in their three-piece suits, awake enough that their eyes darted to the door frequently, obviously hoping for an interruption that would allow an escape. While Thérèse recited her trials with the milliner of her new bonnet, a bizarre headdress of ostrich plumes, Mother Riant listened attentively with a claylike face. Regina struggled to make conversation with Cousin Mathilde, who was her age and who had been staying with them for some weeks but whose self-consciousness and tendency to pick at her acne made interaction embarrassing for all. The Colonel, smiling his abstracted Easter smile, stood by Mother Riant's chair. It was for his sake that Regina, the ruby cross visible on her chest, charmed Mathilde, even had her giggling at one point.

At half past eleven the entire group walked up Government Street to the Cathedral of the Immaculate Conception. They strolled up the center aisle to the front of the church—the altar crowded with Easter lilies, the choir rehearsing the Panis Angelicus—and filed into the Riant pew, the Colonel remaining in the aisle shaking hands until the first notes of the organ opened Mass. Regina stood next to Cousin Mathilde and shared her missal with her for the Kyrie. The Colonel's eyes were bright, but his face was pale and beaded with sweat. The bishop boomed "*Gloria in excelsis Deo,*" the choir responding with the joyous "*et in terra pax hominibus.*" Mother Riant maintained a statuesque reverence, and her sons punched one another's arms and mumbled now and then among themselves. Cousin Mathilde kept her eyes on her feet. Regina's stomach growled as she thanked God for the gift of life. Thérèse had difficulty getting off her knees in the pew to walk up the aisle for Communion and revealed an unpleasant glimpse of her slip as Mother Riant pulled her to her feet. Regina felt many eyes on her as they exited the church, and she thanked the Almighty for her good fortune as she stopped here and there to wish Happy Easter to her father's friends.

The Riant family returned to the house, where they gathered in the dining room around a breakfast buffet of fried ham, grits and sweet rolls, sipping hot chocolate and repeating the same things they had said before Mass, commenting on the beautiful day, mainly, and suffering through an even more detailed history of Thérèse's bonnet.

Thérèse and Josie left at last; Cousin Mathilde and Mother Riant went off to nap. The Colonel headed for the front porch with his newspaper—neighbors would come to wish him a Happy Easter throughout the day—and the brothers commenced with their cards and sherry behind the parlor's closed doors, while Regina, adding shaves of ice to another cup of chocolate, meandered out to the back porch and sat in her favorite rocking chair, removed her shoes and propped her feet on the railing.

As she sat there, in the quiet of the afternoon, she knew she was attractive but didn't think it did her any good. She had an instinct for fashion but the decency not to flaunt it. She knew, for instance, that the skirts were getting shorter and the hats smaller, but she avoided trends. She felt the back of her head with her hand, musing that she had the type of prettiness that spoke of sense and good nature. "Lord help me," she mumbled through her smile. "Why am I thinking of such things?" She had a pale, small face and thin, straight brown hair with reddish accents that fell to her waist and which she had pulled up and folded expertly at the nape of her neck. She had cloudy green eyes, a tiny nose, thin lips, pointy chin and a bell-clear voice. She looked down at her beautiful dress. Again she felt the

back of her hair with her hand. At least she had a moment free of
Mathilde. Why was she feeling so restless? She considered taking a
drive to Spring Hill but knew her mother would be angry if she did.
Mother Riant didn't believe in ladies driving, but her father had
hired a driving teacher for her and she, the first woman in Mobile to
drive a car, was said to be a better driver than her brothers.

She unbuttoned her sleeves and rolled them up to the elbows.
She unbuttoned her neck and fingered the chain of the ruby cross,
poking its edges under her thumbnail. Her mother wanted her to
finish replacing the silk-covered buttons on the cuffs of her cream
gown, but that was just too bad. It was Easter and she wasn't doing
chores. She couldn't tell if she had a headache or not. Was it the
chocolate bringing one on? With the shadows of the magnolia tree
on her face, she adjusted her eyes to the edge of the lawn and noticed a man with thick black hair and red pants pacing on the other
side of the iron fence at the edge of the lawn. She didn't trust the vision. She had bad eyesight, which made things look more pleasant
than they actually were, and she often confused objects, mistaking
one thing for another on a landscape—and got a little thrill when
the object moved back and forth between two or three possibilities.
The pattern of a lady's scarf, for instance, might undulate with umbrellas, paisleys, ocean waves. A baseball glove left on the lawn was
also an ant bed, a pile of cornmeal and the head of a dirt-colored
crocodile.

But here was a man. Definitely a man approaching. A maid came
onto the porch to ask her to check the table setting just as he reached
the bottom step. Having never seen a Chinese man, she could not
hide her delight. Motioning the maid off, she peered into his lumi-
nous face and asked with a directness that shocked her, "Are you
Ahlong?" So slowly did he climb the steps and stand before her!

In spite of the warm day, he wore a deep blue velvet coat, impeccably cut. A red silk scarf tied loosely around his neck drew attention to his dark pink, finely etched lips. His face was large, his skin dull pearl, the color of pull-candy just before it crystallizes. Dotting his forehead and coordinating with the color of his lips, scarf and pants, a few tiny pimples added to his beauty. She noticed them with some relief: so he must be close to her age.

"Yes, and you're Regina," he said, his black eyes glossing over with merriment and wisdom.

Rising from her chair, she glided toward him and took his hand, scarcely knowing what she did. "Pleased to meet you," she said quietly. His hand was as cool as marble. At this first physical contact, they both laughed. She admired the ornate gold fob chain dangling from his vest pocket. He was just a few inches taller than she was. "I have a blue velvet coat just like yours," she said.

Ahlong was silent. He released her hand and moved to sit in the chair beside her, his hands between his knees. She sat back down, saying nervously, "I've read so much about China. Mother has four plates of the famille rose, from the Manchu dynasty. I've read all about Peking, and of course nowadays about President Yuan."

"Would you like to travel there someday?"

"Yes." Her heart was pounding with anticipation—would he offer to take her there?—but he said no more. Gradually the two began playing with the rhythms of their rocking chairs—one slow and steady with the other improvising over it—until the dinner bell announced the Easter feast. "Are you an emissary?" she asked, lightly clapping her hands.

His rocking stopped. "I am interested only in beauty." He stole a glance at her.

She raised her chin to give him her profile. "What type of beauty?"

"I'm a scientist." He chuckled noiselessly, looking into his palms. She turned on him in time to catch the smile draining from his face. The thought that she was being teased made her furrow her brow, but he looked at her with what she took to be infinite patience, and exhaled. "The beauty of nature," he said. "Ask me what you want to know."

He spoke the words so softly that she wasn't sure she heard correctly and didn't know what to say. She looked at him expectantly, long enough to note his high cheekbones, but he didn't repeat himself. The dinner bell rang again from deep inside the house. "Do you know why they paint the ceilings of the porches light blue?" she surprised herself by asking.

"No."

"To trick the wasps. If they think the ceiling is sky they won't try to make a nest there." He seemed to be contemplating this but said nothing for some time. "Why are you so silent?" she asked.

"When his students asked him why he was silent, Confucius answered, 'Sky says nothing.'"

Now it was her turn to fall mute. She was thinking of all the ways the sky expresses itself: the thunder, the rain, the wind and the variety of clouds, but she decided not to mar the loveliness of Confucius's comment by disputing it.

He went on. "'Everything is; God is everything that is not.' I can't remember who said that one, though," he added, grinning. "I converted to Catholicism several years ago, but I still derive satisfaction from my heritage." He turned to her with a raised eyebrow. "And what is the God you see?"

"God is love," she said emphatically. She thought she heard him snicker. Her knuckles went white on the arms of her chair as she pushed herself to her feet to hide her embarrassment. "You can't see God!"

"Fine," he said, rising and smoothing his pants. "Granted."

Though she was not in the least impressed with his fancy quotations, she felt his hand like a bolt of lightning on her elbow, guiding her into the house.


COLONEL RIANT sat sipping sherry in his large carved armchair in the window of the dining room, reflecting on Christ's sacrifice. He liked to be early, liked to listen to the maids chatting as they polished silver in the next room, liked to watch the table being set, the dishes brought out. He took a deep breath to stretch the sides of his waistcoat, the arms of the chair pressing into his skin. His stomach was not well; gastritis they called it, and hypertension, and something with the kidney. But today he would relax. *Thank you for giving me so many chances.* By name, he prayed for his wife, his sons, his parents and brothers and sisters gone to their rest in the hope of rising again, his cousin Thérèse and Josie, poor Cousin Mathilde, and all the friends he had known. He shed a tear from one eye as he thought of his daughter, Regina. A phrase of prayer crossed his mind: *When my cheeks, pale and livid, inspire the bystanders with compassion and awe, and my hair, bathed in the sweat of death, stands up upon my head and declares my hour is come, merciful Jesus, have pity on me.*

He took another sip of sherry to push the thoughts out of his mind. Deep in reverie, he ignored the dark mahogany paneling that bore down into the top of his handsome silver head, the rectangular frames of the high white ceiling crisscrossed with mahogany beams. He took another sip. Waves of renewal flooded his mind and body; he felt light and breathed more deeply. A tiny smile covered his face as he smelled the imminent Easter feast, then the words of an advertisement came to him: *Why didn't I reduce long ago?* He promised to lose a bit of weight but knew he was forgiven. *I am so unworthy!* He looked around, giving thanks for all the things he knew were beautiful—the cut crystal wineglasses, the lavishly stocked sideboard, the succulent roast that awaited them.

He leaned back, soft hand on his stomach, feeling warm and majestic. Life was hard for everyone, he thought, biting the sides of his cheek and struggling not to cry. He had worked so hard, he had his share of grief and powerlessness—he resolved to be gentler with his wife—but he did not blame God for any misfortune. He tried to look forward to death. "God is my last end," he recited, "and as death is the door through which we go to him, I may desire it." Try as he might, he could not desire death, though he wouldn't mind eternal rest. Rest was the thing, and peace.

The dinner bell rang and his wife entered on its heels, stiff in her layers of cream lace. He stood and drew toward her, smiling and taking her hands. "Happy Easter, darling."

"To you also," she said, the lines of tension protruding from her neck as she turned to give him her cheek. He kissed it, sat back and increased the pace of his sipping. He couldn't think of anything to say to her. Their four sons entered noisily, and Mother Riant jumped up to give each of them a kiss on the cheek and brush lint from their dinner jackets. Cousin Mathilde—how long had she been there?—hung back behind Colonel Riant's chair. "Sit down, Mathilde, right here next to me!" he boomed kindly as he patted the chair to his right.

Mathilde moved in front of him, squeaking "Heavens!" as she caught sight of an odd-looking man leading Regina into the room. Colonel Riant twisted around in his chair, spilling sherry down his front as he struggled to his feet. Mother Riant and her sons ceased their chattering to look. Mathilde hid her face in her hands in fear of the stranger, but Louis stepped forward and took control—"Ahlong!"—and shook his hand warmly. "I'm so pleased you could make it. I see you've met my sister." Regina turned bright red before her family.

"I met your son at M.I.T. He's extremely talented, as I'm sure you know," Ahlong explained to Mother Riant, taking first her hand, then the Colonel's, then the rest of the hands, one by one. "It's a pleasure to meet you all." Not looking at Regina, he seated himself at a place beside her at the massive table, around which they all stood with eyes cast to their plates.

"His name means 'Dragon,'" Louis boasted. The Colonel said grace, and the meal began. Esperanza circled the table serving cold asparagus soup, a look of extreme anxiety on her face, which Regina chose to ignore. Mother Riant sat up straighter than usual, wearing a triumphant smile; suddenly she loved Easter. Felix and Peter were attentive to every word Ahlong spoke as he and Louis exchanged news of classmates. Mathilde was mesmerized. Regina studied him out of the corner of her eye. A slight smile played at the corner of his mouth, but the rest of his face was placid. His powder-white skin shimmered in the dining light, cut by a deep black eyebrow and topped with thick, blue-black hair. The bowls were removed and Colonel Riant rose to slice the roast.

Ahlong tried to take her hand under the table but she flicked it off, her heart throbbing with a desire she had never known. Mother Riant asked Felix to pass the rolls. Colonel Riant sat back down, his face mottled red with the festivities. He drank his wine almost as profusely as Ahlong did. Mother Riant asked Regina to pass the sweet potatoes. Colonel Riant faced Ahlong. "And what do you do, Mr. Ahlong . . . ?"

His secretive smile grew deeper, almost mocking the old man, and timing out his answer. "Edit," he said softly while Regina exulted, the candles casting diamonds of warm light across her eyes.

"Saint John of Bosco," whooped Mathilde, "is your patron saint," and got a string of okra stuck in her windpipe.

"The newspapers then," said Colonel Riant, his eyes fixed on Ahlong's mouth, his voice loud enough to compensate for Mathilde's coughing.

"Actually, I'm working on a book about Venezuelan fauna—on their fossils, to be precise."

"Fascinating!" the Colonel exclaimed, easing back in his chair and radiating pleasure.

"Indeed," said Mother Riant. Regina had read *On the Origin of Species* and knew quite a bit about fossils, but her mind was utterly blank. In fact, she was on the verge of a laugh attack, in the midst of this, what she took to be the most crucial scene in her life to date, and Felix, she worried, would come along with her if she started. She turned slightly away from the table toward the window and concentrated on the azalea bush, concentrated on lifting herself from the scene, concentrated on breathing. Then Ahlong said, "I'm actually leaving in a few weeks on an expedition up the Orinoco"—her stomach tightened—"but I hope to have the pleasure of visiting with you all in the meantime."

Regina was devastated at the thought that he would be leaving but covered her emotion by asking, "And are there many spots of exposed sedimentary rock along the Orinoco?" Her brothers and mother all turned to her in surprise, but the Colonel beamed in satisfaction.

"I hope so," Ahlong said. "I'm looking chiefly for petrified shellfish, which are unusual to find, since they lack an internal skeleton. I hope I will find cases where the water has dissolved the original substance, replaced the substance with minerals—thus leaving its form."

"But isn't the Orinoco a famously tumultuous river?" she asked.

Mother Riant gave her a look of extreme disapproval. Women weren't supposed to know so much.

Ahlong was about to answer her when Louis interrupted. "He's an engineer as well."

"My!" managed Mathilde. Esperanza came in to take the orders for coffee.

"Yes," Ahlong said. "I have a theory about the connection between sine and cosine waves and the divine proportions of invertebrates. Not to mention that they are beautiful creations. I just like looking at them." Regina flinched at the word "beautiful" and felt that if she couldn't calm herself down, she would die.

"Certainly," said the Colonel, as everyone turned to the plate of charlotte russe before them. Then George launched into the lengthy and provocative analysis of Father Lusch's sermon, which he had been storing up all day, but Colonel Riant, his other sons and Ahlong turned the conversation back to science. Mathilde coughed intermittently. Mother Riant continued to stare at Ahlong, who lit a cigarette and signaled to have his glass filled. Regina was uncomfortable for him: no one smoked in the dining room. Her father said nothing, however, and the charlotte russe was cleared. The brothers took Ahlong off to play billiards. Regina and Mathilde pushed back their chairs. She approached her father, bent over and kissed him on the cheek. He gave two strokes to the back of her head. "Happy Easter, Papa," she said. "I love you."

AHLONG FOUND REGINA ON THE PORCH as she knew he would. Camilla, waiting for the streetcar, was settled in an old rocker under the purple shadows by the railing, and Mathilde hunched in a chair just outside the front door, slurping coffee. Regina and Ahlong edged into the dimmer light at the opposite side of the porch.

Regina's sighs intensified the cadence of the crickets. Ahlong smoked silently. While she studied his hand—long, gleaming fingers with pointed nails, soft palm and narrow wrist—a dove cooed sadly from an oak tree to their right. He lowered one foot to the top step and Regina reached for his hand, which vanished, and he was pressing her against the column, kissing her, she letting herself bathe inside it and trying to breathe. She pushed him away, glancing anxiously at Camilla's dark form. Stroking his mustache, he slinked down three more steps. He turned back to her. "Will your father accept me?"

"Accept you?" she asked in wonderment.

"I'm sailing from Miami in three weeks," he said, descending to the bottom step and pausing there with his back to her, looking toward the gate. "Please come with me."

She reached the step directly above him. Her face lowered, whispering at his back, she asked, "You mean be your wife?"

His body collapsed slightly, and he faced her, his eyes narrowing as she again gave him her profile, her hammering heart nearly preventing her from hearing him say, "I'll come early tomorrow." Then he kissed her cheek and held his cheek to hers. "I love you," he said huskily to her earlobe, turned and was gone, his blue coat fading immediately into the late evening.

"Where are you staying?" she called out, surprising herself with the hoarseness in her voice.

"The Cawthorne!"

She stood there waiting for the sound of the gate but didn't hear it. Now the porch light had been turned on and tiny moths were diving into it. She returned to her rocking chair and put her feet back on the railing and unbuttoned the high neck of her dress. "I'm afraid" was all she could think.

Darkness came emphatically, cold and spell-less, and she opened the front door and entered the house. The laugh of one of her brothers came to her over the sound of the phonograph as she crept past the parlor door. She closed the door of her bedroom, sat at her dresser and unpinned her hair. She rubbed cold cream on her face, then climbed under the sheets, opened her book and wrote with the new blue ink in her fountain pen: *Mary, Mother of God, thank you for* . . . But before she could finish she fell asleep to the sound of dogs barking in the east yard. It was a sleep shadowed with stone walls angling in *X*'s behind her as she moved through halls full of pigeons. A glass of water by the side of a pond, the face of Mathilde, a future child bloated beyond recognition, she, saying good-bye to each crack in the walk. Actually skipping over them, arm in arm with Ahlong.

She woke with a start and saw it was only midnight. The pen had bled into an enormous stain on her sheets. She balled them up and put them under her bed. After a glass of water, she returned to her bare mattress, where she spent the rest of the night flipping, tossing, readjusting pillows and thinking about what she would say when they next met. Just when she thought she would never fall asleep again, she woke to the sound of Esperanza on the back steps. In a flash she remembered Ahlong.

She rinsed her face in water from the basin and, clutching the ruby cross, debated what to wear. She put on a pale green silk dress that was a few years old, her close-fitting straw hat, and added a veil pinned neatly together behind her head. Then she grabbed her blue coat and crept down the stairs. On the back porch, she sat in her rocking chair and returned her feet to the railing. She watched the sun sear the sky. She didn't know what she would say to him when he came. All she knew was that she should stay and take care of her father.

The milkman arrived and swapped bottles at the door, smiling cheerily at her. Then he noticed her huge exhausted eyes. "God bless," he mumbled, and bolted to his cart. But Ahlong did not arrive before the maids, the eggs, the newspaper. Regina moved to the window of the library to avoid the commotion of the morning house. She watched her father cranking up the car and driving off, not realizing it would be his last day at work. At ten she ran to her room for her sewing basket—her brothers were not yet awake, her mother was talking to Esperanza in the kitchen—and returned to the back porch. For an hour or more she worked steadily on the lace cuffs she was crocheting, glancing every few minutes to the top of the drive. Beads of sweat formed constantly at her hairline and upper lip, which she dabbed away with a handkerchief embroidered with the letters *RAR*.

# Her Idea of Geography

October 21, 1918,
*By Nell Brinkley*

The girl he left behind him when he went away to the War, "just naturally his last worl' wah!" once knew quite a glib bit about geography. She sat on the tubs of her mother's kitchen close to the place where that busy little mother passed back and forth, when her skirts just touched the round of her boylike knees, and while she industriously pushed her hair back as tight as an onionskin with a "back-comb" she dumbfounded her amazed family with information about the capitals of the world and the folks in them, and how many there were.

She examined her chagrined and ignorant father on the length of the River Amazon, and when he couldn't answer how the natives were able to get their motorboats up to Lake Titicaca, on the top of a volcano and whiz about thereon, she cried aloud: "Well, De-e-ead! Didn't you ever go to SCHOOL?" She was bursting and crackling with information about the world she lived in until the heads of her family spun.

Years crept by, and her skirts edged lower and lower, and she pulled her hair down over her forehead instead of swiping it back off it—and a lover came along. And during this time she was an ignorant young American and forgot the River Amazon, only that boa-constrictors lived on it! Information on this whirling, warm and cold, beautiful and terrible little world vanished into the limbo of pale blue back-combs and a Prince Charming who just had to have a certain color hair and eyes when he came along or she couldn't love him! Nevertheless, and, oh, my, and oh ye-eye-eeess! she knows more about geography now than in those Miss Statistics days. For then Germany was a greenish-yellow on the map and France was a red country, and so were England and Italy, and Belgium was Roman gold. NOW they are more than that.

Besides the 'stonishing way that France has drawn near across the ocean and become "over there," and England is the land of the language we speak, and Germany is a place she's goin' to go around carefully when she goes traveling sometime, and Italy is our brother we fought beside, there's one very important thing they mean to her.

Her lover went over with a Canadian girl, with green eyes and Scotch coloring. He went through England, and everybody knows that the English girl's eyes are deep and blue, and her hair soft and long and her complexion so peachy that it doesn't look real—only you KNOW it is! He arrived in France and fought and lived there; now France is not a "red" country—it is just the tantalizing, chic, piquant face of a smiling girl with a tipped nose, odd cheeks, winsome eyes and chin, slim little trotting ankles and an air about her clothes and manner. Italy, Belgium, Russia; he was long enough over to have been in them all! Italy is no longer a "boot," but a dusky woman in vivid green and coral, sloe-eyed and slow-eyed, pomegranate-lipped, golden-skinned. He MUST have seen a million of her—or worse—only one or two. And, maybe, he carried her sheaf of grain and walked beside her. He would, of course, and ought!

Miss Betty grows worldy-wise, pondering on the marching of her soldier lover! And while she twirls the globe to find this last country he served in before coming down on the ocean trail for home—she sees this land and forgets even "Bolshevik"—sees only an odd, lovely face so different from our own—the "sculptor's" face—high-cheeked, whose smile is Mona Lisa's to us who do not understand her, mystery-eyed, broad-browed, a dark jewel set in snow and white fur, a Madonna and a siren.

"What garbage!" Regina tossed the *Chronicle* on the floor near her feet, annoyed at herself for having read the entire thing. She had no lover gone off to war, not even a brother to track across Europe; they had evaded conscription. She had larger worries than the war, looked toward the clock on the mantel: fifteen more minutes before her father would be home and it would be time for the cold compresses. At her feet was a basket filled with garments that needed hemming: two pairs of her brother's trousers, one of Mother Riant's innumerable black skirts; plus the smocking of a blouse needed re-working, the lace of a camisole—not that these were worries. She craved a cigarette but her brothers had gone out. Felix had taken her father for a new treatment that used X-rays to eradicate the cancer. The doctors had warned her that it would leave burns on his skin, and she was afraid, really afraid, to see it. Was this just another one of Dr. Freret's theories? And what was really wrong with her father? What were all these cancers?

Though it was chilly outside, she moved out to the porch for the third time that morning, sat in the rocker next to the one Ahlong had vacated more than two years ago. He probably had nothing to do with the war either, she thought, rocking rapidly: he, a scientist, would not sully himself with the petty boundary battles of war. Still, like the idiotic Miss Betty, she had studied the atlas, had tasted the strange names of Venezuelan cities, traced her finger from Miami to Santiago de Cuba, to Isla de Margarita to Caracas, trod mentally across the perilous Andes as far as Bogotá—and wondered if he still loved her, if he had ever loved her, and if he had, how that love could possibly have dwindled as rapidly as it did. In two years she had heard nothing from him.

Ahlong had postponed his journey and performed flawlessly all that spring before he left for Miami. He had visited her every day, had spoken with her father about his intentions, catered to Mother Riant, ingratiated himself with her brothers, even offered to wait an additional week to allow her time to pack, then another week to make sure her father had stabilized after his fall. He always arrived, she noticed with some amusement, about a half hour before the dinner bell and stayed until just after dark. He ate heartily, smoked and drank too much, and his teeth were yellow, but she and the entire family overlooked these facts in the face of his charms. Dinner went remarkably smoothly, since appreciation of Ahlong was the first topic Colonel and Mother Riant had agreed upon in some years, and as long as he spent the requisite hour or so with her brothers in the parlor after the meal, doing God knows what, they demonstrated a growing respect for him, which, knowing her brothers, pleased and offended her in equal degrees: the world of men. Even Mathilde, her fear thawed by a pair of Chinese embroidered slippers, cooed and nodded with his every comment.

Meanwhile, she sat with him in the same spot on the porch

drinking lemonade, listening to his theories of the world. "Every man and every woman is a star," he said repeatedly in the midst of his talk about the size and mysteries of the universe, "in the company of stars." The things he said to entice her also scared her, but she was attracted to the precision of his speech and the growing liberties he took with her body. They were kissing more and more deeply every evening, so that she sensed in parts of her body that had never before stirred the lengths to which man and woman could travel physically. "When my research is complete, we will build a sailboat and take it in a perfect circle around the world. The world is not a perfect circle by any means, but we will encompass it with our love, making it perfect."

"Why won't we just take a steamer?"

"My love," he chortled, "there's a right and a wrong way to do things. I do things the right way."

She sat up straighter, put her hand on his knee in excitement. "Will we go to Vienna?"

But that annoyed him. "Why do all Americans want to go to Europe? As if that is the only part of the world that is safe for them? And the world is so much larger than Europe, other parts of it are so much more interesting."

"Oh," she said, deflated. "I just want to see the opera. I love opera. I've heard that the performances are best there."

"Well, Vienna then. *Wien*. There is not a port there, but it could be our gateway to further travel east. *Sprichst du deutsch? Nein?* No? Well, I can teach you in a few days, I imagine. You're a quick woman. We'll start our lessons when we get to Caracas."

Meanwhile, the two extra weeks stretched into a third, then a fourth, during which the Colonel stabilized without recovering. Before his fall he was more than pleasant with Ahlong, treating him with deference, seeming to derive amusement from his esoteric intelligence and telling Regina in a private moment that she had his every blessing.

"Do you think I'm making the right choice, Papa?" she had asked.

"Yes, but it's not my choice to make. It's yours and yours alone."

She looked into his face. "I think I'm making the right choice."

"Well then my mind's at ease. I'm not worried about you, Regina. You have a good heart by nature, and if you keep yourself close to God you will be blessed in this life. Your brothers, on the other hand . . ." He grimaced. "But let's not speak about them. You have my every blessing."

But then he fell. While he was in his study before dinner, reading Rousseau, the first and second discourses, Belinda, a hen, flew in through the window and settled on the Colonel's desk. He captured her, carried her down the back steps and released her into the yard. Turning on the walkway, tripping on a lose piece of slate— the post of the banister was suddenly not where he thought it was— he went down. He called out, laughingly at first, but it was just after the dinner hour and no one was about. The shooting pain in his right arm told him something very serious was broken: his collarbone? his arm? his elbow? his wrist? all of them? The pain was disorienting; it was some minutes before he remembered to call again for help. There was no movement in the house or yard. He thought he would be able to stand up and go into the house, but when he put weight on his arm, he blacked out for a few minutes. Coming to, he shifted onto his bottom and sat there staring between his legs at the piece of slate that had felled him, the hen clucking around him, waiting. It was Mathilde, on her way back from buying the chocolates she liked to keep stashed in her knitting basket, who found him sitting on the walkway, his face blank with pain.

A fall, the very nature of which is unexpected, often signals the beginning of the end in the sick and elderly. If he had supported the match with Ahlong before, after the fall he became insistent, ferociously so. "You must go ahead with your plans," he said when she was finally allowed to see him, late that evening. He was in his pajamas, a white sheet up to the middle of his chest, his eyes half closed with opiates. "The last thing I want is for a weakness of mine to deflect any opportunity from you, especially one so blessed."

"How did it happen, Papa?"

"I don't know what happened," he said, irritably. "Please don't ask me that. If I knew what happened, I wouldn't have fallen, right?"

"I suppose so," she said, more worried than before.

"I'll be out of this bed in a week. You'll marry and leave as planned."

She stroked his silver head. "I want to stay, to be here to help you."

"No one can help me now but the Lord Almighty," he said with force, smiling. Then he laughed until he was coughing. She held a glass of water out for him but he didn't take it. At last he said, "Please follow your love. That way, while I'm recovering I can imagine you traipsing through the rain forests, seeing parts of the world that I never had a chance to see."

But the Colonel, at seventy-one, would not recover, and Regina knew it. Until the fall he had enjoyed remarkably good health, with the exception of gastritis and a small skin cancer on his nose that the doctors were able to cut off. Regina had always assumed that his disinclination for doctors was a result of the fact that they had been powerless to save the first Regina Riant and her father. Now she suspected, with some pity, that he had had good reason to keep them away from him, that he had known of his multiple illnesses and had hoped that, by ignoring them, he could stave off his own inevitable disintegration. Now they came out in a torrent of ugliness over the weeks following the fall: not just gastritis but cataracts, chronic bronchitis tending to emphysema—he cursed for the first time in his life when told he couldn't smoke—malignant dyspepsia with possible liver complications, and all the cancers—skin, bone, blood.

"I'm sorry you've waited so long for me," she told Ahlong finally, at the beginning of June. "But I can't go. I suppose I knew all along I couldn't go. My duty is to my father."

The anger she'd anticipated did not materialize; there wasn't even remorse. "'Do what thou wilt shall be the whole of the law,'" he said. "'Love is the law; love under will.'"

This time she didn't bother to ask whom he was quoting. "Love is sacrifice," she said meekly.

"Then sacrifice your father for my love," he said, and waited for the effect of his words on her, but she sat there, slouched in the chair, saying nothing, except after a moment: "Maybe you can come back for me in a while."

He shook his head slowly. "*Modo et modo non habebant modum.* 'By and by never comes.' St. Augustine."

She began to cry. "There's no chance?"

"There's always a chance," he said, "but the one thing the Chinese believe is that chances always change." He stood up.

"I'm sorry."

"Don't be sorry. Be anything but sorry, for my sake," he said, glancing at the gate.

"I'm sorry for myself," she said miserably.

"That's worse," he said coldly, evidently eager to be on his way. "Good-bye, my dear."

· · ·

THE NEXT DAY SHE WOKE to her regret, the weight of which could not be alleviated, no matter how solicitously she cared for her father. During her coffee she realized that she had made a mistake and called the Cawthorne to learn that he had checked out. Either he was on his way to the house to apologize to her, to offer to wait with her, as long as it took, or he was on his way to Miami, where he would realize he couldn't live without her and would return for her. So, as she cared for her father with a flawlessness that was also a symptom of her unhappiness, the rest of her days passed in impotence.

Time still: She expected his return as sure as she was alive. Her body kept vigil while panic rose to the top of her throat. Time widening: She recognized the amber silk of the month of September's cape with the receding sound of Dr. Freret's tires—the pink sasanquas were blooming—and as an abandoned woman lumbers forward through time as if it were water, she redoubled her waiting traces up and down the steps between the porch and her bedroom. Meanwhile, she allowed herself to diffuse in the air of Ahlong's absence and was amazed as his contours, his gait, his long elegant fingers blurred in the bright light of her memory of those precious weeks with him and, overexposed, taunted her with their gray activity. Then it was easy to remain there, ignoring everything but her father's health.

Mathilde spent her days in the hallways, following her cousin back and forth from the porch to her room like a shadow and sitting just inside the front door for most of the night, picking at her fingernails, duplicating Regina's waiting, once removed. Mathilde's idea of preparing for Ahlong's return was to swaddle herself in all the clothing she owned, layer upon layer, so that her body appeared stuffed with material. With its irritated pimples and beads of sweat, its trim of tight, dull brown ringlets, her face puffed into four globes, creating the effect of a bitter and curious pincushion waddling through the hallways after her cousin.

The rest of the family was less sympathetic. "Come on and have a cigarette," Felix said one afternoon when, coming out of the house, he encountered Regina on the porch. She took one, he lit them, and they began to smoke. "Why are you sitting on the porch, day in, day out?" he asked after a minute. "Did he tell you he'd come back for you?" She didn't answer, and he repeated his question.

"No," she whispered.

"Then you're making a fool of yourself, Sister. I don't mean to offend you, but you ought to move on. There's other fish in the sea!"

"I don't care what you say, Felix." She frowned. "Don't you dare tell me about fish in the sea."

He shook his head with exaggerated sadness. "Suit yourself," he said, and walked off to the streetcar.

"Ever heard of onanism?" Louis stopped in front of her chair. "Look it up," he said, and went into the house. Peter and George avoided her altogether.

"If you insist on sitting here day and night, you may as well mend some of your brothers' socks," Mother Riant told her, dropping a huge basket of socks next to Regina's rocker. "I've even brought your scissors, so you needn't move."

"Thank you, Mother," she said, and promptly began stitching all the socks together into a sock quilt, which she spread over her knees as she continued to sit there through the quiet, chilly evenings, imagining why he hadn't returned. Perhaps he had been caught in the treacherous Maipures rapids, shipwrecked against the rocks, and only by giving himself over to the current had he floated to the relative safety of a native village. There they convinced him to remain, he teaching them of Chinese medicine while they shared the secrets of the medicinal powers of local vegetation. Or a gambling debt in Caracas had him fleeing at knifepoint one night, and now he sails the Caribbean in the common boat of a kindly fisherman with a rebellious streak and gets into all sorts of scrapes, keeping the police at bay, filtering salt water, fishing, braving storms and longing for her all the while.

With such fantasies, so diverse and yet so similar, percolating in her head, she sleeps in and out of nervous coughs and starts: a storm snarling at the spot where he'd stood at the top of the drive, kicking up sand and vegetation with his twirling reptilian tips. With a metal pole, she fishes out his black-and-white head from the center of the pool while he rides bareback on a zebra in a purple velvet suit. She is slipping on the tiles that cut blood, and, pasting along with the breeze, she tries to signal him with her mind, watching the red hourglasses on the backs of the black widow, suspended inside their fragile silver halves. "I have faith in the largest," she says to her visions, "but something will crack."

So she wrapped the sock quilt around her shoulders and sat there composing letters. *Dear Ahlong, Dearest Ahlong, Dear One. Don't laugh at me for saying love at first sight. I feel the understanding between us can only be a gift from God, our oneness. . . . If you think I'm going to wait forever you are quite mistaken, sir. . . . I am writing to tell you never to return to this house. I think of you all day. I have no intention of leaving with you and never have had. You are a vagabond in my heart, a ne'er-do-well whose necessarily coarse nature could never complement such a gentle faith as mine. Plus I didn't like your shoes and you were rude to my family. . . . In short, I detest you. Why don't you come for me?* And on and on. Of course she had no address.

One afternoon in the middle of December her father came out to see her. He stood next to her, leaning heavily on his cane, and asked her what the matter was.

"Nothing," she said. "I'm just sitting here. Is there something wrong with that?"

He moved gingerly toward the rocker that Ahlong had occupied and pitched himself into it before saying, "You don't seem happy. Did you notice the sweet olive is out?"

"I'm happy." She crossed her arms over her lap.

"Don't be one of those people who makes herself unhappy just for the drama of it."

"I'll try, Papa," she said wryly.

He winced and put his hand to his side. "Are you taking me seriously?"

She faced him. "Are you?"

He took his hand away and feigned good humor. "Which? Taking myself seriously or taking you seriously?"

She scowled and turned away again. "It doesn't matter."

"Your mother told me what you did with the socks. She's furious." She could feel him smiling but did not acknowledge it. "Let me tell you a story," he said, taking her silence as consent. "When I was in the Richmond hospital with malaria—Gettysburg raging to the north—the newspaper filled with lists of dead men, my childhood friends dying by the truckload, and I lay there picturing them, dead bodies crumpled in the mud. And all the gunsmoke and fire, the sounds of moving troops and wagons and train whistles and the endless speculation about what would happen—just the noise of war—it was the Sisters of Charity who gave me the one spot—"

"I've heard this before, Father."

She sensed his body shift in exasperation. He ran a hand through his fine head of silver hair. He squeezed one hand with the other, then rubbed his fingers for circulation. It took him some minutes collecting his breath. "My point is—I'm not suggesting you become a Sister of Charity."

"I have no intention of becoming a Sister of Charity."

"I can see that." He stared off toward the garden, taking his time to get to his feet. He moved to the door, clutching the railing as he went. She could tell he wanted to get away from her, a thought that made her wretched. He shifted his weight from the railing to his cane, looked at her for several seconds, swaying on his cane; she kept her head down. "You're tired." She didn't dare look up until he had passed her chair. "Get some rest," he said, his hand on the doorknob. When he was gone, she cried with new vigor.

## The Revelers

THE FOUR BROTHERS WERE SHAPED in the same womb, there was no question about it. Differences among them were so minor as to go unnoticed by the girls coming out. Equally tanned and attentive, they had height and complexion in common. Their hair was shiny and dark, all four scalps parted on the left. Teeth white and suits well cut, they tried to put themselves together with an individualistic dash, but the nuances of these were, at the end, untraceable. They shared or had so many duplicate clothes that aesthetic admiration was hard to fix on any particular one. If a girl appreciated a gold cigarette case engraved with the letter *R* on the table near a brother, she was sure to observe it at the next function in the hands of another. By the time the brothers were in their thirties, the differences in their ages could not be detected, and vivacious party games revolved around guessing the order of their births.

Smelling of leather and lavender-musk, they were a ubiquitous presence in drawing rooms, from Advent to the end of June. Then they retreated into their parlor, their romantic pressures and letters declining noticeably, though they always emerged for High Mass.

To avoid the yellow fever in July and August, they disappeared to the springs at Mentone, stopping all activity in Mobile. Year in, year out, white-clad debutantes cast out lines for one of the Riant brothers, only to be disappointed at the end of the season. A girl who expected a proposal based on the wording of a letter was left empty-handed by the following fall, and woe to the girl who scorned another man in the hopes of catching a Riant brother. Most girls, falling for all four of them at one time or another, were clever enough not to take them seriously. The Riant brothers charmed without making love; they were too polite; they never took without asking, not even a kiss. Something was not right.

Even still, they were considered fine catches, encapsulating as they did the harmony between progress and the past. Plus they were rich. The sound of locomotives blending with the lapping of Mobile Bay seemed to accompany them as they entered a room. They owned automobiles but were excellent horsemen, and their peculiar combination of piousness and laziness was a model to all modern gentlemen, itself an oxymoronic term. Their chivalrous manners were unrivaled, yet they were too self-centered to propose marriage. They spoke grandiloquently against the Florida land boom but drove over there on weekends to trade blue books, which gave no more than the dimensions and location of property for sale.

Colonel Riant bequeathed the *Mobile Chronicle* equally among his five children, but the running of it was left up to his sons. Dividing labor and sharing authority, however, were not their strong suits, besides that they approached their collective office without interest or direction. Only to keep it running was the plan, and that, they figured, should be simple enough. At least one brother went to the offices every day to counteract a decision his brother had made the day before, spreading confusion among the staff. Peter gained notoriety for firing writers for filing stories that contained anything unpleasant; Louis appointed himself sole contributor to the long and highfalutin "Sunday Science" section; Felix miscalculated and recalculated profits; George wrote sonorous columns on manifestations of the Virgin Mary, his specialty being the prophecies of Fatima. Only when the number of advertisers dropped substantially did they admit that it was time to attend the monthly board meetings. There, when they weren't standing two at a time to make a statement, they sat back watching the discussion with amusement.

Their lack of interest in the newspaper business left time for betting, primping, fishing and writing letters. As they were already a foursome, bridge was an obvious diversion many afternoons and evenings, the stakes between them astronomically high because it was in the family anyway. At least one of them lost heavily at monthly horse races. Euchre they enjoyed with lady players, always letting themselves lose. Maintenance of the person was an even greater challenge, as it required a balance between the hard and the soft. Every week they were placing orders for some new product—mustache oil, lavender-musk soap, muscle-building tonics, saddle polish, tobacco. Fishing they considered a passion. Twice a week they motored to the house at Bon Secour and checked the soft-shell crab nets. On bourbon-hazed fishing trips to Point Clear or Pensacola, they considered it a triumph to catch two red snappers. In the Riant box at the theater, they fell asleep as soon as the lights went down.

Despite all this variety of pursuits, their only callus was between the fore- and middle fingers of their four right hands, for letter writing was their particular forte. Letters were the reason for those four imposing rolltop desks that crowded the study; letters were the reason they bothered to have friends, family or romantic interests. They enjoyed only the heaviest, wettest rag paper and envelopes, the finest of pens and every accessory under the sun, blotters, wax seals and lensless spectacles. Like dogs they listened out for the mail truck, raced to the base of the stairs and fought viciously to be the first with his hands on the pile of mail. They expected to get back what they sent, one to one, and held grudges against anyone who failed to answer a letter within three days' time.

The four of them writing to young ladies, not to mention aging aunts, old friends and cousins, as well as notes to one another, produced an average of twenty-five letters a day. God knows how they must have strained to include an interesting tidbit, for their lives were a sea of monotonous luxury, the surface of which was punctured by feats of uncleverness and tasteless pranks. Undoubtedly they had help from *The Men's Etiquette, Personal Letter-Writing Outline*, which each kept in his top desk drawer:

*Dear _____ (comma)*
*1. general questions about the recipient's condition*
*2. several paragraphs detailing the writer's news (keep light and humorous, at the same time building in emotion—thread together with relevance to the recipient)*
*3. in-depth response to an issue mentioned in the recipient's most recent letter, or mention plans to meet*
*Love (comma) your affectionate* (insert relationship—i.e., brother, friend) *(comma)*
*X (your name)*

True to form, they conducted the main thrust of their various courtships through the mail. New debutantes received two letters a week from each of the brothers, all reporting similar poetics in the same cloudily seductive manner:

*Dear my dear,*
*How are you? I can't get the smell of your hair out of my head or*
*the feel of your silk dress out of my fingers. I'm pretty sure I feel*
*strongly for you. I won today at bridge, with Peter as my dummy.*
*We're trying to get Mother to replace the green billiard table with*
*a red one. Pray that we pull it off. It's been two days since I last*
*saw you, and I'm still well. Write to me your feelings on this, as*
*it's been intolerably humid. I may or may not come by for a visit*
*Sunday. I can't make any promises, you know. Good-bye, dar-*
*ling! Write to me! Your affectionate suitor, X*

Older women still on the wedding market no longer received
such nonsense from the brothers, as they had long ceased writing
back. To their credit, it took the ladies of Mobile less than five years to
discover that something was seriously wrong with the Riant brothers.
They then picked up the song with vehemence and the spirit of re-
venge, devoting all sorts of powers of elocution to the subject. Where
once the matrons had sighed, saying, "Permanent bachelors, those
Riant boys," they now dug deeper, speculating on the nature of the
trouble and its possible roots. "Colonel Riant is beyond reproach,"
they agreed, "now that he's passed. I'm inclined to blame the
mother."

"She always was rather . . . wasn't she?"

"And still is, if you ask me."

"Holy," tooted Margaret. They sipped.

"She's spoiled them; they're rotten solid; there's not a firm bone
in any of them!" exploded Lottie, followed by miniature poofs of
breath from the circle around her, a chorus of sighs.

"Well," said Margaret.

"Well, well," said Mercie and Susan.

They sipped. "Calm yourself, Lottie," someone said quickly. "It's not too late."

"No, indeed, she'll recover," said Mercie, who had a penchant for the dramatic. "And if she's smart she'll warn the young ladies of Alabama off of those confirmed bachelors, she'll raise her voice in admonishment!"

Lottie was amazed. Margaret reached for a tart. "They're lazy," she said.

"Yes, but that's rather attractive, couldn't it be?" Susan leaned into the circle. "I think they're too . . . how do you say . . . ?"

"Close to one another."

"Yes."

"They make frequent trips to New Orleans, is all I know," she continued. "One can only speculate on what they're doing there, but I'll wager it's not done in daylight."

Someone gasped. "Well," said another. Lottie raised her eyes sadly toward the ceiling. "Well," Mercie chirped, "we can only blame the mother."


According to Mother Riant, there was to be no returning to the house at unseemly hours, no throat clearing, no voice raising, no sitting while a woman stood. There was to be no lending or borrowing, no bad breath, betting or blaspheming, no smoking in the dining room or front porch, no adjusting clothes in public, no eating while in motion. No detail of graciousness went overlooked, no chance at attentiveness went unseized, no thank-you notes unwritten, no funeral flowers unsent. There was no excuse for not attending Confession Saturday evenings at five, fasting from midnight on Saturday to High Mass at noon the next day, observing the holy days of obligation and fasting during Lent. Mother Riant accepted no excuse. Never on Friday was there meat.

Mother Riant insisted that all four brothers dressed for dinner, were prompt, clean-shaven and with shoes shined. The food served, one of them said grace, a duty that rotated among them each week. There was to be no coughing, blowing noses, burping, flatulence or elbows on the table, no eating with the mouth open or talking with the mouth full of food. Nor was there any eating or drinking to excess. Mother Riant tolerated no conversation relating to the body, sex or sickness, and anything sounding even remotely like gossip was unforgivable. Nor was anything personal to the family discussed when the servants were present. This account will spare the mention of each cutlery rule and napkin convention required by Mother Riant. Her idea of the appropriate was so clearly defined the sons had no choice but to obey to the letters of her law—or so it seemed.

Among the four of them it was relatively easy to keep her satisfied. If she asked one to change his clothes, he said, "Of course, Mother," and did as she recommended without complaint, only to change again and stay out of her sight for the rest of the day. If she begged them to organize their desks, they said, "Of course, Mother," knowing that they didn't really have to, certainly not anytime soon. If she wanted a lightbulb replaced, they said, "Of course, Mother," only to vanish into the house in pursuit of a bulb, never to return.

It was the errands they loathed. It had been easier before Regina married and moved away: Regina had run all the errands. Now the brothers had to fetch Mother Riant's spectacles, chocolates from Mr. Leitter's, or refill her laxative bromo-quinine tablets, or the three-grain Cadomene tablets for her nerves, or the five-grain Arbolone tablets for flesh reduction, or a four-ounce jar of plain yellow Minyol for itching scalp. She had so many goddamn treatments! They ran these errands for the most part, taking all day just to run to the pharmacy if necessary. Sometimes they came home to report the strangest things—Mr. Leitter closed at one in the afternoon! The sweets counter out of lemon drops! Perez out of trout! They forgot and misplaced a lot of things as well. Forgetting to call on Father Lusch, forgetting to post her letters, forgetting to . . . They lost receipts, shopping lists and jewelry, keys, checks and change.

At this point in her life, Mother Riant clung to the illusion that her marriage, if not happy, had been pleasant enough. She didn't dishonor the memory of Colonel Riant in thought or deed after his death, though she wished he had taught these boys to be more care-ful with their money. A bill from an eel farm in Nova Scotia detail-ing an outrageous sum—hair oil, wrinkle treatments, masculine compresses, foot cream?—drew her attention to other extravagant expenditures, but she was too reserved to mention specifics of the masculine toilette and said nothing. When she calculated the num-ber of acceptable marriages that had already passed them by, season after season, she reckoned it would be impossible to find four women as unique as her sons and took their choosiness as some-thing of an honor to her. She was not blind to the tremendous sim-ilarities among them; even she confused their names more often than not. But then, it wouldn't be easy for men so gifted as her sons to mix with average Mobilians.

She never slept well at night, but it wasn't until Colonel Riant had taken sick and been moved to a room on the first floor that she became aware of her sons' nocturnal recreations. All night long she heard them passing back and forth across the floorboards, opening and closing the front door and creeping into the dining room—for the bourbon, she realized. Through her open window, she could hear them urinating on the azaleas in the side yard, followed shortly by breaking glass and the sound of arguing over the billiard game. She would never, she swore, get them a red table. Once she heard a woman's laughter, and for weeks after, she agonized over whether or not to confront them. Perhaps they were sowing their wild oats for a few years, as gentlemen do. Though she didn't approve, she took their reckless ways as a symptom of their good breeding and was almost proud; she chuckled to herself, imagining them breaking all the hearts in Alabama.

Then Colonel Riant died, after which she was given the drops and she slept undisturbed, until one night, when she had forgotten to take her medicine and found herself wide awake. She pieced together the sound that had roused her, a loud crash. Giggles came to her through her transom. Were they in the hallway? "Hello!" she called. The giggling stopped.

Shuffles to the stairs and then a thud, a moan, "Mother . . ."

Wearily she put on her dressing gown. At the top of the stairs, she saw his form, splayed on his back between the second and seventh stair, his head resting on the upper hallway. Another figure stood on the dark landing, laughing up at him who couldn't stand, then scurried away. She bent over her son and lightly slapped his face. "You disgust me," she said. She saw the whites of his eyes in the darkness, staring at her without recognition. She straightened and kicked his shoulder with her slippered foot. "Get up."

He shifted to his elbows, rotating his torso as if to push himself up, but he bumped down four or five more steps, moaning and laughing as he went. Standing there, listening to his heavy breathing in the darkness below her, she wanted more than ever to sleep. She heard him stirring about and watched as two matches were lit and extinguished in succession.

"Mother?"

She refused to answer. In the light coming from the first-floor hallway through the space between the two flights of stairs, his hand shot up, grabbing unsuccessfully for the banister. A series of shiftings: his profile was visible for a second, then she heard his back slam against the wall, his footsteps heavy and slow coming up the steps toward her. His breath, and then he was standing in front of her, the flash of his teeth through his smile. "Mother!" He threw his arms around her and put his head on her shoulder. The flesh of his cheek dug into the knob of her shoulder bone, which now supported the weight of his entire head.

"Stand up straight." It was Peter; suddenly she felt sick.

"Stand up straight?" He reeled backward. "I am standing up straight, aren't I, Mother?" The shape of the curls made it Louis.

"You disgust me," she whispered.

"I know it," he said, pivoting on his heel, teetering and grabbing again at the wall. She, too, grabbed at the wall when she realized it was Felix. He stumbled in the direction of his room. Was it George?

She was sad and furious in equal amounts. The remainder of the night she spent planning their deprivation, but the next morning she hid in her sewing room until dinner. By one o'clock they were seated and served. She waited until the last servant left the room and closed the door. She was pleased to see her sons exchanging nervous glances. The peas were passed in silence. "Sell the newspaper," she said at last.

Felix turned flaming red; Louis cleared his throat; George looked at his plate.

Peter arched his eyebrow. "Four is our habit, and four it will be," he said, throwing both arms over the back of the chair, looking into the eyes of his brothers one by one. "Let's vote."

"Fine," muttered Louis. "Why not? It's not as if we pioneered the 'Sunday Science' section or anything."

"Yes, why not sell it?" echoed Felix.

"Three is my habit, and three it will be," said George, looking to Louis, who shrugged his shoulders.

"I said fine," he laughed, reaching for a roll. "Of course"—his
smile died down quickly—"I could still write the science section
and just not own the paper." They all waited for George to speak.

"It's settled then," said the fourth.

*Such nothingness,* Mother Riant thought. She had expected some
resistance. Her hand had made red marks on them as toddlers; now
she could make no impression. "Are you gentlemen?" she asked
quietly. Peter and Louis rolled their eyes.

"Ribbit," said Felix. "Excuse me, Mother."

"Ribbit, ribbit," said another, supported by ripples of his brothers' laughter.

IN JUNE 1919 THE NEWSPAPER WAS SOLD and the money invested in a
mixture of high-risk and solid stocks, all on the advice of Felix. With
it went the Riant brothers' last pretense of industry. Now they had
no reason to leave the house, except to escape Mother Riant, who, in
turn, exerted herself more desperately than ever on their behalf. Peter slept shamefully late and wouldn't rouse himself at all, even for
the most important errands. Louis persisted in writing the "Sunday
Science" section, though it was cut to biweekly. To Mother Riant the
column was more unintelligible than before, so she pored over it,
asking the leading questions of an intelligent layperson and giving
him line-by-line suggestions for lightening the tone.

Felix began taking business trips whenever the mood struck
him. The fall just after the newspaper was sold, Mother Riant offered him the assistance of her family connections in Savannah. His
eyes betrayed such a strange, stifled amusement she never dared
again to ask him for details. George was meanwhile devoting himself entirely to his studies of the Virgin. As one of his women friends
had already joined a convent, Mother Riant spoke with wild enthu-

siasm about any girl he mentioned and prayed continuously that one of them would pity him enough to take him off her hands.

The brothers saw no reason to keep up their front of obedience after the sale. They missed breakfast and appeared sullen at dinner, red-eyed and without appetite. She endeavored to keep their attention by chattering about this and that or criticizing their manners in a loving tone, and though they mumbled the requisite "Excuse me, Mother," she began to digest that it made no difference. They had nothing to say to her. Supper they took out or stayed shut up in the parlor playing bridge.

Mother Riant expressed her discontent with a very real sickness of the stomach, diagnosed as nervous gastritis, which relegated her to a strict diet of avocados, applesauce, catfish and mashed potatoes. For a while she valiantly hid the sudden pains that struck her as she sat across from her sons, eating cheerily, but she grew so thin that obviously she was ill. Another cook, Sylvie, was hired especially for her needs, and Mother Riant was persuaded to take her meals, with the exception of Sunday dinner, alone in the sitting room off her bedroom.

As she grew sharper and sharper to what she admitted was the impotence of her progeny, Mother Riant weakened physically. Arthritis, establishing itself in her joints, became more and more crippling. The doctors could do little for her, beyond recommending that the heels of her shoes be softened and lowered, and doubling the dose of her sleeping drop. She napped two or three times a day and even when awake maintained the state of somnolence. A broken hip resulted from a nasty crash into a horse and wagon on her last trip downtown, and she took up the silver-plated cane that had been her mother's, but the more disgraces she observed from this place of keen inactivity, the less strength she had to discipline.

Her rules were too numerous, even for her. It was impossible to reprimand them on so many various fronts, so she contented herself with uttering about a fifth of her complaints, to no noticeable effect. Peter lay in bed longer and longer—she shuffled to the door of his bedroom at noon and banged on it with the head of her cane, announcing her orders for the day. "Peter, run this recipe over to Miss Charlotte on your way to Mr. Leitter's. I need you to pick up some oysters too, and return this book to Sister Mary Joseph." The whole ritual took about an hour and a half, as he would never stir until a cup of chicory had cooled on his bedside table. He would get up and go out but return having completed none of her requests.

Louis had only men friends. His "Sunday Science" section grew in obtuseness, and she began to see it as adding further to the shame already growing around the family name. When the newspaper discontinued it, she encouraged him as best she could in his study of the classical flute, but as she prided herself on having perfect pitch and had been, as a girl, something of a talented pianist, she couldn't resist correcting him the rare times he practiced—until he stopped altogether. Felix she suspected of being a gambler and never addressed him without a tone of disapproval. As he aged, he reminded her most of her late husband, so she stopped looking at him. As for George, after three of his women friends had become nuns, he took up a halfhearted dog-breeding hobby, but she refused to let the beasts onto her grounds and forced him to rent another property for the enterprise, which he soon abandoned.

Had there been too many rules? Had everyone else seen the dissipation of her sons long ago? Was it too late? Such thoughts were unbearable. What had she done wrong? In her many hours alone, she chastised herself for creating dilettantes and told herself she was as worthless as they had learned to become. Her lady friends visited less and less, and she understood why. Now she could read her sons' posturing; now she had no illusions about them. They had defied all of her sound advice.

As much as they tried to stay away from her, to keep out of the house, the brothers remained imperceptibly longer and longer under the same roof with her. Part of it was Mother Riant's doing. She had inherited everything except the newspaper from the Colonel—the dairy, the bank accounts, the property—and was able to cut their allowance so they could no longer afford to drink out. They continued with their letters. As much as they disregarded their mother, with great success, she still made them feel bad. Though unwilling to change their ways, they were capable of feeling awfully guilty—especially after Peter, falling out of bed one night in late September with a lit cigarette, set his mattress on fire; Louis smelled smoke, ran to the room and put it out, beating it with a blanket and pouring the water from the washbasin on it. Even so, Felix called the volunteer fire brigade, and they all evacuated. Standing on the lawn in their robes, mother and sons in the purple predawn light did not recognize one another.

The following day the house made great efforts to return to normal. Felix, who had taken over the finances after Mother Riant had shattered her elbow, purchased a new bed and mattress immediately and set a maid to work scrubbing the soot off of the walls. No one mentioned the fire, but the brothers were scared. Overnight Mother Riant's hair had gone white and brittle. All four sat down and wrote a letter to Regina, insisting that she return home. Mother Riant also sat down and wrote a telegram to Regina—she needed help—then got on the phone and hired a woman to come once a week and rinse her hair with reddish purple dye. This act confirmed that she would never again leave the house, for Mobile would never know her as a woman who dyed her hair.

## The Pearly Gates

DIVINE PRESENCE WAS NOT A LOGIC PUZZLE. For Regina, human consciousness, with all its strange, unspoken combinations—line, memory, the pull of water; word, dream and mountain; note, thought, the silence of the desert—was enough to suggest the existence of God. She knew that it could not be proved, and that the very nature of faith was this inability. The problem of evil: she didn't see evil as God's fault. There were plenty of people eager to promote it without any assistance—just look at the war. She liked how the church attacked her senses and provided an interview with the Power that one returned to after death, she hoped, in some form or another. And she had made it a practice of believing. "Faith takes work," her father had always told her, but she hadn't worked hard enough, evidently.

His funeral made her think of dirt so much she couldn't bear it. The body of her father in the earth. In the face of death, her casual kind of faith, she realized, was lost. She couldn't imagine him returned to God and didn't want to live without him; she didn't have the strength for it. What love—she could remember so many of her father's kindnesses, and those scenes flashed across the screen of her mind, each no more than a half second long, but picking up pace until her eyes were blurry with tears again. Crying again! She couldn't stop. She remembered once, when he was helping her with her word problems at the dining room table, seeing him proud of her mind. There were a thousand learnings with him: to speak and swim and read, to ride a bicycle, to stand up straight. He approached her on the porch a second time after Ahlong had left without her and said, "Behave like the lady you are. God has another plan for you. Maybe that man Ahlong—and I liked him—would never have made you happy. He wasn't like you. He didn't have your faith."

"No one is like me," she blubbered anew. "That's why I have no faith."

That subdued him, seemed to make him sad. "Faith takes work," he said finally. "And you'd better start working on it or you'll have a nervous breakdown when I die, I who have loved you since you were nothing." Her face blanketed with grief, she had always been sure of his love for her, as she would never be sure of anything again. But faith is too much to simply say and get away with. No one knows what it means. What makes up life? Work, of course. Testing oneself against the board game of commerce, against the wits of other men, against time. But she was a woman. To use their God-given talents to the fullest was one of life's challenges for women. And the other, love, was just the interstices.

Now that her father was gone, she didn't know what to do with herself. She knew she was being selfish to begrudge him a painless place. She hadn't wanted him to remain suffering, nor was she ready to relinquish him to the ranks of angels. Perhaps it was a lack of vision: when she tried to imagine him among the cherubim and seraphim and saints, she hit a wall. What if the Colonel hadn't made it to the top? And how could any such inequality exist in heaven?

·  ·  ·

As the result of a dispute with Mother Riant, Dr. Freret had left off his ministrations in June of 1918, and new doctors were brought in for the Colonel. Now his excruciating cough could be heard in all rooms of the house and as far as the magnolia tree near the front gate. When he took to bed with fever for a third time, his family knew the end was near. Two doctors confirmed pneumonia. One said simply he would die. Another said cancer of the spine and applied more X-rays to his back, leaving wounds that, no matter how many times Regina applied the dressings, never healed. He weakened. An expert from Atlanta was brought down to announce that the Colonel was exhausted and should stay in bed. His eyes yellowed and his skin darkened and cracked, as the fever rose and fell each day. Regina spent most of her day and night by his bedside tending to him and saying the rosary. When it became obvious that she was the only one who could calm him, Mother Riant never returned to the sickroom, which was moved to the first floor at the beginning of July.

Mother Riant disapproved of her daughter's assiduousness in the sickroom and often barged in to chastise her. "We can afford nurses, dear," she told Regina scornfully, or, "Regina, dear, you really can't neglect the rest of your obligations to sit here crying. It's unseemly. You've got to show a little more fortitude," but Regina didn't care what her mother said, especially now.

Visitors flowed through the house throughout the middle of August, and each of the Colonel's sons appeared at his bedside at specific times to weep alone with the prostrate form and presumably say his peace. He worsened, spoke of heaven. Regina kept a little notebook and pencil on the bedside table to record her father's last wishes, which streamed from his mouth in endless catalogs whenever he was lucid. The nurse, who took her place while Regina was sleeping, recorded up to thirty such proclamations in the early-morning hours.

*Widow Sabatier—first floor of prop. on Old Government*
*R. Chalmette—OOM's cig. case and cufflinks*
*Jules Meunier—cows*
*Francis Decatur—poniard with Yankee bone handle*
*Ursulines—theo. library, Studebaker stocks*
*Paperboys—ties*
*Uncle Sawyer—deed to bicycle track*
*Felix—pay your debts*
*A. Dismukes—maps*

"I have nothing," he would rasp to Regina after an extended spew. "Regina, I don't really have anything to give." Yet she filled a book and then another book. All the men at the newspaper were to have bottles of brandy. Georgie and Cedric, his pigs. Gibb, his rolltop desk and war letters. Camilla, his sister Alice's Three Fates cameo. Sometimes he spoke of his mother, how she hadn't approved of his mentor, Major St. Peter, how she had been cited in the newspaper for passing counterfeit Confederate dollars—Regina couldn't follow it. He spoke of seeing angels on earth and sang the Agnus Dei. He coughed, begged the air for forgiveness.

The Colonel's boyhood friend Cardinal Straw arrived from Baltimore at the beginning of September to give the Last Rites. The heat was insufferable, not breaking until the beginning of November and then only slightly. She sat at her father's side, sponging his face with a damp towel and holding his hand, massaging it a bit. She fanned him with a palmetto leaf and said "Just rest" every time he shifted in frustration. She kept his hair combed. She tried to talk to him and he tried to speak, but the sick, even the most faithful, are often too tired for last words. Everything she'd wanted to ask him must already be asked, and so she just sat there watching him doze, wishing he had been able to see her children before he died. She opened the slats of the shutters to let in the evening drafts.

How she had fallen in love with Charles Morrow during her father's long illness was a mystery to her. A year before, she thought nothing of Mr. Morrow except that he was an excellent horseman, lived at Spring Hill and was not Catholic. He had come to dinner several times as a guest of her brother Peter, years ago when they had taken English-riding classes together. In those days his conversation had been easy for Regina to ignore.

Through the fall of 1918, Charles came to see her many Sundays in a row before she realized he was courting her, but by then things were in motion without her: they were seated alongside each other at dinner parties, mentioned together in the newspaper. Matrons made flattering references to him when talking with her—embracing Charles had become a pastime with them. She started receiving invitations from his sisters on the hill. Peter claimed he was one of his best gentleman friends, and Felix made a practice of reconstructing the Morrow family tree. Louis spoke in impressed tones of Charles's chosen industry—everyone knew that lumber had replaced cotton as Mobile's chief export. George gave her supportive smiles from across the parlor during visiting hour, and Mother Riant went out of her way to be courteous, though she would always object to the match on religious grounds. They were all relieved that Regina never talked of Ahlong after Charles appeared on the scene.

Charles was a delicately boned man with elegant reddish facial hair. He gave the impression of being reluctant to take his hat off, and as he was shifting near the door, she noticed his angles—his long hands and feet, his narrow shoulders and hips, his thin legs.

For the most part, he was silent and seemed indifferent to the activities around him, but he kept himself occupied—refreshing drinks, striking matches, stoking fires. Regina prized his drowsy, pale blue eyes, which had a capacity for showing a naive excitement and by turn eternal sadness, making him seem both younger and much older than his twenty-eight years. His skin was tanned, with pallor underneath, his light brown hair too silken to stay in place. Two dimples on each side of his soft, broad lips he employed frequently in smiles either to himself or to strangers, while moving around a room with the stiff grace of one on stilts. Though youthful, he maintained an air of having tapped in to the sad undercurrents of life; at times he seemed barely able to lift his eyes from them, but when he did—to her at least they were warm and wet and loving.

There was also something of the clown about him. He dressed well, but always with some quirky touch of his own, a splash of color in his tie or socks or suspenders, a flower in his buttonhole. When, a week before her father's death, she was told he was waiting in the parlor to see her, she knew enough to put on a nicer dress before going down. She opened the door, and he strode forward wearing an unnatural grin. "I hope your brother told you I was coming by . . ."

"Oh yes!" She had no recollection of it. Her hand was swallowed by his. She was standing closer to him than ever before and backed away.

"Then you know why I'm here."

"I suppose so." Should she offer him coffee?

"I don't think so," he said, taking her by the elbow to the couch. He said, "Now that we're sitting down"—before they were sitting—"I don't mind admitting to you that I'm confused. I want to make you proud of me, proud of my growing lumber business. I realize I don't have anything to work for but you."

"Me?"

He jumped from his seat beside her and began pacing in front of the couch. She settled back to watch. "What is this thing we call life? And I keep thinking that if I have you for long enough, you can tell me. When does it begin?" He ran his hands through his hair. "Take these trousers, for instance. Why did I choose them? I mean, what do they mean? That's not a good example. Why are there so many things that we have to do, so many petty things to choose from? Not to mention the big things! I don't like it!" He was standing before her, cheeks aflame.

"Those are questions I have, too," she said. "Every thinking person does."

Suddenly Camilla was in the doorway. "The Colonel's calling for you, Miss Regina."

"Of course," said Charles, clasping his hands.

"I'll be right back," she called to him from the hallway.

But the Colonel was not having a good night. For a half hour or more, she sat by the bed, sponging his face, watching him thrash with fever, giggling and shivering, his face like a sheet of crumpled paper, his lips dried in cracks, his eyes jeweled with cysts. Twice she got up to leave but his urgent muttering called her back to his side. Finally she asked the nurse to tell Charles to go home, that she would be all night. "Well, here you are on your deathbed," she said to herself, and took up the rosary beads again with a haggard sigh.

She had run out of prayers. It was as hard to stay true to love as it was to say there was something called "true love." She had treasured Ahlong because she had dreamed the farthest with him and everything else fell away, but life is harder than a dream. She would care for her husband because he would protect her from the world, which is not love, she reasoned, though she wouldn't mind feeling safe. There were other things involved with a marriage that she supposed she would enjoy. She tried to think of her father united with her mother, or the first Regina, in the afterlife, but that didn't feel like the answer, as she knew relatively little about their intimacies. There were many kinds of love, and she had, at twenty, done her best to honor them, as daughter, sister, friend.

He began burbling about what she guessed was the newspaper. She put her ear to his lips but could make no sense of it; she tried to get him to sip water but he wouldn't take it. ". . . afraid," he said, but she couldn't tell whether he'd said "I'm afraid" or "I'm *not* afraid." She rearranged the pillows, rubbed rosemary oil into his chest, calves and forearms. Still his breathing did not steady. "Pierce . . . ier . . . ce . . . P . . . ," he rasped. She didn't know if he was referring to Pierce Circumbers—or how her heart felt for the past year and a half, as she watched him fade away. "Don't worry, Father." She was exhausted, put her hand on his forehead. "It's Regina," she said for the fourth time, and he seemed to calm down.

Then he was silent for some time, and, continuing with the Hail Marys, she turned her mind to Pierce, whom she had seen briefly before her father's most recent relapse. Pierce had driven fast. "Have anything you want, darling," he had said as they sat at the shiny wooden counter at Antwerp's. Then he talked about improvements he was making to his stables. She wanted a chance to ride his horses—that was one reason she remained polite when the Negro boy who sold newspapers came in and asked for a glass of water. "You can have anything you want, boy," Pierce had said. The boy's eyes lit up with excitement and he edged closer to the counter. "Do you want chocolate water, vanilla water or strawberry water?" And laughed. Mr. Blum's hand was limp over the counter. The traffic in Bienville Square seemed to quiet. Pierce laughed again, swiveling back to Regina on his stool. She had tilted away from him, smiling thinly, and while she was pretending to

glance out the storefront until Mr. Blum had given the boy water
and guided him out, she was actually looking at her reflection, wondering if her face was bright red in mortification.

Her heart was not broken in the slightest. She knew that Pierce
would never do even before he botched the proposal. One Sunday
after supper in the parlor he made himself comfortable with a cigar.
Regina rattled on about the book she was reading aloud to the
Colonel in his sickroom, *Life of Mrs. Elizabeth Ann Seton, Afterwards Mother E. A. Seton,* but she could tell he wasn't interested and
trailed off. "Let's talk about something serious," he said, holding
her gaze. She asked him what he thought of Annie Spotswood's engagement. "You can't avoid me, Regina. Tell me something very
serious."

"My father is ill."

"I'm well aware of that," he said. They fell silent. Feeling herself fill up with tears, she looked out the window, wishing he had
compassion for her, wishing he understood. She sensed him idling
behind her. *He wants me to say I'm fond of him,* she realized, and
there were things she liked about him, but when she turned to face
him, his smug expression repelled her. Just then the nurse came in
to say the Colonel was asking for her. "I have to see my father," she
had said. "I'll be right back," and rushed out of the room. She
hadn't seen Pierce Circumbers since.

The Colonel was restless, but she held his hand and said a prayer
over him, imploring him to help her and asking him that, if he had
to die—and she was willing to let him die—that he try to look
down on her from heaven and guide her, through God, in times of
need. That was all she asked of him and, loving him and thanking
him with all her heart, she stopped her crying. Things would be
all right. Through the gaps in the shutters, moonlight dipped into
the room, making shadows of prisoner stripes on the white sheet,

mummifying him. His cheeks were sunken and ash-colored, his eyes bruised, his throat quivering with sleep. When she rose to leave, he stirred, inspired to speech, and she glided halfway back to his bed. "Kind," she thought he said. Her kind? Kind-natured? Kind of something? Light? Lime? Moonlight. She sat back down in her chair, but he said no more for the next half hour. Then he was suddenly awake. "Read to me," he moaned, and she picked up her missal.

*Charles Morrow would have bought the boy a chocolate soda,* Regina thought as she read. Charles loved chocolate, took so much pleasure in ordering chocolate sodas all around, so she felt that telling him chocolate gave her a headache would break his heart. They were writing and visiting almost every day now. He knew all about her plans for the red silk skirt, about her father's progress, her taste in music, her favorite streets in Mobile. She even told him the story of going to see the great Indian War chief Geronimo at Mount Vernon when she was a girl. Which reminded him of Choctaw Bluff, the most beautiful spot in the world he called it, where he stayed during the lumber season. And the land he owned at Spring Hill and his plans to build a house there. He was an excellent horseman; she had seen him ride. It was understood that if they were married, they would go to Choctaw Bluff for the first six months so he could sell the property and use the money to build them a house at Spring Hill and set himself up in business in Mobile.

Colonel Riant stirred again, and she realized she had stopped reading maybe ten minutes ago. "A long . . . ," he gasped, "short light." Light again? Life? Ahlong? She leaned her ear to his lips. He shook his head rapidly against the pillow, cleared his throat and tried to sit up. "No, Father, you've got to rest." She guided him back to his pillow, but a remarkably strong arm tried to push her away. "Ata!" he cried. She put one palm behind his neck and pushed him back down with her other palm on his shoulder. Suddenly he sagged in her arms. She nested his head back on the pillow and refolded the sheet under his chin.

Again she picked up her *Saint Vincent's Manual* and began reading "A General Prayer for All Things Necessary to Salvation," one of the Colonel's favorites. When she woke up, her neck was stiff, her forearm imprinted by the upholstered chair, her dress wet with perspiration. By the sounds of the birds and the color of sky through the slats in the shutters, she guessed it was almost dawn. Still there was no breeze. She could hear the whistling of the nurse's nose as she slept in the corner armchair; Colonel Riant slept peacefully. Without looking at the chamberpot, the medicines cluttering the bedside table, the pile of dirty towels, she moved wearily through the room and into the hall, turning out the electric lights and the gaslights as she went. She would lie down in her own bed for a couple of hours. The house was silent, but a strip of light showed under the library door.

She shrieked upon seeing Charles Morrow, who shifted in the shadows of the sofa when she opened the library door—had he been waiting all night?! What night was it? Had she forgotten some engagement? Had the nurse forgotten to tell him to go home?

He put down his book and strode toward her, pale in the light of dawn. "I'm sorry to scare you."

"Why are you here?"

"I hope the Colonel is resting."

"No one recovers from age," she snapped, turning to the window.

He flinched, stepped back, ran a hand through his hair, stepped forward again. "Regina . . ."

She faced him, trying to remain composed. "I'm so tired," she said. "I can't talk. . . . I can't think. . . . Please leave."

"Regina . . ." He put his hands on her shoulders and she fell forward, releasing the posture she had held for so long, pressing her cheek against his chest. "Regina, I love you." She cried in his arms and then he kissed her for the first time. "I love you," he whispered again.

A week later, on November 25, 1918, two weeks after Armistice Day, Colonel Riant passed on and the cyclone commenced, with Regina at its eye: in black, spun by everyone around her. Charles, who had called it into being, was on the ground beyond the swirling air; the terrain over which it swept was her mind, as the wedding date grew nearer, blown sand-clean of all pretensions and romantic ideals of a perfect life. Regina married Charles Morrow six months after her father's death. Still in mourning, she made for herself a black wedding gown out of taffeta and beaded lace.

Everyone conspired to make it go off without a hitch; everyone was so happy for her—what an excellent match. Only Mathilde withheld her congratulations. She acted as if she herself were being betrayed by the act of marriage, as if everything, including love, were being scandalized by the union. "I have to try something else," Regina said when she saw the look on her cousin's face. "Ahlong's not coming back."

"Find him," said Mathilde, shifting from the doorframe to a position on the trunk at the foot of the bed, so that Regina could see her cousin's scarred face in the mirror of the vanity where she was putting on powder.

"I don't know where he is."

"If you set out, you'll find him. Desire is the key."

Regina laughed until she realized without looking up that Mathilde's face was grave above her pale green gown. "I'm too far into this. It wouldn't be right. I'm decided."

"Searching for him and not finding him would be better than this. An endless search would be better than this."

Regina turned around on her stool and looked at Mathilde with the patience she would have shown to an unpromising child. "Leave me in peace, please, Mathilde. And wish me well. That's all you can say."

Mathilde put her chin to her shoulder mumbling, "It's not too late."

"One day you'll see that life is imperfect," she said, turning back to the mirror, the fingernail of her thumb tracing the flower pattern on the back of her sterling hairbrush. "That's what I've realized. There is no purity."

Mathilde said again hoarsely, "It's not too late," but when Cousin Thérèse and her daughter Josie came into the room a second later, she exited without further plea.

Everything was beautiful and went exactly as planned, as puppets move through a dream, a bubble of soap swirling the colors of the rainbow, beautiful but without delineation. Because she wasn't nervous at all saying the words, had steeled herself against regret, and because she was admired and supported by everyone, it didn't hurt. A glance at Mother Riant gave her the only justification she needed to follow through with her promise to Charles. With time she forgot almost all of the ceremony except a moment at the end, when she stood at the doors of the library of her father's house—they couldn't be married in the cathedral because he wasn't Catholic—realizing it was irrevocable before God.

# An Ideal Husband

THE TENNESSEE RIVER west of Lawrence County threads into the Warrior-Tombigbee Waterway, connecting Birmingham to the Gulf of Mexico at Mobile. At the top of this junction the town of Choctaw Bluff stands as a gateway to more than sixteen thousand miles of navigable inland waterways. In 1919 the town consisted of a cluster of produce stands, one small saloon posing as a dry-goods store, which Regina loathed to enter, and a general grocery that placed orders through the Montgomery Ward catalog and also served as a post office.

Saturdays, Regina and Camilla drove into town for the shopping, and though it was their one day out of the house, neither took joy in the excursion. The shadeless streets were filled with Indians not wearing shoes, men covered in sawdust, wrinkled women with their unspeakably ragged children, and every type of mild scoundrel, who had been churned to this outpost for one reason or another and whom they referred to as Yankees.

One of Camilla's pretexts for coming north from Mobile had been her relatives among the Chickasaws, but she had done nothing so far to locate them. Both women had fallen victim to backwoods lethargy. They didn't think about the past or the future—no longer recalled the features of Mobile—but moved through the days as if in a swamp, forgetting their resolutions and confusing boredom with exhaustion. On shopping day the dust seemed to hang in a cloud of warbling heat over the town, and it was difficult for Regina to breathe. She was frustrated no end with the shops, stocked with vegetables long past their prime. The dry-goods store with its festive air and many drunken men repulsed her. Charles came to dread her returning home from the shopping, for she was always in a foul mood. One Saturday she insisted he stay with her in the bedroom while she cried and talked, quietly enough that Camilla wouldn't hear, about how she was lonely, how she worried for their child who was developing in such horrible heat and dust. As the crying slowed, she lay on her back and closed her eyes.

"I wish you wouldn't go to town anymore," he spoke to the tops of the window frames. "Camilla can manage."

"But where will I go then? I have nowhere else to go!" she groaned, putting her elbow over her eyes. "It's so hot!"

"It's no hotter here than Mobile, I think." He sat beside her and loosened her collar, used the tips of his fingers to push up her sleeves. "Can I get you an iced handkerchief?"

"No."

"Lemonade?"

"No."

"I'm doing the best I can, Regina," he said evenly. "What more do you want?"

"Nothing," she said.

He struggled for patience until she began crying all over again, this time for her weakness, for her fear, for being such a burden to him. With his shoes on he lay down beside her, pulled her head onto his shoulder and put his arm around her. She promised to do better. He told her it was all right. She said she loved him. He said he loved her. After a few minutes of silence, "It's too hot," she whispered, detaching herself from him, but he was already asleep. She kissed his cheek and pushed back the hair that was stuck to his forehead. He murmured something with a small smile on his face. She stroked him behind the ear with her middle finger. "I love you," she told him softly. Then she shook him gently. "Charles, I'm not going to act like a baby anymore, all right?"

"All right," he said, thick with sleep.

Charles seemed to fatigue more and more with each passing day, and it worried her. She figured he was working extra hard to bring the lumberyard to a point of sale—to close it as quickly as possible. He had told her about a man at the sawmill losing his leg and that they were paying for the medical treatment, which was a drain on the liquid capital, but she didn't know about the turpentine still he had bought.

The turpentine trade had been a successful transition economy of forty years before. She knew that from having many conversations with her father's friends, but this particular still needed expensive repairs. She had noticed on her way to Choctaw Bluff that the pine forests were remarkably thinner than they had been ten years before, that outside Mobile they were already cut over, but she didn't know Charles's logging crew was demanding a pay raise, that he was trying to switch from river transport to ox-drawn carts, a method that had defied logic by becoming cheaper than river floating. Or that he was beginning aggressive replanting of his land.

Charles knew Regina wanted desperately to leave but could never know the extent of her physical discomfort. He was doing the best he could, he told himself, and combated her growing dissatisfaction with gifts, which he was able to procure through his friendship with various steamship captains who stopped to do trade at the bluff. Not a day passed that he didn't bring her some new treat—from little desserts to hard candy or caramels to special gold thread, a gold thimble or lavender sachets for the drawers; things for the garden: a camellia bush, sweet peas, and sweet potatoes; things to stimulate her appetite: fresh oysters and shrimp, limes, merlitons, mangoes, watermelon. His overactive, even stressful, gift giving she buffered with selflessness. The violet silk he expected her to use for a maternity frock she converted into curtains for the dining room. The flower-printed cotton was made into a bedspread for Camilla and pillows for the couch in the parlor; the pineapple was made into an upside-down cake.

From the back porch, Regina and Camilla watched the grass darken and the cracked clay ground of high summer cover with lizards. Sitting there, they were not ashamed to raise their skirts to their knees so that the smallest breeze might dry their sweat-wet legs. The sun burned the backs of their necks if they dared to cross under it and by two o'clock pierced directly into their eyes, fat and old and loathsome, until they contrived of nailing up cheap muslin to make an awning for the porch. Periodically the water pump went dry, but they put out the cooking pans to collect the hot rain when it fell for a few minutes in the afternoon, so that they might soak dishcloths in it and, applying them to their foreheads and using hand fans to dry the wetness, have a bit of relief. Or they sucked on cubes of ice, took them out of their mouths and put them on their foreheads, necks and behind their ears. By August there was no such thing as cooking. Lighting the stove was unbearable, and they had no appetite anyway. Egg salad, tomatoes, strawberries, cold chicken and cold spoon bread constituted their every meal.

Regina's hands and feet swelled, her back ached, and the smell of the cabin's new wood baking in the heat drove her mad. Sleep, too, she found impossible. Nights after Charles had fallen asleep, she crept across the floors in her bare feet—risking splinters—and returned to the back porch. There she tacked up the muslin to welcome the air and sat back, put her feet up on the railing, letting her white underwear glow into the darkness, admiring the arches of her feet, looking at the progress of her belly and thinking that to try to force love to be perfect is missing the whole point. Sitting there in the peace of midnight, she bonded with her unborn child, looking forward to its birth with an almost unbearable excitement. Then a profound sense of love for Charles would wash over her—until she felt sleepy. She would return to bed but couldn't relax, would creep into the kitchen and set up the next day's breakfast, consider waking Camilla but decide against it. And so her nights were passed.

Her days were spent in such an impossible mix of tension and collapse and missing Charles that Camilla sympathized with Charles, imagining she knew the reason he returned later and later each night.

Regina noticed everything: that Camilla was miserable, that Charles found it impossible to wake up in the morning, that evenings when she tried to get him to talk about the house at Spring Hill, the subject was as dog-tired as he, but she didn't know what to do. All her charms failed to lighten the strain lines in his face. In her frustration—she feared later—she may have overquestioned him, begging for his confidence, while his inability to give it made her pity him all the more. "Oh fine, just fine," was his nervous-eyed response when she asked him, more and more tenderly, about his day.

"How can it be fine when I'm not there to keep you company?" she asked, as she had the first night at Choctaw Bluff. Now without gaiety.

"Right," he said with a lowering of the head.

She regretted the words, one by one, as they came out of her mouth: "What do you do all day that makes you so displeased?"

"I'm tying up the ends," he said, sighing deeply, "as I've told you many times, so that we can leave, but I have to identify the ends first. At the same time, I have to pretend not to be doing what I'm doing, understand?" One look at her told him he had gone too far with his tone. "I'm sorry, but you're not helping. You can't help."

"I thought you wanted to sell it," she said in a small voice.

"Well, I can't sell what's broken, can I? But please," he said with a heave of his chest, "let's don't talk about it . . . I . . ."—he grimaced—"our home is not the lumberyard, is it? And besides, look what I brought you."

"Are you all right, Charles?" she asked as she opened and closed the heavy sterling jewelry box, the third he had given her that month, but he just stared off. "Thank you for the box," she said, and kissed him on his chin. Now he picked up the newspaper with satisfaction. She took a deep breath. "Charles, you don't have to worry about me. I'm sorry if I've been whining too much, but now I'm doing well."

"I'm glad, darling."

She went on. "I'm . . . I'm worried about you. Glanton came by . . ." He turned the pages of the newspaper rapidly, making her rush headlong into the speech she had planned. "He said you'd given all your workers a five-dollar bonus and that, well, he thinks that's bad management, but he said you won't listen to reason. Now, I . . . I think it was very kind of you to give the bonus to your workers, but I thought I'd ask you why Glanton is coming to tell me about it." He had stopped at a page of advertisements and appeared to be reading the fine print about Lyko, an energizing tonic. "Talk to me, Charles," she pleaded, her hand grabbing his wrist. He shook his wrist free and turned the page.

She waited several minutes, watching him pretend to read, before, in desperation, turning to her letters. Since she had been at

Choctaw Bluff, she had received countless epistles from her four prolific brothers, at least one a week from each of them. *Dear Sis,* read one dated August 12,

> *Race, sleep, write, sneak, all four well-peppered with details. Here all is well, though Mother took it upon herself to throw the book at us again last night over nothing whatsoever. As a result I'm locked in my room this night. "Denial is right," she tells me, and "Discipline is freedom." Well, I am close to innocent; lost twice at euchre, an hundred each. Cherries well. Last week we had a delicious pork, rose-petal and cherry pie dinner, and well, what else is there? Don't be afraid of snakes or natives, Sis, and write me a letter. I hope this finds you well. Regards to Camilla. Love, your affectionate brother, X.*

At once she noticed that letters from different brothers were almost identical, thus their information blurred in her mind. In the week of August 12, for instance, all four letters contained the term "throw the book," mentioned the cherry pie and included at least one rhyme. All but Felix's suggested she return home as soon as possible, that Mother Riant needed her. Though they depressed her, she would read one or two here and there to remind her that she didn't want to go back to Mobile.

Then she was further confused: where did she want to go? Sitting there next to her husband, a half-read letter in her lap, wishing she could express this, she heard the newspaper drop between Charles's knees to the floor. "Glanton is an ass," he said. "He doesn't realize that in thirty years this property is going to be the most valuable in Alabama, thanks to me."

"I know, darling!" she said eagerly. "I thought it so impertinent that he came to talk to me! Maybe you should get rid of him."

"And I don't feel the need to explain myself to you, with regards to the workers' bonus."

"Then you don't want to sell it?"

"Sell what?"

"The property."

"I'm going to bed," he said.

THE WEATHER BROKE COOLER, bringing earlier evenings and a sense of lost time. Her flower garden rotted; the small cabin seemed cluttered. Regina lay in bed through the cloudy, warmish afternoons, trying to visualize the leaves turning yellow on the desolate road in front of her house. Lying flat was the only ease from her terrible backache, and, drifting in and out, she convinced her daydreams to turn into catnaps until a headache woke her. She tightened scarves of palma Christi leaves around her forehead and lay back, feeling more and more comfortable with an agony that, at the same time, never failed to surprise her. Camilla brought her three or four cups of hot sugar-milk but otherwise sat for hours on the porch with her thoughts, ignoring Regina.

All that ran through Regina's head as she lay there were prayers for Charles and for the baby, alternating with a burning desire to attend Mass, but there wasn't a Catholic church in Choctaw Bluff. She was lonely. Charles was almost never home. Even Sundays he wanted to visit his comanagers and drink. In one of the last conversations they had before leaving for Mobile, he accused her of not socializing with their wives.

"Rod and Glanton aren't the sons of my father's partners, I want you to know," he said slowly, as if he had practiced. "The sons of my father's partners sold to these men, whom I'm dealing with now."

She opened her eyes in the darkened room and studied the shadows of the half-pulled curtains on the opposite wall—she had been asleep since early afternoon. She tried to piece his face together in the shadows. Closed her eyes again.

"They're originally from Chicago," he went on, "which means they are more difficult to deal with. Things might take longer than I thought." He let out his breath loudly, ran his forefinger across the side of his nose. "I want to sell out to them, as you know, but they are driving a hard bargain, actually. And now that the war is over . . . business is, well, I think the industry is full of potential, but . . ."

"We have to wait for another war?" she said with a voice that hadn't been exercised in some days.

"I need you to make efforts with the wives, is my point, darling."

She was confused. This was the first time she had heard mention of any wives. If only she had known earlier! She wanted to tell him she'd make efforts, but it took her a long time to collect her thoughts. "I'll make efforts," she scratched out, her head falling to the side. "I'll invite them to tea, Charles," she said louder, lifting her head back up and bringing the room into focus. But he wasn't there; now it was long after dark.

She sat up, wrapped herself in shawls and hobbled out to join Camilla on the porch. While they watched squirrels and swallows passing in the gray sphere beyond the porch light, both knew that the other was wishing she were somewhere else. Insects smashed against the lantern's glass. Regina wanted to return to Mobile, though not to the house of her mother, but months ago she had ceased boring Camilla with accounts of the house Charles would build them at Spring Hill. Around the same time, Camilla had stopped mentioning a man named Harold who was opening a carpentry shop—now she just longed for her daughters, Regina supposed. When a chill rose off the wet grass, they went inside and lit the kitchen fire, had cups of tea and kumquat jam sandwiches.

The next day she received the telegram from Mother Riant—the thirteenth of October. It was the last time Regina succeeded in waiting up for Charles. She was five months pregnant and, having not sat up for days, she was uncomfortable in the parlor where they sat now. "'Can't believe wilderness doing you good STOP,'" she read to him while he sipped coffee, his head on the back of the armchair, his legs outstretched, his eyes half closed. "'Am worse STOP Brothers worry lack the necessary gentleness STOP Mending STOP Come by first STOP Is your duty to assist holidays STOP Alive STOP Mother STOP' Can you believe she says that about the mending?"

"If I know your mother, she wouldn't write unless it was serious," he said with a sarcasm she missed.

She looked to the sputtering lamp, to the window, to the carpet. "I don't know what to do." Tears rolled down her face; she sniffled, but when Charles didn't move to comfort her she found them difficult to sustain.

"Aren't you glad to have someone who gets sad when you get sad?" he asked. She stared at him: in the dim light he appeared to be smiling, but was he? "Or is it a burden? Both, right?"

She felt herself go cold. "You always seem sad, Charles."

He concentrated on refolding the newspaper as he spoke. "I just don't know that I'm ready to leave here. I'll need at least another month to sort out my affairs." He tossed his head. She sighed because she didn't understand. Her vision was blurred, and she was making a game out of chasing the black spots that swam in the liquid of her eyes. "I love you, Charles."

"I don't know about you"—he shot up from his chair cheerily—"but I'm going to bed."

A deluge of letters from her brothers, all more or less identical, arrived on the thirteenth of November. One from George read:

*Dear Sis,*
*How is the wilderness? Things continue well on this end with us, but well, Mother has fallen, broken her elbow and needs your help. She hates us, it would seem, and we aren't well disposed to her either, though she is our mother and we love her. She is your mother, too. She needs your help. Help us, Sis—it would help if you could be here tomorrow or the next day, at the latest. Telegram us back and let us know when we can expect you. I guess you can tell we're desperate for your help. Also, Peter set his bed on fire. I hope this letter finds you well—that would make at least one out of the six remaining Riants doing well. Regards to Camilla.*
*Love, your affectionate brother, X.*

But neither her mother's resolve nor her brothers' pleas could persuade her to leave Choctaw Bluff. She simply added their names to her daily round of rosaries. It was the morning that Charles didn't make it to work and, in truth, the day he would never again return to work at Choctaw Bluff that made her insist on returning to Mobile.

The bacon burned and the entirety of the small house filled with grease smoke, so Regina and Camilla opened all the doors and windows, letting in a freezing air that chilled the coffee immediately and put out the small fire Camilla had begun in the grate before going out to feed the chickens. But it had rained the night before, the wood on the porch was damp, and there was no newspaper left.

Regina loved burned bacon but Charles did not, which started her thinking about the finances and whether or not she should try to pawn the gold-and-coral brooch—which was gorgeous—that he had given her the day before. And where could she find such a place, without a car, without an excuse for such a mysterious errand? There were no pawnshops in town. Having for some time now made one week's food allowance stretch into two and giving Charles's food to Camilla, she knew there would be no more bacon. "You look beautiful," he said, coming up behind her at the stove and putting his hands on her belly before moving them lower and trying to pull up her skirt as he kissed the side of her neck.

But the plate of burned bacon made him sob. Camilla, coming in with the fresh eggs, fled the room in shock. Regina approached him, pushed aside the table, straddled his lap and stroked his hair, face and the back of his neck. She kissed his eyes and the front of his neck as he continued to weep and weep, coughing, gasping and rubbing his nose until some evidently sad thought, old as the moon, triggered a new avalanche of sobs. When she put his head to her breast he cried even harder. "Thank you for loving me," he croaked.

She lifted his head, pressed her mouth to his forehead. "Loving you is my favorite thing to do," she said, kissing his wet eyes. "Just tell me what you need."

"I don't know what I need," he moaned, fresh tears on his face, dropping his forehead onto her shoulder. "I love you, Regina!"

Starting to cry herself, she rubbed his back. "Don't go to the lumberyards today," she said into his hair. "Let's just stay together." He nodded, blew his nose and let her lead him back to the bedroom, where they lay down side by side and discussed names for the baby. They both fell asleep and, when they woke up, remained talking in each other's arms. He confessed that he had spent a great deal of money replanting the land and buying the turpentine still. They considered whether or not to return to Mobile, though she was sure at this point that it was the only thing that would help him—to get away. They laughed about how much he overpaid his workers, and she was proud of him, kissed him exuberantly all over his face. She lay on his shoulder for a time, reached down and touched him. She shifted and pressed herself against him but he was already snoring lightly.

ON THE SEVENTH OF DECEMBER, Camilla covered Regina with blanket after blanket and then stood in the dirt at the front of the house, waving them off. Even still, Regina was freezing and moved closer to Charles on the bench. The ground was hard, the countryside brown and brittle. The bumps in the road noticeably caused her pain, and he applied all his driving instincts in avoiding them. The sky was cloudy; a winter sun hung directly in front of the windshield. Because she said she needed one, the first half of the journey was spent looking for a place to stop for a toilet. At one point a few dozen wet snowflakes dissolved on the windshield and she became so excited that she kissed Charles on the cheek, who warmed up a little bit at this, though his worry-lined face could not thaw entirely. "Don't you love Christmas?" she asked feverishly.

"Yes." He smiled out of the corner of his mouth but kept his eyes on the road.

"Aren't you excited to go back to Mobile? To see your sisters?"

"Of course." His smile petered out.

"You're not that excited, I guess, are you, Charles?" she asked out of the silence.

"Well, I would have liked to have finished up with my business. As it is, I'll have to return."

"When?" He didn't answer. "I'm sorry," she sniffled.

"Please don't cry," he said, his eyes fixed on the road, his jaw tight. Working on her face with a handkerchief, she started to explain that she was crying because she didn't feel well but kept her tongue and, turning to look out the window, began simultaneously praying and thinking up names for their child. She wouldn't discuss it with him again until she had ten—no, twenty—names that she loved. Then she would let him choose. She checked the mileposts to be sure they were getting closer to Mobile, then thought of how her father had named her. Mother Riant had been lying in, but she had given Colonel Riant explicit instructions to name her fifth child, her only girl, Angela Mary. She understood why her father had changed the names at the Baptism. She liked her own name. But could he have known that naming her Regina Angela instead of Angela Mary would make Mother Riant treat her with so little love? Was that really the reason? A name? She wasn't looking forward to seeing Mother Riant.

They drove on. There were no more snowflakes or rain. They took no notice of the sun, somewhere overhead dimmed by clouds. Her vision constantly blurred over with tears as she thought of her love for her father, thought that they were at last returning to Mobile and that if she could just be in the house of her childhood for a while, she would remember how to make things good with Charles, how to make him, and herself, happy again. She closed her eyes and concentrated on her breathing. Charles followed the road without seeing it. There were no other vehicles in sight.

"Darling?"

"Yes?"

"Can you try to avoid some of the bumps?"

"I am trying to." His voice was testy. "But the roads are hard and—"

"Fine." She winced. He rubbed his eyes and increased the speed. She slept for twenty minutes, woke and unwrapped the sandwiches.

Because she wanted the egg salad, she insisted on giving it to Charles, but he expounded on how much he preferred ham until neither could remember what they liked. Quickly he ate the egg salad. She opened the window curtains to throw out a piece of ham fat and let in enough dust so that she couldn't finish her sandwich, which Charles urged her to rewrap until she recovered her appetite. She slept again, woke and began talking about Christmas presents she wanted to make for his sisters, her eyes unnaturally bright.

*Part Two*

THE SON

# King Sloth

AFTER CLOSING UP THE HOUSE IN CHOCTAW BLUFF, Camilla arrived with the trunks in mid-December and was amazed at the state of the house on Government—not even a year after the Colonel's death. On the back lawn geometric patches of grass grew longer than the rest, indicating a distracted mower. Weeds encroached onto the unswept walkways of the garden, and where there were usually rows of poinsettias and beds of winter orchids, there were no flowers to speak of. Four brightly painted, motorized bicycles cluttered the lawn at the side of the carriage house. The columns were scarred with patches of missing paint; the side porch was wet with dead leaves; the swing hung unevenly. She stopped in the kitchen, which was empty, then found several Negroes she didn't recognize on the back steps. After telling a woman named Janie to unpack the trunks, she knocked on the door of the billiard room, behind which she could hear the brothers talking. They didn't answer her knock. She knocked again, opening the door a crack, calling out, "Sirs, this Camilla!"

The sound of them bounding toward the door scared her. They

threw it open, jumping into and out of her arms like four huge fleas. "Camilla's back! Camilla's back! Hooray! Hooray!" sang Louis, the hoorays echoed by George, Felix and Peter, who danced the old Lu-Lu-Fado around the red billiard table as they sang. She was glad to see them, too, but the sour smell of the room alerted her to the half-filled glasses, full ashtrays and glasses used as ashtrays, which covered almost every surface of the room. "Y'all a mess!" she said matter-of-factly.

The dance dissolved. Felix feigned astonishment. "What do you mean?"

"You expect me to work for pigs in a pigsty?"

They laughed heartily, leaning on their pool sticks and taking sips of wine.

"Where Esperanza?"

Peter shrugged. "Who knows?"

"Come to think of it, I haven't seen her in a while," said Louis.

"Yeah, me either," said Felix. "What happened to her, do you think?"

"Who knows?" repeated Peter.

"Y'all fools!" Camilla exclaimed, stepping back, breathing deeply. "And your sister ain't nothing well neither, but she's got an excuse."

"It's true we're fools," said Felix, "but we like it that way."

Louis added, "Don't be mad at us, Camilla. You know how we are. We're worthless by nature. But without you, we're downright, what's the word . . ."

None could think of it. George went down on his knees to her. "Please help us, Camilla."

She backed away until he stood up, grinning. The other three brothers laughed again. "You want me to help you?" she asked, incredulous. All four nodded solemnly. She looked down at her feet, saw a molding coffee cup against the wall and said under her breath, "Jesus give me strength." The bizarre situation at Choctaw Bluff had been just about enough. The cramped house, the weirdness of Charles, the loneliness—all had her on the verge of quitting. She never went through with it though, because there were plenty worse white people than the Riants. What she wanted most at that moment was to walk out the front door, leave the house once and for all and go home. She couldn't wait to see her daughters, to walk into her little shotgun, which would be exactly as she had left it, and chat with her neighbors over some rum, telling them all about the sad state of the Riant house. And she thought about seeing Harold again, imagining how she would tell him, "Man, oh, man, a family like the Colonel's gone to ruin. Wonders never cease. Things always gonna change, thank God," and then later, when they would kiss.

"Please?" George squeaked.

Returning her attention to them, she asked, "Where's Regina?"

"Somewhere upstairs," grunted Peter, turning back to the billiard game. The other three followed suit.

*Every girl baby needs two mothers, a black one and a white one,* Camilla thought as she climbed the stairs rimmed with dust. Motherhood is one place where love is free, and the only place between black and white where free things got thrown back and forth in equal amounts. Whenever she thought of all the other places where black and white met, Camilla would say—she never cursed— "There's another one of them doggone lines," and the white people around her would titter. They knew what she meant, but to them she supposed it was just one of those funny facts of life that they wouldn't lose any sleep over. But they all, black and white, lost sleep over it, one way or another, Camilla knew, and she felt sorry for them both, mainly the whites, whom she considered having less of a chance of getting into heaven.

Camilla had been working for the Riants since she was fifteen. Beginning with the first Regina Riant and staying on under the second, she served as the nursemaid to the four brothers and the third Regina. She hadn't intended to love the third Regina but she did, and Regina was very affectionate to her in return, though neither one of them thought the other was in any way equal. For one thing, they were different colors; for another, Camilla was older—it was her job to discipline Regina. They shared moments of closeness that mothers and daughters will: power battles over clothes, bedtimes, body odor, acne, menstruation, manners. They loved each other, and over twenty years they had developed a language all their own that they both prized highly and took joy in exercising. They both thought the other suffered from excessive thinness and, both were proud to say, could stretch up to an hour and a half a discussion about which tonic to use.

At the same time, each spoke a native language that the other could understand but would never use. In the whole of their friendship, if it be called that, Camilla never forgot her place, never forgot that it was she who worked for Regina, but she made do with the strictures as best she could, remembering lines and behaving differently when she and Regina were being watched.

Camilla didn't think that whites and Negroes were equal in any way. She allowed Regina to take her for granted, and she in turn got "white help." Regina paid her significantly more than the going rate for a Negro domestic, gave her paid time off and financed several trips to visit her sister in Birmingham. When Regina gave her money for groceries, unless it was a large bill, she didn't take the change. In a bank account, admittedly not large, she stashed away funds for Camilla's retirement. During their time at Choctaw Bluff, Regina had even tried to teach her how to read, but Camilla was too unhappy to concentrate and none of the lessons stuck.

She had been excited when she got the invitation to come help with the pregnancy because she missed Regina and considered it an honor to be part of her having her first child. She was initially amused at how difficult it was for Regina to take to being pregnant. Then she had to make efforts not to judge the poor girl. All bodies are different and physical pain is forgotten once it's gone, like, she told Regina, "how people dream of summer during the winter, forgetting that the heat is equally rough." So it is with pain, Camilla knew. She had delivered two daughters but they were grown and she couldn't remember suffering at all from them. She thought of her daughters almost constantly, especially as she became annoyed by Regina's perpetual demands. Lying in her bed at night, she wondered how she had gotten so far from her own people, from her family, on behalf of a white woman. Yet she hesitated to quit and resorted instead to praying, day and night, that they would return to Mobile.

There were good whites and there were bad whites. Everyone knew bad whites: the ones who made you use different plates and silverware, who made gifts of molding cheese, rotten fruit, bug-infested grits to take home to your family, who blamed you when they were the ones making the mistakes, who tried to get away with paying you less than the agreed-on wage, accused you of stealing and even raped you if they had a mind to do it.

Far less common, good whites were the ones who weren't lazy and who helped you when you were in trouble, and on this front her girlfriends, who all worked as domestics in white homes, envied Camilla, for the Riants paid her well enough that she was able to send money to her brother in Chicago whose steel work never seemed to cover his expenses. Particularly the Colonel and Regina went beyond to help her and her family, demonstrating a kindness and thoughtfulness unheard of in white people. The Colonel sent

huge pots of flowers to her daughters' weddings, paid for her eye-
glasses, teeth and trips to the doctor, and Regina made a lace Baptism gown for Camilla's first granddaughter. Regina and her
brothers stood in the sun all dressed in black outside the funeral of
her mother, Amelia, to hug and kiss her cheek as she left the church.

Camilla could do without Mother Riant, but she let herself be
charmed by the four brothers. Finding them handsome jokesters,
Camilla rarely refused any of their special requests, after which
they would kiss her on the cheek and dance around with her in what
they called "the kitchen jig." Because she couldn't keep them
straight, she never called them by name, replying "Yes, sir" or "Yes,
sirree" or "Yes indeed, you right there" to everything they said. She
was fond of them in spite of their indolence and even prayed for
them, that they would settle down, get married and take on some responsibility—for heaven's sake, they had no excuse not to. And so
she was appalled and depressed when she arrived in Mobile and saw
what had been going on in the Colonel's house on Government and
saw that the god of change had already visited.

After the Colonel's death, word had spread quickly through Sandtown, the Negro neighborhood adjacent to the mansions on Spring
Hill, that working for the Riant brothers was the best job around. You
didn't even have to pretend to be working, it was said, and could
while away the hours sitting on the steps off the kitchen sipping coffee. A housekeeper, a head cook and two assistants, three maids, a
laundrywoman, four dairymen, two gardeners, a stableboy and a
driver were already on staff. As a result of recommendations to the
brothers, the ranks spread to include a glass washer, a walk sweeper,
an alphabetizer, a bookkeeper, a silver polisher and a chicken feeder,
a beekeeper, a travel agent and a spirits purchaser. None but the glass
washer and laundrywoman did any work.

The brothers had many clothes and required precision in the dry-cleaning and the ironing department, always requested at the last minute, but were indifferent to everything else, so it was unnecessary to work at all steadily on their behalf. It was the same to them whether their sheets were changed, whether their corners were swept or the grates of their fireplaces mopped. They insisted that the letters in the shared study were "just so," and more than once they flew into a rage over a missing paper and sent a well-intending duster out of the room in tears. Nor was there any point in sweeping, as they organized their correspondence on the floor. Since they were always in the billiard room and didn't appreciate interruptions, it was impossible to tidy it up until dawn the next morning, when one met with such mess as to discourage the highest-paid among them.

The brothers noticed the creeping disorder but they didn't know what to do about it. They sympathized with the servants—the very word "work" was odious to them—and to keep the house clean without anyone's having to do any, they turned to the Sears, Roebuck catalog. Peter purchased a battery-powered shoe-shiner and introduced it to the staff; Louis spent the summer trying to install a timer on the percolator. Felix championed a solar-powered carpet-cleaning powder that didn't work in parts of the house without direct sunlight, and Cookie mistook it for a dishwashing fluid. George ordered pounds and pounds of artificial flowers, made of expensive linen, but no one took any pleasure in them.

Esperanza, an excellent cook who had worked for the family since the time of the first Regina Riant, quit after the brothers had a food fight. Her replacement quickly learned how little difference her efforts made. The brothers were often too tight to taste, or they decided to eat at a restaurant without notice, and an entire meal was laid for nothing. They never complimented specialty dishes, even when given hints, nor did they criticize the inedible fare that came more and more commonly to the table. Laughing that the bath-tub bourbon had burned off the brothers' taste buds, the servants gathered in the kitchen as the sun went down and stood around Esperanza's replacement as she distributed provisions of ham, turkey, potatoes and greens, which were toted from the house under cover of dark.

The brothers observed the lack of flavor in the small portions they were served but didn't like to say anything about it directly. In-stead they presented the kitchen staff with gadget after gadget de-signed for their ease. Electric lights, already used in the rest of the house, were installed in the kitchen and pantry, but Janie couldn't stand the buzz they made and used them only to please the brothers. Louis's implementations—an enormous faucet sprayer for dish-washing and a special bread-rising bowl, which supposedly con-ducted "taste atoms" into the yeast—the kitchen help stashed under the sink. The electric mixer inaugurated by Peter caught on fire when Sylvie used it to grind catfish for catfish cakes and they all fled, abandoning the room ablaze, the damage from which took a week to repair. Then the kitchen was torn up for the installation of an electric stove, but the head cook sorely missed the subtlety of fire, so this improvement resulted in either burned or raw food.

Confining herself to three or four rooms, Mother Riant made requests to the general staff through the mouth of Sylvie, whom everyone else resented and who was another reason Esperanza had quit. As Mother Riant's personal servant, Sylvie cooked, cleaned and catered to the old woman, a job that kept her so occupied she really couldn't be bothered with the goings-on in the rest of the house. She was unable to complete even one request before being bombarded with three more from those wrinkled lips, cracked with fuchsia lipstick, whose every utterance made Sylvie jump. All the livelong day she spent opening and closing windows or curtains, moving the rocking chair closer to and farther from the fire, administering drops, rubbing feet, adjusting shawls, doing the prescribed elbow exercises, wiping Mother Riant's mouth with the corner of her apron, bringing things in—the chocolate-covered soda crackers, the tea, the rosary, the newspaper—and taking them out again. Nothing she did lasted more than fifteen minutes before it went back to the way it had been before she touched it. Most of the food she prepared was thrown out.

But Sylvie didn't mind all the errands—the more the better, she figured. She wanted to be gone from Mother Riant's room as long as possible and even invented pressing matters—that Mother Riant needed a hot-water bottle or a special pillow—in order to excuse herself from the sickroom and, roaming the house, reflect on how awful her job was. During these extended perambulations she never saw a single other person doing any work and noticed the gathering filth, but the last thing she needed was for Mother Riant to get wind of the situation. Therefore, she encouraged her to stay in her quarters at all times, even resorted to saying that the servants had coughs and that, in venturing to other parts of the house, Mother Riant would risk infection. She tried to anticipate Mother Riant's requests for sewing materials or conversations with her sons, so there were no impulsive moves. If it became necessary for her to change rooms, Sylvie put extra sleeping drops in her tea, made sure the passageway was poorly lit and, guiding Mother Riant by her shattered elbow and confusing her with chatter, led her rapidly to the next room.

IT HURT STANDING, hurt moving, hurt sitting down, but she struggled to keep her distress to herself. "I'm not leaving this house," Regina told Charles and her brothers when they pressed her to come with them to various holiday socials, but confined to her father's house she was even lonelier than she had been at Choctaw Bluff. As she sat with her mother in the upstairs parlor in front of the fire sewing clothes for the baby, she felt more intensely helpless than ever. The extreme heat of the room combined with Mother Riant's conversation exacerbated her headaches. She had already produced enough lace for four Christening gowns, and Mother Riant, who never sewed, had made a bonnet in every color of the rainbow, but both women continued their sewing anyway, as in a factory, getting faster and faster with repetition. Regina missed her father deeply, so that one of her regular prayers became, *Father, I hope my life is some kind of happiness, joy, peace to you even while you are dead. God help me to live with this objective always.*

She had seen the rest of the house. The silver and candlesticks were tarnished beyond mention; chipped teacups were in use. The windows were unwashed and the tops of the curtains were gray with dust, balls of which tumbled down and gathered under the furniture. The carpets were covered with dog hair, little white flecks and the remains of spills not sufficiently cleaned. She would deal with all that later, she vowed, after the baby was born. For the time being she had to stay in the upstairs parlor.

She missed Camilla. Regina saw far less of her than she used to, and to keep herself in good spirits, she replayed the conversations they had had at Choctaw Bluff, during which she had learned so much about Camilla's life—all about the daughters she had with a husband, Will, who had passed away some time ago and whom she spoke of as both the dashing man she had loved and the cause of what she called her "ruin." Regina learned more about other white people than she ever cared to know, through stories Camilla had gotten from their domestics. She heard secrets for spicing red beans and ribs and ate them vicariously in the backyard with Camilla's friends. Regina paid more attention when Camilla had mentioned men and their silliness and could recite their trajectory: Jeremiah was a no-good, Paulie was slightly insane and Camilla didn't have the strength to deal with it, though she loved him. Tobias had tried to charm her, but his ways were dissolute. Harold was the new man on the scene, and Regina had taken pleasure in advising Camilla that he seemed like the best one so far.

Camilla didn't know how to read, though she loved to have Regina read to her—whatever—be it the newspapers, *Ladies' Home Journal*, *Mansfield Park* or *Evelina*—those nutty English folk made her howl with laughter, and Regina would laugh, too, and then explain how this was serious, this maiden in distress. Camilla began to take it all very seriously and would even bring up poor Tess time and time again in conversation, when she wanted to make a particularly strong point about innocence, sacrifice or stupidity.

But as Camilla grew more and more distant after their return to the house on Government, these recollections faded, and worrying that Camilla would abandon her became one of the storms Regina put into circulation around her worry-board. Others were, in order of importance, the health of the baby she carried, what to do about her husband, how to make the holidays special enough to bring them all back together again.

"Oh, my joints are aching!" Mother Riant shattered a silence.

"My back is killing me," Regina said. "I feel as though I'm about to die."

"Oh, grow up," the older Regina rejoined. "My legs are swollen."

"I'm sorry."

Each had been bored with the other's ailment, their only safe topic, for some time. Both forged ahead with the sewing in silence until Mother Riant closed her eyes at last. Her head fell back against her chair; finally she was breathing steadily. Regina watched the scarf slip off her mother, revealing a neck doubled in size, which seemed to undulate with shiny strips of cartilage. The rest of her mother was shockingly thin and gave the impression of being ready to splinter, like the dry twigs currently cracking in the fire. Regina forced herself to push away the thought of Mother Riant burning in the fire and thought of the summertime at Choctaw Bluff, almost longing to return there. In her abdomen a sharp pain leveled her. What if she should be unable to deliver a healthy child? As she sewed she said Hail Mary after Hail Mary that everything would please be all right. Then Mother Riant was awake and shifting. Regina managed a grim smile. "I have a headache behind my eyes; it's hard to concentrate on such fine lace," Regina said by way of an excuse that her eyes had been closed.

"I'm retaining water," Mother Riant said, and rang the bell for Sylvie. Then she put a few more drops into her coffee.

Regina wished she had some drops for herself. "Mother, how many times a day do you take those drops?"

She rang more insistently for Sylvie as she spoke, "Well, last I heard, it was three times a day but I'm in such *constant* pain I just take them whenever I need them. Not the full dosage, of course."

Sylvie entered. "What is it?"

"Sylvie?" cawed Mother Riant. "How many times have I told you *not* to enter without knocking?"

Sylvie didn't respond. Looking shyly at Regina, who gave her no support, she helped Mother Riant move closer to the fire.

"Well," said the two Reginas at the same moment after Sylvie left, then lapsed into silence. Mother Riant slept again while Regina, to keep her thoughts from an unspecified dread of the baby, began playing with her anxiety over Charles, whom her brothers had recently swept under their wings of decadence. She rarely saw him these days that he hadn't had "a little something," as he called it, and his forced gayness at such times irritated her. He slept like a dead man; they never had a chance to talk. Mother Riant woke with a loud sniff, so Regina deflected her thought of Charles by mentioning her brothers. "They're as wild as ever," Regina said, then regretted it. She expected her mother to take their side, but she didn't.

"If you mean your brothers, I've washed my hands of them and they of me, which is a shame, a crying shame, after the thirty years I've spent serving them." She paused. "Maybe I spoiled them, as everyone said, and so I'll pay for it on Reckoning Day, if I make it that far."

"I don't think so, Mother."

Mother Riant snorted and reached for her handkerchief—was she crying?—and said nothing more for several minutes until, "That they're rotten is a fact."

Regina looked up from her crocheting. "They should marry," she said. "Can you hand me the threader?"

"Oh, they'll never marry," her mother spit, shooting the threader across the room, so that it clacked against the wall before rolling to Regina's feet.

She was unable to see beyond her stomach and groped the floor for it before finding it, sitting up and catching her breath, "Well, they're rich," she said.

Mother and daughter thought about this for a moment. "That's the worst reason to marry," Mother Riant said, "but I confess it's the only one I can think of. That's the reason I married your father, after all. Poor Papa was suffering financially; I didn't feel I had a choice."

Regina was appalled to hear spoken aloud what she had some-how always known. Was that what it all boiled down to? Money? She hadn't married Charles for money, yet she had to admit that the fact that their money was hers and not his caused a rift between them. Not because she cared about it, but because he did. "I haven't been out of the house in so long," Mother Riant went on. "Are there any pretty girls in poverty around Mobile these days?" She paused for quite a while, muttered "I don't care anymore" and fell asleep during another pause.

As her mother slept, Regina continued to think that Christmas would solve the problems of the house. She envisioned them setting up the Nativity on the mantel, then, bundled up, walking down Government to midnight Mass. Christmas morning they wake late, drink hot wine and lounge around the tree, a fire blazing away in the fireplace. That evening, after the feast, Mother Riant sings "Ave Maria" to them, and as the candles are reflected against the windows, the tinsel and sparkles, Regina sits close to Charles. And she already knows what she will pray for: thanking God for the birth of Christ and asking that she be worthy of the child she carries, that she have the endurance.

On a trip to New Orleans before her wedding, she had picked out presents for her brothers, four reading lamps in the shape of knights, each in a different pose. The seams of the knights' armor shone with the light, and they were already boxed, wrapped with green paper, decorated with berries and stashed in the back of her closet. Her present for Charles was among them: a copy of Wordsworth, his favorite poet, which she'd had hand-bound at the bookbinding shop on Royal Street in midnight blue Moroccan leather and letterpressed with gold. The week before Christmas she stayed up late into the night to finish the red silk evening bag she had made for Camilla, which was beaded with a pattern of birds.

Then Mother Riant was awake again and continued the conversation as if she hadn't dozed. "I don't care about your brothers anymore," she carped, gaining volume as she went on, "I tell you, it's not easy being a mother. You work your entire life for the happiness of your children, never thinking of yourself, and then they refuse to become what you've designed for them. I mean they reflect back badly on you—they want nothing to do with you—they stomp on the very values that made you such a good mother. I tell you, I don't envy you at all, my dear."


CAMILLA WAS SO BUSY SHE DIDN'T REALIZE it was Christmas Eve until she saw the corn hens in a pen by the back steps. Then she scrambled to think of something to give Regina, but she eventually decided that nothing would be good enough and gave up. She was bone-tired and just didn't have the spirit. The presents from Regina and her brothers she accepted ungratefully and got small satisfaction in offending them. But in the days after Christmas, she thought more and more about the red silk evening bag Regina had given her—she was planning to wear it to a New Year's party Harold was taking her to—and she felt sorry, sorry enough to brave Mother Riant one afternoon and sit with Regina, who matched her mother in coloring, the coloring of someone who hadn't seen the sunlight in years. But Mother Riant so openly disapproved of her visit that conversation was strained, and Camilla left after a few minutes, feeling even lower than before.

Regina, who had made it through Christmas with false gaiety, the mask of which she was petrified to remove, felt the heavy air more keenly than anyone. Nothing had worked out as she'd planned. When she'd dressed the windows with red bows and candles, the dirt on the sills and panes got the better of her and she resigned, leaving the bows half done. Then she'd attempted her famous gingerbread, but the pan slipped out of her hand as she went to put it in the oven and the batter spilled all over the floor. She nagged her brothers to find the boxes of ornaments for the tree but saw with dismay on Christmas morning that the tree was bare. Louis took apart the lamp she gave him and couldn't put it back together. Unwrapped, Wordsworth remained under the tree, covered in pine needles. Mother Riant had launched into the "Ave Maria," but her voice was so wobbly that everyone but Regina had snickered. The turkey had been raw, the potatoes cold, the gravy overpoweringly tangy and the charlotte russe had not set. But most of all, Regina was upset that she hadn't gotten a present from Camilla.

Now there was only one more day to get through: New Year's Day, 1920. The dinner began typically. "Peter, please put your napkin on your lap only after the water is poured, not when you first sit down. Thank you."

"Thank you, Mother."

"Mother, should we drive—"

"Please stop doing that, Felix."

"What?"

"You know what."

"On the contrary, Mother, I haven't got a clue."

Her lips puckered at him until he realized that he should have put a helping of butter on his butter plate and buttered his bread off that instead of buttering it directly from the communal dish. "Excuse me," he mumbled, in his confusion dropping the bread facedown on the tablecloth. They all watched as he, turning redder and redder, picked up the bread and tried in vain to lift the butter off the tablecloth with his fish knife, finally wiping it with his napkin, leaving a large grease spot on the green damask. Mother Riant sighed loudly.

"Can we open a window? It's hotter in here than it is outside in July," said George, who had been eating green beans with his fingers to see if he could attract his mother's attention.

Now she studied him. "George, please watch yourself. You've got sauce on your lip."

"Mother, do you need us for anything this afternoon?" ventured Peter.

"Please don't speak with your mouth open."

"How else am I supposed to speak?"

The brothers and Charles laughed at this, souring her further.

"You know very well what I mean."

No one said anything for some time until Regina spoke, very slowly, "I think we're all adults here. Perhaps we can discard this line of conversation."

"Mnn," said Mother Riant, sucking a string of meat from between her two front teeth and arching her eyebrow. "What do you think, Charles," she smiled, turning to her son-in-law. "Do you think my sons are grown men?"

"Yes," he managed.

With Mother Riant's attention on Charles, Regina felt the way the stuffed hens must have felt five hours ago. "But then, you don't know how to sip," her mother said. Regina's face, neck, ears and arms went hot. Her brothers increased the speed of their eating. Mother Riant smiled again. "And no one likes to hear the workings of your throat. It's only a recommendation." Charles put his fork down and looked out the window, his face splotchy.

Serving himself gravy, Louis asked, "What's going on?"

At the same time, George asked, "Can we open a window? It's hotter in here than it is outside in July."

Regina cleared her throat. "Can't we all put these things behind us for the New Year?"

"There's no such thing as a New Year," snapped Mother Riant.

"Actually what we're celebrating is the Feast of the Circumcision," piped George.

A wave of nausea swept over Regina. She would have to be excused to take some breaths outside the room, but how to bring it up? Rivers of saliva filled her mouth. She put her fork down and, looking over her brother's head at the wall, waited for a break in the silence.

But Mother Riant waited for no such break. "I'm sure you'll excuse me," she said. "I'm not feeling myself, and the eating habits of my sons and son-in-law upset my delicate stomach." Then she stood, clutching onto the table for balance, looking at Charles in defiance and ringing her little bell. When Sylvie appeared hovering in the doorway, Mother Riant turned to Regina, "You'll accompany me."

Regina was about to rise when Charles said, "She'll finish her meal."

"Sylvie!" Mother Riant hollered, tossing her head, and Sylvie rushed forward with the cane and took her elbow. "The other elbow!" she screeched, and waited until Sylvie repositioned. As she hobbled out of the room, she gave instructions to Sylvie in a loud voice. "Please have tea brought to the upstairs parlor immediately. No, on second thought, I'll take it in bed, and bring me my missal, the faster to remove myself from the memory of this low company." All stared at Felix's grease stain on the tablecloth until the door had closed behind her, until they had heard the five feet make their way to the foot of the stairs and begin to ascend. Only then did Louis say, "Lord help us and save us."

After a moment, "Jesus, Mary and Joseph," George volleyed with a grin.

Regina took tiny sips of water, holding her stomach. "Well, you all might have behaved yourselves for her sake or, just this once, for my sake," she said, giving a stern glance to each of them. Charles slapped the table, making the china jump, and threw his head back in laughter, so unable to control himself that all the others were forced into a moment of mirth.

"The same could be said of her," said Felix. "She makes me so self-conscious I'm bound to make a blunder of some kind."

"Mary, Mother of God," said Peter, wiping his eyes. They were silent for some time, tension gone from their stomachs. All but Louis had given off eating. Charles stopped laughing long enough to sputter, "I wonder if there's a school I can attend to teach me how to sip!" and reinitiated the chuckles of the brothers.

Refilling their glasses and gulping them down, they waited for Charles's sporadic giggling to stop so that they could go play billiards. "I'm cold," Regina told Charles.

Felix stood. "The window's closed."

"Are you kidding, Sis?" asked George as he pushed himself away from the table. "It's hotter in here than it is outside in July." Louis rubbed his finger over his plate and licked it, stood up. Charles leaned back on two legs of his chair and looked at Regina admiringly.

"Wait a second," said Peter, who was still nursing his cognac.

Felix turned his back to the table and moved toward the door, pausing with his hand on the wall. "This wall is on fire," he said and his hand edged along the wall until it reached a point above the light switch. "It must be electric." All eyes fell on Peter, who had insisted that the chandelier in the dining room be replaced with an electric one, then to Louis, who had done the wiring himself, then to Charles, his smile vanished. "Go to the front porch, Regina," he murmured as a strip of fire appeared, stretching from the light switch, up the wall and across the ceiling to the chandelier.

Rebelling against its occupants, the house chased them out. Now lines of flame connected across the wallpaper to points in the ceiling, now curls of smoke eased themselves through every seam in the walls, now waves of heat smacked them as they turned each corner on their way to the porch. Charles's fingers dug into the nerves above Regina's elbow, and he thrust her forward and she tripped and fell into Felix who caught her. "Charles!" she screamed, as he turned and charged up the stairs—part of the banister was crackling. The front door was bottlenecked with servants she didn't recognize. Through the French windows she saw Negroes in uniforms of white streaking across the lawn toward the street. As she waited to pass through the door, she knew the baby would die of the smoke and knew there were tears pouring down her face though she couldn't tell if she was making any sound.

On the lawn at last, bending over and gulping for air, Regina saw a maid with her apron on fire flash past and called out to her after Camilla but got no answer. The next thing Regina knew, she was in the air, carried to the brick rim of an empty flower bed and placed on one of her brothers' jackets. Now the front of the house was burning in patches; her brothers were about her, mouths agape, pacing, ogling, turning away, and the noise of the gigantic fire added to her disorientation. Was she, like the neighbors and passersby who had gathered in a semicircle behind her, really watching the house burn to the ground? The only thing she was sure of was that Charles had gone up the stairs for Mother Riant and had still not returned, but against the roaring house, she couldn't have said why she knew this.

"Where's Mother?" one of her brothers asked.

At the question George fell to his knees next to her on the jacket, took up her hand and wept, choking on his Hail Marys as Peter charged toward the house only to be rebuffed by the exploding glass of the front windows. The volunteer fire brigade arrived. His face covered in blood, Peter ran back and took over for Felix, who yelled at the firemen to be faster about attaching their hoses and dispatching men into the house after Mother Riant.

Louis wailed, "There's nothing to do!" over and over as he ripped the bottom of his shirt into pieces and used it to dab Peter's bloody face. In the meantime, Felix had located a ladder, brought it to the side window of Mother Riant's parlor and was climbing it, until the ladder caught a lick that spread, at the tenth step, to his pant legs, to his coattail and up his back. He dropped to the grass.

The roof caught; the roar. The house was dissolving in front of her eyes; blood was mixing with soil was mixing with burn was mixing with glass. Suddenly she didn't have to worry about Camilla anymore—Camilla was at her side, moaning, "Oh, baby, you're safe, girl. Thank God, you're safe." She fell into the black woman's arms and didn't see the third floor drop into the second—she heard it.

*Pecan Pie*

MOTHER RIANT LIVED. Helped out of the back of the burning house long before Charles climbed the stairs to rescue her, she was uninjured except that her hearing had been impaired, inexplicably. She carried on in the new house much as she had before. Instead of her upstairs parlor, she ensconced herself in front of the gas heater on the closed-in porch off her new room in a dark green wicker rocker, alternately saying the rosary and playing Skip-Two, a rapid card game that evades strategy—she won only once in the ten-plus years she spent in the house on Dauphin Street before her death, during which she played more than forty games a day. Or she added another shawl to her shoulders and looked through the windows at the magnolia leaves.

Mother Riant loved trees but she hated the house her sons had bought. Had they bothered to consult her, she would have explained the foolishness of having trees so close to the porches during hurricane season, a lesson they would learn in 1926. Dumaine had once been a nice name to have, though it hadn't for many years stood for money. Devastated by the death of her two brothers in the war, the young Regina Dumaine had watched her father's shipping company dwindle. Even at five she remembered the first signs of decline—the thin spread of silence, the money extensions. The Dumaines had been in Mobile since the Spanish seized it from the British on March 14, 1780, during the American Revolution. The Spanish language had been lost by Mother Riant's time, but as a girl she had listened to her grandmother speak it with Captain Fry, the Cuban martyr. She didn't speak French either and had always hated it when the Colonel had spoken it with his childhood friends.

Turning the cards without even looking at them, she felt death hover beside her and was grateful, she admitted to herself, for his company. Sylvie had deserted her the morning after the fire, and her new personal helper was a woman named Nikkatai, a Chickasaw who never wore shoes. Nikkatai was far worse than Sylvie, and Mother Riant was lonely enough to wish death drank tea. She had nothing to do but ruminate on her own presence, ponderous and silent, as she bored through the floorboards into the tops of the heads of her sons, who scurried below her, following specific splinters of their construction. Dimly she heard hammers, saws, shouts of men, but could not determine from where they came, nor did she make sense of the wagons or the white-clad painting crews. From her window she saw them come up the drive but never saw them leave. By and by, her sons visited her room to present her with plans and corresponding expenditure reports, but she couldn't hear them and watched their lips for the signal to say, "Isn't that nice? That's lovely."

While Regina and Charles convalesced in the Cawthorne Hotel, buying a new house was left up to Regina's brothers. They toured the Dauphin Street house just to please the estate agent; they had already made up their minds. It was essentially a farmhouse, though of grand proportions, with a wide central hallway that cut front to back, with parlor and library to the right, dining room and the small room Regina would sew in to the left. The second floor was identical, with the same hallway and two bedrooms on both sides of it. The house was wired for electricity. A stifling-hot third floor, unsealed, was filled with dusty, broken furniture of the previous owner, a cypress baron. Mahogany paneling in the dining room, library and hallways, broad two-tiered porches that circled the house, and the magnolias and oaks, lining the various driveways were other of the baron's marks. It was the fourteen acres of pecan orchard, however, that struck the brothers' collective fancy. The basic productivity of trees was a delicious revelation to them so late in life. That they could profit from this productivity with little effort was hilarious to them. They loved pecan pie. "It's a gold mine," Felix announced.

"Isn't the house itself a bit small?" George objected feebly.

"We're obviously going to build, George."

"There's plenty of land," said Peter.

"It's a little rustic for Mother?" George suggested to Louis, who replied, "Well, her eyes are failing her."

Peter said, "We'll make her room incredibly nice," and signed the papers that afternoon.

REGINA SHARED A SUITE IN THE CAWTHORNE with Charles, who was being treated for the severe burns on his hands. Nightfall made her cry, and she locked the door against the nurses and climbed into his bed with him while he, staring into the low white ceiling, stroked her head with his bandaged hand. For most of the night they remained silent, except for Regina saying again, "I'm so sorry I failed you."

And he would whisper, "Nonsense. Hush."

Her weeping had become inevitable. "I was such a coward, and now I am punished," she hiccupped, her sobs intensifying. "I had no faith . . . I'm so sorry, Charles. I was too afraid."

His neck and shirt were soaked with her tears and mucus. "I'm hot." He shifted, removing her head from his shoulder. He rearranged his white boxing-gloved hands so that, bulging in the center of his chest, they glowed in the moonlight that came from the small window. The doctor said he would lose between 35 and 75 percent of the feeling in either hand, but it didn't matter to him what happened to his hands.

"I was responsible for the life of our child," she gurgled, "and I lost it. I lost it."

From far away he listened to her cry. He worried that she would never stop, and he pulled her back to his shoulder, said, "Quiet down."

During the four weeks they spent in the hotel, neither of them relished visitors, not that they had many. Camilla came once with a lemon pound cake, but Regina couldn't speak freely in front of Charles and sent her away with a nervous kiss. Her brothers came to flash the deed of the new house before them. "It sounds wonderful," she said, glancing at Charles, "as long as there's no electricity." Charles said nothing. "Do as you please," she told them. "We aren't terribly interested." That was their last visit. Her old friend Charlotte came religiously, and half the times Regina told the nurse not to admit her.

They had already extended their stay in the hotel twice because they weren't sure where to go. Charles mentioned returning to Choctaw Bluff, but the doctors told Regina she was too weak to travel, and she refused to let Charles go without her. Neither spoke of the house at Spring Hill. To Charles's "I need time to think. Why don't you go on and stay with your brothers?" she said she didn't want to be alone. "But you'll be with your family," he said.

"You're my family, Charles."

This he took silently, staring at his hands, so that she, too, became confused by the blanks in her vision: a baffling substructure of unknown towering over Charles and her. Despite her vigilance, the hole had come. Here it hung over Charles; here it blanketed his eyes. Adrift without her, he had let loose, but she didn't yet realize that lost contact couldn't ever be recovered. At such junctures of miscommunication she would, not knowing what else to do, launch into a story she had gotten from the sermon of a Jesuit in New Orleans, the point of which was that only through our wounds can we become Christ-like for others.

The more Charles visualized Christ's wounds, the more he looked forward to the end of the world, but he noticed how the story seemed to make her stronger and happier each time she told it, after which she beamed and kissed him under the eyes. "And so, I'll have your son," she concluded. "I'll have another chance." The morning his bandages were removed, she kissed each one of the tips of his fingers, again and again, pressed them across her cheek. The tips were red and smooth, like the skin of a newborn, but she refrained from making that comparison. Now he had no fingerprints and she, remarking that he could rob a bank and never be caught, imagined that he chuckled along with her.

"Then we could move away from your mother," he said, which she took as a further joke and abandoned her heart to optimism. She stood elated, clutching the muscles of his upper arm as he signed them out of the hotel.

But the pitch of activity Regina and Charles found when they arrived at the house on Dauphin Street shocked them, so recently recovered. Felix crouched with tape measure and string, staking out dimensions of a new wing, while Peter wielded an ax against the wood to their left. Only Louis, who circled the activity with a sheaf of papers, paused to greet them. Already an old smokehouse had been torn down to make room for the modern kitchen they were adding off the dining room. From there, he explained, they would build another large, low-ceilinged wing, which would sprout three or four more rooms of as-yet-undetermined function. In front of this wing, they intended another porch and above it an A-lined attic with skylights—for a small meteorological studio, which would connect to the nearest second-floor bedroom, which was Louis's, by way of four winding steps.

In the first few weeks of their residence, while Charles was bedridden, Regina organized a cleanup crew to trail behind the workmen; developed a system for ordering Mother Riant's medicine, vegetables, ice; set a laundry schedule; fired Nikkatai and sorted through the items that had been salvaged from the flames. Every other minute her brothers dragged her into the parlor, where plans and proposals and blueprints were draped across the backs of chairs and layered over the billiard table. They needed her advice on the design of the kitchen, or needed her to be the tie-breaking vote in one of their decorating disputes. Or they would say, "Come out to the porch and have a cigarette, Sis," and divert her considerably with descriptions of a recent visit to Aunt Eugenia or any of their other captivating pursuits.

From the northeast bedroom, Charles complained about the noise and scowled at the contractors stalking back and forth from one end of the house to the other, tracking dirt, but Regina was inspired by their crude sense of self-importance. She thought the constantly rotating architects contributed favorably to conversation at dinner, where Charles sat like a boulder, and she was on friendly terms with the workmen. She brought cold, fresh lemonade to them on the back porch, where they lounged after lunch, until Charles told her it was inappropriate.

Charles claimed that his breathing was affected unfavorably by the sawdust, that the constant noise prevented his resting. Every afternoon when Regina took him up for his nap, he pleaded for an end to the construction. "They may as well drive nails into my eyes," he told her.

She walked around the bed. "Heavens, Charles, it's not that bad, is it?" she asked, and moved to close the windows.

"Don't close the windows," he barked. She stood by the bed and held his head up to settle the pillows. "It's so hot," he moaned. She eased his head down and adjusted the wet rag over his eyes. "I can't stand it another minute, I've told you before."

She perched next to him on the bed. "Maybe you could go out for a little while this afternoon," she said soothingly. "Visit Alfred Babineaux or something." She rose and started to the door. "Or we could drive out to the hill and see your sisters."

"I don't like Alfred Babineaux."

She stopped in front of the dresser and looked abstractedly into the mirror, removed some hairpins and replaced them. "Maybe you want to take a walk. It's actually not very hot out there at all. It's just May, you know."

"No thank you."

She crossed to the fan and tilted it more directly on Charles, went back to him and stroked the wet hairs off of his forehead. Slowly she bent forward and took a deep breath in the warm air beside his neck. "You might feel better with some fresh air," she said, kissing him behind the ear.

He twisted away from her and the wet rag slipped to the floor. She straightened up. "I'd feel better without this constant Riant cacophony, of which you are no small part!"

"I wanted to tell you something important," she said, stooping to pick up the rag, "but I'll wait until you feel better," and went off to find Camilla. Charles couldn't dampen her good mood. Everything she had tried had worked. A small calendar that she kept between the linens in the linen closet and about which only Camilla knew testified to the regimen she had followed for the past six months. Eating raw eggs on certain days, drinking the juice of cooked collard greens on full moons, boiling her lingerie with a cube of yucca and a pinch of paprika, rearranging her bed so that it was parallel to the gulf—these were small tasks compared to that of seducing Charles. She left her camisole opened and left her hair down around her naked shoulders. She hiked her skirt roundly, removed her stockings achingly slowly, but he gave no reaction until she became ashamed. "I don't feel well," he often said when she was more overt, or "It's too hot," or "It's too messy, Regina."

She lay there, waiting for him to be midsleep. Then she took his hand and put it on her breasts or between her thighs, or when that failed, she put her hand on him—until he was quickened forward onto her, kissing her in the anonymity of sleep and admitting to her body in the talkless half-light. At such times she felt she was able to love him. Afterward she was glad to hear him sleeping more soundly. She covered her neck with a small scarf and listened to the fan, to the breath of the gas heater—which Charles ran simultaneously—and was nostalgic for the girl she was when she had known Ahlong. If Charles was drunk he noticed her more, pinched her nipples without the slightest provocation and pulled her behind the door, any door, which she would run back to, to shut, to lock, telling him to hush. She was always ready, but either way she never relaxed, never minded, stayed not minding, thinking it was all for one end, not the process.

Her prayers and her patience had worked, she thought, smiling broadly as she carried the supper tray up to Mother Riant. She balanced the tray in one hand, kicked open the screen door and turned the porcelain knob with ease. The room was in shadows save for the golden triangle of light from the small window near the makeshift kitchen. Regina put the tray on the marble-topped dresser and lit the gas heater for the coffee, took her time cleaning the percolator in the bathtub and returned to the kitchen to measure out the coffee, still smiling. Behind her she heard the door to the porch being pushed open with a cane and Mother Riant's "Where have you been? I've been missing you for hours," but her mother's tone didn't bother her this time. It's true she had strayed, had sat on the windowsill off her sewing room and craned out to look at the sunset. She had predicted rain, and it hadn't come, though she was sure it wanted to. On such days the clouds were frustrated with their lack of expression and put a particular magenta into their sunsets.

"It's just eight," Regina said. "Where do you want to sit?" Her answer was the sound of the porch door swinging into place. She listened as her mother hobbled to her rocker and fell into it. She stood with her lower back to the dresser, watching the light come through the slats of the door to the porch, waiting for the coffee to boil. Then she picked up the tray again and brought it out.

"You're late," Mother Riant said accusingly, but the gentle way Regina set down the tray and the fact that she took the chair across from her—she never sat down—disarmed Mother Riant into silence. To compensate for her mother's poor hearing, Regina screamed, "Can I sit with you while you eat, Mother?"

"No."

Smiling even more, Regina slowly added sugar to the coffee. She was already practicing the infinite patience of motherhood. "That's too much," said Mother Riant with annoyance. But Regina could only smile even more widely as she thought how unlike Mother Riant she would be. She would sing with her children when they weren't outside climbing trees, running up and down the drives, collecting specimens. She descended the stairs with a dazed grin on her face as she thought of how her brothers would love her child, would spoil him. Stopping outside the parlor, she considered announcing the news to them, but she decided it wouldn't be fair that they know before Charles. Tonight she would make mayonnaise. She imagined how busy she would be when the child came at last, the disgusting things she would learn to love: feces, vomit, impetigo, breast milk, teeth, thumb sucking, puree. And she looked forward to being so busy, so drained and fulfilled, finally able to answer for her herself, for her time, for her love for Charles, for her existence.

## Getting and Spending

CHARLES WAS SURPRISED AT HOW EASY it was to take the road north. The more distance he made from Mobile, the more elated he was with possibilities for the future. The windows were open, the warm autumn wind churned his hair, and for the first time in memory he had no doubt that a return to Choctaw Bluff was the answer he'd been seeking. The sun was hot on the black dashboard and occasionally he closed his eyes as he drove, letting the car go forward where it would, then swinging it back onto the tiny dirt road. This was a game for him. An optimism he had not known since he had first loved Regina washed over him. With delight he thought of Little Charles, whose birthday was approaching, and how, when he turned eighteen, he would make his son the gift of the land at Choctaw Bluff. By then the replanting he had already done and the further planting he intended on this journey would be lucrative. Perhaps he would borrow against it to buy more land, which he could also replant.

Passing the Negroes on the edge of fields of squash, turnips, corn, and the mule-drawn wagons of traveling preachers, tonic salesmen, a circus, the white wooden crosses of the country graveyards, the dusty general store where he stopped for supplies—he surged with love for all the things he noticed.

His three children had taught him this: curiosity. Anna was fascinated by the smallest things—a single ant, the sand between the floorboards of the porch, the rainlike quality of rice, the burring sound she could make with her spit. Isabel was content to sit on his lap and play with his buttons while he read the paper, and Little Charles, whose quiet intensity he recognized as his own, loved storms and would stare at the wind vane, count seconds between thunder and lightning, collect and measure rainwater.

Charles often answered their questions at length until he bored them, and he envied his brothers-in-law the good-natured games they played with the children. He never saw them without being observed by Regina, who beamed at them as if they made a portrait that she owned, but he didn't begrudge her this small satisfaction. His children loved him indiscriminately. None could go to sleep without three of his kisses, he thought with pride as he drove to Choctaw Bluff, and Little Charles liked to do the same things he did—wear a tie, carry a briefcase down the stairs every morning, ride the streetcar, sit on the porch after the midday meal.

"You're a wonderful father, Charles," Regina told him. "The children admire you so much." For the first time in his life he believed her. Any discomfort he felt with his children he dispelled by stealing into the newly decorated nursery after Regina had gone to pray. There he sat rocking in the dark and listening to them sleep. Sometimes he picked Anna up and held her, pretending that she had started crying or had had a bad dream and needed his comfort. Or he stood over their beds, watched their peaceful faces and tried to synchronize his breathing with theirs.

As he drove he kept his eyes open for land for sale, thinking that if he found something close enough to his acreage, he would make bids on it by the end of the week. Through the success he would make off the land at Choctaw Bluff, his children would one day know the extent of his love for them. It was this new purposefulness that made him so happy. It amazed him that the grave responsibility he felt to his children gave him a hitherto-unheard-of sense of liberty. In the next two years—he swore aloud to himself—he would build his family a house at Spring Hill. Maybe Regina was right: he should borrow some money from Felix. With such thoughts fueling him, he made the journey to Choctaw Bluff in record time, and back in the pine cabin he had built with his own hands he fell instantly asleep. He dreamed he was wandering through his great-uncle's satsuma orchard and woke the next morning stiff from the chill air of the open window. As he sipped his coffee, he walked from room to room in the silent house, approving his handiwork and remembering the young Regina, whom he loved.

THE CHILDREN HAD THE EFFECT ON CHARLES for which Regina had prayed: he showed initiative. That something so small was yet so perfectly formed, so delineated in personality, had made Charles tender, even to Mother Riant. His eyes gleamed. His mind began to turn again, if only on the one axis, that of the house at Spring Hill. This turning, which intensified with the subsequent births of Isabel and Anna, did not make the house at Spring Hill any more of a reality, but at least he bounded out of bed every morning with a plan, however erratic. In an intimate moment with Regina, Charles expressed his feelings, that if only he could get himself and his new family there, he would become the father and provider he was qualified to be. Only in the house at Spring Hill—his house on his land—would he wake up and, like his wife and her brothers, know how to live. "You're a wonderful father, Charles," Regina told him repeatedly. "The children love you so much."

So he had rented a little office on Bienville Square, across the street from the newspaper and in direct line with the Colonel's old office, but he just sat there at the desk, doodling floor plans. He took contractors out to lunch, leading them to believe, as he believed, that construction on the new house would begin any minute. He instigated a competition among several firms, which he baffled with wildly different start dates. Evenings he drove out to see his older brother William, who was installed on the family homestead adjoining Charles's land, and stayed too long there discussing geology. He so didn't want to go back to Dauphin Street that he often stayed at his brother's for supper and didn't get back until after dark, when the children were already put to bed.

All he needed to build the house at Spring Hill was liquid capital. He had known since before his marriage that the best way to get liquid capital was to sell the land at Choctaw Bluff, which he was loath to do. So he put about a fifth of his total energy into five different things. First he decided to open a motion-picture theater, until he discovered after one negotiation that entertainment people were phony. He was excited about dry cleaning, pastries and importing Irish tweeds. He contemplated writing a book on lightning photography, then resolved to focus on the Civil War. He typed all of Colonel Riant's letters and sent them off to a historian at Emory, who told him that the names and battles needed to be footnoted, cross-referenced and indexed, the thought of which demoralized him. After the hurricane of 1926, he considered buying an orchid farm. He planned, with the help of the new refrigeration techniques, to ship the orchids as far as New York.

"Just choose something, Charles," Regina told him tirelessly. "You're so talented. You can do anything. It doesn't matter what it is as long as you follow through with it. Even if you fail, you'll learn something." Her faith in him was such that she had, without his knowledge, asked Mother Riant for two loans on his behalf, and was refused. The denials only reassured her that Charles would be brilliant as soon as he found the right business. She supported the orchid business to such an extent that she mentioned it, regardless of Mother Riant's presence, at the Sunday-night dinner. "Charles has a new business scheme" was barely out of her mouth when she realized her mistake.

Felix took up the topic hungrily. "What's this?"

"Charles has a new business scheme," Regina faltered, but her brothers were all attention.

"Is that so?!"

"Let's hear it, man!"

"Don't be coy, Charlie!"

Charles shifted uneasily and directed his stammer to the center of the table. "I'd rather not discuss it." Regina sat by, her head bowed. "It's in the early stages," he said. "I'd rather not discuss it."

Louis began to hum the chorus to "My God, How the Money Rolls In!"

"So it does exist, though," Peter insisted. "Something exists and you're calling it a plan."

"I'm not calling it anything," Charles said, suffering. "You may call it anything your heart desires." He shot a look at Mother Riant, who gazed at him, shaking her head slowly.

"You discussed it with Regina; why don't you discuss it with us?" Peter whinnied.

Felix's voice came on the heels of his brother's. "Give us a hint, Charles. Come on, we're family!"

"I can't," Charles stuttered, his eyes filling with water. "I mean . . . that . . . you'll know it when you see it."

Mother Riant heard none of the previous conversation. She finished her food and kept to herself as she followed the music in her head, the Mazurka from Delibes's *Coppélia*. Meanwhile, she grinned at her sons, who were talking excitedly as usual, passing her eyes over Charles and Regina—until she sensed that the tone had suddenly changed. She scanned the table for signs of distress and caught her eye on Charles, his face white, his hand shaking around his knife. Her boys continued to chatter but something was wrong: the dining room echoed strangely to her. *It's my turn,* she thought, *I can say something to change it all, to make it good. I can lend Charles money for one of his enterprises. Hasn't Regina asked me that once before?*

"It sounds big!" exclaimed Louis.

Regina knew Charles couldn't speak and was wretched for him. "It has to do with refrigerated orchids," she said evenly. "I'm sure Charles will ask for your advice when he's ironed out the details."

"Let us invest!" Felix hooted. Above his brothers' cheers, he continued breathlessly, "I want in, Charles. I demand that you let us invest. Think how wonderful it will be, all of us working together."

Regina sat tensely, waiting to hear what Charles would say to this. She knew he needed investors, and she was tempted to take Felix up on his offer herself, but she refrained wisely. Charles persisted in silence, a smirk carved on his mouth. Her brothers were perplexed by this and did the only thing they knew how to do when they encountered things they didn't understand—mock. "You'll be our boss, Charlie!" Peter interposed. "We'll do whatever you say."

Desperately Regina turned to Louis and asked in reference to an earlier conversation, "So where did you run into Lizzie Powell?"

But Louis was offended and called out to Charles, "Don't you think we have enough business experience? Do you think we're going to cheat you or something?"

Felix laughed loudly at this.

"We do have some business experience," George said softly. "I think you should trust us a little more, Charles." Felix's eyes gleamed with amusement.

*I am the savior,* Mother Riant thought again, *and this is it, this is my last chance.* But she didn't know what form her saving would take and, more than that, didn't know what to say. Again she strained to hear, but she couldn't even tell who spoke, much less what was said, and the realization of this separation brought her to the point of panic. She would give them all more money, is that what she should do? She looked again to Charles, thinking for some reason that he would know what she should do, but his face was contorted, one shoulder was up to his ear, which was bright red; his neck, too, was red, and he worked his throat constantly. Next to him, Regina's face was a mask of misery. He and Regina should go on a trip, she decided, a trip to Lithia Springs. People who went to Lithia Springs got well. And she would give them the money for it. Then the moment had passed. *I'll not forget what I'm supposed to say,* she promised. *I'll tell it to Regina: a present of a trip.* Then she lowered her chin onto her chest and traveled even farther from the table, into the half sleep of the aged.

Meanwhile, Regina realized there was nothing to be done. She had tried in vain to signal George with her eyes. Her brothers would toss Charles's ego back and forth until the last plate was cleared. "You can order us around, Charles. Think about that. You've always wanted to. Right, Charles?"

"We'll make you proud of us, Charles."

"Charles, we're every bit as smart as we look."

CHARLES PULLED UP WEEDS from around the front steps of the cabin and sauntered into the office around noon. Inhaling the sweet smell of sun-baked pine, he accepted a whiskey from the man behind the desk, whose name was Glanton, and who said, "Fancy running into you here!" as he handed him the glass.

"I've got some fabulous ideas," Charles said, eagerly taking a seat at his old desk. "First of all, replanting. I want those hundred acres on the northwest replanted by January. And I want to sell our plots on the road to Thomasville, remortgage our twelve-year lots in order to buy back the land and replant it. I've known all along that this will work, and I'm here to do it." Glanton said nothing and Charles gushed on, "Look, the Roman and Lawrence plots are done for! They don't have more than four years left. By then, we'll own the most one-half and three-fourths planted property. We'll borrow against it to buy out Roman and Lawrence." He swallowed the whiskey in one gulp, gathered his breath. "I know it's long term, but looking ahead is the only way to make money. We'll sell the turpentine still and use the money to buy old Dashell's mill, and we'll have five or six years to get it running. Well"—he sat back, grinned, crossed his legs—"I think we'll be very rich men."

Glanton waited a minute to make sure he was finished before saying quietly, "Rod is with the lawyers now. We've sold out."

"What?"

"We're selling out," Glanton repeated. "We wrote to you but we never heard. Not a sound." Charles was stunned and the man went on, "For the past four years we've been in the red. What with all the lumber you gave away the last time you were here, the exorbitant salaries. And the still has never made a dime, you know that, Charles." The man sighed. "Bigbey mill caught fire twice and we repaired it twice. When it caught a third time we realized no one would fix it for us; we owed too much money. We tried to honor your way of doing things, Charles, which was a mistake. We have to let it all go. At this point, we owe almost as much as every tree is worth."

"You didn't write to me!" screeched Charles. "And you can't do this without my consent. Your deal with the bank, whatever it is, is void!"

"It's called bankruptcy." Glanton leaned forward to fill Charles's glass.

Charles shot back its contents, came up flushed and exuberant. "Well," he said, slapping the desk, "I'll buy you two out, then."

"Look at the papers, Charles," the man said, his voice even, sorrowful. "It's all right here." He pushed a file over the desk. Charles took it up and studied it for some time. "It's a done deal, my friend. I'm sorry." The papers spilled onto the floor. When Charles dropped his head into his hands, Glanton said it again, "I'm sorry."

"You're lying," Charles whispered. "You never wrote to me. Pour me another one."

The man obliged and filled his own glass as well. "It's not that bad, the deal. When all is said and done you get forty-five hundred dollars. Rod and me each take two thousand."

Charles tossed back his drink before exploding, "Forty-five hundred!"

"That's *after* our debt is paid!" Glanton said, raising his voice for the first time. "Face it, Charles! Look at the numbers!"

Charles stood up. "We're going straight to the bank."

The man shook his head woefully. "It's a done deal, Charlie."

"Get up, Glanton. We're going to the bank. You may be able to pull off your little deal but I'm getting the mineral rights to this land if it's the last thing I do."


SHE SPENT THE REST OF THE EVENING in the nursery, watching over Little Charles, who had begun to lose weight and who today for the first time said his legs hurt. She tried to entertain him, but she felt too terrible about the spectacle at midday dinner. Why had she opened her mouth about the orchid business! Equally without spirit, mother and son lay next to each other on the bed reading the second *McGuffey Reader*. While she read, she applied part of her mind to the details of Charles's humiliation at the hands of her brothers and, when he didn't appear at supper, grew increasingly afraid of what he would say to her. She was surprised to find him in her sewing room when she went in to get the basket of socks to bring to the radio room. He looked calm and happy and said, "Sit down for a minute, Regina."

She sat close to him and held his hand, apology in her eyes. "Charles," she began, "let me apologize for my brothers, and for myself. I shouldn't have brought—"

"Forget it," he said. "I want to talk about something else." She waited for him to speak. "I'm going to Choctaw Bluff for a month or two, or as long as it takes, really"—she waited—"to get that old noose from around my neck."

"What albatross is that?"

"I said 'noose.' The lumber company. I know I can make it work, Regina. I'm going to replant the other half of the land. That's my inheritance, my fate, after all, and it always has been. Forget the frozen orchids, though you are so sweet to encourage me. Sometimes I feel I can do no wrong in your eyes."

"Oh, Charles!" She brought his hand to her cheek, kissed it and put it back on her cheek.

"I have made mistakes, plenty of them, but this isn't one of them. I can make it profitable within two years. I know I can."

"I have no doubt that you can, Charles," she said, feeling his excitement in this prospect. "I've always known that the lumber company was your passion. Especially since it belonged to your father. You have pine in your blood. And I've always believed in your plans for replanting, you know that."

"Then we'll start construction on the house at Spring Hill, and we won't have to watch"—he detached his hand from hers, waved vaguely toward the window through which they could see a double-decker gazebo, designed by Louis, advancing ponderously toward the magnolia canopy, and she realized he was drunk—"another Riant atrocity." A burp. "Excuse me. I might even buy some more land out there."

"That's wonderful, Charles." She wondered if she should tell him about Little Charles. Instead she said gently, "I know Felix and the rest were rude at dinner, but they don't mean to be. They'd really be honored to lend you money, I'm sure, if you need it to buy land."

That comment deflated him, but she didn't notice right away. "'The world is too much with us, late and soon . . . ,'" he said, putting his head back against the chair, trailing off. "'Getting and spending, we lay waste our powers . . .'"

"I think it's going to work splendidly, Charles. The children and I will miss you, of course, but we'll write."

He sat up suddenly—her chest went cold with fear. "We're not spending another penny of your mother's or father's money or Felix's money or anyone else under the sun's money," he said, his voice rough. "I don't care if the queen of England grants us an allowance. Or better yet, the pope. I don't care if the pope invites us to be his lifelong guests at Vatican City, I'm not going."

Not knowing what to do, she laughed. "Well, I certainly wouldn't want to live there, Charles."

"Yes you would, you'd love it."

"I'd only go if you wanted to go, but I wouldn't like it."

"Ach!" He pulled at his hair, seethed at the mouth. Rocking back and forth on his chair that wasn't a rocking chair, he pressed the palms of his hands into his eyes.

"I'll leave you alone," she said standing. "I suppose you've had enough, Charles."

The next morning he was gone.

INSIDE THE CABIN HE PACED, his hand caressing the walls until he lay down on the floor to pass out each night in a different room. Charles lost at least a month to a haze of gin until one morning he woke up missing Anna, jumped in the car and headed back to Mobile. On the road he made terrible time. Driving slowly, he stopped for drinks to buck up his courage. He stopped to rest his eyes and, approaching Mobile, he drove more and more slowly, wondering what to say to Regina. As soon as he pulled into the driveway, he knew something was wrong, but as usual he thought it was himself. Unrelated signs in the landscape conspired to tell him that nature had turned against him, he thought through a splitting headache. A magnolia branch didn't hang right, the light was an eerie prestorm yellow, the design of the ant beds in the red clay of the driveway were off-color. The grounds were empty: could the brothers' construction have ceased at last? What could he say to Regina?

Inside, servants glided out of his way without looking at him. "Black suits you," he said absently to the girl who took his coat. Regina was not in the sewing room. Wearily he mounted the stairs to the nursery. His brothers-in-law, shadows across their brows, came forward at the top of the stairs, shook his hand without a smile and peeled away. Could they already know of his failure? Dread filled his heart as he came to the door.

Regina sat still in the rocker. Her eyes were dry, pinched, rimmed with pink, and she looked up at him as if he were a ghost.

For the first time he realized he had no idea how old she was. He heard himself ask, "What in the hell is going on?"

She swallowed and wet her lips with her tongue. "You got the telegram?" she asked hoarsely.

"No. Did you hear what happened?" he asked in a high-pitched voice. Then he noticed Camilla, who came forward from behind closed bed curtains and lingered between Regina and the door. He shot her a glance of annoyance but she didn't move.

Regina continued to look at him in bewilderment, asking in a raspy voice he didn't recognize, "What happened, Charles?"

He hesitated, looked to Camilla, who still didn't budge. He noticed that her eyes were smarting with tears. All at once he saw the sickbed, the pale, sleeping child, the evidence of ministrations; now his throat was constricted. All three stared at one another, locked in a triangle of postponement, until finally Regina worked herself to her feet, came forward, took Charles by the elbow and hobbled with him toward the window. They looked at the surface of the glass without seeing beyond it, their backs to Camilla. "Charles, Little Charles has leukemia. We sent you a telegram."

# On the Rosary

ON THIS PIOUS EXERCISE, the Reverend Alban Butler, in his *Lives of the Saints*, writes: "It is an abridgement of the Gospel, a history of the life, sufferings, and triumphant victory of Jesus Christ, an exposition of what he did in the flesh, which he assumed for our salvation." The Rosary ought certainly to be the principal object of the devotion of every Christian, always to bear in mind these holy mysteries, to return God a perpetual homage of love, praise, and thanksgiving for them, to implore his mercy through them, to make them the subject of his assiduous meditation, and to mould his affections, regulate his life, and form his spirit, by the holy impressions which they make on his soul. The Rosary is a method of doing this, most easy in itself, and adapted to the slowest and meanest capacity; and, at the same time most sublime and faithful in exercise of the highest acts of prayer, contemplation, and all interior virtues.

The principal mysteries of our redemption, which are celebrated in this exercise, are fifteen in number, and the prayers are divided into fifteen decades, or tens, corresponding, one to each mystery. Each decade consists in reciting the Lord's Prayer once, then the Hail Mary ten times, from which it is called a decade, or a ten. We repeat the Hail Mary oftener, because that is the prayer which contains the view and intention which is proper to this devotion. But this does not imply that we honor the Blessed Virgin in this exercise more than God. God forbid! Such a blasphemous thought we abhor and detest. Indeed, the adversaries of our holy Religion lay this to our charge, but most unjustly; for though the Hail Mary be immediately addressed to that ever Blessed Virgin, yet it is evident, from what we have seen above in explaining it, that all the praises therein given to her are referred to her Divine Son, as the fountain and source of all her excellence. All the praises given to the Blessed Virgin in the Hail Mary are only offered because she was the Mother of Jesus Christ, and consequently they all belong much more to him than to her.

The Rosary, when said with proper dispositions, is a powerful means to obtain favors from God. How many public favors, attested by the Church in her public offices, have been obtained by this means! How many private graces are recorded to have been received from the same source! St. Francis of Sales, in attestation of its efficacy, says, "The beads are a most profitable way of praying, if you know how to say them in a proper manner." It has been strongly recom-

mended to the faithful by many Popes, who, to encourage us to practice it, have granted great indul-
gences to those who do so. Experience itself will soon
convince all, who apply to it in earnest, how powerful
a means it is to obtain our petitions from the Almighty.

Regina strove to align herself with the Virgin, who had also lost
a son, but it gave her small comfort. Her son was not Christ, and his
death could not save them. Things with her husband were worse
than ever. He had kept her up most of the night with his drunken
sobbing. At dawn she left him snoring lightly and, unable to sleep,
sought solace on her knees at her prie-Dieu. It never occurred to
her to worry that in saying the rosary she was honoring the Virgin
more than Christ. She thought the *Saint Vincent's Manual* a little
outdated and took it with a grain of salt. She didn't use the rosary to
gain favors from God either; indeed, she scarcely knew what to ask
for. But the repetition soothed her.

Now, as she reached the end of a decade, she focused on the
church bells and counted: quarter to ten. She was running late. In
the *Saint Vincent's Manual*, which she had opened on the top of her
prayer stand, she flipped through the rosary section to the Five Do-
lorous Mysteries and rapidly said the two final decades of that cy-
cle: Jesus Carrying the Cross, and the Crucifixion. Then she ran
across the hall to dress Isabel and Anna.

Back at the house after Mass, she changed her clothes, put Isabel
and Anna in their play clothes and convinced them to sit on the
floor of the dining room, where she could keep an eye on them
while they built houses with playing cards as their uncle Felix had
shown them. She met Camilla in the kitchen and got the status:
Lucy had not shown up for work, but already the shrimp was
peeled, the oysters shelled, the crab gone through for bones and the

chicken stock simmered in a huge pot on the stove. Regina picked up the wooden spoon and stirred it, saying, "Give me something to do, please, Camilla."

Camilla, who from this day forward would be cook rather than the children's nanny, sat with her feet up on the rungs of the chair next to her, her skirt raised to her knees, fanning herself with the Sunday society section. "Well, there's the tomatoes, okra, onions and such," she said sluggishly. "I'm fixing to make the cornbread."

"To chop?"

"But I don't think you ought to, though, sugar. Why don't you rest?"

Regina ignored her. "Let's get some music in here, right?" she said, and went off to roll the phonograph from the library into the dining room so they could hear it while they worked. She passed back through the dining room, saying, "Girls, you're responsible for changing the records," but they were already gone, a deflated card house scattered near the legs of the table. Gathering the cards, she got a splinter in the side of her ring finger, which reminded her that the floors needed to be oiled. Then with alacrity she chopped to Prokofiev's ballet *Cinderella*, tossing the tomatoes, okra, carrots, green pepper, celery and onions into a large mixing bowl. "Is it time for the roux?"

"That stock's been going on three hours now," Camilla answered from the table where she stood pouring the corn mixture into square pans. "And the celery's chilling, the silver's ready for setting, no thanks to that doggone Lucy."

Regina melted a cup of bacon grease in the frying pan and added flour to it, stirring constantly. "Have you seen Mother this morning?" she asked.

"Oh yes! She was up with them birds as usual, wide awake and waiting for her coffee when I went on up there around seven or so.

Had Joseph drive her to the eight o'clock Mass, I believe. This here is ready to go," she said, wiping her hands on her apron. She untied it, mopped her brow with it, cast it onto the counter. "We gotta get this in right away," she said, heaving open the oven door. "Tomorrow's beatin' biscuit day, you know."

"Did Mother say she's coming down for dinner?"

"I never know her to miss a Sunday dinner. She was dressed up like she usually is. All her pearls, you know." When the mixture of bacon grease and flour had turned dark amber and smelled like it had started to burn, Regina turned off the heat. Camilla came over and held the strainer while Regina poured the stock through it, into the pot with the roux. Camilla returned to the table, where she sat rolling a cigarette. "I'm taking care of these dishes a bit later. Don't you touch them."

Stirring, Regina said, "It's just that Father Slidell is a bit difficult to handle without her."

"Ow! I can imagine that!" Camilla cackled.

Regina's giggle was short-lived, "It's amazing how well they get on, even though she can't hear. He's done so much for this family since . . ." She swallowed, gazing into the gumbo, her vision blurring with tears.

"Well, he's gonna get a delicious meal today, I'll tell you that much," Camilla said. "I sure can smell it!" Unable to answer, Regina added the vegetables, the Worcestershire sauce, the Tabasco, tomato paste, sugar and black pepper. Camilla watched her back with pity. "You get out of here, Miss Regina," she said finally. "It's all under control. I'm gonna fix us some iced tea and we're both takin' a break, you hear? Then I'll just do the final touches. We aheada time, you know."

Regina took her iced tea out to the front porch and sat down on the rocker, feeling her feet lighten, the drying perspiration raise the hair on her arms. She looked forward to the gumbo and had nothing to do but change her clothes before dinner; Camilla was making the rice. It was the end of June 1926, the hottest week of the year so far, but thoughts of Little Charles made her shiver. It was almost a year since his death. She was sick of wearing black but didn't want to discontinue it. She had been wearing black for most of her life, it seemed to her, as she crossed her legs, folded her hands over her stomach and let her neck collapse against the chair. She wondered where Isabel and Anna had gone and decided she ought to go look for them when their shrieks came to her ears as they passed the edge of the porch on their bamboo horses. She opened her eyes— weren't they getting too old for that?—and caught sight of a speck of gray suit in the bush by the gates. *It's Papa come back from the dead to deliver a message to me!* But, doubting the vision and its accompanying thought, she closed her eyes.

She thought of Charles, immediately after their son's death. There he was locked in the room; there he was staring at the wall; there he was with whiskey spilled all over the bed. He didn't answer the door when she invited him to go to daily Mass with her. He barely spoke at all, in fact. Regina, Isabel and Anna joined him whenever he let them in, and occasionally they ate their meals in the stuffy, foul-smelling room. When Isabel and Anna asked what had become of Little Charles, she told them he was in heaven with the angels. They wanted to know what angels looked like, what angels did all day and what songs they sang, but a glance at Charles, whose eyes were gushing silently, whose nose and neck were bloated with sorrow, made her throat too thick to respond.

And Charles still hadn't recovered. He came down to breakfast occasionally but that was it. Ach! How could she turn her mind to other thoughts? She opened her eyes. This time she saw for sure that a figure was approaching the porch. Who could it be at this, the hottest time of the day? All of her brothers were inside. Was it Charles's brother William? No, he would be driving and this man was too short. Anyone with a delivery would also have an automobile or a wagon; anyway, it was Sunday. Try as she might, she could not place the approaching man. There was something familiar about the situation. It struck her: Ahlong! Then she saw that the man's hair was light brown. By now her heart had risen and sunk so many times that her nerves were on edge, which made her predisposed to dislike whoever it was. She considered going inside to avoid him—she meant to go to her room and say a rosary—but had already waited too long; he had spotted her, and going in would be rude. He was closer and closer.

His "Good afternoon, madam!" startled her.

The light was in her eyes as she turned to the voice. She rose and went to the edge of the porch, shielding them with her hand. The man below her shone with sweat. His rounded face, gone hollow, offset his bright brown eyes and high, sunburned cheekbones. He held a black bowler hat against his breast. "Good afternoon," she said hesitantly, noticing that his suit was well cut, shaped at the waist à la Zouave, and of a gray linen with wide, lighter gray stripes.

"Mighty fine weather, wouldn't you say?" With the arm that was holding his hat, the man gestured in a general way toward the landscape behind him as if to present it to her for the first time.

Something about him made her simper with graciousness as she looked into his bright brown eyes. He needed a shave. "Yes," she said, conscious that she was blushing through cheeks already hot with the sun.

"Not a cloud in the sky," he boomed, and replaced his hat.

She lowered her hand from her forehead. "No, indeed."

He shifted back and forth on his feet, grinning. "The birds are singing and the leaves are blinking in the sun."

"Yes, I suppose so," she said, now puzzled. "What can I do for you, sir?"

"Madam," he lilted in a voice she thought was beautiful, "I've walked all the way here from New York City looking for work. Any kind of work. I'm a bond trader by training, have a right head for figures and persuasion, but I'm quite a handyman, a gardener, a cook—you name what you need. Short-term or long-term, I'm your man, and I'm from these parts originally so you needn't think of me as a stranger."

Again she was irritated: She wasn't sure what to do with what she admitted was an attraction to him. She didn't believe for one second he was Southern and found herself matching his overblown way of speech, playing the Southern lady to his Northern gentleman: "My land! New York! I thought they had every kind of work under the sun up there."

"That they do," he said unhappily.

"Your family's from Mobile? You came down here to be with your family?"

"No, madam, Pensacola. If you want to know the truth"—he paused, the shifting of his feet more pronounced—"I went bankrupt on a phony holding company is why I'm returning, but I'll be happy to be home again, that's for true." He hung his head.

"Oh." Her sympathy roused, she softened her tone. "And you walking all the way! You'd better take a chair and rest a bit out of the sun."

As he mounted the steps she noted he wore shoes of fine Italian leather like her brothers', but the soles of both were detached at the front and one was missing a heel. He seemed to feel her scrutiny. "Thank you kindly," he said quietly, then wavered, not knowing which chair to take.

She waited patiently—a drop of sweat passed down her inner

thigh, down her calf to her ankle—until he chose a chair and settled into it. Leaving an empty chair between them, she sat herself, wondering what kind of job she could give this man. After a time she said, "I'm afraid we don't have any work."

"As I said, I'm willing to do anything and I'll not be proud about the wages."

He rocked furiously as he said this, which inspired her to speak gently. "I'm afraid we have all the help we need at the moment." They lapsed into silence, but she felt the tension come off him and was ill at ease, even guilty. But it was true. Construction had stopped since the death of Little Charles, and all the household and gardening positions were overfilled. She thought she might be able to come up with something if she could make better sense of the man, of his position in the world, but she couldn't place him anywhere, and it wasn't in her nature to pry further into his misfortune.

"Who's 'we'?" he asked suddenly.

"I beg your pardon?"

"Would there be a Mr. Pretty Lady in this house? Maybe I can speak to him."

She flushed with humiliation, suddenly aware that her dress under her arms was soaked. She thought of Charles. She had not looked in on him since the morning, but she knew she would find him still in bed, sweating under his blankets. Recently he claimed that Little Charles was communicating to him from the beyond. If she believed him, she couldn't help being jealous: Why wasn't Little Charles giving *her* signs? If she didn't believe him, the whole frustration of the afterlife was on her in full: where had Little Charles gone?

She turned her head as far away from the stranger as it would go. "I live with my husband, my four brothers, my mother and my daughters, not that it's any of your business," she said, tempted to ask him to leave or to leave herself. "And my word has as much authority as you'll find around here. If I say there's no work, there isn't."

"I've offended you!" His tone was penitent. "I'm terribly sorry," he went on after a pause. "Madam, I didn't mean it. Please forgive me. I'm run across rough times, as you can tell. It makes a man lose himself a little."

"It shouldn't," she said curtly, but she had warmed to him again. They fell silent. The tension between them was so unbearable she had no recourse but to offer him a glass of iced tea.

"I don't deserve it," he said, "but I accept." She rolled her eyes at his naked charm but smiled as she moved to the front door. "Madam!" he called again when she was just inside. She came back out onto the porch, conscious that he was looking at her figure. "I don't mean any inconvenience, I truly don't, but if you have any leftovers in the way of a sandwich, I'd remember you forever for your generosity." She was taken aback, and he added, "I'm a long way past hungry."

"Of course," she said, her voice gravelly. "Please just keep an eye out for my daughters."

In the kitchen she regretted the gumbo would not be ready for several hours. "Camilla, honey, help me," she said. "There's a starving man out there on the porch needing a sandwich." Camilla set to work cutting slabs of pork roast, while Regina heated collard greens in the pan with the bacon grease she didn't use in the roux and cut two slices of bread. "Let's make another one for the road," she said as she arranged the plate and poured iced tea into a glass. "He's walked all the way from New York."

"Heavens to Betsy!" Camilla cooed. "I'll make two more."

Grabbing a napkin from the dining room, Regina returned to the porch and placed the snack in front of the man on a dark green round wicker table. She knew his eyes were wet with gratitude and kept her own averted. She resisted the impulse to ask him his name as he crammed the sandwich into his mouth. She left him alone, going back to the kitchen for the other sandwiches, which Camilla had wrapped in waxed paper. "I'm bringing them out," said Camilla. "I want to catch a look at the man who's walked all the way from New York." The two women lingered in the hallway, peeking through the screen door to see when he had finished, then stumbled over each other out onto the porch. Camilla shoved the sandwiches at him and studied him from a place behind his chair until Regina suggested that she go check on the rice.

"Please sit down." He pushed out the chair that was next to him, and she sat in it, smelling the old sweat that came off his forearm, which rested just inches from her own. He put down his plate, wiped his mouth and fingers with the linen napkin she'd supplied and took a long draft of the tea—she could hear the workings of his throat as he swallowed—before he pocketed the extra sandwiches. He sighed and sat back. They stared off the porch. He had become as satisfied from the food as she had become anxious. Her mind flew upstairs to Charles's bedside, to the gumbo, then to Father Slidell, to Mother Riant, to her daughters, to Camilla, who would turn down the burner, add the shrimp at the last minute—and back to the man beside her. Suddenly she was afraid. Would he try to kiss her? She wished he would leave. Equally she wanted two things: for him to kiss her and to say a rosary before dinner. "Lady," he began and stopped, took a large breath, held it for a moment. He clasped his hands and stretched them behind his neck, let out his breath. His arms fell back to his sides. "It's all going to hell," he said.

"What?"

"From the looks of this place you and your family have some money—stocks and bonds, probably, and money in the bank. Well, get it out. It's all going to hell and it's just a matter of time." He finished the tea in a gulp, put down his glass and shifted to the edge of his seat, facing her.

"I don't know what to say."

"Don't *say* anything. Trust me," he said, his eyes boring into hers, his friendly demeanor all but vanished. "And get it out. As fast as you can. It's only a matter of time," he said again.

She fixed her eyes on her lap. "I don't know anything about all that," she said nervously.

He sighed, looked away, stood and hitched up his pants. "Suit yourself," he said, replacing his hat, "but you said you had some authority around here."

"Well . . . I . . . ," she stammered.

He grabbed her hand and kissed it roughly. She yanked it away. He sighed again, rubbed his forehead and became a picture of his previous amiability. "I can't be taxing your kindness any longer and I'm aiming for Pensacola by dawn. Many thanks to you and your family." With that he was down the steps and heading for Old Shell Road.

"Good luck to you, sir!" she called.

"Get it out!" he yelled from halfway down the drive, without turning around.

She watched his back recede down the drive, then lurched up out of the chair and bounded down the steps. She should call to him, invite him to dinner, invent a job for him, give him a room in the house, fall in love with him, marry him. But the thought that she was already married, that he was younger than she was, that he himself might already be married, stopped her in time. She went back up to the porch. "Isabel!" she screamed at the top of her lungs, but she got no answer. "Anna!" Nothing.

Up in her room she knelt, drew her beads out of the top of her paisley upholstered prie-Dieu, crossed herself—*In the name of the Father, the Son, the Holy Ghost, amen*—and pinched the first bead. From the onset of Little Charles's illness, she had spent every free moment on her knees, not that she had had so many, though she also couldn't have said what she had done with her hours—except sit by his bed. She had watched his tiny body get smaller and smaller, his eyes get brighter and brighter with the silent plea that she, his mother, relieve his pain. Yet she could do nothing but pray. While he slept she took up the beads; while Camilla fed him she took up the beads; while her brothers entertained him she took up the beads; when sitting with her husband, who looked as if he was always on the verge of vomiting, she took up the beads.

There was the treatment that was very expensive and was the last hope that was no hope. Her brothers offered to pay for it, but Regina did not suggest it to Charles. She saw him drive off one afternoon in the direction of Spring Hill and knew he would strike a deal. He deeded his property at Spring Hill to his brother in exchange for seven thousand dollars. "Don't, Charles," William said when he heard the proposal.

Not trusting himself to speak without crying, Charles took up a pen and began writing out the contract. William watched him in misery. He shoved the papers forward. "Sign," he said.

"Let me make you a loan," begged William.

"Sign," said Charles. "When Little Charles is well, I'll make the money back and buy back the land, with a fair percentage increase in property value. If Little Charles doesn't get well, nothing will matter."

She knew what he had done without having to be told. They never talked anymore. They'd sit there reading, eat without talking, dress without talking, fall asleep in estranged positions. As soon as the pages are numbered, as soon as the counting starts, there is nowhere to go but forward on the path—which gave her the sense that everything that would happen to her had already happened. In panic she took up the beads.

The money had not saved Little Charles. The beads had not saved Little Charles either. She had known at a certain point that he would die, but she kept with them, reversing her grief as best she could as she prayed, so that she was thanking God for granting her a son, if only for five years, and asking God not that he wouldn't die but that he would die peacefully and be taken straight up to heaven. Then she had prayed that Charles might have the faith to cope with his son's death, when it came. At one point she even prayed that her son would die soon, so that her husband could be that much closer to restitution, so that their lives could return to normal, so that Isabel and Anna could get the attention they needed.

On the insistence of Camilla, who could not be persuaded that leukemia was not infectious, Little Charles was moved to his own room. Isabel and Anna were left to their own devices in the nursery, while Regina and Camilla and the brothers all tried to amuse Little Charles with coloring books and blocks and toy fire trucks. Charles watched the charades from the doorway; Little Charles grew thinner and thinner. Her brothers poured money into the barrels of toys, which they brought to the sickroom every day. When they saw that their charades as wild animals on the carpet made Little Charles smile, they fashioned an elephant, a tiger, a giraffe, a monkey from papier-mâché, so that the room became a veritable jungle. Regina saw little of her daughters, had been too distracted by death to play with them, but all the while she prayed for them.

Today as she took up the beads her mind strayed from the envisioning of each mystery, traveled down to the kitchen and the pot of gumbo, and she thanked God for Camilla, wondered about the man she had met that day, how she hadn't ever gotten his name, but she prayed for his safe journey. As she imagined the Virgin Mary on the road to Calvary, she wondered how far the visitor had made it on the road to Pensacola, where he would be by nightfall and where he would sleep. It occurred to her that she had no idea where her finances stood. The land at Spring Hill was gone, she was sure about that—which reminded her to pray for Charles, that he might be stirred to life once again. She knew he wouldn't appear for the dinner. Then she went downstairs to check the table setting, went back up to retrieve Mother Riant and back down to greet Father Slidell, back up to make Isabel and Anna change into Sunday clothes, and back down to dinner.

Something was missing. Had the bay leaf been forgotten? Nor were the oysters as plentiful as they should be, but she cleverly put most of them in Father Slidell's bowl. Since Little Charles's death, Father Slidell came out Sundays to dine with them as a comfort to Mother Riant, who took her meals in her room every day except this one. The cold shrimp dish accompanied by the iced celery had been fine, but it was clear that Mother Riant and at least one of her brothers—Louis, she thought—had noticed the flaw in the gumbo and was trying to cover it up with excessively vivacious conversation. Father Slidell had just been to Baltimore and had the pleasure of dining with Cousin Beauford and Mrs. Polignar and had seen the two Miss Dangerfields and Uncle Antoine, so fortunately there was much news to exchange. Pecan pie and black coffee were served.

Father Slidell had a tendency to overstay his welcome and could be long-winded on topics about which he was passionate, such as the proper conditions for growing hibiscus—his, cultivated in his greenhouse, had won several awards—the Jewish presence in Moorish Spain, the persecution of the Jesuits in Mexico. And he chain-smoked, which made her brothers smoke more and made Regina crave a smoke. She wanted him to leave so she could ask her brothers about the finances, but she had to wait. "And to think Mexico is right below us," she said, as she guided the party into the library, hoping a change in scenery would bring a change in conversation. Mother Riant smiled like a baby as a cordial made of sand pears was passed around.

"Yes, there are heathens in our midst," Father Slidell lamented.

# *Welcome*

IN VEGETATION'S CHOKING SCRIPT, the property signed away. In the desiccated forests surrounding Mobile, a consciousness discarded. In the dust-struck land inherited no longer—*God, help me*—he can barely get out of bed. Afternoons to be out of the house, he shuffles around Bienville Square, perspiring in a seersucker suit. He absorbs into lowered eyes the glare off the sidewalk, off the glass of the storefronts, and bends his mind to the deserts of a better age: skin, warmed by whiskey, glowing against the red felt of a billiard table, or the reflection of crystal goblets on an ivory face across from him, a face he once adored. Or candlelight, glazing the side of a duck as it circles the dining room—to all circles—to the rhythm of his footsteps around and around Bienville Square.

*God help me I can't*. He can barely get out of bed. He prefers to lie, letting time and substance winnow through his fingers. His hands fiddle across his lap. He sucks on a bourbon-coated ice cube. He has no thoughts. He shrivels against his thoughts. He cannot bear the hidden truth of his ruined heart, his boredom with Regina, his dead son, the land at Spring Hill that is no longer his, the intolerable fluctuations of life leading down. He has no money. *Why don't you seem in league with the others? You know we owe. I'm praying for you, why don't you this, that.* Regina seemed to want to whine him to the grave.

As he pours drinks from the bedside table, everyday sounds irritate Charles Morrow: mosquitoes coming close to his ears, cackling in the side yard, chairs scraping floors, the rapid shucks of Regina's sewing machine. Sometimes he sees himself as if it were tomorrow. He stands at the head of the table to make a toast, a worthwhile feat that would please them, but he freezes on his feet, his hand holding the glass shakes uncontrollably, a grin of alarm spreads across his face. *I can't.* In his mind he crouches inside himself, knitting the tendrils of memory into a fist. *Charles Morrow*—his name, the name of his dead son. He can't remember. Again he skims the catalog of his misfortune, looking for a crack that could lead him out, but concludes he is not equal to the search. He leans into the bedside table. Even his prayers are deposited in a bottomless well, a space infinite and unable, so that he walks away from reconciliation. Nothing lands.

REGINA WATCHED HIM CAREFULLY, endeavoring to protect him from the flies of reality that swarmed around his sickbed but puncturing this protection with quick lashes of blame—in equal measure. She couldn't help herself. When, in the bloated figure before her, she recognized the features belonging to the prince of her lifetime, for there would not be another, she pitied him and vowed to serve him, to nurse him whether or not he could return her love. Other times she spent waiting, waiting for something to change.

Mornings as she opened the double oak doors, paneled with mirrors, and crossed the dining room to see about the coffee, the smell of Harold's moonshine infuriated her, and if she discovered broken glass pushed clumsily under the couch, she felt she had run out of worry. She couldn't care anymore. "What did he promise me?" she asked herself in vain. Nothing specific, nothing spoken. She couldn't even entertain the idea that this was not right—she loved him; God was right, she was guided and safe. She tried to think of ways in which she was blessed, resolved again to be good for him, graceful in the way that he needed. "Darling, why don't you call Alfred Babineaux?" she suggested to him at the breakfast table.

He rubbed his eyes. "It's hot."

"Yes." Putting her hand on the nape of his neck, she stroked his hair, there and behind his ear, but the breath coming from his nose, the smell of old sweat and alcohol repelled her. "You could go by there and just see what he says," she sweet-talked, removing her hand and sitting back.

The jerk of his head belied the dullness of expression. "Tomorrow."

"What will you do today?" He shaded his eyes with his fingers, scratched the side of his head, crossed his legs and began shaking his foot, keeping his eyes averted. She knew she was making him miserable. "Do you want another cup of coffee?"

"No, no thank you."

She poured herself another cup and used it to help her swallow the toast. She shifted in her chair. "Did you sleep well, darling?"

"No."

She waited another moment before asking, "Do you want me to help you bathe?"

"No."

Then it was on her like lava: impatience. She took a short breath to stop herself. "I ran into Mrs. Carr and pledged twenty dollars to the United Cath—"

"Please," closing his eyes and lowering his forehead into his hands, "Please, Regina."

She poured them both another cup of coffee, took a sip, stared at him in impotence, at the unshaven flesh draping off his cheekbones, the lips of blue rubber, his wrinkled suit, his misbuttoned dress shirt. He persisted with ticking his foot. She put her hand on his shoulder and when he didn't move she continued, "Charles, I'm expecting——"

He looked up at her, his cornflower eyes soaking with pain. "What?!"

Her hand dropped. His head lowered. She expected nothing. "I love you, Charles," she said pitifully. To keep from crying she reached to the center of the table for a piece of toast, straightened it on her plate next to the other, half-eaten piece and began scraping butter across.

"Please don't make so much noise with your eating." *Please.*

Both stared at a different raised flower on the damask cloth; their eyes pulsed with helplessness. "Please forgive me," he said a long moment later, putting his hand on her leg to help him rise. "I know——that everything there was to do, I've done wrong." She watched as his hunched back made its way through the dining room, returning to bed.

AT HER SINGER, Regina set to work on the darts for a suit she had seen in *Harper's* and was making for Cousin Mathilde's birthday. To prove to her that handmade clothes were just as beautiful as ready-mades, Regina would wrap the suit in a Hammel's dress-shop box and have it delivered during the birthday dinner. Why she needed to prove such a thing she didn't know, but it gave her small amusement, thinking about the surprise. She had spent weeks deliberating on the material, and now that she had the peacock blue piqué, it was a delight to work with. She laid out the material and glanced over her notes for the bodice: *0.5 at their thickest; 9 long, 1.5 from bottom; 4.25 from side seam.* As she measured, drew out the triangles and pinched the lines with pins, she thought of Charles and how he had come to this—the "this" rising and falling on her subsequent reflections. She decided to do the pale blue silk lining simultaneously, stretched it out on the table and began cutting. How she loved Charles for the very qualities that made him miserable: his inordinate degree of feeling, exhilarated or upset, how he threw himself like a child onto every wave so that by the end of the day he was exhausted, vulnerable, his little boat shattered against a rock, and he straggling to shore, only to be skinned alive by the Indians.

It was hot and stuffy in the library, and though the four French doors were open onto the porch, the air did not stir. The sweat of her hands began to stain the silk. She wiped her lip and forehead with a handkerchief, went to the kitchen for iced tea and returning, turned off her working light and moved the iron to the other side of the room. She knew by the heaviness in the air that it would rain sometime after dinner. She studied the *Harper's* again for a minute and sketched out ideas for the lapels on sheets of pattern paper. Then she went to the kitchen to make the gravy. She took a dinner tray up to Mother Riant's room, came back down and set the table.

Only her brothers turned up for the meal. Camilla made a show of ringing the bell, which purported to signal Charles to the table, but it was evident that he would not appear and they commenced without him. Regina ate in silence. She ignored her brothers' attempts to rile her by keeping their elbows on the table and talking crudely of the Laborde girl. Until three she remained in her chair, presiding over an empty table, her brothers gone to their midday respites. Isabel and Anna—she hadn't seen them since breakfast—ought to be napping also.

. . .

THE BODY WAS FOUND, later that evening, in the life-size dollhouse
that stood beyond the orchard on the western edge of the property.
Isabel and Anna, aged seven and five, were allowed to play more or
less unsupervised there, where they had everything that a real
house has. Light pink streamers wound around the two pillars on
each side of the dark green front door, and lace curtains hung on
their two front windows. A small oak table, four matching chairs
and four miniature mahogany beds, carved with roses on the head-
boards, ranged about the inside. Two sets of damask napkins
and tablecloths, one pink, one white and embroidered with roosters, were secreted in the cupboards. An old icebox filled with boxes
of Heavenly Hash, made by the sisters at the Convent of Mercy,
stood in the corner by the door. Paint kits, playing cards, story-
books and pieces to the ivory mah-jong game that had belonged to
Colonel Riant's friend Captain Fry, the Cuban martyr, were scattered about.

As mistresses of the dollhouse, the girls enjoyed a private world
created just for them. Harold the handyman added knobs and
hinges to a wooden crate that functioned as a play stove. He at-
tached legs and little wheels to cast-off wooden pallets so they could
spend the afternoons on their front porch, rolling instead of rocking. Camilla gave them old pans, mismatched bits of silver-plated
cutlery, any china she didn't consider fine enough for the main
house, and fashioned pairs of stilts for them out of coffee cans and
string. Their mother sent old perfume bottles, torn fans and pocketbooks in their direction, made green satin aprons for them out of an
old evening dress and was constantly at it with the needle, repairing
the dolls' clothes. Uncle Felix made horses for them out of bamboo
shoots, with string for reins, the tails of which would swish behind

them as they rode, back and forth from the main house to the doll-house. Even the iceman, who drove his cart up to the back of the house every morning, made a special trip by the dollhouse to give them shaves of ice.

The morning started as July mornings usually did. The girls were up very early, and their mother insisted that they swallow every morsel of corned-beef hash and eggs before they could go off to the dollhouse, but Anna said, "I don't want to be the husband to-day," as soon as they had opened the small front door and pushed back the curtains.

Typically Isabel, as the mother, decided what the husband, mother and children were supposed to do, when they needed to nap or were hungry or thirsty. Anna always played the husband and sat in a roller on the porch with the empty tonic bottles while Isabel flitted around with the linens, dressing and undressing the dolls, taking them in and out of the beds and covering and uncovering them. "Fine," said Isabel, "but it's harder to be the mother. It's Thursday, and the mother has to clean the entire house on Thursdays."

"All right," said Anna cheerfully.

"You'll have to sweep the porch, make the beds, dust the furni-ture and fold all the linens while I sit on the porch relaxing."

"All right," said Anna, who folded dish towels and blankets to the tune of her sister's disapproving grunts.

"You're not doing it right," she said finally. "You're too young to play the mother."

"No I'm not, Isabel! Why can't we both be the mother?"

Her sister pushed her toward the door. "Go sit on the porch, husband."

Anna's shoulders drooped and she slunk out onto the porch, sat on the steps and cried softly while Isabel worked behind her in the dollhouse. She considered going back to the main house to sit with her mother while she sewed, but it was too hot, she was scared to go without Isabel, who knew where all the ant beds were, and Rowena wasn't around. Rowena, who came every day to help clean—with the additional duty of keeping an eye on Isabel and Anna—didn't actually pay much attention to them. They kept at their play for hours at a time, so that she left them to it, often enough, and returned to the house to chat with Camilla and help her with the cooking. Anna was still on the porch, watching a lizard, when Isabel came out. "I just remembered, husband. Thursday is Visiting Day. We've got to take the children visiting around town."

Anna was obedient, if quiet, as they dressed the dolls in their best clothes. Then they were on the bamboo horses tearing across the yard with two babies each, tucked into the front of their black bloomers. Rowena, who had gone to the dollhouse to call the sisters to dinner, saw them fly by with the bamboo horses between their legs, the leaf tails stirring up dust as they went. She called to them, and they waved without slowing their pace. Her arthritis prevented her catching up, but she saw them turn to the eastern side of the house. By the time she reached the clearing, out of breath, she found nothing but the bamboo horses, tied neatly to the horse posts by the porch. That was before the storm, about half past two.

CHARLES HEARD THE DINNER BELL as a church bell resounding in an empty village. Or the village was full of people and he, far removed from it, heard the bell from the top of a mountain. And the blizzard thwarted him from something, he no longer knew what. He was hungry but couldn't bear to face any of them at the table. Maybe if he had another drink: he couldn't pour, couldn't sip, couldn't swallow. *Couldn't.* God had gone out of him. His bed was a bathtub but the water was freezing, and bottomless, and he felt himself descending layer upon layer in the only direction he knew: toward the hour of lead. All had left. His body was a log, and there was no grass, no birds or foliage, no air or sun around him. Where was his love? Could he make it down to the parlor to read the paper? The twenty-eight-odd steps seemed to him as painful and difficult as Christ's steps on the road to Calvary. His brain was thick; his body bloodless. To be old. To be old and sick. To be dying. To remember that every step he had made in this life had been a wrong one.

He concentrated on determining what day of the week it was but only got as far as July. July! There was so much to do in July; he decided to make July the pinprick of light that would sustain him, but a second later that light had gone out. "O when this glorious nature lies before me so rigid like a little varnished picture, and all the joy of it cannot pump a drop of bliss from my heart to my brain." His urine warmed him momentarily, then went colder. He had lost his inheritance and all his money. His children, he didn't know where they were. His son was dead. Where was Regina?

IN THE LINEN CLOSET WITH CAMILLA, she enjoyed the rhythm of folding, and just the presence of Camilla calmed her, but it was cramped in the small closet off the second-floor hallway, which was barely large enough for both of them to stand on either side of an old pine table. It was simply too hot in there. The open door allowed the puniest draft to stir the damp backs of their necks. Camilla ironed napkins, tablecloths and handkerchiefs on the ironing board, the iron only slightly hotter than her skin, while Regina folded. It was too hot for talk but to Regina's dismay, the silence was not peaceful and rather built in tension as it lengthened. Camilla slid the second large laundry sack out from under the table and wiped her forehead on the forearm of her dress. Pausing, she looked at Regina and ventured in a low voice, "You all right, honey? Most white folk takes a nap after dinner, and that's where you should be."

Regina shifted on her feet, murmuring unintelligibly and continuing to fold, only to stop a moment later to loosen the collar of her dress. They lapsed into a silence that didn't break until Regina had finished with her piles of sea green napkins. "And Isabel and Anna?" she asked. "How do they seem to you?"

"Oh, Rowena says they as fine as can be." Camilla breathed deeply and used her untucked shirt to fan her stomach. "They don't give her trouble at all." The room grew a few degrees hotter. Regina was now so hot that she began to feel chills. Camilla put the iron on its back foot and held the edges of the table, bending forward at the waist; she was nauseated. "What we going to do about this heat?"

"I don't know." Regina reached for the crimson pile of napkins and began folding, her pace quickening slightly under Camilla's gaze. She stopped in the middle of a square and stared at her hands, which remained in position around the second-to-last fold. "I don't know."

Camilla reached for the folded stacks and placed them on the shelf behind her. "Don't worry about any things, honey. It'll all be coming along as it should." Reluctantly she picked up the iron and continued her work. "There's nothing under our Lord's sky than what should be being."

"I'm praying constantly for Charles . . . ," Regina stuttered, "for Mr. Morrow, as you know."

"I am, too, child." Camilla worked silently for a time, intensifying her concentration on the creases of a blue napkin. "But he's traveled off by himself; by now he outside all understanding, barring the Lord's."

Regina's hands caught. Twice she took out her fold and began again. She wanted to contradict Camilla, to scream at her for impertinence, but she lacked the strength to lie. In her confusion she stopped altogether. Camilla carried on steadily with the iron, smoothly changed the subject. "It's impossible to get the temperature right on these terrible 'lectric contraptions! I just as soon leave it for the next generation to figure out, heaven help them. I wouldn't mind," she went on, "one of those 'lectric washing machines, though. For everything but the linens."

"Or one of those refrigerators," Regina said.

"Ha, ha!" Camilla broke into laughter. "I knew you was wanting one of those!"

Regina laughed, too. "How's your grandson, Ezel?" she asked at last as she reached for the blue pile with a smiling sigh.

"Oh, he's fine as can be. My daughter Rose's been teaching him how to read, you know, and he so smart. He so smart."

"How old is he now? Because I have some clothes of Little Charles's . . ."

But Camilla, who was getting on in years, misheard "how old" for "Harold" and didn't listen to the rest of the sentence. "Same old, same old," she said. "He's still peddling his 'shine, if that's what you mean." Regina left off her folding to stare at her. "Oh, I asked him to stop like you tell me," she went on, "but he don't care what we say, Miss Regina. Your brothers are his biggest customers. He don't have to care."

A moan erupted from Regina's throat but was trapped in time by her lips, which disposed of it with a poof, undershadowed by a short, high-pitched cat noise. She closed her eyes tightly, then flicked them open and bored them into Camilla, who looked away. "It's *Mr. Charles* who's his biggest customer," she hissed.

Camilla's cheeks filled with air, which she slowly exhaled,

carefully ironing the same blue napkin over and over again. "I ain't profiting none from you," she muttered. They stood there, Camilla now furiously folding Regina's abandoned pile, while Regina held a red napkin like a deflated flag in her hand and stared at an indeterminate space on the floor beyond the table. "Ooweeh," Camilla intoned after a moment. "There's something headed our way in the form of a storm this afternoon," she said.

"I know," said Regina, snapping the napkin and placing it gently on the table. "Forgive me, Camilla. I have to get some air." Then she turned into the hallway and descended the stairs in search of Felix.

ROWENA COVERED THEIR PLATES and put them on the counter. On the backs of two recipe cards she marked the letters *I* and *A* with a pencil and put them on top of the covered plates: Isabel didn't eat carrots and Anna loved spinach. She went back to the east of the house and sat on the porch, keeping a watch on the bamboo horses. If the girls were somewhere in the house, their mother or Camilla would pin them down and send them to her. Otherwise she would catch them when they came back for the horses.

They were in the house—it was Visiting Day—but neither their mother nor Camilla ever crossed paths with them, and Rowena, who walked back to the dollhouse at the first rumbles of thunder, missed them entirely that afternoon.

Visiting was no small feat. They began by planting the dolls around the house, at various spots where Mobile society obliged them to call. Martha, their least favorite, they left in an old high chair in the still-unsealed part of the third floor, where she would have tea with Aunt Eugenia Des Moines. Veronica they left in charge of Captain Fry, the Cuban martyr. He lived in a magazine basket on the stone sunporch off the parlor and was famous for his shortbread cookies. Germaine, poor soul, they left in a secret spot, on blankets inside the log of the oak tree felled in the hurricane of 1916; she would snack on fairy dust. Sofia, Isabel's favorite, had the honor of calling on Madame Octavia LeVert, Mardi Gras queen, on the red velvet ladies' chair in the corner of the parlor.

Then they had to distribute the food. They circumvented Rowena by going out the door of the west wing toward the ant beds in the side yard. There, with two bowls taken from the kitchen—they saw their dinner plates on the counter, but Isabel wouldn't let them eat until their duties were done—they prepared the squashed ant and pecan stew on a bed of Alabama clay. All that remained was dessert. Back on the floor of the dining room, in two more bowls they ground gingerbread, soda crackers and corn cakes to a fine pulp. After all the food had been delivered they sat on the pink couch in the corner of the darkened dining room. "Oh no!" exclaimed Isabel. "They'll need something to drink!"

Anna closed her eyes and lay back. She was starving. "What will they drink?"

"Here, husband. Take them this lemonade," said Isabel, miming the handing over of a pitcher of lemonade. Anna walked out slowly, stopped in the kitchen and, standing, ate part of her dinner with her fingers. Then she returned to the dining room.

"Where have you been?" demanded Isabel.

"Hunting."

AT THE BOTTOM OF THE STAIRS, Regina forgot why she had come down. To find Felix. She paused before the closed door of the parlor and hauling it open, stared into the scene that she had triggered to action: Charles picking up a newspaper from the floor, cradling it for a moment in his lap, placing it back on the floor. He rose to his feet, turned to her and stood, shivering in the shafts of dusty light that emanated from both sides of her. When she could not bear to face him any longer, she dropped her eyes to his shoes and strode forward to the middle of the room. "Where have you been?"

He shuffled in place. "Hunting . . . ," he said, and cleared his throat. "Does that please you?"

She paused a moment, perplexed. "Hunting?" Then she charged at him. "Why are we in trouble?" she whimpered, her nails digging into his soiled smoking jacket. "Tell me!" she wailed, her face red, her tears splashing onto his hands. "I want to hear."

Stupidly he patted her head, which she jerked out from under his long, thin fingers. Over her shoulder she could see Isabel and Anna through the window, sitting side by side on a log in the driveway, arguing earnestly in the afternoon light, their childhood foreheads already creased. Murmurs of thunder rolled across the silence. "I love you," she said, but the words, tinged with a nag, were deflected by his adopted resistance to her pitches. "I love you," she repeated solemnly. It sounded the same as other things she said. Now she heard herself speak in the voice of a pitiful child. "Do you love me?"

He seized her upper arms, rattled her. Closing his eyes he pushed her away. "It'll be all right, Regina!" he screamed, a clap of thunder hooding his voice.

She stood at a distance but her fervor increased. "The girls love you so much, Charles. Are you listening to me, Charles? Let's get away from here, from my brothers and my mother and this house. We can go to St. Louis. I've always wanted to go to St. Louis, or no, or anywhere *you* want, Charles, just tell me. Let's go back to Choctaw Bluff."

"You are prodigiously kind, madame, thank you," he said, bowed low and hurried from the room.

. . .

AT FOUR O'CLOCK ROWENA LEFT her post on the porch and headed to the dollhouse. Seconds later Isabel and Anna appeared by their horses, removed Germaine from her place in the old log and began arguing about who was to feed her the smashed ginger cookies they had just prepared on the floor of the dining room. They dropped their horses on the lawn beside them and sat down on the log to hash it out, facing the house. "It's one for you and three for me," Isabel said, ignoring the dusky drumroll of thunder to their left. "Always. I'm older and I'm always going to be older." Against the purple afternoon, the windows of the brightly lit parlor stood out to them. They could see their mother and father talking within.

"But it's my turn," Anna said.

When the rain started, they ran with Germaine for the cover of the west porch and sat down on the top steps. They brushed the water off their hands, arranged their clothes and fell to silence as they gazed back at the log and the bamboo horses cast beside it. "Horses need water," Anna said, repeating her mother's reason for leaving them outside the house. "They like it. It cools and cleans them." She sat back and prepared to watch them soak in the storm.

Isabel clutched Germaine. "I'm sure Sofia will be afraid to be without us in the storm," she forecast, looking warily around her. "She'll start crying, and no one wants to witness that."

"I'm sure she'll be fine," Anna said as scribbles of lightning over the Labordes' property drew their eyes.

"Husband," said Isabel, "you're going to have to take Germaine to the dollhouse. I'll pick up Sofia and meet you there. She's scared. I can hear her crying in my heart. She needs to be home during the storm."

"I don't want to, Isabel. She's not scared. She's sleeping."

"We have to pick up Martha and Louisa. And our umbrellas, which are at the dollhouse. Oh, what are we to do?" Isabel wailed.

"My horse is cooling off right now, so I can't go anywhere. I'll wait until he's finished."

"You're no husband of mine!" shouted Isabel, but a clap of thunder silenced her. They held hands, watched the rain. Anna began eating the ginger cookie dust from the porch. "Please don't make so much noise with your eating," Isabel said, herself taking a pinch or two of the dust. When the rain had slackened, she stood up. "That's for Sofia," she said, stomping on Anna's hand in the ginger cookie. Then she stalked off toward the dollhouse.

AT THE TOP OF THE PORCH he crossed paths with Harold. "Take cover, Mr. Charles," said Harold pleasantly. Charles stood there dumbly, drooling and clutching a newspaper. He fell against Harold's shoulder.

"You're a lucky man, Harold," he moaned as he pushed himself off with his cheek and stumbled down the steps.

Harold gazed down at this man who swayed back and forth on the pavement with glazed eyes. "There's fixing to be a bad storm, Mr. Charles. You best be getting indoors."

Charles held on to the horse post, rocking for a moment from foot to foot before he bounded back up the porch steps to Harold. "Good luck, sir," he saluted, tripped backward down the steps and crashed to the pavement on his back. A gust of wind stirred the crepe myrtles, which pelted their rotting pink blossoms on his head. He struggled to his feet.

Harold was beside him. "Come on up here, sir. Sit with me and we can watch it roll in." Harold led him by the elbow up the steps and into a chair, took the newspaper from his clasp and fanned him with it, until Charles relaxed into a stupor and closed his eyes. Harold sat near him on the top step, dragging away at a rolled cigarette, following the clouds bruised with thunder as they advanced on the property, coloring the lawn gray and turning the air with the smell of salt water. Charles snored lightly. A splinter, then a crack that sounded like the crack in a bone: the thunder surged up the driveway. Charles's breathing stopped dead, tripped down the steps of his throat and transformed into a gruesome snort. Awake, he gulped for air and snapped his jaw. "There is no peace," he said. "I didn't even dream."

"You dream waste, Mr. Charles," said Harold. More thunder came like furniture being dragged across the sky's hardwood floor.

Charles slumped, muttering curses, but something in Harold's stiffening posture made him stop. More boulders of thunder pushed toward them from a magenta patch over the Labordes' property. The massive magnolia trees were seized up in the air's disturbed current and rustled in increasing waves across the yard. Behind them in the house a screen door slammed. "I didn't make it." Charles stood and tossed his limbs down the steps for the third time. At the foot of the steps he caught his breath and looked up to Harold, who was looking at the sky. "Thank you for waiting with me while I slept, Harold. I appreciate that. Usually I'm afraid to wake up." He lowered his gaze to his feet.

Harold looked up to catch Charles's eye, but he had already turned and was weaving his way into the distended gray clouds streaked with midnight that waited for him behind the double oak trees at the gates. A clap of thunder obscured Harold's "You all right, Mr. Charles?" Charles hesitated, seeming to recognize the signs of the imminent storm for the first time. Harold watched him cut right in the direction of the orchard and stagger out of sight. A few yards behind him, Rowena was hobbling in the direction of the dollhouse. Minutes later it began to rain.

REGINA STOOD STILL in the center of the parlor, crowded between the four walls that meant nothing to her; nor did the chandelier, the carpet, the crystal hurricane shades—all of which seemed to jump out at her in her shock, begging for a recognition she could not assign. *It's the end,* she thought, but there would be no end. She understood that the power had gone out and in the gray rain light that came through the windows, a vague foreboding of violence flashed across her mind. She thought of whiskey, she considered glass or cutting knives, she thought of stuffing herself with pound cake, or a cup of coffee. She wanted to go home but there was no such thing. Then she thought of Camilla. She found her on the small porch off of the kitchen, under the tin roof with Harold and Rowena, watching the rain.

"I need you, Camilla," she said, "to help me with something in the parlor." Camilla exchanged a wave of worried intimacy with Rowena and followed Regina, saying nothing. She stopped in the hallway to sweep up a pile of gingerbread crumbs into her hands.

Regina stood aside to let Camilla pass into the room, then closed the door behind them. "Where are the girls?" In her voice was a hysterical tone Camilla had never heard. The wind picked up steadily and sent rhythmic sheets of rain against the glass doors of the parlor.

Camilla had no idea but knew from Rowena that they were not at the dollhouse. "They're with their dolls in the attic."

Regina rolled her eyes as if twisting her thoughts to the attic. "I don't believe you," she said sadly. "I'm beginning to doubt everything you tell me. You must get rid of Harold." She paused. "Camilla, tell me honestly, am I repeating myself?" Her eyes were glassy. They stared at each other in mutual confusion. The rain had stopped.

"They's up there, Miss Regina. I'll go find them and bring them down."

Then they heard the shot.

"No," whispered Regina. For a moment she stood in front of the other woman, immobile in grief, her face contorted with agony, her hands hung large and limp at her sides, her back curved like an ape's. Then she began to weep.

Tears came to Camilla's eyes, and she rushed to Regina to lead her to the couch. "Sit still, sit here, don't cry, baby, breathe and wait here. I'm going to bring you a cup of tea. Don't worry. Just close your eyes. Calm down. I'll be right back. I'll get the girls." And with that she quickly left the room.

Imagining with the firm closing of the door that she was locked in, Regina began to sob uncontrollably, her tears building to a frenzy until she was crying generally for all the sadness in the world. At length she was scared that she would not recover her breath. This calmed her for the time it took to gather her strength and tear across the room. She tipped the marble plant stand, a hurricane shade, Great-Grandmother's mirror and the glass doors leading onto the veranda, though she made no effort to leave through the now-open door. She ripped down two bookcases, their books mixed on the floor with glass, soil and plant matter. For a while she paced around the pool table, attempted to knock it over but didn't have the strength and collapsed on the floor crying quietly. At the sound of her pitiful wails, a chill ran down the spine of Camilla, who stood behind the closed door, holding a cup of tea.

. . .

CALMLY CHARLES CLEANS HIS PISTOL over another bottle in the carriage house. Suddenly it occurs to him that he hasn't even noticed the rain until now, just before it stops, and by then *I am careening down the walkway to my daughters' dollhouse.* He finds himself in the center of the floor by the play stove, legs spread to clutch the gun between his thighs. He will use the gun to make some cornbread. Sarcastically, determining to raise himself up, he smiles at his own foolishness, loving himself a minute. Like all cowards he turns and looks over his shoulder to the open doorway. Nothing. A breeze barely stirs the Spanish moss on the oak tree, scattering leftover rain. The small white-blond head of Isabel the angel appears in the doorway to convince him that he has already done that which he now realizes he can do: the letting go. The piano keys of insanity pound at the top of his throat. He will clean his guns again, put some cornbread in the stove. A scale up, a scale down, a trilling. He doesn't hesitate. But loads and shoots.

# To the Market

IN THE MADDENING QUIET OF HER HEAD Mother Riant was often confused. Her sons came close to her ear; she could feel their hot breath on her cheek, the vibrations of their larynxes and their bodies at large—she felt them all, but she couldn't, God bless her, hear a goddamn thing, and she was forced to make guesses based on the mood around her, the expressions, the body language, and second-guess herself and guess again. "Isn't that nice? That's lovely" she took as her standard response unless she realized it was the wrong response.

By straining her powers of perception, she aimed to sort the communication from her sons into one of two groups—good news or bad—and taper her responses accordingly, but she knew her sons tended to lie; she could never be sure of her interpretation and made many mistakes, which served later as the butts of jokes. For example, when they told her that Little Charles was ill, she said, "Isn't that nice? That's lovely." But for the most part they left her alone and she was grateful for the long stretches when they didn't visit her. The pretending drained her.

After the death of Little Charles, she took great pleasure in strolling the grounds on Camilla's arm, for outside was the only place she could rely on her sense of smell. These walks restored her strength. Awake most of the night, she made it a habit to take a slow, unassisted walk to the gate at dawn and pick up the newspaper, though she never even glanced at the front page. After dinner on Sundays, when she ate with the family, she and her two canes, one ivory, one silver-plated, took the back path under the rose arbor, followed the driveway's turnaround, down the slate path to the edge of the orchard, past the banana trees and between the hibiscuses to the spot where she had a wicker armchair and a table placed, under a magnolia. The fire ants and mosquitoes plagued her, so she wore her wool stockings, wrapped herself up to her neck in long black gloves, a hat and a veil, and marveled at the fact that she no longer perspired as she sat there watching the grass grow, the deck of cards in her lap.

Her deafness was more than just the impenetrability of sound. The first time she caught herself forgetting, it was that Charles was dead, easy since she hadn't understood how it had happened and was too afraid to ask Regina. Really, she hadn't wanted to know. That way, she could explain Regina's grief as the grief of a young wife pining for a missing husband who was off somewhere, at Choctaw Bluff probably, toiling for his family. Nights she slept lightly and woke with a start as fresh gaps cropped up in her deafness: mostly faces. Her husband's was one of the first to lose its definition; then his eyes were gone; then the more she tried to remember things he had said to her over the years, the more she forgot the sound of his voice.

Her clearest memories were of instances furthest away, of her childhood; she remembered every detail of the face of her brother Damian, who was closest to her in age, who had gone off and died in the Civil War. She replayed their games, his clothes, his laugh. Next she retraced the horses she had loved; the nuns who had taught her;

Easter meals before her marriage; suitors and girlfriends. She knew she was hopelessly mixing up the facts, but she wanted to tell them to someone. She wanted to explain what was happening to her on the threshold of death, bombarded with the sweetest memories of life, but she didn't trust her voice. So she talked to Camilla, kept her in the afternoons after Camilla gave her the bath. And, better than anyone, Camilla knew how to make her comfortable, how to tuck in the sheets, how to pour coffee an eighth of an inch from the top of the cup, fix the pillows.

Camilla adjusted the blinds so that there was both darkness and flowing air, and helped her onto the porch where they played double solitaire, making one hand last for up to three hours as Mother Riant soliloquized. And she knew she was amalgamating scenes: Colonel Riant coming to ask her father for her hand; she was celebrating her Confirmation. Her brother is dead; her favorite aunt is also there, and it is Christmas, the Christmas she got the dollhouse. Camilla smiled as if the memories were sweet to her, too, until it was time for her to go down and fix the supper.

Mother Riant was no fool, but she had become something of a fixture unto herself and the household: there she was in a reading chair, there she was in a rocker. Her noiseless circuitry was a constant surprise to her sons, who, talking among themselves, heard a voice saying, "The old do not perspire," looked up and were surprised to find her there with them in the room, speaking into an empty fire grate. In 1928, spring had come with its typical garrulousness. At last it was April, and the weather cleared itself of indecision. In the brighter air the brothers felt high above the mud, though they sensed they had become older. They were not bad boys. They were good boys, but they tended to talk about how to make their mother comfortable without managing the slightest solicitation.

A year for every year of Little Charles's life, they put a five-year moratorium on construction on the house, leaving several of the third-floor rooms unsealed. Their fatalistic sensibilities closed the door on many other projects, but there was no shortage of things to investigate. One or more of them jumped on the tail of any fad that came through Mobile, and there were enough fads and enough brothers to keep pretty well abreast of things, especially since, with the help of catalogs, magazines, newspapers and radio, they heard of goings-on well beyond Mobile. They crossed, crisscrossed, and cross-referenced their calendars with engagements at the brokerage, appointments at one court or another, tennis, basketball, meetings at the links, seats at game tables, boxing matches—and they always had the clothes for the occasion.

Becoming president of Mobile's chapter of the Mah-Jong League of America, Peter wrote treatises that received national attention on how to break the wall and when, exactly, to call pung. Louis considered himself the least selfish of all the brothers, so he concentrated on the technology sector. He sought to support the household by way of refrigeration, electric irons, phonographs. He also became known for his particularly smart golfing suit.

Felix played tennis for a while, then joined Louis on the green. He thought about investing in miniature golf but decided against it, saying, "In this economy there's no reason to think small," yet he pored over crossword puzzle books and could be found mumbling "'Braggart's problem,' forty-seven across. 'Like the nobility,' starts with *l*. 'Stagnant'—shoot, that's six. 'Bring about in a jiff,'" and then out loud, "Regina, I need your help with this one." He followed the market, especially the shifting of blue chips, and talked of forming Mobile pools that would compete with the best of them.

George threw himself into wireless telephony, kept himself up to date with the latest in live broadcasting of orchestras and insisted that they all sit around the new "radio room" to hear the daily improvements in transmission. He had had a wireless set since the end of the Great War, taught himself Morse code and spent entire nights tinkering over the set to pick up messages from ships at sea and from land stations equipped with sending apparatus. By day he followed hungrily the development of soundproofing and talked of nothing but the great quartz breakthrough.

But the brothers took sparse joy in these pursuits. Collectively they were so self-centered as to believe that they were either the cause or the effect of everything that happened around them. If something went wrong in the midst of a project, they dropped it as though they had burned their fingers on it. They believed that if any one thing gave them too much pleasure, they were putting themselves in a position to be betrayed by it—that it would hurt them back for loving it. So it was in the case of the house construction on Dauphin Street. They had started the construction in an effort to please Mother Riant; to alleviate some of the burden Regina and Charles carried around with them, namely their dream of the house at Spring Hill; to give their nieces a fantastical place in which to grow up. But it had instead ended up being, to their minds, the cause of the deaths of Little Charles and Charles.

They shared the guilt: Perhaps they had been overconfident, perhaps they had behaved as though they were responsible for their own salvation—when only God was responsible for salvation. They had tried to play God with four-by-fours and fancy architects and now they were punished; they had brought God's wrath upon the household. So they took to gambling, a release they had always enjoyed, with calculated zeal.

They would demonstrate their faith in God by casting their fortunes in the hand of fate, where they would have no one to blame but chance. But, the brothers reasoned, because the size of their risk corresponded to their faith in God, God would employ his steady hand to make sure they stayed even. They believed the stock market was a perfect forum for such a test. It was also something they could watch from afar, like a sporting event. "I like the sound of that," they would say when reading the words of Billy Durant, head of General Motors.

"Anaconda Copper. Anaconda," mused Peter. "I'm going to name my daughter that."

"I'm going to name mine Data," said Louis. "Isn't it beautiful? Latin, you know."

And God rewarded them. They danced around the room when the evening papers came in and they read the latest stock quotes. Mardi Gras of 1928 and '29, they passed out favors, sterling mint julep cups, red lacquer cigarette boxes, and green enamel compacts for the ladies. They dressed in their best suits and stayed out until their comrades in revelry could no longer stand up. Lent did little to dissuade them. Each night they came home and sat in the parlor in various poses, watching the fatigued light of dawn come up through the windows. Unable to stop drinking, they couldn't go to bed. Peter tapped his feet to music that no longer played. "We ought to make a trip to New York to see this spectacle for ourselves," George suggested early one dawn at the end of May.

"Don't be such a minnow!" exclaimed Peter. "Why should we go up there and gape when we're in the game, same as anybody else? Besides, we're already traveling with them: straight up!" They made the motion of toasting glasses but were too lazy to actually connect.

But they were all attention when Felix interjected. "There's talk of an asbestos-gypsum merger," he said in the voice of someone to whom it was not a game. "What do we think? Maybe it's the wrong time to talk about it. We're soaking wet." All remained silent, and after a time he spoke again. "I wanted to get five thousand of the Shenandoah but the word on the street is it's oversubscribed."

"So what!" scoffed Peter. "We've got to ride the blue chips. I keep telling y'all, those securities are for minnows!"

"You're drunk," said George. "Quit calling everyone a minnow."

"Minnow!"

"At how many points should we, you know, cut out?" Louis asked his brothers generally. "I'm getting worried about wheat."

"Forget wheat," mumbled Felix. "We—"

"Boys," Peter slurred in a loud voice, "listen to me. We can't lose. Don't even *think* about wheat. We can't lose."

With a stern look to Peter, Felix persisted with the comment he was going to make before being interrupted: "We need to split ourselves among American Cyanamid B, GM, what else? You know, I want to get some more U.S. Steel. I'll handle that one. But there's Montgomery Ward, Houston Oil, RCA, Studebaker."

"Take your pick, boys!" Peter yelled to the ceiling.

"Quit calling us 'boys,'" muttered George. "We're men, aren't we?"

Louis patted Peter's knee. "Be quiet, Peter," he advised. "You're smashed. And the rest of you listen to me. I ran into Deek at the post office. They're organizing a pool around Commonwealth Edison."

As soon as it was out of his mouth, all but George—who asked, "Who's Deek?"—exploded with derision.

"That news is older than the Bible, brother!" whooped Louis.

Peter shouted, "Deek is such a minnow!"

"Oh be quiet, Peter," said Louis, his face sour. "You're too wet to talk sensibly. You're not even listening." He rose and went to the sideboard. Peter and George exchanged glances. Felix studied the quotes in the morning newspaper that had just arrived.

"I can't help it if you're swimming in the wrong pool, brother," slurred Peter to Louis, who stood at the sideboard with his back to them. "Just admit that you're a fool and let's move on."

"Yeah!" said George. "Don't be so sensitive!"

Felix cut in softly, "You're the pot calling the kettle black, brother."

At that, George looked at his feet. Louis returned from the bar and sat back, now commanding attention through his sulkiness. "I thought," he said, "that we were only keeping half in the blue chips on half margin. I thought"—he looked at each of them—"that's what we agreed on."

Felix heaved a sigh. "Relax, all of you," he said. "We did say that, Louis, but now we're changing our tune. Above all this—we have to *feel* what's right. That's the only way to win, don't you see? We can't just choose based on what other people are saying, especially minnows like Deek." He paused for effect and went on, "I, for one, like radio. Maybe you should take over that account, follow that one for a while, George, since that's something of a specialty for you."

"A specialty!" groaned Louis, who, considering himself a master of technology, resented George's passion for radio.

"All right," said George.

Felix stood and picked up a cue. "Business interests are good, but there's a drought in the Midwest that we have to watch carefully," continued Felix as he paced around the billiard table, using the cue as a cane.

"I'm starting to lose track of all this," moaned Peter. "Everything's spinning."

The other three brothers looked at one another in exasperation. Peter was useless.

Louis ran his hands through his hair. "I'm worried about wheat."

George rolled his eyes at Felix, who said, "We all read the same paper, Louis. We all know about wheat, but let's don't jump to any conclusions. It's scientific but it's not. Industry, products, automobiles. They can't lose because they've just begun. Forget the crops! It's just too Southern. I think we should go in for something . . . what? Something more exciting. Up the ante, as they say, and jump the train before we get caught."

Peter's eyes flew open. "We're in with the big boys now!" he cackled.

"Whoa, are you serious?" asked George, giggling. "All right, I'm game."

Felix smiled and made the gesture of a toast. He looked to Louis, who hadn't moved. "You and your blue chips. Put more in if you want, just quit being so proud about it."

"Yeah," piped George. "Quit being such a minnow."

*Afterlife*

EVEN FOR THE PROTESTANTS, the funeral was subdued, as befitted the unusual circumstances of his death. It was held in the library of the house on Dauphin Street; Charles's brother William, and two sisters, Tilly and Faith, Mr. and Mrs. Alfred Babineaux, Peter, Louis, Felix and George, Isabel, Anna and Mother Riant were in attendance. Never more grateful for a veil, Regina cried silently through the service, the procession to the cemetery, words by the grave, the reception for the family.

She paid no heed to the suspicions that surrounded his death. "Cleaning his pistols," she told Isabel and Anna to tell their friends at the Visitation Convent. "It was an accident." She did her shopping in black, her head held high, and continued to plan the menu, iron the linen and sew with somnambulant efficiency. Mother Riant ailed steadily without taking a turn for the worse, and Regina took over the duties that concerned her mother, bringing her all her meals as well as teas and drops and frosting-covered crackers at exceedingly regular intervals, just as Sylvie, Nikkatai and Camilla had done. The brothers carried on exactly as they had before; she did her best to be tolerant. Isabel and Anna seemed to thrive. At times, she admitted to herself, she felt relief. The suspense was over once and for all.

But she was the wife of a dead man. She missed him every second of every day, was crippled by missing. She couldn't eat and went about the house with a thick throat, stopping in darkened corners to dab her eyes with an apron string. She couldn't bear to listen to music and went to bed earlier and earlier, though she struggled for hours to fall asleep. As she lay there she prayed that in death he might reach a peace he had not achieved in life, prayed that God would take him in because he had been such a loving man, more disturbed by temporal troubles than anyone she had ever known, an angel really, not meant for this world. At some point in the middle of the night she would get up, go to the library and sit with her sewing in her lap.

In a soft voice, she kept Charles updated on the affairs of the living, how their daughters had taken to the new school year, the craze for flagpole sitting that had come to Mobile, the stunt George had played on the streetcar, the health of his horses—things he had not had the strength to listen to in recent years. Occasionally she read him a very funny editorial from the paper or went deeper into the currents of her dreams, her frustrations with Mother Riant, her brothers. She even asked him what she should do now that he was dead, but after an hour or so she would lose purpose, lapse into silence and understand that he was not with her. Then she would remember the sweetness of Little Charles—blurring with her husband in her mind, and then she had something new to pray for: that they were together in the afterlife, united in spirit.

Eventually the nocturnal conversations took place only in her head, where she replayed their last scene in the parlor, this time seizing him to make him stay with her, or she imagined his last moments in the dollhouse, his ridiculous personage drunk and dancing, but she could never get to the part with the pistol fire. She remembered the feel of her hands pressing into his head—*I'm praying for you, I'm this, that, I'm expecting*—and winced at the memory of her voice. She begged him, and God, for forgiveness for every instance when she had been unkind, startling herself with the number and poignancy of such instances in her memory until she forced the talk to more pleasant things.

Sometimes she pretended he could help her in a practical way. She would ask him to kill a roach or discuss the advantages of GM, asked if he wouldn't mind bringing her shawl, asked him what she should do with herself now that he was dead, but as the weeks passed in their merciless way, she lost touch with where he was except that he was no more.

Back in the bedroom, she stood looking down at the bed—a ship that wouldn't budge on its pitiful wooden ocean. She lay down on it and closed her eyes. *This is grief, it will pass, it will all pass,* she thought. She was not innocent, she was not courageous, and she figured she was old and ugly. In August she would be thirty-one. She caressed her neck, rose and stood in front of the mirror, but she didn't cry over her flesh. And Charles's flesh? Had he killed himself? No. Had he been killed by accident? There are no accidents. Charles had made a sad choice not to have the strength, not to have the desire. Her love had not been enough; he'd been afraid of her love; her love had been too much. But how can there be too much love? And now she was the wife of a dead man.

After midday dinner she often sat in the library, where she turned a sock inside out, right side in, examined the hole. Sighing, she slipped the darning egg into the toe. Gently she pulled the silk threads together. She could hear her brothers in the parlor with their brandy, chatting stocks and shooting pool; their billiard balls clacked incessantly in her head. She closed her eyes and concentrated on her head-ache, heartache and collapse. Maybe this was her end. Maybe she could just slide right off her chair, join Charles wherever he was.

"Mother!"

She opened her eyes and focused on her daughter. For a long moment she couldn't place her: yes, Isabel, eight and a half. Four feet tall, her black bloomers gathered around the reed of her body; her white starched shirt covered nothing.

"Anna won't be my friend," she said, clenching her fists at her side.

Regina drew her forward by the hands. "Why not?"

Isabel looked at her feet. "She won't do anything I say. She doesn't like me anymore."

"I see," said Regina. Putting her arm around her daughter's waist, she brushed the fine, light blond bangs out of her eyes, wiped her cheekbones with the flat plane of her knuckles. "Maybe you're bossing her around."

"I'm not!" bawled Isabel. "I'm older!"

"Stop crying and I'll tell you a trick," she said. After a moment Isabel stopped, and Regina went on. "Play by yourself and pretend like you're having a marvelous time. Within a half hour she'll come and want to play with you."

Isabel stamped her foot halfheartedly. "I don't want to play by myself!"

"Why don't you play with me? I'll show you how to make a skirt for Sofia."

"I don't want to make a skirt!"

"All right, then," said Regina, and she picked up the sock. "Why don't you play Hop Flower? Hop Flower is a really delightful game," she went on casually, "though it's not easy. You have to jump from flower to flower on the rug. First you jump on each one; then you skip one; then you skip two . . ."

Isabel was soon enthralled with jumping across the Oriental car-pet while Regina cut out the collar and lapels of a new mourning suit. By the time she started the basting, Isabel had disappeared, and she relaxed her pace, allowed her mind to run back and forth over possi-ble escape routes: She thought of heading west on foot, abandoning everything to take to the open road, where she'd be accosted by a murderous cowboy who would recognize her as a lady and, seeking to protect her from men like himself, whisk her to safety. She would cry from fear and gratitude and retire behind a screen to remove her wet clothes. In the firelight she would remind him of his wife, whose death had caused him to lose faith in ever being happy again. She would enjoy the hot buffalo stew while he scolded her for being alone on the road, and she would fall asleep to the sound of his voice telling of how lonely he had been on the settlement. He'd sit up, watching her sleep. The next morning he would propose, explaining that life was hard in the West but he would make it as nice as possible for her. She'd send for her children . . .

"Miss Regina, there a reason why there's a pan of tea on the back steps?"

She opened her eyes. "What?"

Camilla in the doorway, hands on her hips. "There's a pan of tea on the back steps?"

"Oh, yes, I couldn't find the matches."

Camilla shook her head in annoyance tinged with wonderment.

"So . . . so," Regina faltered, "I made sun tea, like the Indians."

"Your brother Peter just kicked it over."

"Well, I might have known . . ."

Camilla's scowl deepened. "I'll make it on the stove, then."

Eyes closed, Regina called to Camilla, "You're losing patience with me, aren't you, Camilla?"

"I'm close, I'll tell you that much, honey," she answered, her head bowed with the curve of her back, her hand on the doorframe. "I'm real close."

Maybe Regina would be captured and killed by the Indians, but that was all right, too. She would even welcome such an end. As long as she was scalped *after* she was killed. Maybe the West was too wild for her, after all. She wouldn't like it, having to make her own butter and whatnot, plus the dust and the emptiness of the prairie and the fact that her imaginary lover was poor.

She spoke some French, bits picked up from her father and Cousin Beattie on trips to New Orleans, and she pictured herself and her girls parading around in white frocks. Not Paris, but possibly Nice, somewhere where sun sparkled on aqua, where there was an element of underhandedness, smuggling, sections of town with women of ill repute, sand, absinthe.

She didn't hear Father Slidell until he stood directly behind her chair. She smelled his cigarette before she heard him say softly but firmly, "Regina." He waited. "Can I offer you some comfort?"

"I don't know," she croaked, not turning around.

"I'm praying for the souls of Charles and Little Charles," he went on, "as I know you are. That's all you can do for them anymore is pray. But there are a lot of things to be done for the rest of your family and the children you share with him."

"I'm trying," she whispered.

"I know you are, and I know you know that Isabel and Anna are a gift from God."

"I know," she sobbed.

"Bless you," he put his hand lightly on the top of her head.

She dabbed her eyes. "Thank you, Father."

She woke to make a fresh stab at the material in front of her. It was a dream, she supposed. She would ask Camilla later if Father Slidell had been by. Preparing to stitch both sides of the lapels together, she realized they were different sizes and didn't have the strength to cut them out again. But no, she'd never been to Europe and didn't, in her heart, even really feel like seeing it. Europe was something she was perfectly happy to miss. It would take too much effort, really—not that she minded effort, but effort in the land of strangers just didn't appeal to her. Nothing appealed to her; she would go nowhere. A woman like her could not change. She was too gentle, truly, to go roughhousing in the West, too dignified to throw herself at the mercy of men without references, and too familiar with being respected to start over, to vanish and emerge as someone else. For one thing, they wouldn't let her—her brothers, Camilla, her daughters; their existence demanded sameness from her, and she amazed herself at how normal she could act in an effort not to disappoint them.

At mealtimes she watched her body perched on the edge of a chair while she winced inwardly over every false movement she saw herself make. Her only hope, she reasoned, was to join Charles in death. Lacking the strength to kill herself, she resolved to fast. At first she avoided all desserts and any sweets that might appear on the coffee tray, particularly her old favorite, charlotte russe. Then she expanded to deny herself sugar in her coffee, then eggs, then coffee itself, until a gnawing appeared in her side. Not enough. She cut the pleasures of scent, soap, shampoo. She cut the pleasure of hot water, cut water itself. She took each denial as a new hole and cherished the growing dirt on her hands and feet. Ceased bathing.

The more she disciplined herself to these various holes, however, the more her dreams craved to fill them—her night mouth crammed with chocolate dirt, nostrils with cotton candy, ears with honey, breasts with syrup, their milk melting into the fire. And everything—holes in the walls stuffed with ham. Holes transposing themselves into the centers of her eyes became, for a time, a permanent part of her vision. Dirt disappeared as she walked through the garden, crumbling inward under her feet, dishwater in whirlpools, spirals in the air. Her body a ball tumbling down an uneven slope, her daughters balls from her hole with holes themselves: the vagina. Holes, holes or a lump, rotting at the base of a cave. During Holy Week she was a model faster, but she wasn't very good at fasting for Charles, whose purgatory, as time passed, became more and more vague—especially since he never answered her. And she had an intellectual sense of the futility of discipline: there would be no end to cutting pleasures when everything eventually became a pleasure to cut.

This was her lowest point, which might have gone lower if it weren't for the interruptions, which were nonstop. Twice Peter backed the car into the Labordes' fence and needed her to telephone them and promise repairs. Administering Mother Riant's medicine was itself a full-time job.

*Mother, Anna's stuck up in the tree.* Regina suspended her thoughts and sat up "What? What do you mean?"

Camilla entered the sewing room on Isabel's heels, continuing, "Her bloomers are caught in them branches. She's hanging upside down, crying her head off. We've got to cut her down."

"Well. Cut her down, then," Regina said.

But Camilla wouldn't take that. "For heaven's sake," she said. "I need you to hold her while I cut."

"Oh."

There she sat for two years with her thoughts, demand drifting in and out of the doorway, leaving little impression on her. She was more than busy. There was always gravy to make with Camilla on Sundays, beaten biscuits on Mondays. Peter and Felix came to her, one after the other, to have their wedding suits altered. They married older women from Montgomery and brought their wives to live in the house for long stretches, so that sometimes Regina had her sisters-in-law for company and sometimes not. There were a million discussions about the end of the Florida land boom, as well as chimney repairmen and landscapers, who brought their questions to Regina, who answered them and paid them and watched them leave. House painters came that same year to fulfill Mother Riant's final request, that the house be painted white, the last time it would ever be painted in its entirety.

The air filled with the smell of burned coffee, grape jelly and cigars; the leaves turned brittle and red; pecans fell, twice. Twice the girls needed alterations to their school uniforms and set off in the crisp air, full of expectation and industry. A Christmas tree came into the library, was decorated, danced around and removed, twice, washing over her without effect. The lawn-mower men came, week in, week out. Father Slidell came every Sunday for dinner. There were thunderstorms, birthdays, nightmares, chicken salad and iced tea, mayonnaises made again and again, silver tarnished and repolished a dozen times and the news: the Scopes trial, the rise of U.S. Steel, the election of Hoover, the new car models, the endless talk of fashions and mergers, the heat. She watched it all, not uncurious, and prayed for Charles.

*Part Three*

THE HOLY GHOST

## One End

"I HEAR YOU, CHILD," Camilla said as she sponged a plate. "That woman Naw has been dancing on my nerves for two weeks now. I don't see how you can stand it."

Regina dumped the silver into a tub of hot soapy water. "I think they'll be gone soon," she said, taking up the drying rag. "We can't carry on like this for too much longer." She added, "Surely they know that."

Camilla shook her head. "I know that and you know that. But your brothers are another story."

"I know."

The sound of Mother Riant's bell made them freeze. Slowly Regina put her lower back against the edge of the countertop and stretched her legs forward. Camilla glanced at the mirror-paneled door that led to the dining room. "Hand me that platter," she said. "Thank you."

Camilla began scrubbing it while Regina scraped plates, but both women stiffened again when they heard Mother Riant's furious bell a second time. "I think the ladies'll be moving into the parlor by now. You join them, Regina."

"Honestly, I don't think I can bear it," she whispered. "I just want to stay with you."

"Fine by me, child," Camilla said, turning back to the sink in disapproval. Mother Riant's bell cut through the air a third time; now they were both afraid. "I'll get her," Camilla said. "You go on into the parlor."

Regina put her hand on Camilla's forearm for a minute before heading up the back stairs. "That ain't the way to the parlor," Camilla said.

She stopped on the steps. "I'm getting Isabel and Anna and bring them down. They're good buffers."

"Uh-huh." Camilla wiped her hands and headed out.

Entering the dining room, Camilla recognized the cream silk backs of Naw and Agee as they scuttled through the door on the other side of the room and into the hallway, but otherwise she had no idea what to make of the situation. Mother Riant was throwing bits of food into the center of the table. Louis stood guard at that door, frantically ringing the bell until Peter, who caught sight of Camilla, lunged for the bell and silenced it. Felix, his face stony, rounded the table clearing plates, something he had never done in all his days. George was flattened against the wall by the sideboard. Mother Riant had pulled her plate close to her chest and was breaking off parts of uneaten chicken and throwing them at her sons. Each time she missed her mark, a fresh store of tears streaked her face. She was coughing and bawling and throwing. Camilla was at a loss as to how to proceed and saw her ignorance reflected back to her in the faces of the sons.

"Call the doctor," said Peter to Louis.

"*You* call the doctor," retorted Louis.

"George, call the doctor," said Peter. George hesitated for a moment, then hurried out to the hallway phone, the back of his head hit by a dinner roll as he fled.

Mother Riant had knocked a burning candle out of its candlestick in reaching for the rolls. Camilla approached her from the side. Felix righted the candle and continued his stiff ellipse around the table. Camilla put her hand gently on Mother Riant's shoulder, but she didn't feel it. *"You boys are worthless!"* she hawked, but she was so upset no one could make out what she was saying. *"You lose everything! Everything I've given you is wasted; everything I've taught you is disappeared. My life . . ."* Her chin dropped to her chest. She let her hand be taken by Camilla. Felix swooped in and whisked the plate and breadbasket away from the spot in front of her. Louis and Peter studied the floor as Camilla pulled her up and led her out of the room.

The entire time it took Camilla to get her to the top of the stairs, into her room and into her rocker, to hand her a handkerchief, adjust the blinds, prepare a cup of tea with the sleeping drops in it, run her a hot bath, bathe her and dress her in the most comfortable black skirt and soft white blouse and black sweater, Mother Riant said nothing except, "Thank God for you, Camilla." Finally, when her thick socks and shoes were on and tied, she said in a choked voice, "I want to see my sons."

Camilla groaned inwardly. "I think they's in the radio room," she said. "You don't want to be hearing all that rattle."

"I want my sons."

FOOD THROWING MAY HAVE BEEN Mother Riant's way of drawing attention to her financial fears, but she was not the first to sense the gravity of the situation. Regina had known something was wrong for months prior to her mother's tantrum. Her brothers avoided her. None had invited her for a cigarette in the past weeks. There were other indications: the morning papers said the worst was over; the afternoon radio reported smaller and smaller numbers, after which they suppered in silence, with the invariable exception of one of her brothers' putting his hands on his stomach, sighing and saying, "Well, I think the worst is over."

The days continued thus, until Regina felt she would die of not knowing. Late one afternoon the parlor was empty. Her brothers were napping, she guessed, and she snuck into their sanctuary looking for clues, pieces of paper, letters postmarked "New York," telegrams, lists of figures, but all she found was half a rough draft of a letter from George to Cousin Mathilde, which she skimmed without much interest. She decided to check the files in the desk but found it locked. She returned the next afternoon to scour for the key, only to flee when she heard a noise on the floorboard above her.

So she had to content herself with the newspaper. It became her habit to steal it out of the parlor every afternoon and, while they slept in the house behind her, read it on the porch. Perhaps because she was unaware of exactly the extent of personal significance in the material she read, she was able to detect notes of horror behind the flood of assurances. *These men don't know what's happening either,* she realized. *How could they have expected it to happen, yet done nothing to stop it? They say it's natural. Then why were they caught by surprise? It really doesn't make sense.*

"Your nose is going to turn gray."

She jumped and was annoyed to see Louis beside her. "Ah, Louis, you scared me. What?"

"Your nose is going to turn gray." He reached out and snatched the newspaper out of her hands, playfully. "I was looking for that."

"Oh, I'm sorry," she said saucily, and stood as if to leave.

He folded the paper in half, fourths, then he sank into a wicker chair. She looked at him for a minute in irritation, then sat back down beside him.

"So what's the latest in fashions, Sis?" he asked jovially, crossing his ankle over his knee. He made a roll out of the newspaper, musing, "You know I was thinking of you the other day. What was it? Oh yes, I saw an exquisite fuchsia, Italian flannel, it was. Elise said she wants to make a suit of it, and I told her you might be willing to help her. I hope you don't mind."

"No," she said. "But there would be no need for such material in this climate."

He said nothing, and they both sat there, looking out across the yard. It was a day in late October, which managed to be gray, bleak, warm and humid at the same time. Rain came in ten-second bursts, making it impossible to say if the shower was coming from the sky or a shaking of the trees. Her view was obscured by a withered banana tree. Mobile was too cold for banana trees, everyone knew that, and Louis's phosphorus implants had not been effective.

"Your tree's not doing too well," she said.

"Why does everyone always bring that up?" Louis exploded. "It was an experiment, for Christ's sake! Hasn't anyone ever heard of the scientific method?"

"Calm down."

"Peter and Felix are coming down with their wives," he said as if to explain his outburst. "They'll be here Monday, sometime in the evening."

She turned to Louis. "What's going on?"

"Just get everything in order, if you could. You know, give Camilla enough time to make up the rooms," he said. "They'll probably want some kind of supper when they arrive."

"How much do we have invested in this racket?" She gestured toward the paper.

"Sister, I never thought I'd hear you use the word 'racket,'" he said with a red face. "What have you been reading? Don't tell me you believe the newspapers?" He pulled out a handkerchief and blew his nose. She contemplated the landscape despondently. He went on with a nervous chuckle, "I feel kind of embarrassed saying it, I don't know why. I'm getting married, you know. Elise and I have decided, well, we decided last week."

"Congratulations!" she exclaimed, taking up his hand and pressing her lips against it.

But her gesture made him even more nervous. He stood and stared out toward the rosebushes, his eyes frozen with apprehension. "I suppose we'll have to wait until all this smoke clears."

Regina studied him, said what she was supposed to say: "I'm sure Elise will make you happy." As an afterthought: "I'd do it now, though. Don't wait."

THE BROTHERS BELIEVED that what happened to them was different from what happened to everyone else. So they met the excitement of the panic, when they finally acknowledged it, as one meets a hurricane that is rumored to be about to pass through the town. They gathered a party in the mahogany-paneled radio room, with cards, whiskey, hard candy and cans of deviled ham, and assumed the air of people listening to rain and wind all night long. They clutched one another's arms at the crashes, laughed and placed bets on which tree had just fallen.

For a while they embraced the dogma that all was not lost, that the whole thing would rise again, even higher, and that this latest calamity was just another test of their faith. Reassurances from the dons of Wall Street; soothing from Hoover, economists and scientists; reports of organized support all contrived to keep them calm. What had happened was "a necessary readjustment to the speculative fury," they quoted to each other for a while over the phone, and "just a shaking down of prices."

Peter and Felix arrived in Mobile at the beginning of December and set up their wives, Agee and Naw, in the library with Regina every afternoon. Louis's fiancée, Elise, joined them more and more frequently as the wedding date approached, was postponed and approached again. The women rummaged and fumbled, distributing their supplies and outdoing one another with ambitions. Agee was embroidering a cummerbund for Peter—"He's thickened, you know," she giggled—and spent weeks with her colored pencils, dreamily sketching the design. In the most comfortable chair sat Naw, her high heels and loose-fitting silks unable to disguise her ample poundage, stitching by hand an entire wardrobe for her favorite porcelain doll, a Mary Haze that had become something of a collectible. Every few minutes she rose and got the others to help move her chair so that she could catch the weak rays of light from the window. "Regina, honey," she called now and then, "come look at this. I've destroyed this godforsaken hem," and Regina carefully put down the school uniforms and fixed the mistake. Only Elise sat ticking her foot. She played with her engagement ring and asked on the half hour for a hot cup of coffee.

For long stretches they sewed in silence, their ears tuned to the conversation in the parlor, where the brothers were conferencing incessantly, their tones starting in whispers and growing raspy with their attempts to stifle the noise of their disbelief as one by one the facts and figures piled up against them. The women's faces were a kind of thermometer, slowly draining. All they caught were snatches of conversation.

"Play with our fortunes . . . in cycles, I tell you, getting rich . . . gentlemen . . . the economy goes . . . the wise man . . . like in '28"—and then Felix booming over them all, "Not at the first sign of trouble!"—but they were better able to follow the tones, the long periods of silence, the outbursts, the laughing fits. Regina often left off her sewing and took to the cards. For great extensions of time, Naw and Agee did nothing at all, just sat with their sewing in their laps, heads bowed, ears cocked.

When Camilla came in with the coffee, they made their first valiant efforts at small talk. "I had wanted to honeymoon in Palm Springs, but Louis says it's not the thing this summer," said Elise as she reached for a cigarette. "Of course, I've been thinking about destinations since last fall."

"Oh no, dear, not at all." Naw spoke with the most exuberance she had displayed all afternoon. "Everyone you want to see is going to Newport. Not to sunbathe, I imagine, but to look at the water and contemplate more important things in these times of trouble."

"I'm not sure how to do that," laughed Elise, reaching for the matches and lighting the cigarette.

"Oh, just watch everyone else," said Agee, her face shining. "You'll get the hang of it."

Camilla handed out the cups of coffee. "You shouldn't smoke," Agee said to Elise. "It'll give you a mustache."

The young woman ignored the advice. "But I'm Southern! Why would I want to go all the way to Newport? And more than that, why would I want to contemplate?" Elise said laughingly, and Regina joined her.

"Thank you," Regina said pointedly when Camilla gave her the cup.

"Don't be intimidated, my dear," said Naw, pursuing the topic with perfect seriousness. "Louis tells me you come from one of the first families in the country. You ought to take your place with the best of them."

"But they're Protestant!" groaned Elise.

Regina gasped in spite of herself. Did Elise not know that Naw was Episcopalian? Naw glared at them, then snapped her head to the window. Camilla finished pouring the cream and set out crackers and crab pâté on the marble side table by the door. "Well, Palm Springs may be all the rage again by the time we have a honeymoon, if we continue at this rate," said Elise, looking to the three women with both dimples showing. No one answered her. At the moment they could hear Louis's voice clearly from the parlor:

"This is not a sign, Felix! The thing has already happened!"

And then a voice mumbling—probably Peter's from the tense light in Agee's eyes—"We missed the sign."

"It's a question of faith," someone pronounced.

Elise's questions masked the voices. "What do you suppose they're talking about in there?" she asked, though they all knew what they were talking about. "How can they talk so much about one thing?"

When no one answered her, the voices from the other room were audible again. "You always say it's a question of faith, Felix." Regina knew it was George by the slow enunciation. "But faith isn't always rewarded."

"That's because you don't have any," Felix replied. "But that's all right, let's vote then. Oh, don't take it like that, George! I was only kidding. Come on! We have to stick together here!"

Regina looked straight at Elise. "Why don't we go in there and ask them?"

Elise seemed about to rise, but Naw interrupted. "Look at this for a minute, won't you, Regina? Your eyes are better than mine. I've just slipped a stitch. Dear Gussie!" But when Regina had the material in front of her, she saw there was no slipped stitch. Naw glowered at her; she was not to say anything further in front of Camilla.

Regina turned away in disgust; she knew that Camilla was as smart as a whip—Camilla probably knew more about what was going on than she and her sisters-in-law combined—and she didn't see the point in bothering to hide the truth, especially since they were all in the same boat. Death is not an end, she knew, but most illusions have an end date. It would all come to the surface sooner or later, she figured, and tried to stay patient. Often she blamed herself for letting her brothers dismiss the prophecy of the man who had walked all the way from New York. "Why would you trust a vagabond more than your own brothers?" they had asked after she told them the story. "We're just as smart as we look."


MOTHER RIANT HAD NO VISITORS. Her sons never came up to her room anymore and avoided her eyes at Sunday dinner. She had tried on several occasions to sit with the ladies in the library, but their shifty eyes and jerky movements as well as the overwhelming smell of Naw's perfume unnerved her. Why were they all sitting like this—suspended? And why, with Elise's wedding dress on the chair awaiting alterations, was Regina playing card games? And how was it that she never won? Mother Riant knew that the odds for winning at solitaire were better than Regina's results. Was she paying so little attention? Through the French doors, Mother Riant noted the plumes of smoke pouring from the parlor windows and saw the little groupings of her sons on the stone porch, their ties loosened, their vests unbuttoned, their hair standing on end. Once when she stared at Peter, her eldest, as he came into the library, he turned around to meet her gaze, and shock, barely visible, coursed through his body. He rushed back into the parlor.

Even Father Slidell had not been heard of in some weeks, and Mother Riant's loneliness reached an awful pitch. She rang the bell for Camilla. "Take me to my sons," she said, already standing at the door armed with two canes, one headed with a silver-plated eagle, one headed with an ivory-plated tiger.

"They's in the parlor," Camilla said apprehensively, starting to take the old lady up by the elbow. Mother Riant would accept no assistance. Camilla was careful to stay close behind her as she descended laboriously. When at last she reached the bottom, she stood for a moment outside the two closed doors: the parlor, behind which her sons were making a mess, and the library, behind which their women sat with pinched faces, keeping secrets. It soon became apparent that she could not muster the courage to intrude on either party. "Take me to my chair, please, Camilla," she said.

Camilla led her down the front steps and into the side yard, where she eased her into a chair under the dying bananas; Camilla was her only friend. Camilla was a Negro woman—how low she had sunk! She felt revulsion for her sons, her daughter and those moronic daughters-in-law. "Sit with me, won't you, Camilla?"

Camilla stood because there was only one chair and listened, shivering as Mother Riant poked about, tried on different truths. "Well, the boys came back to sort out the finances, that much is clear," Mother Riant said to the falling leaves of the sweet olive tree. "Though I think it's a mistake to divide it, and I've always told them that. I suppose since Louis's getting married they think these things are necessary, but they're wrong. They should have asked me."

Camilla patted the wrinkled arm and said, though she knew she could not be heard, "No need to be getting all worked up."

"I want the wallpaper replaced in the parlor," Mother Riant or-
dered in a tone that set Camilla's nerves on edge. "Can you tell
Louis it would be the appropriate thing to do before the reception?
And this lawn could use some work. What month is it?"

Camilla answered that it was December, but Mother Riant
didn't hear her.

"I suppose I'll call over to Mr. Howard. What about the girls?
What are they going to wear? They look so sloppy most of the
time. I don't know what Regina thinks about ordering the lace, but
I'll just go ahead and do it, don't you think?" Camilla nodded, and
Mother Riant resumed after a moment. "I'm proud of him," she
said. "The girl Elise is pretty, don't you think?" Camilla nodded
again, waited another minute, then signaled that she was going into
the house to get a wrap.

Mother Riant didn't understand Camilla's gestures; as soon as
she was gone she realized how cold it was. She cried a little but it
only made her throat thick with mucus. She spit into her handkerchief. There was no real reason to replace the wallpaper in the parlor except that it would disrupt her sons. She had asked for favors
from her family, but since she couldn't hear, she often doubted
whether others heard her—she couldn't ever be sure she had spoken the things she meant to speak. For instance, she kept asking
Camilla for the newspaper but never got it. She looked down at her
feet, observing the various colors of wet magnolia leaves—brown
for the most part, but varied and strangely bright. She thought it
was bizarre: the look of her own brown shoes resting on top of the
leaves. How many different shades there were! She smelled a fire
burning and realized that she might die right now in the chair. If she
ever made it back to her bedroom she would have a fire.

All at once Isabel and Anna were beside her; Camilla was visible in the distance on the porch, holding the door of the west wing open for them. "Girls," Mother Riant said, spitting again into her handkerchief and crying a little more, "I'm about to die."

"No you're not," said Anna. "Not before dinner."

"WELL, THE WORST IS OVER," said Felix as he stood at the head of the table and carved the Sunday bird.

"You said that last week, darling," said Naw. Silent as a ghost, Camilla moved around the table clockwise, serving greens.

"Everything looks delicious, Camilla."

"Thank you, Mr. Felix," Camilla said automatically, while Regina rolled her eyes at George, referring to Felix's charm.

"The marketplace is self-correcting," Louis was saying as Camilla exited, "so we have no worries in the long run."

Mother Riant coughed and spit a piece of gristle into her napkin. To cover up the embarrassing moment, everyone took up the conversation with vigor. Naw looked to Regina for help. "Is this marjoram?" she asked. "Regina, is this marjoram I'm tasting?"

"Probably," Regina answered, "but Camilla knows more specifically."

"Delightful!" cried Agee, who had had too much wine. "Of course the market is self-correcting." She spoke loudly and slowly, so that everyone but Mother Riant turned away. "Like nature, right? That's how Pete described it to me and I've been explaining it to the ladies that way." She turned to her husband. "Sit up, darling," she said softly.

Regina noticed that several plates were already clean and took two quick bites of her yam.

"Have you ever tried cooking the turkey in brandy?" Naw

asked. "My own mother used to insist that it be prepared that way. It takes that unpleasant feather taste out of it."

Mother Riant looked around the table, sniffing another rat in the gaiety around her and wondering at Peter, who she could tell was three sheets to the wind. She sensed that things were not going well for her sons and their wives and for her only daughter. The bird was not grade A. She endeavored not to glance toward the head of the table, where Felix presided with a new tension in his forehead that made him even more handsome. Naw was picking at him; Mother Riant could see how Naw's speeches made him cringe. George was playing the good-natured center, Louis looked as if he had decided to say nothing at all, and Regina had on her best inscrutable face—which meant she was determined to make it through the dinner without any kind of scene, but even she who was so strong pleaded a need to help Camilla in the kitchen and excused herself before dessert.

Annoyed that Regina had beaten her to the exit, Mother Riant decided she would look for an opening in which to leave the table. Did she really have to wait until the coffee was served? The conversation went on, she noticed, though she didn't hear it. "Business conditions are good," George said flatly. "They—whoever *they* are—say we can expect a full recovery by spring."

Mother Riant reached under her chair for her bell and rang it loudly enough that she could hear its dim fringes. All turned to her with exasperation. Agee put her hand over the bell and, easing it out of Mother Riant's hands, replaced it under the chair.

"The main concern," Felix pontificated in a voice that all but Mother Riant had come to despise, "is that the quotations on the exchange do not represent the situation fairly. So we see the function of illusion—a psychological component to the whole affair, and we've somehow, somewhere, lost the confidence to sustain the numbers."

Louis judged it was time to contribute. "What about the Federal Reserve?"

Mother Riant shocked herself and everyone at the table by breaking her crown rule and asking, "What are you doing with the money?" She had forgotten that she wouldn't be able to hear what they said back to her. Felix said something indignant. Louis shifted in his seat. Peter wore a sad smirk. "What are you talking about?" she burbled self-consciously. Agee put a comforting hand on her wrist, but she snapped it away, grabbed a piece of chicken off her plate and threw it at Agee's forehead.


REGINA, NAW AND AGEE sat bolt straight in the library. They had been there for some time—too long—and it was growing dark, but they were too stunned to turn on the lights. Isabel and Anna sat on the floor by the French doors to the porch, using the sparse light to cut fashions from the court of Louis XIV out of a new book of paper dolls. The door to the hallway opened and they all heard George emerge into the hall and telephone the doctor, who was apparently off delivering a child, and leave a mangled message with his wife. "She's shouting and throwing things. She needs a sedative, I believe."

Regina considered going into the dining room to clean up the mess, but she decided against moving. Then they heard the four brothers filing into the parlor and closing the door, then the clinks of the making of cocktails. Isabel and Anna worked out in whispers their disagreements over which doll would wear what. "It's cold in here," Naw said at last. Regina and Agee both looked up at her blankly. "Couldn't we have a fire?" None answered her, and she said after a minute, "It's not as if it's wartime."

Regina thought Naw must have asked for light, and she rose, lit the lamp and returned to her chair.

"Soon it will be time for the wireless," said Agee. "I wouldn't mind having a cup of coffee before that ordeal."

Again Regina made no response. Naw and Agee showed each other their raised eyebrows. Now, with undisguised curiosity, Naw and Agee watched Anna approach her mother. "Mother." She wheedled her way closer to her mother's knees and put her hands in her mother's lap. "Couldn't we have an automobile for Christmas? That's all we want."

Regina smiled in despair and embarrassment. "No darling, there's no chance of you and Isabel getting an automobile for Christmas. Put it out of your mind, please. You won't be able to drive for another few years anyway."

"But Mother!" Anna whined. "Uncle Felix said we would have one this year for sure. We need our very own. We'll just drive it around in the yard. We won't have any accidents in it, we promise. That way, by the time we can drive on the street, we'll be excellent drivers. It's safer."

Regina pushed her away gently. "It's better if you put it out of your mind immediately, Anna. You'll not have an automobile, and that's the last I want to hear about it."

"It's not that expensive!"

"Anna . . . ," she warned.

"Come here, child," called Naw. "Let me look at you." Anna went forward, looking back at her mother and sister, who, oblivious to the drama around her, continued to cut. "How old are you anyway?"

"Eight."

"Regina, don't these girls have something a little prettier to wear in front of their aunts?"

"Oh, hush, Naw," said Agee under her breath.

"You can try, Naw. Dress them in whatever you please," Regina said. "I'm going to make the coffee."

Crossing the hallway, Regina glanced at the closed parlor door and felt frustration toward her brothers well up inside her, for the hundredth time. Their presence did her no good. When would they get out of the house and take their wives with them? She wasn't upset about the money, whatever they had done with it. She knew so little about money and stocks and bonds that she couldn't imagine they had lost enough to change their lives drastically. They'd asked her to cut the household expenses by ten percent, but that was all.

She put the coffee on, carried Felix's piles of dishes into the kitchen, swept up the tablecloth with all its debris and took it to the linen closet. At the top of the stairs, she listened at Mother Riant's door and was comforted to hear the running of a bath. Back in the kitchen, she turned off the coffee and slowly set out the tray of china, creamer, sugar and little silver spoons. She sat for a long time in the chair where Camilla always sat, and put her head in her hands.

Then she carried the tray into the library. Agee had got the phonograph going, and Isabel and Anna were in the midst of dancing to *The Nutcracker Suite*. The Russian dance ended. "It's very Christmas, isn't it?" Agee asked apologetically, turning the volume down as Regina appeared with the coffee. Isabel and Anna were red-faced and breathless with their exertions. "You'll have to show me the other ones tomorrow," Agee told them. "That was splendid. You all are fine dancers, indeed."

Naw waited until Regina handed around the coffee. "That was beautiful, girls," she said belatedly, sipping with a sour face. "Regina won't let us have a fire. Do you mind closing the drapes for me? The draft is simply cutting into my joints."

"Oh, you poor dear," sympathized Agee. Regina sighed.

Naw sipped the coffee again and winced. "It's a little cold, Regina."

"What?" Regina asked. "Oh, you'll have to forgive me," she

said automatically. She had finished her own coffee and poured some more, heavy on the sugar, not even noticing it was cold.

"Maybe you should hire another girl to help you around the house," Naw went on. "Do you ever think of that? Not that we'll be here much longer, but for your own peace of mind. Of course, they're so difficult to train, but once that chore is over, you might find things run more smoothly. And you being the only woman in this huge house! I know I'd be terrified."

Regina looked at Naw in disbelief. She really couldn't think of anything to say. The door opened and Peter burst into the center of the circle. "It's time for the wireless," he announced, his eyes falling on the tray. "Is there more coffee?"

"Uncle Peter!" cried Anna, galloping forward.

"No," said Regina.

Peter took up Anna in his arms and swung her around while Agee looked on her husband with pride. "Hello, little goop," he said to her head buried in his neck.

"I'll make more," said Regina. Naw stood smiling peevishly, and the company, joining with the other three brothers in the hallway, advanced to the radio room, a small sunporch off the dining room. All averted their eyes from the dining room table as they passed it. The radio room was the most casual room in the house, but three of its four walls were windows and the room was chilly in the evenings. Regina pulled the curtains closed while Felix lit the gas heater, in front of which Naw situated herself, saying nothing for the time being. Isabel and Anna clamored to be allowed coffee. Regina said they couldn't, but Louis overrode her by granting them small cups—half coffee, half cream. George sat in the corner, his watch in one hand, his other hand poised over the radio dial. Peter went off to fetch Agee's shawl while the rest of them arranged themselves in chairs.

"Uncle Felix, Mother says we can't have an automobile," Anna said loudly.

Felix, the only one still standing, had pulled the curtain aside and was looking at his reflection in the black pane. "Oh dear," he said, turning absently to her voice. "You know you can have whatever you want."

"Felix . . ." Regina gave a forbidding stare to his back.

"How many days away is Christmas?" asked Isabel from the floor near her mother, where she concentrated on cutting out a difficult bustle.

George frowned at his watch. "We're going to have to have silence in another minute."

"How about some music while we wait?" asked Agee, but when no one responded, she said, "No, I suppose that's a bad idea."

Naw smirked.

"How many days away is Christmas?" asked Isabel, louder.

"Seven," said one of the brothers.

Felix faced them. "It's going to be a splendid Christmas."

Agee swallowed, Regina sighed. As Naw gave her a look of disdain, Regina rubbed her eyes, cleared her throat and spoke softly, her hands still covering her eyes. "I don't know how you feel," she began, "but I'm so tired of this routine." She raised her head and her voice. "I don't know what we hope to get from this contraption," she gestured to the radio, "which says the same thing every night. There's no volume—in trading, I mean. It's staying the same. Instead of expecting it to change one day, maybe we need to face what the present facts mean to us, which is obviously a great deal."

"Here we go, here we go," George spoke above her as the radio cracked to life; Anna clapped and danced around the room to the tune of a beauty commercial. The door opened and Mother Riant entered on Camilla's arm. "She wanted some company," Camilla explained as she deposited her in the seat closest to the door and put the bell under her chair.

Naw sighed loudly and adjusted her wraps. "I don't know that we're the best company for her after that little—"

Camilla cut her off. "Y'all need anything else?"

"Are we having supper?" asked Agee with a lopsided smile; the rest of them had turned away from Camilla.

"I'll set something out on the sideboard, honey, but it ain't gonna be hot."

"Fine, fine."

Camilla cast a look at Regina. "Now, what about these chilluns? You want me to take them away?"

"No! No!" Isabel and Anna echoed as the opening song of the news program came on.

"Hush," hissed George, "or you'll have to leave." Camilla closed the door softly behind her. Regina longed to follow her. *"Today on Wall Street, trading continued at a disappointing volume. News of extra dividend declarations came from—"*

"Mother, if we can't have an automobile, can't we have a—"

"HUSH!" yelled Felix, charging forward as if to strangle her.

Mother Riant flinched in her chair and looked at Felix in horror. She had heard him! She had heard him say hush. Had she been talking? Why did he say hush? Should she ring for Camilla?

*"All the gains of August have disappeared and the nation holds its . . ."*

Anna sat in Regina's lap, crying softly.

*". . . looking to Washington. In his annual speech to Congress, President Hoover reiterated his belief that conditions were . . ."*

Felix stared at Anna murderously.

"Calm down, Felix," said Regina.

"... *When asked about falling prices and unemployment, he said he believes* ..."

"Why don't you take her out of here?" asked Louis.

"Could we just have some quiet in here? Is that possible at all?" screamed Felix.

"... *the numbers. The Dow Jones Industrial Average lost 2.70 in light trading* ..."

Anna cried louder. Mother Riant, thinking he was yelling at her, was scared to be in the same room with Felix. The entire room stared at her in disbelief as she rang. The bell, resounding over Anna's crying, only emphasized the same news they had heard for two months now.

"... *American Can down 2.6, American Telephone and Telegraph down 2.2, Anaconda Copper down 1.2, General Electric up one-fifth of a point, General Motors down* ..."

Regina jumped to her feet, flinging Anna off her lap, and wheeled around to George. "Turn that thing off!" He complied immediately; Anna stopped crying, and only the bell sounded. Naw reached for it, but Mother Riant fought to keep it and to keep it ringing. All waited for Camilla, who didn't come and didn't come. In one motion Regina seized the bell from her mother. "All right," she said, standing in the center of the room, the bell clutched to her breast. "I assume we've lost everything. That our father's fortune is gone. Am I right? Please don't look so guilty. Am I right?"

All the brothers looked at Felix, who sneered, "Most of it."

"How much is left?"

Peter came forward, whispering, "Don't you think we ought to have this conversation in private?" He tried to guide her back into her chair, but she wouldn't move. She looked beyond his shoulders at the others in the room. George, Louis and Agee all stared at the carpet. Isabel and Anna stared up at her from the floor. Felix had moved to a position behind Naw's chair and looked at her with alarm in his eyes. "Really, Regina," Naw said disapprovingly. "It's not the right time." Peter, continuing to block her, now grasped her elbow.

"Please let go of my arm." Peter let go, wiped his forehead and aimed for a chair beside Agee.

"We can handle it, Regina," George muttered.

"It's a difficult time," said Louis soothingly. "We're all anxious, but this kind of thing doesn't help."

She made a circle in place, speaking to them all. "I don't trust you. I've been waiting. I'm tired of this silence. I have a need to know what's going on—obviously I'm affected by these things, not to mention my daughters. I'm trying to prepare for their futures and I need to know what I have to work with. I'm surprised you all would be so inconsiderate of that."

"Aw, come on, Regina," said George.

"Maybe it's time for you all to get jobs," she said.

"Maybe it's time for *you* to get a job, Sister," snarled Felix.

# The Eye of the Needle

"Is she in pain?" asked George, leaning forward.

"No more than she has been for the past seven years." Dr. Freret waited for his words to take effect on the gathering in the library before he sighed, looking at each of them over the top of his reading glasses as if they, in their health, were complicit in death. "She has her laudanum, which I've increased so she will not panic at the sight"—he sighed again—"of the jaws to the beyond."

"Very comforting, Doctor," Felix said dryly.

But the good doctor just fixed his enlarged eyes on him. "I delivered all you children and I was present at your Baptisms," he went on in his slow, creaky voice, falling into an armchair near the fire. "I, too, am old, and I can't look at anything rosily. It is the matter-of-fact that has made me useful in this life and the matter-of-fact that will take me out of it. I've seen it all," he continued. Peter and Louis began to snicker at the doctor's verbosity, but he just ignored them and shook his head at the fire. "Affections and afflictions of every degree, and I've never ceased being amazed, amazed at the bizarre turns this life will take." He fixed his jaw. "Not that there is anything unnatural in your mother's decline. On the contrary— it's as natural as the setting sun."

Glaring over at Peter and Louis, who had their hands over their mouths and were trying not to look at each other, Regina asked, "Is there anything we can do?" Felix wore a look of rebellion. Peter concentrated on drinking. Louis got to his feet and went over to poke at the fire in an effort to bring what was becoming a laugh attack under control. Such laughter is the beginning of guilt.

"Yes. Humility is one of many saviors," the doctor held forth. "There is no constancy, nor is there any temporal success that the body can't betray. And none deserve what happens. Death. The great equalizer. Be humble before that! Death is the most—"

"Please, Dr. Freret," Felix cut him short with no effort to hide his frustration. "Be direct. I'm sure I've heard all this before. Please just tell us what we should do."

"I *am* direct, young man," the doctor cheeped, "and I have seen man. I have seen woman and child in all states of decline, so I should think I know what I'm speaking about."

"Of course, I didn't mean to imply that you—" Felix broke off and with his elbows on his knees, rested his eyes in the fleshy part of his palms.

Dr. Freret removed his glasses, took a handkerchief out of his vest pocket and wiped the lenses. He breathed hot air onto them and wiped them again. He replaced his glasses, folded and replaced the handkerchief and, with a hand on either knee, looked down at the floor between his feet. "Olla!" he yelled. "There's a slug down here on the floor. Boy, I wouldn't want to step on that in the middle of the night. Those doggone things move fast! You know they can make it up the stairs and onto the ceiling of your bedroom within six hours," he chuckled. "I've timed it. It's amazing, this thing we call life."

Rudely clearing his throat, Felix looked into the fire with the rest of them. Regina spoke up. "How long does she have, Doctor? What should we do?"

"Not long, my girl, not long," he said woefully. "None of us do."

Felix stood and signaled for everyone else to stand. "Thank you so much," he said. "You've given us a lot to think about, but we'd just as soon be with Mother now."

Regina walked to the door of the library and opened it, a departing smile on her face, but Dr. Freret remained seated. "Do not agitate her, children," he warned, his voice deepening. "Do not. Any concerns you may have are but granules to her on Our Lord's eternal beach."

"Heavens," said Regina, her face twisted at the doctor, her body turned toward the hall.

"I think we understand." Felix took him up by the elbow and strolled him to the door, the others following silently. Thank-yous and promises to call tomorrow and details of how often the medicine should be administered followed. The door closed behind him; Regina and her brothers stood without looking at one another in the vestibule. Naw and Agee hung back at the door to the library, holding the shoulders of Isabel and Anna.

With a nod to them, Regina led her brothers up the stairs to the sickroom, which was dark but for the line of ten or so prayer candles on the mantel. When they entered, Mother Riant stirred briefly, seeming to recognize them each as they kissed her. She asked for more medicine and croaked that she wanted the hallway wallpaper replaced. Eventually she fell back onto her pillow, and they took up their positions around the bed.

Regina distributed the beads and they settled into the rhythmic mumble of prayer. "Hail Mary, full of grace, the Lord is with thee. Blessed art thou among women and blessed is the fruit of thy womb, Jesus. Holy Mary, Mother of God, pray for us sinners, now and at the hour of our death. Amen. Hail Mary, full of grace, the Lord is with thee. Blessed art thou among women and blessed is the fruit of thy womb, Jesus. . . ."

A shudder went through Regina's body and she opened her eyes. Across the bed she could make out Camilla's form bent over Mother Riant's hand, her eyes squeezed as if imparting strength to the old woman. Regina looked toward her brothers, who were ranged at the foot of the bed, their bodies seemingly carved into the wood of the chairs in which they sat. George and Louis had their eyes closed, their fingers moving along the beads, their lips moving soundlessly. Peter appeared to be mesmerized by a spot on the bedspread, his eyes glassy with tears, the beads limp in his hands. Felix was looking at Mother Riant's face and, feeling Regina's eyes on him, looked up. With Mother Riant gone, there would be nothing between them and death, his expression said: they were next. He smiled. Regina shuddered again, and, still clutching the beads, she took up Mother Riant's hand.

The candlelight played across the wrinkles of Mother Riant's face, which was like the surface of water, constantly changing. One minute she was grinning, the next she wore the merciless expression of a devil, or her face was melting, or waves of peace crossed it. "It's the passing," Camilla whispered. "She's gonna have to choose."

Now her face was contorted in a silent giggle, now she looked frightened. Her cheeks were hollow and full by degrees. She turned her head slowly on the pillow as if saying no; her eyes pinched shut and then relaxed; her mouth twitched as if a wet feather were stroking her cheek. Through the window that led to the porch, they could see the sky beginning to lighten. George and Louis were asleep. Peter had his head down on the foot of the bed, but his eyes were wide open. Felix stared at his mother's face.

Sometime before five in the morning Mother Riant was no more. Camilla rose to close the blinds and went downstairs, Regina knew, to start the funeral coffee cakes. The brothers rose and stretched and had a brief spat, no less fierce because it was whispered, about whether or not to put gold coins on her eyelids and, if so, whether they should be Confederate. Regina had a headache, but she knew by heart the routine that would occupy them for the next week. She went downstairs, drank a cup of coffee, made two café au laits for Isabel and Anna, cried for a second in Camilla's arms, then went up to her daughters' room and told them of their grandmother's death. Isabel and Anna wept hysterically at the news, less because they would miss her than because they were horrified at the very concept of an end. "Is she with Father?" Anna asked huskily.

Regina hesitated to answer, as the image of their union in heaven was not auspicious.

"What about Little Charles?" peeped Isabel.

"Of course," Regina said quickly. "They're all together—your grandfather, too—having a feast. They're sad to be without you, but they're looking down on you. If ever you need help, you can call up to them and they'll help you. They can talk to God if you need any special favors."

This made Anna cry again, and her crying set Isabel off. "Now, calm down, girls, you know Grandmother wouldn't like you all to be crying," she said, stroking their heads. "Try to stop, dears, if you can. Be happy for her that she's in heaven, that she's out of pain. And pray for the passing of her soul." They cried even more. "You'll see her again when you die," Regina pleaded. "You'll be with her in heaven." But they cried louder than ever. Finally Anna climbed into her sister's bed and Regina lay down between them, one daughter on each shoulder. After a short time, all three had fallen back to sleep.

They survived the funeral, which was held in the cathedral two days before Christmas and was well attended by those contemporaries of Mother Riant's who still remained on earth. Father Slidell said the Mass, including a few words on her strong moral character and her generosity. The food was prepared, accepted, eaten, the hands were shaken, the sympathy cards opened, the flowers arranged and then thrown on the compost pile, the body put in the ground next to Colonel Riant.

"I'm getting the hell out of here," Felix said after the last guest had left. "I really can't stand this anymore." No one commented. The brothers and their wives sat in front of the library fire, while Regina cleaned up plates and cups and put them on the tray by the door. The ever-faithful fiancée, Elise, was at home in bed with the flu. "Sit down, Regina. We have to talk," Felix said. She grabbed a few more plates and put them on the tray before sitting.

"I'm getting the hell out of here," he said again, loosening his tie. He scanned the room for his wife. "What do you say?"

"Fine," said Naw, a thin smile on her lips.

"You needn't put it so rudely, Felix," Regina said. "We heard you the first time."

Peter stood deliberately, went over to the round table and poured and began passing out tiny crystal goblets of sherry.

"I've decided to move to Birmingham. A friend of mine there, a fellow by the name of—"

"I don't want any, Peter," called Regina.

"We're all going to toast Mother before we have this conversation," he said firmly, handing the last two to Isabel and Anna. All stood up and met in the center of the room with the glasses. "To Mother," said Peter.

"To Mother," they chorused.

"Any excuse for a toast," mumbled Felix.

"What did you say?" demanded Peter.

"You'll stay through New Year's, I hope," Regina addressed Felix, who grimaced. The others settled back in their chairs looking at something else. "I don't know," said Felix, "I suppose." Isabel and Anna sat in child-size chairs that they were too big for, taking scared sips of the red liquid.

George, now weeping copiously, slouched back in his chair with his face covered. "She's gone!" he sputtered.

Anna went to him, kicking over her sherry, the spill of which occupied the others while she said, "Don't cry, Uncle George. Christmas is in two days."

George pulled her up to his leg without looking at her and continued to cry. They all watched him in distracted sympathy. Louis tossed a handkerchief in his general direction and it landed on the top of his shoe. Lifting his patchy face, he gurgled, "I'm leaving, too, by the way! I'm going to South America and nothing you say can stop me, Felix."

No one knew what to do with this latest development; Anna went back to her mother's side. "There's work to be done there for the church. They need all hands, willing and able"—he made a face into the fire—"and I will be that. I've got to strike out on my own and make something right. You heard what Dr. Freret said. We don't . . . Life is—"

"Oh, please!" spit Felix. He got up and refilled his glass.

"Don't go, Uncle George," whimpered Anna.

George jumped to his feet. "You'll be quiet, Felix!"

"What about Christmas?"

"Sit down!" Everyone turned in astonishment to Regina, who had screamed above them all. "Why don't we try to talk calmly? Sit down, George," she said again.

He sat, sulkily.

"Go if you must, George," said Peter. "Sounds exciting."

"Yes, go, God bless you," said Felix. "Just spare us the rhetoric."

George looked at his brother with hate. "I'm not asking you for a dime, Felix."

"Good, because no one has a dime to give you." He threw up his hands. "It's gone, George! It's all gone!"

Regina raised her voice a second time. "Please stop this," she said. They held their tongues.

"No need to cry over spilled milk," Agee rejoined. The comment perplexed everyone, and they were silent for some minutes, thinking how to answer it. Peter took Isabel's glass away from her and sipped on it. George stared into the fire. "I love your dress," said Agee to Regina.

"Thank you, dear. I've had plenty of opportunity to wear it."

"Black is so difficult!"

"Thank you."

"Let's talk about my wedding," said Louis suddenly. The other three brothers scowled. "It's been postponed three times now. I'm getting anxious." He paused. "If it's all right with you all—I mean, if you think it's appropriate—I'd like to get the whole thing over with as soon as possible," he tittered. "Clear the plate, so to speak."

"Clear the plate?" Naw guffawed in her cruel way. "You don't know what you're talking about, obviously."

He stammered on, his face red. "It could be small, private, at the house. I'm sure Father Slidell—"

Naw cut in, "You have to wait at least six months, Louis— everyone knows that much. It's a gesture. What kind of impression do you hope to make? Think of your wife!"

"Oh, forget it all!" Regina exclaimed. "I'm so exhausted by these mourning rites. We can't wait to begin living again—there's no time. You heard what Dr. Freret—"

"Oh, please," said three or four of them.

"Let him get married next week," she continued. "Why not? For the sake of what?"

"Let's get it over with," Felix said vituperatively. "I'm going into the insurance business, and Peter is coming with me. Right, Peter? In Birmingham. And I'd like to get rolling as soon as possible. Let's have the wedding the day after New Year's. Then we'll all be clear about what we're doing."

ISABEL AND ANNA WERE SAD to return to school after the Christmas holidays, the usual joy of which had been dampened by their grandmother's death. They blamed Regina for the absence of their uncles, who had pampered and coddled them and, between the four, provided more or less constant games and teasing. They did not get their automobile, yet there was the usual trumpery, parade of dolls and ribbons and sweets. But they were given with shifty eyes, given reluctantly. Yes, they were given a little less, and the New Year's toasts were uttered with a new, inconsolable tone. The Christmas ham, the turkey-tight throats calling for prosperity and more than that, thanking God for what they had as if they had nothing, the making sure to be grateful for what they did have, however little. It was that kind of year.

Anna decided that she didn't really like her mother, while Isabel clung to her, seeking to feel safe, to understand through closeness. But February was bleak and boring. The joy had gone out of the world, it seemed, and everything went gray along with it. Though they grew and learned, newness was never reflected back at them, not replaced or cleaned, and so gradually did things become gray as they grew older—they were eight and ten by now—that in seeing the world for the first time with mature eyes they saw it thus: black men lining the streets with signs demanding free electricity, white men in black suits selling pencils.

"It's dumb to sell pencils," Isabel said. And everyone in lines. Lines at the Iberville mission, lines at the unemployment office, lines of men doing roadwork. Lines of women in worn dresses fishing along the waterfront.

The week after New Year's, 1930, the house on Dauphin Street was as empty as Christ's tomb. Mother Riant had willed the house and the property on which it stood to Regina, who, left alone there with her daughters, immediately began to cut corners. Gone was the relaxed relationship she had enjoyed her entire life toward spending. Now she would have to forgo new material and all the excesses she had enjoyed since birth. Not excess, just the best, which is, she began to realize, a form of excess when others have nothing. In their own households, her brothers were making similar adjustments, she assumed. The five of them had agreed to bear the denial equally. It was only prudent to do so until things cleared up. That the brothers did not hold up their end of the agreement, that they spent just as competitively as before, really made no difference. Nothing would clear.

Gradually they adjusted, ate less meat, more from the garden. The servants went painfully out of their way to insinuate themselves in favor, hoping to be spared. Regina kept them all on for as long as she could, but by the beginning of March, only Camilla remained. Regina sat in the silent house reading, her daughters gone off to school, Camilla drifted to some remote porch. In time there wasn't even anything left to sew. There was no one to see, nothing for her but a comfortable chair and a cup of tea. But things were bad with Camilla. All of a sudden they had nothing to say. With Naw's departure went the last unified point of derision between them.

Nor was there any work to share. They had spent the initial days cleaning up after the holidays, washing the floorboards and sheets and remaking the beds where the guests had been, but soon there was nothing to do. Most of the rooms were not ever even walked through these days, and whole sections of the house went out of use. Quietly and rapidly the dust settled. It took preparing only two Sunday dinners of the caliber they were used to—cold appetizer or soup, meat or fish, three hot vegetables, bread, two desserts and coffee—to realize that there were too few mouths to feed, that there was no longer any point in putting on such a show. After the first Sunday, they spent the rest of the week trying to eat the leftovers, but the fish spoiled right away, the bread was soon hard, the greens brown. The following Sunday they looked over the feast, realizing the uselessness of their efforts. Regina and her daughters weren't terribly hungry, and afterward they loaded the whole meal into the car and drove it down to the mission on Iberville.

For some reason this act of charity offended Camilla. After that Sunday she drifted even further, to the edges of the property, wandering the grounds on Mother Riant's old trails, sunk in depression. Once or twice Regina, coming up to her in the kitchen, smelled alcohol on her breath and finally asked what was wrong. "I just can't conceal it, Miss Regina," Camilla burst forth, as if she'd been waiting to be asked. "It's already over?"

"I suppose so, Camilla. Please don't make me cry."

"Child, I'm the one gonna cry. I just can't believe this is it. I'm just shocked, I guess."

Regina looked at her, perplexed. "Over what? Sit down, babe."

But Camilla remained standing. "All the people. Dead and gone, gone to the wrong side and not caring. The money disappeared. The years adding up on my back. The house empty. Not a trace left of what I knew. The Colonel and Mother Riant gone to their rest."

"You need to get out of the house," Regina said. "Take a couple of days, go to a party, see your daughters. Get some fresh air. Maybe that will help."

"You need to get out of the house yourself," Camilla countered, her eyes fixed on Regina, who laughed, embarrassed.

"I've got my books," she said.

"Books ain't no substitute."

"I'll make up something, soon. I'm just resting. All right?"

"For sure!" Camilla called. "It's all right. Didn't mean to interrupt."

But Regina didn't pay too much mind. The death of her husband and Little Charles had been worse than this. She was used to the vicissitudes of life and gained a strange strength from the fact that nothing was stable. She took it as a challenge—she would not die from this—and in the economic fall, she discovered a certain freedom. Things would change—they would have to change. Also, she gained a new perspective on Charles's death. He may have died because he thought himself a failure—when it all failed anyway. It added an extra degree of tragedy to the event, which hurt her more than ever, at the same time that it gave her resolve. There had to be a new solution. Everything and everyone would fall in the end, and only in such leveling could one discover everything latent: courage, intelligence, heart—the formula for prevailing.

The cash stores lasted for the next year and their credit even longer, but Regina could tell that a closed door was imminent. The prices were slashed, but the shops were empty of customers. The shelves at Mr. Leitter's were half full. Gratuitous or imported items—apples, olive oil, tea, anchovies—vanished altogether. Even flour was hard to find. People in battered hats loitered outside the St. Jude Mission on Iberville all day long, though the soup wasn't given out until four. It was only a matter of time before the Riants would feel it, too, Regina knew, in spite of her brothers' assurances. "It's only a matter of time," the man who walked all the way from New York had said. She knew what she had in front of her was an opportunity to change but she didn't know what to make herself into.

In the South, wealth had never trickled down, but this was poverty from the top, bringing poverty at the bottom to new lows. Daily stories flooded in of people being ruined, and people added themselves to the numbers on the street. Spring came and nothing changed. There are few things more depressing than a spring without new possibilities, where the uninhibited, unasked-for growth around them mocked the dearth in which they lived.

Letters from her brothers said the same things: conditions would improve any day and to hang tight and wait. Wait she did, meanwhile cutting back in every way possible. On March 1, Mobile National Bank announced that it was bankrupt and could give only twenty-five cents to every dollar. At last she knew what she had to work with, a certain sum that would only get smaller with each week, with each move. So she tried to make as few moves as possible. Life ground to a halt.

They made do with eating the eggs from their own chickens for breakfast and egg salad for lunch, and would roast a ham once a week and eat it cold for supper each night. They had bread without butter, coffee without milk or sugar, and leaned more than ever on their own garden for the collard greens, the okra, lettuce, sweet potatoes and peas.

All summer long Regina and Camilla discussed whether it wouldn't be prudent to buy a milking cow. But the food was the least of their expenses anyway and the easiest to adopt new routines for. By summer, the Mobile paper mill had laid off half its workers, evicted a third from the company houses and reduced work schedules to about a tenth of what they had been, so that men were working about ten hours a week. Black women lined up at Regina's door, asking didn't she need some domestic assistance, and the men, black and white, appeared with tools, begging to fix a sagging arbor or paint her porches or cut her grass. She sent them away with some vegetables for the family, more than she could spare. They dreamed of going up to Mentone that summer to escape the heat, but stayed in town with wet towels around their necks.

It was the wearing out that took longer to appreciate. Anna's birthday came in October and was celebrated with a new dress Regina refashioned out of one of her old gowns. All of their shoes were repaired instead of replaced. Banisters that needed fixing went forward into disrepair. Everything that could be was put off, but still the expenses piled up. Camilla cut the shopping list in half, but there were always staples to run out of unexpectedly—tooth powder, pepper, hair tonic, rice. One day Regina went downtown and sold one of her brothers' cars to pay the girls' tuition, the balance due to contractors her brothers had hired years ago and to Camilla's salary.

Camilla continued her drifting, did little work, drank even more and came to Regina only to announce some new, unanticipated expense—that the plumbing was broken in the main kitchen, that the grass was getting messy on the side—did she want her to get a team to neaten it up for only a dollar? Regina minded least of all that she was toting off food from the kitchen and taking it to Sandtown every afternoon; what she minded was that they were no longer friends, that she saw Camilla only to hear some new expense, that Camilla seemed to resent the cutbacks more than anyone and to blame Regina for them.

"You gonna plan something, Miss Regina?" she asked one day.

Regina looked up from her book. "You mean about the cow?"

"No. You gonna sit here while the house collapsing around your ears?"

"Maybe so, Camilla. What should I do?"

"It ain't my house."

Regina sighed. "I never asked for this house either."

Camilla moved away and made some motions to straighten up the clutter of unopened mail on the round table by the library door. "Your daughters shabby," she said, her back still turned. "Your mama woulda never let them out the house looking like they do."

"I'm not my mother, God rest her soul." She leaned back in her chair and stared at the ceiling. "What can I do?"

"You right there. You ain't nothing but a reading fool!"

"Camilla!" She tossed her book from her lap, which clattered to the middle of the floor where the carpet had been removed for the moth holes—the sound was too loud for both of them in the empty house. "I'm sorry," she said. "Be nice to me, Camilla. You're drinking too much."

"I'm sorry, Miss Regina, but I'm 'bout to lose my mind. They ain't no purpose to this behavior. You got to think up a plan. It's getting cold, and we got to get a shipment of firewood, lest you expect me to go out and chop down the trees, which I can't." Regina fell deep into thought. Camilla watched her thinking until her patience ran out. "I hate to leave like the rest of them done, Miss Regina, but this here a sinking ship. I gots to care for myself."

"What?"

Camilla didn't answer.

"Don't leave me, Camilla," said Regina absently. "I'll think of a plan."

Camilla came forth, crouched next to her chair and put her hands on Regina's knees. "I'm sorry, honey. I'm gonna be a beauty culturist." She gushed on, crying pitiably. "My sister's friend deceased and left her a shop. She wants to make me an agent to Madame C. J. Walker, the colored beauty scientist. She'll take me as a sales representative in Atlanta. I gotta do something fast 'fore I die in this house."

"Camilla!" said the astonished Regina. "Are you moving to Atlanta?"

"Yes, ma'am."

"But won't it be hard for you in a new city? Is Madame C. J. Walker really hiring?"

"Oh yes!" Camilla put her hand to the floor and pushed herself to her feet. "She's dead. But her company ain't." She caught her breath. "My sister gonna give me six clients to start off."

Regina's face was set, her mouth lined with alarm, though she tried to sound casual. "That's wonderful, Camilla! I'm happy for you. You'll be making more money, I hope."

"Oh, yes, ma'am."

Regina instantly regretted the impropriety of asking Camilla about her salary. She reached out and patted the back of Camilla's leg affectionately. "I don't know that I can live without you. We've been together for so long."

Camilla stepped off. "Don't wait for your brothers," she said. "They useless."

Pausing, Regina switched tactics. "Oh Camilla!" she teased. "I wish you would stay. I'll think of a plan, you know I will!"

"The first of the year, I'm leaving," Camilla said solemnly. "I 'pose I'll stay with my sister till I get on my feet."

# Employment

By the time they reached the ages of fourteen and thirteen, Isabel and Anna had learned to be proud. They were the last daughters of one of the most prestigious families in the South. Their grandfathers and great-uncles had been generals in the Confederate army, and at one time their family had owned half of Mobile. Because it was never spoken of, they knew little of their story except that they'd lost their money; the newspaper and land at Spring Hill had been sold, the diamond bar pins cast into the fire. Finally, their father had died alone while cleaning his pistols. Unable to remember a time when their circumstances were not reduced, they felt the family rely on what it represented rather than what it was.

Sprouting against this backdrop of decline, the sisters ran wild. For them the house was everything their uncles had intended it to be: well versed in magic and a refuge for magic's Southern sisters. There was nothing shameful about it. They had grown up traipsing about on their bamboo horses, chasing the remaining cow, stringing wire between two pecan trees to ride a pulley swing between them and walking on top of the hedges. As they were only a grade apart in school, their lives were intertwined. They went everywhere together, studied together. Attending high school at the Visitation Convent on scholarship, they studied French, Latin, history, chemistry, religion and literature alongside girls who had much more money than they. At sixteen and fifteen, they were invited to three graduation teas a day. Between teas they would rush home and change their earrings and swap belts and purses—but the other girls had three entirely different sets of dresses, shoes, purses, belts and jewelry in which to appear.

As a result, Isabel developed a lust for beautiful things, and Anna came to dislike social obligations. Isabel saved her every penny for a peacock blue silk pleated skirt, a Chanel copy, while Anna, believing it was impolite not to go where she was invited, soldiered through the long teas in inferior clothes, taking refuge in her mother's adage "It's better to say anything than to say nothing at all." Kinder girls knew she was poor and went out of their way to make her feel comfortable. The sisters didn't learn to sew or bake sweets, though they tried. Isabel followed Regina around the kitchen for a span, asking questions—when to make a roux versus a cream sauce, when to use bacon or butter, how to whip egg whites, how to make mayonnaise, when to add gelatin to the charlotte russe. But she forgot all her mother's answers.

Many times Regina had offered to teach them to sew. She was tired of putting so much thought into finding a material that wouldn't rip, following the different degrees of rayon, mending their school uniforms and concocting things for them to wear about. But they showed no interest. Meanwhile, Anna sought her mother's help in crocheting six place mats—an assignment for her sewing class at the school—but on the night before it was due, Regina

finished five out of the six mats, her needlework so clever that Anna
was sure Sister Barbara Jude knew it was not hers.

Though the Morrow sisters never spoke of their missing father,
they treasured the few pictures that existed of him, and scenes inspired by these pictures from time to time cropped up in their
dreams. Nor did their mother speak of him often. Instead she told
them about the charms of her own father, the Colonel, and one of
the regrets they carried with them throughout their lives was that
they had never known him. Their father's absence they took for
granted. "Tell us the one about the Can't Get Away Club," they
had said when they were children; they loved the story of his escape
from the New Orleans prison, but now they didn't ask about their
grandfather either. The silence of maturity had come to them, and
it was in sharing this silence that they became so intimate.

The house was large and the bedrooms were empty, and the sisters spread themselves around liberally during the day. They slept
in the same room every night, however, because they had found
that sleeping in separate rooms was scary. One Tuesday afternoon
they were lying on their beds reading, having just finished a discussion about how Isabel had hoped to get a part-time job at Hammel's
but was not quite old enough. How their mother had sold another
plot of land, the money from which ought to last six months. It was
1934. Anna wanted a job at the department store, too, in the book
department. Now they lay on their backs. Isabel was reading Tur-
genev's *Fathers and Sons*; Anna, Longfellow's translation of Dante's
*Inferno*.

"I'm bored," said Anna. Isabel continued reading. "Let's go find
Mother." They tossed their books aside, and after searching unsuccessfully on the porches and the sewing room and the kitchen they
found Regina on her knees, facedown across the top of her prie-Dieu,

her forehead between her forearms on the padded pew. She was sound asleep. "Mother!" they shook her awake, and she got to her feet instantly.

"How was school?"

Isabel was perplexed. "Fine."

Anna giggled. "Mother, you have marks across your forehead from the fabric."

"Go on and make the coffee and I'll meet you in the radio room." Regina smiled sleepily. "I just need a few minutes." She washed her face, brushed her teeth and lay down on the bed for a minute, her arms folded under her head. She stared up at the lace canopy, then looked to the bookshelf on top of which sat her favorite doll. Then she went downstairs to help the girls with the cups and saucers. Soon they sat around the card table in the radio room pouring out the scalding brew.

"I can't believe I fell asleep like that!" Regina began. "While praying!"

"You must be very tired, Mother," said Isabel.

"God will forgive you," Anna said.

"Well, I was praying for Cousin Mathilde. I got a letter from her this afternoon. She was on Dauphin Island for a retreat, but she's back in Mobile and has joined the sisters at the Visitation Convent. She might be your teacher someday. I understand she's going to teach physics."

"Oh no!" cried Isabel. "I'm going to have to study that!"

"It'll be good for you," said Regina.

"She's young!" Anna said.

"Well, she's only five or six years younger than I am."

"How old are you?" asked Anna, but Regina didn't answer.

"It's about time! She's been a novice forever. I see her every day in the hallway after lunch," Isabel said.

They lapsed into silence. "Yes, well, your uncle George has been in love with her all these years. Of course, he's in Venezuela."

Both girls grew pensive at the news. "No wonder he always wanted to drive us to school," reflected Anna.

"I think it's romantic," proclaimed Isabel. Anna rolled her eyes.

"Yes, well, the whole thing's rather sad," Regina mused. "Maybe you all can write him to cheer him up."

They fell back into a comfortable silence. "Why's he so sad?" pursued Anna after adding more coffee to her cup. "Because she's joining the convent and he loves her?"

Regina nodded, and Isabel repeated that she thought it was very romantic. After a time Regina spoke in a faraway voice. "I used to think of becoming a Sister of Charity," she said, "but your grandfather was against it." She paused. "But they say you either have 'the calling' or you don't. Sister Mary Francis told us that when she was a little girl she ran up to a nun after Mass and, trying to impress her, said, 'Sister, I'm going to be a nun,' and the nun looked down at her and said, 'Yes, I think you will.' I was never called like that."

"Mother, I don't have 'the calling' either," said Isabel. "At least I don't think so. Maybe it will come to me."

"I don't either," grumbled Anna.

"Well, I didn't either," said Regina, "and your grandfather thought it would be too hard of a life for me." She took a sip of her coffee, folded her hands and sighed. "But life is hard! I tell you that much!"

Isabel looked at her lap; Anna gazed at the camellia bushes on the other side of the glass. Regina talked into the air over their heads in a voice they had never heard before. "Your father didn't kill himself, you know. He would have had no reason to. We were in love. We were going to work everything out."

Isabel and Anna said nothing, and Regina, unable to think of anything to add, resorted to talk of the weather. "They say there's a tropical depression in the gulf."

"I know!" cried Anna, and they proceeded to discuss the storm.

"By the way, girls," Regina said as they rose for dinner. "I've thought of a plan. I'm going to need your help."


THE STORM DIDN'T HIT, and at eight o'clock the next morning, a chilly Saturday at the end of October, the skies were blue. Isabel and Anna stood in their oldest clothes and oversize gardening gloves, staring in disbelief into two empty pails. "Let's get to work, girls," Regina called cheerfully as she came down the front steps with two glasses of warm buttermilk for them.

But they proved to be lazy workers, eating a good deal of the pecans and complaining that it was boring and too hard and it was cold out there and they wanted to go to their friend Mary's house, but their complaints only fueled their mother's resolve. Her mind was already expanding the business, thinking about designing and printing labels that she would attach to the wrapped pies by way of a pretty ribbon. She would also sell gingerbread and peppermint pull candy. "You all better get used to this. This is our new job."

"Why?" wailed Anna, while Isabel lined up pecans to make a frowning face in the dust of the driveway.

"Because we're poor now."

"Why?"

"It doesn't matter except that we are."

Regina was so sure her business would work, she went so far as to thank God for her brothers, who had shown the only foresight of their lives in buying a house with a pecan orchard, an orchard that would now be her livelihood simply because she had the gumption to harvest what was right under her nose. Figuring that the pecans on the ground must be rotten, she realized what she needed was a ladder. But no ladder was high enough, so she added a pail to the top of one and stood on the very top. She was so scared of falling that her insides were tight, her crotch nervous all the way up to her throat, out to her palms, which were sweating. The tips of her fingers tingled.

The only thing that could steady her was the tree limb itself. When she shook the branches, pecans pelted her face and head and fell down the neck of her dress. Protecting herself from their on-slaught, she teetered dangerously several times, once finding her-self hanging from a branch, the bucket kicked off the top of the ladder, her feet unable to reach. She screamed for help—Isabel and Anna had drifted off—her arms about to give way with the effort, until Camilla came running out of the house.

"You a monkey now?" she asked angrily climbing the ladder. She replaced the bucket and guided Regina's boots to its top.

Regina said nothing until she was safely on the ground again, her heart pounding. "Evidently not," she snapped, "though maybe with a little practice . . ." She looked at Camilla, utterly still, her eyes wide with fright. "Do you want to help, Camilla? I'll give you half of whatever we make."

"I wasn't gonna pick," she said, "that was the deal."

"I know, I know," Regina said quickly. "But you still want to make the pies, right?"

"Yes," she said, "indeed."

"All right, then. If I can get Isabel and Anna back out here, we can have enough for two dozen pies by suppertime. We'll bake into the night."

Camilla turned her face away and mumbled something; Regina didn't know what. She retrieved the bucket and sat down on top of it with a sigh. "Camilla, dear, you don't have to do anything you don't want to, you know that."

Camilla started to head toward the house but changed her mind, swung around and came back to stand in front of her. Annoyance showed in her brow, which was framed by the blue sky as Regina looked up at her. "You 'furiating me, miss. Why you have to work?" Regina could smell the sour coffee on her breath and leaned back. "What about them brothers? They doing nothing, never have done nothing."

Now Regina was annoyed. "So you won't help me? Is that what you're saying?"

Camilla sent a cut of air out from her mouth, her eyes narrowing. "You don't need a ladder to gather no pecans," she said. "They fall to the ground when they ripe."

"Oh!" Regina said. She fell down in the grass and bent double with laughter. "Well, that ought to make it even easier." At the end of the afternoon, she trod into the kitchen with the rest of the pails held gingerly in her blistered hands, her face shining with sweat. Camilla stood over the counter working the nut grinder, a strainer full of washed pecans next to her in the sink. She appeared determined to say nothing but took one look at Regina and shook her head again. "It ain't gonna work," she said under her breath.

"Oh, be quiet," retorted Regina, but she was nervous. Collecting pecans and making pies was easy compared to what awaited her—trying to sell them. She had planned to ask Camilla to sell them, but now she knew she couldn't. She tried to imagine herself with a little stand in Bienville Square, but that was just as impossible. She didn't need to sink that low yet. She stayed awake all night in spite of her exhaustion getting up the courage to sell the pies. At last she decided to take them to Mr. Leitter's shop and sell them on consignment.

At dawn she fell asleep for an hour, woke, washed in cold water, dressed and made herself drive to Mr. Leitter's without thinking,

but the man behind the sweets counter was not surprised to see her
or hear her out. "Mrs. Morrow, we'll take your pies because you've
always been a valuable customer," he told her, "but they aren't
likely to sell, especially since we've got a dozen women bringing a
dozen different confections to us every morning." She was speech-
less. "There aren't many occasions for pies these days," he added
nervously.

"There's Christmas," she said, appalled at the desperation in
her voice.

"That's true," he said with a lopsided smile.

"Damn," she said when she was back in the car, because there
was no one to hear her, and smacked the steering wheel with her
palm. Camilla, who was cutting squash, looked at her with curiosity when she came in to make her toast and coffee, but Regina offered no information. She spent the rest of the morning making
gingerbread, and when Camilla came to call her to the telephone,
she looked at her as if she were interrupting something impossibly
difficult. "It's your sisters on the hill," said Camilla. She wiped her
hands and went to the hallway phone.

"Regina!" Charles's sister Tilly had never gotten used to the
phone. "We're opening a bakery business out of our home!" she
screamed.

"Well, that's wonderful news." She reached for the coatrack to
support her. "What are you going to sell?"

"Oh, pecan pie, pralines, dinner rolls and breads, of course, angel food cake, caramel custards, meringues—just about anything
you can name. Tea cakes, Aquinas candy, peppermint pull candy,
rum balls, cheese straws, pound cake, gingerbread. We've already
perfected all of our recipes!"

"Well, that's wonderful news." She could see Camilla out of the
corner of her eye, hovering at the foot of the stairs. She struggled to

keep the earpiece close to her head and asked quietly, "Do you need any help?"

Tilly ignored the question. "We're sending you a sideboard! We're setting up a counter of sorts in our dining room and one of the mahogany sideboards has got to go!"

"Well, I don't need a sideboard, Tilly."

"No!"

"No. I don't really see any need or want for a sideboard."

"But it's already on its way!"

"What?"

"It's on its way! Some men just left with it in the back of their truck. Don't sell it, though, whatever you do with it, we want to keep it in the family! Thank you, dear!" Tilly hung up. Regina waited a moment before saying into the phone, "That sounds good, then. Yes, I'll bring you some confections later in the week. All right. Bye." Then, ignoring Camilla, she went to the kitchen, washed her dough down the drain and took the back stairs up to her room, where she lay facedown on her bed and cried.

AFTER SHE HAD GIVEN UP ON HER BAKING, she went back to reading. Two years had passed; Camilla hadn't left yet, though she'd begun to receive packages that contained iron combs and certificates in the mail. Regina stopped praying. She spent longer hours with a book, a hem, a sock on her knees—it scarcely mattered which, her pace had slowed so considerably. Flashes of her dreams—she was strolling along with the Colonel, meeting old friends on a street corner—recurred to her in this new space of hers, but she was afraid to leave the house for fear of spending money. Only the hope that Isabel and Anna would eat kept her laboring at the table until her plate was empty. But she knew the unsavory food wasn't Camilla's fault, it was her own.

Even so, it wasn't until just before Christmas that she motivated herself to action and decided to make a navy blue wool-blend traveling suit for Camilla and, from the same pattern, a dark mauve suit for Isabel and one in dark green for Anna, with skirts for all three a little longer than midcalf. Of course, her recipients knew she was making something for them, she had had to measure them, but they didn't know the nature or the color, for she worked at night behind closed doors, and the sense that she would make an impression on the world with her talent, however small, delighted her as she worked. She had splurged on the wool, though she used a synthetic for the lining. It was an investment, she figured, for looking good might actually earn them money. Again her mind turned to money, as it did more and more frequently, until she wondered if she was dangerously equating God and money in her brain. Wasn't it this equation that had stopped her praying?

After several days of enjoying the feeling of purpose sewing afforded her, she realized, *This is my talent. Everyone has always said so. I could make some money this way.* And then she progressed from imagining the face of Camilla as she opened her present to imagining clients waiting expectantly in the outer room for her to work her magic. And as she studied her handiwork under the lamp, she talked back to these clients, smiled modestly, whispered thank you, said, "I added this topstitch for detail. No, no, it was simple, really." Perhaps she could make up little cards, advertising her services. She would use a false name but the proper address so that if anyone recognized the address, they could assume it was her maid who needed the extra work.

She grew satisfied again, this time with very little, and almost unconsciously she began to pray again. She prayed for relief and for a sign of what to do, for a success of her sewing venture and for a turnabout in the economy. She didn't expect any miracles, just a change for the better. She gave up feeling bad; now she knew things would improve. *Like a child,* she marveled, *I've ended up exactly where I started—sewing and praying.* She didn't even feel guilty for those cloudy months in the fall, when she hadn't prayed; it had been beyond her control. Indeed, abandoning her faith had been a thoughtless thing: how was that possible?

They opened their presents on Christmas Eve in what started as a solemn ceremony before the fire in the library. Camilla cried when she saw the suit Regina had made for her, and Isabel and Anna rushed into the parlor to try theirs on. Isabel gave her mother a pin-cushion in the form of a ladybug that she had made at the convent sewing class, and Anna gave her a small notebook, the cover of which was a needlepoint rendering of King Tut's death mask. Camilla had ribbons for the girls, and they gave her a small leather change purse. They made a feeble attempt to drink rum eggnog, which had been the brothers' tradition, but they had made it so strong that it was almost undrinkable. Then Regina took to the piano bench and launched into "Silent Night," but piano tuning was one of those things they neglected to spend money on, and their voices were weak compared to what had once resounded in that room. Anna kept messing up the words. They returned to their seats, sipping eggnog silently.

At eight o'clock the Morrow sisters-in-law from the hill, Tilly and Faith, arrived, laden with packages that proved upon opening to be stale baked goods. Since they had given Regina the sideboard, Tilly and Faith made it a point to visit her with increasing frequency. While they were there, they gravitated to the sideboard, caressed its knobs and said, "We're their aunts, after all," with a wave of their heads to the girls, who were unwrapping fruitcake upon fruitcake with dismayed looks on their faces. The sisters had lived too long in isolation, was the general theory, for they bragged about using their father's silver-plated pistols on anyone who dared to trespass on their property. Most recently, they told her, they had shot the foot off a man who was replacing a neighbor's fence and had cut through their side yard in order to position support beams across the back. The police had taken the pistols away from them, but they were not apologetic. "Oh, we'll get another one," said Tilly, "and in the meantime we'll just use our china."

"We couldn't believe it when we actually hit him!" Faith blustered. "We never hit anything we aim at. Never before, anyway, right, Sister?"

"But how can you be sure they haven't come to buy baked goods from your shop?" asked Regina, giving them each a teacup of eggnog. "You have to drink this or it will go bad."

"Oh, that we can always tell. People coming to buy sweets have a certain look about them. This is delicious!" exclaimed Faith, who took another enormous sip of her eggnog.

"An expectation of pleasure, if you will," added Tilly.

"Don't you sell bread also?" asked Anna, but her aunts ignored her.

Now it was Tilly's turn to say, "This is really delicious, but perhaps it could use a little more rum."

"Add some, please."

"I don't mind if I do," she said, taking her sister's cup without needing to ask. Fortunately the sideboard was right in front of them. "Anyway," she said as she doctored the eggnog, "we can always tell."

"In the meantime we're just going to throw china at them," said Faith. "We have heaps of old plates and lots of incomplete sets in that house."

"Generations' worth. That should last us until we can get a rifle."

"Shouldn't you save those?" asked Regina.

"Oh, for what? It's not going to mean much to us when some intruder kills us and we're in the grave, right, Sister?" She looked to Faith.

"No indeed."

"Better to use our heritage as a weapon."

"I should say so, Sister."

"Well," said Regina, "I just wish you-all would be careful. It sounds a bit wild up there."

"Oh, it is. More than a bit," said one as both of them nodded their heads vigorously.

They left the sideboard reluctantly when Regina said, "Come and sit in front of the fire." She led them to the sitting area and sat down on the couch. They hesitated for a second before sitting on each side of her, rather too tight a fit. The sisters spent some time adjusting their stockings and slips. A heavy fruitcake in each of their laps, Isabel and Anna looked up at them.

"Oh, it's the holidays that turns our mind to poor Charles," said Faith with a sigh, pulling out her handkerchief, but Tilly was not ready to relinquish the previous subject.

"It's these times, I tell you. Negroes and trash coming up—to the front door no less—asking for work, asking for you to pay them to protect your house. The threat being, if you don't pay them, they'll kill you. Now, Sister and I can't pay. We can't give anyone work; we're working ourselves. So we just as soon protect ourselves, too."

Tilly leaned forward, putting her hand on Regina's knee. "Aren't you afraid, Regina?" she asked, her jowls shaking.

"Well, I don't know. I like to think this house is hidden behind all these trees."

"Not for long. Shouldn't we have another cup, to keep us awake until you-all leave for midnight Mass?" asked Faith.

"Of course."

"Regina, fill yours, too, dear!" called a sister. "Fill Isabel's and Anna's, too!" called the other. They sat back with their cups. "Maybe you should get a dog," mused Faith.

"I really don't like dogs," Regina said.

Tilly swung around to look at the children. "My, you-all are growing up. You have to tell us everything about your little lives. We're your aunts, after all."

"Yes, let's hear it."

Isabel and Anna said nothing, and Regina spoke for them. "They're shy."

"Go on. Don't be shy. No need to be shy. It won't help you in this world, not at all. Let me tell you, Sister and I could be shy when these heathens approach us, threatening our lives. But then we'd be dead. You see?"

"What pretty little Christmas suits you girls have. Did your mother make them for you? I know she did. She's famous for that kind of perfection. How do you like the fruitcake, girls?"

"Very well, thank you," said Isabel.

"You probably thought that was the only thing we were going to give you, didn't you?" The sisters leaned forward to look at each other, held hands and spent a few minutes, red-faced and shaking with giggles, while Regina and Isabel and Anna looked on. "Oh, go ahead, Sister, give it to them." Tilly opened her tapestry bag and brought out two little boxes of unwrapped Arden face powder. "You see"—she pointed to Regina with her head—"our little business isn't doing so badly." Isabel and Anna gushed over the beautiful boxes, sang out thank-yous, blew kisses at their aunts and rapturously read the product enclosures. "Of course, I can't resist a beautiful advertisement, as Sister says. But it smells so nice. I use it three or four times a day! I do think it gives me a certain confidence."

"We spend all day talking cosmetics, you know, when there aren't any customers."

"My, I'm falling asleep right here on this couch and it's not even ten-thirty. You've such a lovely room here, Regina," said Faith, closing her eyes. She opened them suddenly. "Fires are so nice, aren't they? We should have fires in our sitting room, too. I think I'm just going to rest my eyes."

"You going to sleep, Sister?" asked Tilly, suddenly anxious. "Me too, then, me too," and she promptly slouched down and closed her eyes.

Regina laughed outright and spontaneously, hugged the sisters, who opened their eyes, confused. Regina had never hugged them, but she felt so grateful for their presents to Isabel and Anna. She no longer begrudged the sisters their bakery business—she had a new scheme of her own, the sewing scheme, which kept her in positive spirits throughout the holidays. Things were going to be fine.

CAMILLA LEFT EARLY ONE MORNING in the middle of January 1934, with a cloth suitcase, an overstuffed leather pocketbook that had once been Regina's and a grim look about her face, the bus ticket she had bought two weeks in advance clutched in her hand, which was rapidly losing circulation with the weight of her bag. It had rained all night, and the sky was dark gray, which, throughout the morning, would struggle to lighten and fail. A wet breeze shook water out of the magnolia trees as they loaded her suitcase into the trunk of the car. Isabel and Anna had made a corsage out of hothouse gardenias for her lapel, and as they stood in their nightgowns on the front porch, waving good-bye, they fixed their eyes on the eerily white petals, the only thing that stood out against Camilla's dark and nervous form.

Regina was already in the car. "Y'all be good now!" Camilla called to them as she opened the passenger door.

"We will!"

"Help your mama!"

"We will!"

"Bye now!"

"Bye, Camilla!" She got in and slammed the door. Regina cranked up the car and headed down the drive. Camilla waved at Isabel and Anna until she could no longer see them. Regina turned onto Dauphin Street, aimed the car toward downtown. She had not yet had her coffee. They arrived at the depot in silence. During the ride it had started raining again, so Regina pulled up as close to the awning as possible, rolled down the window and signaled to the porter, who came up and stood in the rain by her door. "Which is the bus to Atlanta?" He pointed. Regina handed him her keys. "Could you take the suitcase out of the trunk and put it in the bus, please?" Camilla stared straight ahead at the patterns of rain on the windshield.

"Yes, ma'am." It took him some moments fiddling with the trunk, while Regina's sleeve got wet. He returned with her keys; she gave him a dime and rolled up the window.

"Thank you, Miss Regina. I could've done it myself," said Camilla. When Regina didn't answer, Camilla shifted, rested her hand on the door lever. "I'd better be getting on my way."

"You've got time yet."

They said nothing for some minutes. It was dark under the awning, with several spotlights illuminating the parking lot. It felt like the middle of the night. It was cold. Regina wanted to go back to sleep. Finally she opened her purse. "Take this," she said, passing a bill to Camilla with a rush. "Please, just take it."

"Thank you, Miss Regina," Camilla said coldly. Regina began to cry quietly. "Oh, don't cry. I can't comfort you no more."

"You have to go," she choked. "It's time. Thank you for everything, Camilla."

Camilla opened the car door so that her pocketbook and side were immediately spattered with rain. "It'll be a while before we see each other again," she said.

"You're getting wet."

Camilla leaned into the car, "I don't know what'll happen to me, but I know you'll be just fine."

"You'll miss your bus," Regina sobbed.

"Take care yourself, Miss Regina. Bye." As she got out, her purse hooked on the lever, and she struggled to detach it, her suit and hair and the car seat becoming soaked. She slammed the door and ran through the darkness for the bus. When the bus was gone, Regina stopped crying immediately. "All right," she said out loud as she drove away. "Let's see what's left."


BACK AT THE HOUSE, she set immediately to work designing her business cards and drove out to have fifty of them printed, then bought three redfish and some sweet potatoes to make a special dinner. Isabel's and Anna's tuition was due the first of February, and by now she was imagining paying that without compunction, for her sewing would buy their food, and the nest egg, still depleting slowly, would at least deplete more slowly. The card read:

## OLIVIA McKEON

### SEAMSTRESS

### TAILORESS EXTRAORDINAIRE

*Design, Alterations, Refashioning the Old*
*Specializing in details: smocking, lace, pleats, outer-stitching*

### REASONABLE PRICES

She waited in the hallway for the girls to come home from school, but they did not come. She made coffee and turned on the radio to a jazz program. When they finally came in, it was dark and she was just about to go in and fix their dinner. She would teach them to cook, she thought, because she would probably have to spend all her time sewing. "Where have you girls been?"

"Driving out with Janice Strand, and you know what, Mother? She got drunk. She was drinking!"

"It smelled terrible! Scotch it was, she said," gushed Anna. "She was laughing all over the place and couldn't even hold up her head."

"Isn't she young to be doing that?"

Isabel answered, "She's fifteen. We had to take her home."

"And did you all drink, too?"

"No."

"Well, you girls should discourage her. There's plenty of time to be a drunk, if that's what she wants to be. But not now, when she's too young to have something to be really sorry for."

"We will, Mother."

"Well, I need your help." She picked up the cards and stood. "I've been waiting for you. We're going to have a delicious dinner, by the way. Listen, you're going to have to take the streetcar downtown tomorrow before school and take these cards to Mr. Leitter. Just put them on the counter. You don't have to say anything."

"What are they?" asked Anna.

"You like your Christmas suits, don't you?"

"Yes," said Isabel slowly.

"Yes," said Anna.

"I think I can do the same for other people. No one has any money these days, but they still need to look nice. Maybe I can make us a little extra with these. You girls can have more of what you need. Don't say it," she said to Isabel, who was about to open her mouth. "I know all about the Winter Dance at McGill."

"I want to go, too," sang Anna.

"Then you won't mind helping me with these cards."

They took the cards and studied them, perplexed expressions on their faces. "Who is Olivia McKeon?"

"Oh, it's just a disguise," she said, turning red in front of her daughters.

"Why do you need a disguise?"

"I don't, I don't. I just thought some of the matrons would be more inclined to hire Olivia McKeon than Regina Morrow, whom they know."

"But aren't you going to have to see them face-to-face, to find out what they want done?"

"Well, yes, but if they hire me that won't matter."

"I think it's strange you don't use your own name, Mother," said Anna. "The whole town knows you're an excellent seamstress. They'd all want to hire you."

"Yes, well, we'll try it like this first."

That night, for the first time in months, she slept soundly, and the next morning, all three of them in high spirits, she saw her daughters off to the streetcar. Back in the house, she brought a stool over to the table by the telephone and set to work. Using a ruler and pen, she made a calendar. Then she titled three sheets of paper— CLIENTS; WORK IN PROGRESS; DEADLINES—and propped them up against the wall. Waiting for the phone to ring, she imagined all the beautiful materials she would get a chance to work with, and she returned here and there to the comfort of her inner dialogue: *Yes, Mrs. Mercer, I cut it on the bias. Oh, thank you! Yes, I'd be happy to make you another suit—just bring me the picture from the magazine and the material. You're too kind, Mrs. Mercer, really. I've been doing this since I was a child.* But the phone was resolutely silent. By three o'clock she realized that Isabel and Anna must not have delivered her cards.

She waited for them in the radio room again, but today they were prompt and eager to show her what they had found on Mr. Leitter's counter—a half dozen other cards offering seamstress work. She studied the cards at length; some where she recognized the address but not the name she knew were disguises; others were her social contemporaries and fine seamstresses in their own right. She felt ashamed for not having used her real name, but this time she didn't cry. "You're going to have to go there again tomorrow morning and get every one of my cards off the counter," she told them. "We'll just have to think of something else." Anna clicked on the radio and dialed for a station.

"Why don't you open a library?" asked Isabel. "It seems like your favorite thing is to read."

"Because books don't make any money," she said roughly. They listened to a commercial for detergent. "Did you-all get a good lunch at school?" she asked.

"It was all right," said Anna. "Red beans and rice."

"Was there sausage in it?"

"I had a piece in mine," Isabel said.

"I didn't," Anna said.

"Well, the reason I ask is that there's no dinner," Regina said cheerfully. She jumped up and kissed their heads. "But don't worry, little dears, we're going to think of something." A thought struck her at once. "Actually, there might be enough flour to make pancakes. And I'm pretty sure there's a little oil and an egg."

# The Dismantling

THE NIGHT THE LIFE-SIZE DOLLHOUSE was taken apart for firewood, she didn't sleep well, hearing without knowing it the ax going through the little green front door, the prying off of the clapboards, the games and linens, tables and chairs carried out. From hand to hand passed into the sea of the poor, board by board, exposed nails cutting into fingers but not preventing the quickness, and the shoeless feet not afraid of the sharp points of dried magnolia leaves and other hard things on the ground over which they ran in the quiet, not even trying to be quiet. One by one, the way it had come in, teacup by teacup, the curtains and the blankets, the mah-jong set, the dolls, silverware, cribs, the floorboards ripped up, taken out and toted off, even the slate from the roof.

She woke coated in light sweat and knew as she knew at this point in the night every night—though she couldn't remember the season outside, couldn't remember what she had been dreaming—that this vastness was a trap she would die in. She had for the life of her no idea where she was headed in the vastness, which seemed to be the middle of the ocean, and could only tread water, run out of breath and strain

her neck, looking about her for land she would not spot and hadn't
the strength to move toward even if she did. She threw herself over
on her stomach and lay with her head turned, staring at the darkened bookcase. They had two thousand dollars; soon she would
have to sell more land. Her pecan pies, her gingerbread, her dresses—
none had sold; and the ribbons, labels—Regina Morrow and Olivia
McKeon—mingled together at the back of a drawer. She had even
called the paper.

*"This is Regina Riant Morrow. My father was Colonel Riant, who
owned the* Mobile Chronicle *at one time. How do you do?"*

She got out of bed to open a window. That had been two or
three. Now there was the three hundred dollars for Sister Aloysius,
two dollars and four dollars for the new cook and another four for
the electricity (these girls could not keep the radio on the way they
did when they weren't in the room), plus—don't get distracted,
what was the other thing?—the five for the water, then that was
first because it was late.

*"Well, I would love to volunteer, but I was hoping to be paid. . . .
I see."*

The electricity had tripled—had her wire been tapped by the
Hooverville beyond Old Shell Road? But it's a comfort to be
robbed when you have nothing yourself, maybe. Is that true? Plus
material, probably seven total, five yards—no, four. Lord. She
turned on her side and tucked up her knees. Help us and save us.

*"And what did you hope to write about? We already have a fashion
editor."*

Rubbing the tension out of her jaw, she turned onto her back
again. *Our Father who art in heaven*—yes right, they were getting
old—*hallowed be thy name, thy kingdom come*—she would call and
cancel lunch—*thy will be done, on earth as it is in heaven. Give us this
day our daily*—oh, the chicken feed, the lawn-mower men—*bread*

*and forgive us our trespasses as we forgive those who trespass against us*—had they really tapped her wire? And hell, there was no help to be expected from polish anymore; they needed boots.

*"You'll have to keep your sentences short."*

Oh, the telephone, too—that was the other thing. "Sleep! Please!" she said out loud. Tomorrow—today—was the day she would pick up her first set of books for the book reviews. Find that typewriter, too. That would be two dollars a week, which could go straight to food. She reached under the covers and felt along her ribs to check for being too thin. All right, you're not going to die.

*"You'll have to keep your sentences short."*

In the end she had gotten the job, as a freelance book reviewer, and she aimed to make it work, though it would not be enough to sustain them. Her eyes were open. Her back hurt from the gardening. And now that she had let go of the gardener, the rest of the yard looked like the last leg of the road to perdition. All right, let out the sleeves and the hem of that blue frock and take in the waist. Oh, there was plenty of land and jewelry to sell, she knew that, and knew that the time would come; next would be the lot beyond the orchard. But everything was already for sale; there were simply no buyers—she had found that out when she tried to sell the horses.

*"We buy most of our content from the New York papers, you may imagine. No one makes a living writing for us."*

Think of something pleasant. The screens—they would have to rescreen the upper porches before summer. Was summer coming? Plant tomatoes. Oh, okra. She slept.

And while she slept, more about the dismantling reached her from across the yard, and she felt herself being passed from hand to calloused hand, but softly, quietly, and they could drop her at any moment, but she made the decision even in her dream to not be dropped. And they placed her on a bed of hay—she was the baby

Jesus maybe—and sang to her as they took the house apart for fire-wood. It must be winter, she thought as she bit at her thumbnail, but this is all right, they can take it all down. What difference is it to me whether I have wood around me or not? Why didn't I think of it myself? Just take it all down and be done with it; all I need is a bit of hay. And then, as if in answer, a cold rain began to fall on her skin, and she had to admit, though she pretended otherwise, she was un-comfortable.

The hay had turned sticky. The dollhouse was gone. And they—who were they?—had taken her clothes. Yes, she should give away everything she had and not expect to be remembered for any special kindnesses, she who had always been so kind, and now she couldn't move from the bed of hay. There was nothing to save anymore anyway. The rain would have helped her garden, but everything would be picked before it was ready. And their fingers like jaws took another and another bite out of the stables, out of the barn, out of the smokehouse.

She woke at dawn to the hush of rain beyond her screen, light rain but insistent in its fineness. She realized that the side of her mat-tress was damp from the rain blowing in from her open window along with the soft carpet of balmy air it rode in on. What season was it? For a moment she couldn't remember; then with a pang the complications in which she existed were on her in full: the water bill. She lay there for several minutes staring at the ceiling. There was no one left to ask for help. She wished she could look into the future for her own answer; she knew she could come up with something. When she finally thought of it, what would it be? She was more tired than she had been the night before. What else? The gas bill, and to-day was the day she was to pick up her books from the newspaper.

Finally she got up and dressed and knelt on her prie-Dieu and prayed for everyone she knew and for herself and for some relief. Then she went downstairs to make the coffee. She was sitting in the radio room under a reading light, a shawl around her shoulders, a cup and saucer on the table beside her, when the new cook, who had been out feeding the chickens, came to report that the chickens were gone, that the milking cow was gone and that the dollhouse had been pillaged and dismantled. "That's awful!" she exclaimed. Then, to hide her consternation, she forced herself to read the words in front of her—as it happened, a radio schedule. The cane blinds were raised along the large windows that formed three of the walls, but a weak, rainy light was all that reached them. Elmira stayed in the doorway, visibly distressed, until Regina said the first thing that came to her: "I'm thinking of getting a dog."

"I don't like dogs."

"I don't either," she said, struggling to sound nonchalant. "Well, what should I do, then?"

"I'm scared," said Elmira.

"Don't be scared," said Regina kindly. "Get yourself a cup of coffee and sit down. None of this is going to kill us."

"But what about . . ." Elmira twisted her hands. "Maybe you should get a watchman."

"Maybe," said Regina. She folded up the paper and put it on the floor near her chair. "The rain has stopped, I think." She rose, turned a bar on the window and swung one side of it open. Heavy air from outside slowly stirred into the room, but the chill that had been in it for recent weeks was gone. "It's warmer outside than it is in here," she declared. "Is this spring finally?"

"It's a strange day."

"Well, we have nothing to do but just sit back and admire it. Of course," she laughed, "that's not entirely true."

"I got plenty to do," said Elmira. "It's nigh on seven o'clock. And you'd better go on look at that damage. Ain't nothing left to admire."

As Regina strode out across the wet grass toward the dollhouse, she could not explain the lightness in her heart. Indeed, there was nothing left out here. Suddenly she felt very young. "Well, there's no point to crying over spilled milk," she said aloud. She stood still, her black form small against the indomitable green that grew so effortlessly around her, and stared down into the dollhouse's stone perimeter, listening to the growth. The grass edged up her calves while nameless vines crawled through it toward the trees behind her. The bamboo had shot up to twice her height, vines covered the magnolias, and Spanish moss covered the oaks. Everything covered, the future covered, surrounded on all sides by the green and the wet, she stood there for some time.

Had she been able to see herself from a distance, as Elmira saw her from the porch off the back of the kitchen when she came out to dump a tub of soapy water, she would have wondered what such a tiny woman was doing in the presence of such hugeness, so serious in her black dress and shawl, so angular standing beside everything that is beyond control. She might have smiled sadly. *Anything left by the people will be taken by this foliage*, she thought as she turned and went to the chicken house—to make sure they were not there, and to the barn to make sure the cow was gone, too. The animals' absence was no surprise. In the empty pens, she could feel their lives taken elsewhere, and abandonment, because they lived still, but for someone else. "Damn it," she said, marching back to the house.

Inside was cold and damp, and she was grateful to learn that Isabel and Anna had left for school. It was past eight o'clock. She knew that sometime this morning she ought to drive over to the newspaper and pick up her books, but she didn't feel up to it. A great heaviness had come over her, heavier than the lightness had been light. She might have explained it as an effect of what she had just seen, but she didn't allow herself to think like that anymore. She sat in the library and looked at the empty fireplace, thinking that she ought to work on that blue frock and that she didn't feel like that either. Then she looked at the round marble-topped table by the door where all the unopened letters from her brothers were stacked. She rose, picked up one from George and read it standing.

*Dear Sis,*
*Are you well? All is well here in the birthplace of Bolivar, though I eat rather too much fish. I have learned only a few words of the language, thus far, and I rely rather too much on my peaceful disposition and near-fluent Latin to set an angelic example for the natives. I want to come home. I hate it here. I tell you, I can barely bear it. But I can't be selfish where the souls of others are concerned, can I? Let me know what you think, for I got a blister playing lawn tennis the other day and now it's infected. Is this sufficient cause to renounce my duty and return to Mobile? Let me know what you think as soon as possible, for once it heals I'll be forced to stay. You'll never guess who I ran into down here: that Chinese fellow Ahlong. I've called on him a few times but he's extremely busy. How are you faring, dear Sis? Regards to Camilla. Kisses to my nieces.*
*Your affectionate brother, X*

She ripped it, dropped it between the grates of the fireplace and stood looking down at it. Then she set it on fire, took a log from the nearby basket and was surprised to see that she had lit a fire. All at once it felt like a holiday. Ahlong may be busy, but she wasn't. That was fine for him. She was glad she hadn't married him. Today she wouldn't do anything she didn't want to do and everything would work out all right. She wouldn't go pick up those books. Damn the newspaper.

She grabbed the stack of letters, pulled her chair up to the front of the fire and began reading letters and tossing them into the fire, one by one. The next was from Peter.

> *Dear Sis,*
>
> *Hope you are faring well in these trying times. I can't say that our insurance endeavor has taken off like we'd hoped, but we've invested enough that as soon as the economy is out of its present doldrums we should be in a fine position to make a success. I try not to think about the fact that Agee's mother's cousins are staying with us at the moment, adding rather too much of a strain, as you can imagine. Oh, I can barely bear it. I hate Birmingham and want to come back to Mobile. The Communists are here in full force, organizing the Negroes. But I've made my bed here and now must lie in it. Why don't we hear from you? Regards to Camilla.*
>
> *Your affectionate brother, X*

She tore it up and tossed it into the fire. The next two, from Felix, she didn't finish reading. It made no difference that the letters were out of order chronologically. They all accused her of not writing back; several asked for money; there were complaints of never-leaving visitors from the Birmingham faction. All used the phrase "barely bear it," a great joke between them, no doubt. Half used the phrase "made my bed and must lie in it," and three mentioned fear of Negro insurrections. One by one she tossed them into the fire. The drivel was sprinkled by letters from her cousin Beattie in New Orleans, who mentioned a friend of hers, a Miss

Imogene Morgan, who had once had a lover in Mobile and wanted to make a lengthy visit down memory lane, and could she stay with Regina? She would have to write her back. At last she saw the letter that interested her. From Camilla, obviously written for her by someone else.

> *Dear Miss Regina,*
> *My sister is fine and the great Atlanta seem to get on without help from any soul. It being burned down a few times may explain that its ugly tho I don't complain. After plenty waiting Sister made me a Agent and give me a deploma and my firs Sales Kit. I set to work. Sister introduced me about and I'm making out all right tho I'm shy. Then I saw colored women, same as white, drop any sum for beauty, no matter how hand-to-mouth they is. Peoples coming out to find me! That Hair Grower is a fine product and the Softener sell like hot Cakes. It's colder here I spect. How are my girls? Tell them they best right. I pray for yall and beg you keep me in yours. But I know you do.*
> *Camilla*

She sighed—she couldn't think about that now. She tossed the letter into her letter box and opened another. George had recovered from his infection. Felix suggested she sell property and make him a loan. Louis asked for a loan. She threw another log onto the fire. The insurance business was doing well and then doing poorly. Peter asked if she thought about selling some of the property. Louis was searching for a job as an engineer, with little luck. Two consecutive letters from Peter and Louis were devoted to chastising her for not writing back. A letter postmarked "Savannah" was from a Louisa Dumaine, her mother's cousin Modesta's daughter. Louisa wrote to say she was making a study of her family's silver patterns, and did Regina have any that matched the enclosed drawings? A letter from Peter and one from Felix went into the fire without being opened.

The fire was roaring and spitting when Elmira knocked and entered. "Mrs. Morrow," she said. Regina turned to her with flushed face and bright eyes. "There's a man on the back porch here to see you."

"Oh, all right," she said, and got up.

The man she met there was not young, though age would be the last thing to mention in describing him. He wore worn, tan canvas pants and a thin cotton shirt. The cloth over the lower left arm stirred in the damp breeze—there was nothing there below the elbow. His bright brown eyes looked down at her from fully two heads up. "A train accident," he said immediately.

"Aha," she said.

He was lighter than black and darker than yellow, a pleasing shade with undercurrents of red. His face was thin in the forehead, chin and neck, though his cheeks were full. A light pink scar cut through the hair of his left eyebrow. "Name's Willie Slay," he said, smiling wide to reveal a mouth full of gold teeth.

She shook his hand and lowered her head to look at his feet. The canvas shoe on the right foot called attention to the peg that protruded from below the knee of the left leg. "What can I do for you, Mr. Slay?"

"I heard tell of your misfortune and I think I can keep any more away."

"I see." Willie Slay would be the first of many men to come throughout the day to offer their services, she knew, as word of the robbery spread through town. The best thing would be to get rid of them as soon as possible. She shouldn't have answered the door. "I don't need a protector," she said. "I'm thinking of getting a dog. But thank you."

"Yes, ma'am." He looked down shyly, and she reached behind her for the handle of the screen door. "I suppose I don't cut much of a figure for a watchman, is that it?"

"Oh no, it's not that," she said, embarrassed. "I really can't afford to take on any workers, you see. I make do with just a cook."

"I got a shotgun." He grinned down at her.

"Well, I wouldn't want anyone getting shot." The air outside was surprisingly warm, and she felt foolish for indulging in a fire.

"I don't have any of them diseases."

"I'm sure you don't, Mr. Slay." She sighed. "All I can offer you is a piece of bread. I'm sorry. I wish it weren't the case." He didn't speak or move, stood there beaming. "All right," she said, "wait here a minute." She returned with bread and black coffee and left him on the front porch to eat it. Then she went upstairs to put a nicer dress on; she would go to the newspaper after all. She was passing back through the hallway when the doorbell rang again. It was Willie Slay a second time. "I think you should be on your way," she said firmly. "I thank you for offering to help me."

"I can fix this here lawn for you, at least, make it look perty again."

"I can't pay you, Mr. Slay, and you shouldn't be working for free," she said, a note of frustration in her voice.

"You just done got me started with the bread," he said. "It's a known fact I'm out of work, but that don't mean I don't need something to do. Aren't you working even when you sitting in yo rocker?"

She had to admit she was not. She needed to go pick up those books from the newspaper. "All right," she said, "let me show you where the tools are." But when that was done, she went back to the library, stoked up the fire again and settled back down to her letter flaming. She had decided to postpone her trip to the paper until the afternoon. Another letter from Peter asked for money; another from Felix advised her in what order to sell the plots; another and another from Peter asked if she might keep the cousins he was shackled with. All went into the fire. She got up and drew the curtains. In spite of herself, she was curious to see how Willie Slay would maneuver the lawn tools. The mower was no problem, apparently; he could guide it with one hand and push it forward with the opposite hip. Already a quarter of the side lawn was cut, and he was moving along the hedges at the edge of the Laborde property with the clippers, which he held in the crook of his elbow, using his good arm to open and close the blades.

The next time she looked out, she saw Elmira beckoning him to lunch. She took this chance to drive to the paper and pick up her books, and by the time she returned with the stack, he was already back at work with the mower. He paused to wave to her as she pulled up the drive. The side lawn was cut and he was advancing steadily across the front. She found the typewriter and spent the afternoon reading *The Radetzky March*, which she enjoyed immensely, and making notes for her review. She was grateful for the job after all, she realized. Even though it paid pennies, she would have new books to turn to when she couldn't sleep. Then the afternoon was over; the light was golden and waning. The fire had long been out, and only a prism of light, weakly warm, came through the French doors onto the bare floor of the library and illuminated the dust.

Soon Isabel and Anna were in with all their racket, talking about the horrible dress in which someone named Sue had dared to appear, and that the McGill boys were coming to their Easter pageant and how embarrassed they would be to perform in front of them, and that someone had put on Sister Aloysius's desk a magazine, on the cover of which two people were kissing, prompting her to talk about sex the entire class period and say, holding up the magazine, "This is what you should do only with the man you marry," and they had all been red in the face, particularly Janice Strand, whose mother was not a Catholic and who had kissed so-and-so last fall. By then it was too dark to cross the lawn, so Regina told Isabel and Anna that their dollhouse had disappeared in the night. "I'm scared," Anna said. They discussed who had done it and cataloged all that was lost until it was time for coffee.

"But we're not to cry over it," Regina told them as they moved into the radio room, "because we should be happy that it's in the hands of those who need it more than we do. Why do we need a dollhouse when we have a house, an enormous house?"

"A freezing house," said Isabel. Regina lit the gas heater, and she couldn't tell them not to turn on the radio. It was Duke Ellington's Orchestra playing "It Don't Mean a Thing If It Ain't Got That Swing," broadcast from the Cotton Club, and Elmira brought them coffee, and Isabel and Anna had begun dancing a bit to the music when the doorbell rang. "Oh heavens," said Regina. "It's Willie Slay. Go tell him, won't you, Elmira, that I'll be there in a minute?"

"Is that the man working on the lawn?" asked Isabel.

"His name is Willie Slay. I forgot all about him," she said. "I guess I thought he'd already left."

"We talked to him. He's nice. He told us he would take us hunting for possums," said Anna. "He gets a dollar a skin. But you have to go at night, of course."

The doorbell rang again; they heard Elmira open the front door. "Possums are so vicious," Isabel said disapprovingly. "I don't know that I could face them, much as I wouldn't mind them being killed."

Regina was anxious. "I have to pay him something. He did such quick work. I think four dollars."

"That's too much," said Elmira, who had returned.

"Three?"

Elmira shook her head. "Only your mother," she said to the girls, "would hire a one-leg, one-arm yardman."

"I have to give him at least three," she said, standing. She couldn't afford to hire him.

On the front porch, she shoved the money into his good hand. The porch light had gone out and she couldn't see his features. "Help yourself from the garden," she told him. "There are sweet potatoes and leeks. Thank you for your help. The yard looks wonderful."

"I trimmed this whole side here. But I didn't quite finish."

"It looks wonderful, Mr. Slay."

He was silent for a moment. "Then I can come back tomorrow?"

"I can't pay you. Please." She smiled tensely. "Don't make me have to say it again. I wish I could, but I can't."

"You're paying me now."

"Yes, but that's all I have. That's so you won't come back."

He lingered still, shifting from foot to peg. "Pardon my 'pertinence, ma'am, but we need each other."

"I don't think so." She reached for the doorknob.

"It don't have to be so money, money, money. It's the God's truth that I mean no disrespect, but I can take some kind of gardener's shack for my abode. I seen you have one over yonder. And you can feed me maybe and trade me some things you have for my work. Such things like you don't need anymore."

"I've decided to let the yard go, Mr. Slay. I'm going to have to sell some land soon anyway. And I just don't have the strength for more than the vegetable garden."

"I can run errands, too, like, and I know all about the land and planting. I was a sharecropper, been done kicked off my land, and I'm . . ." He trailed off.

"I don't think so. Please, I'm sorry. I've already turned so many men away as to break my heart a hundred times."

"Maybe today's the day you stop breaking it."

She laughed in spite of herself. "Then I'll just feel worse when I have to let you go."

"None of that, ma'am."

She sighed. "All right."

"Yes?"

"Yes."

"Then I'll be back tomorrow?"

"If you would, yes."

"Thank you, ma'am. I'll be here with the roosters. And I don't mean to be bringing up unpleasantries." A shadow crossed her face and she took a step back. He stopped himself. "I mean, no one will be bothering you ladies anymore. Don't worry. I ain't gonna shoot no one neither. I just scare 'em. And they knows me already. They knows I'm a man of the Lord."

"I don't need a protector, Mr. Slay," she said.

"Everybody need a protector."

She took another step back. "All right, then," she said. "We'll see you tomorrow. Good night."

## The Daughters of Modesta

IN SUMMERS REGINA SLEPT on the screened-in porch off her room, and one August morning the wet heat just before dawn woke her and she set about her coffee and sweating much earlier than usual. She swept the front porch and got the girls their toast, and, after much discussion about attire, succeeded in putting them into their suits and into the automobile of a new friend who was driving them over the bay. Yes, they were getting older. She noticed it sometimes when she saw them off but allowed herself no pangs over it. She chatted with Willie Slay for a moment before the heat drove her inside to start reading her latest book. Willie Slay had much less to work with since she had sold two acres of land that were between the front of the house and Old Shell Road and made the back entrance on the St. Francis Street side into the front entrance. She really couldn't afford to keep him on—all the money she made from the book reviews went to him—but couldn't let him go. Of course, she had known that would happen.

She'd loaned half of the proceeds from the land sale to Felix's insurance enterprise, but her half still allowed her to relax. No one had begun building on the lot in the back—she sold to the bank— and she let herself imagine it still belonged to her. On the other hand, relaxing only caused her more anxiety. She knew that the halcyon days would run out again, that she would have to bestir herself soon, but soon was never today. It was this vague disquiet that crossed her mind when she was alone in the house, when she looked up from her book to stare at the wall and take a sip of coffee. Yet she was continually glad for the books that, though they didn't stave off the panicky thoughts entirely, kept them less frequent. There was no sign of Elmira when the doorbell rang, and she went to answer it.

The woman standing there was tall and bony, with a bluish complexion and eyes the startling pale green of luna moths. She was dressed neatly in the matronly style of twenty years before: a skirt to the floor and a silk blouse, both white. In spite of the heat, she had a fuchsia shawl around her shoulders, high black boots and a black cartwheel hat, angled over her left eye, which she took off as she stepped into the foyer, revealing hair that was thick, board straight and the color of unvarnished oak streaked with white. Regina invited her into the dining room, explaining that it was the coolest room in the house, and offered her a glass of iced tea, which the woman accepted. "It's been so long since we've met, Regina," she said from a sunken place on the pale pink couch. "I wonder that we even recognize each other."

"I don't think I'd recognize you if I didn't already know who you were," Regina said tactfully, reaching for the woman's hand and patting it in welcome. "It's so nice of you to visit."

"I remember meeting you at the homestead in Abingdon. We must have been six or seven, or even younger, I don't remember, but we were playing a game with your brothers, and they made me cry for one reason or another—I probably had a spot of mud on my dress." She laughed a throaty tinkling that struck Regina with its beauty. "Anyway, you were kind. You dried my tears on your hem."

Regina flashed a smile. "I'm sure there were many such occasions for anyone foolish enough to play with my brothers."

The doorbell cut off the woman's soft laughter. "That'll be my luggage."

"Your luggage?"

"Yes." She stood, her pretty smile gone, and sighed in a way that indicated the ordeal of traveling had been simply too much for her. "They had to bring it from the station in a second trip. My wardrobes, I had to ship. They tell me they will arrive sometime next week, though I won't hold my breath." Again she laughed from her beautiful throat. "Let me just be sure they all made it."

"Splendid," said Regina, with considerable effort. Her mind was racing down all the branches of the family tree and out onto the narrowest twigs, trying to place this woman as she led her back into the hallway. "Did you change trains in Atlanta?"

"No," the woman answered.

"Oh!" Regina laughed nervously: was she dreaming? "All trains seem to go through Atlanta, no matter where they're coming from, don't they?" No; the luggage that was piling into the hall looked real enough, and Elmira, who appeared at that moment, shooting Regina an annoyed look, was having the men stack it, trunk after trunk, parasol, umbrella, hatbox after hatbox, cosmetic case, prie-Dieu, ottoman, at the top of the stairs. Regina decided to ask the woman how long she intended to stay, but before she could formulate the question, which she knew would be rude, it occurred to her that the woman must be family, and that everything is secondary to family. Then she knew how to proceed. "Come look at the library."

But the woman would not go beyond the threshold and stood

staring at the painting of Jackson and Lee on horseback that hung above the mantel. "I have a portrait of my mother with me," she said. "Modesta Dumaine."

Family! There it was. The now dead—was she dead? Modesta must be dead—had been a second cousin of her mother's. She had three or four daughters; this could be Otelia Morgan, the eldest, who—what was the story?—had married a soldier named LeBlanc. No, because LeBlanc had been lost in the war and she, struck by lightning on the Arkansas prairie, had died shortly after. It might be Louisa, the one whose husband and father—she'd had a different father (now, how had that been possible?)—had died in the same year, the one who had written to her about the silver patterns, the one who was reported to do nothing but make peppermint pull candy in her Savannah homestead. Or Florentine. Florentine had been the wildish one; they'd heard of her running off to New Orleans with a married man named Drozin Rocheblave and turning up in St. Louis a few years later, penniless and looking the worse for wear. And there was a fourth whose name Regina couldn't remember. The woman's next comment put an end to these thoughts.

"If you like, perhaps we can replace Jackson and Lee with it above the mantel. Also, I have one of my brother. Those are coming with the wardrobe."

"How is your brother?" Regina asked, then catching the eye of Elmira, who had reappeared at the bottom of the stairs and waited in the hallway for a clue on how to proceed. The woman sensed the shift in Regina's glance and looked down. Normally Regina would have introduced her to Elmira at this juncture; instead she rambled on in embarrassment. "I can't remember the last time I heard word of him. Put the things in the four-poster room," she said to Elmira. "The green one, please."

"He died last April."

The two women squared off. "Oh, I'm so sorry, I didn't realize!" "Not at all."

"Forgive me," Regina said softly, "I'm a little distracted. I've had more than my share of misfortune"—she rushed on and, taking the woman's arm impulsively, she steered her back into the dining room—"as you might have guessed by the state of the house. Maybe you heard about it from our common cousins. But never mind it." They returned to their seats.

"Yes," the woman said. Her head resting against the back of the pale pink couch, her eyes fluttered closed, then opened on the little blue-flowered porcelain clock on the side table. "Sometimes I think it is better not to speak of such things, but of course one never forgets."

Regina waited for her to say something more but, met with silence, said, "No, indeed," to fill the space. She studied her guest. For the first time, she saw an expression that over the years would become very familiar: a blanket of horror clouded the woman's eyes for a moment and subsided. Regina felt a rush of affection for her and took her hands. "We are so happy to have you with us, dear."

"Thank you." The woman stood nervously, dabbed her eyes with a handkerchief. "Perhaps I'll just go up and rest. I get worn out so easily by—"

"Of course," Regina said, jumping to her feet. As she led the way upstairs, she racked her brain for some words of comfort. At the door to the bedroom they stopped. "I'll show you around the house when you feel better."

"I don't believe you knew who I was when I first arrived," the woman said, now crying openly, "but you are so kind to take me in." Regina clasped her hands and kissed them. "When you didn't respond to my letter, I wrote to your brother Felix"—the woman coughed quietly, her handkerchief held to her lips—"who invited me to visit. I thought he would tell you." A sob escaped her, and she pressed the fingers of one hand to her temples, hanging her head. "I'm mortified, absolutely."

"Nonsense!" Regina reached out and clutched the woman's upper arm. "Calm down, for heaven's sake!" she said gently. "You're in the wrong place for this." The sobs abated. "Take a rest; then we'll have supper. You'll meet my daughters." The woman nodded obediently. "Rest," Regina said again, and watched as the woman backed into the room.

Regina had a little smile on her face as she headed downstairs, but a moment later scouring the letter table did not reassure her. Ripping open letter after letter from Felix, the feeling of sympathy that had been kindled by the woman made way for doubts. Who was this sad woman? Was she insane, and if she were, how would they ever get rid of her now that she was settled upstairs? These damn letters: she had made it through only a tenth of them, finding nothing, when Elmira in the doorway said, "You should have told me, Mrs. Morrow, that we was expecting a lady guest. Things ain't fancy up there as they might."

"I know, Elmira, and I'm terribly sorry. It must have slipped my mind."

"A big thing to have slip," Elmira said, frowning.

"Yes." Regina looked up. Elmira's criticisms had a way of making her rebellious. With her forearm Regina swept the letters into the trash basket that stood next to the table.

"Letters from your brothers!" Elmira exclaimed softly. Regina pointed her eyes at the ceiling. "Mr. Slay want to talk to you."

"All right," she said with a last look to the trash. "All right." Disregarding a hat, she tromped out into the side yard, where Willie Slay was trimming the rose arbor near the stone porch off the parlor. "What is it, Mr. Slay?"

He shifted the clippers from the crook of his elbow into his good hand and faced her. "If you told me you was having a lady guest I woulda finished the walk edging yesterday." She said nothing. "It's not far from a fright, though I been working, I just been focusing on other bits. Not on the presentation bits."

"The truth is, Mr. Slay, I forgot all about it. I wasn't expecting her."

He looked incredulous. "Well, who is she?"

She hesitated. "I don't know."

"No, no, no," he said, and broke into a grin. "Lordy me, Miss Morrow, you falling apart or what?"

Regina started to laugh, then controlled herself. "She's a relation of some kind," she said defensively as she chopped off a fuchsia bougainvillea flower with her fingernail, "and that's all that's important."

Willie became serious, too. "She seem nice."

"Maybe you can pick some flowers for her room."

"That's what I intended," he said, defensively. Then he spoke low. "Maybe you don't need a protector now."

"You're not my protector, Mr. Slay," she said, rubbing her eye. She was allergic to ligustrum. "But you're doing fine work."

"Thank you, ma'am."

"Thank you."


THE IMPRESSION THE WOMAN MADE on Isabel and Anna at first was that of someone who didn't belong, someone who would not be with us long on this earth, not because of any sickness but from the lightness of her bearing, the sheerness of her skin, the nervous fluttering of her hands as she turned pages of a book she wasn't reading, the unsureness of her step. They had the feeling that if she stood too close to the fire she might melt; if she drank too much iced tea she might drown; and if she persisted with that look in her luna-moth eyes, with which she stared at the crucifix above her prie-Dieu, she might be taken, up to heaven, body intact. And because she barely spoke.

By virtue of their ages, the girls were impatient with any medi-tation on grief and so remained oblivious to the causes of the woman's strange behavior. They approached her with simple hearts and, when they learned her name was Louisa, they began to call her Wheezie, and so she would remain. She was a new if im-passive audience for their antics; she made their mother more solic-itous, and they had the comfort now that there were two ladies watching over them, not just one. Also, she relieved them from feeling that they were too silent, so trapped away in the house that the world wouldn't notice a difference if they never turned up again. That the house might as well vanish and they renege on life for all the effect they had on the day to day beyond. So Louisa be-came, in spite of her own celestial presence, an anchor to the living world, a recognition, an impression.

The household at large responded favorably to the new purpose afforded by the mourning guest. Elmira served them now on the Haviland china; the silver was always polished; the food was, though not lavish by any means, at least prepared with imagination and presented with care. Extra vegetables were steamed; larger cuts of meat were stewed to hide their toughness, and where before they sucked on lemonade ice cubes for dessert, they now had chocolate-covered crackers. Willie Slay, in addition to keeping the lawn mowed and the walks edged and swept, now cultivated jonquils, roses, vio-lets, zinnias, everything that would grow—several arrangements of which he cut three times a week. There were vases of flowers in each bedroom, the most beautiful being reserved for Louisa's. Mr.

Slay had quite an eye for flowers, they all remarked, and Isabel and Anna, delighted by all the extra attention, thought each day that much closer to a holiday.

Anna particularly loved Louisa, who had announced quietly and early on that she hated to cook and refused to sew, and Anna thought that scandalous. She often joined Louisa on the front porch when she got home from school and the two of them sat in silence, Anna reading, Louisa pretending to read. Sometimes Anna would ask her about her past, but she always said the same thing: "The happiest women, like the happiest nations"—here she would emit a few chimes of her laugh—"have no history." Or Louisa would ask Anna questions about her plans for her future. The two conversed slowly, with many minutes between replies. "And do you like school?" Louisa asked one afternoon after an extended stretch of silence.

"School's fine. Fun. We're always talking about one thing or another, and I laugh all day long."

"That's good." They fell back to their separate reflections for a time. "And will you go to college?" Louisa asked.

"None of the girls go to college. Well, Sylvia Babineaux wants to go. I don't know why—I guess to meet more men. And there's Laura Coddel, but she's a brain. There's nothing but college for her."

Louisa stared off toward what had once been the back gate and was now the front gate for long enough that Anna returned to her book. "And you're not a brain? You seem like a brain to me," Louisa finally said.

Anna folded over the corner of her page and shut her book. "Oh sure, I've got one. I've got a good one, I suppose as good as anyone's, but I don't see the point of exercising it so much. It's there, it works. Why make it jump rope? It's too tiresome!"

Louisa laughed warily and tilted her head back so that the magnolias reflected in her eyes. She stretched her left leg out in front of her, brought it down again, took a deep breath and let it out slowly. "I see what you mean."

"There's other ways to learn. Of course reading. I'll read anything you give me and be pleased as punch with it. Also, the art of conversation is important. But to sit there and listen to Sister Aloysius teaching chemistry! She's eighty if she's a day and teaching herself as she goes along—that's the only thing about it that's clear—she blew up four test tubes just the other day. Fortunately we were all wearing goggles. It's simply ridiculous."

"Well . . ." Louisa paused, recrossing her legs and arranging the folds of her skirt over her knees. "It's the exercises of the mind that prepare you for your internal traveling: the spiritual journey and the contemplative life."

"Yes, yes, I know, and there're outer traveling, too. There're so many outward demands. I mean, you get invited to so many places, and Mother says it's impolite not to turn up where you're invited. I rarely want to go but I always do. And then there's the conversation, the art of conversation, I mean. I mean, you can't just sit there and be quiet." Anna stopped because Louisa seemed not to be listening.

Louisa arched her back against the rocking chair and, stretching her arms out in front of her, at last said, "Oh, child, I left all that long ago." Both were silent for several moments. "Though I did always enjoy dancing," she mused.

"Of course I enjoy myself once I'm there, I truly do, but I wouldn't mind being something other than I am: a Negro, or a white man, or anything else. No, that's not true. I suppose I just want to be a child. If everyone could be a child again at the same time, you know? So we could all meet each other for the first time, just seize each other's arms and invite each other to play. With

children there's no refusal or strange eyes or anything. And they
don't talk about each other. They don't even talk; they're just happy
to be in one another's company. Like you. That's what I'd like. To
not talk. Of course I'm not off to a very good start this afternoon."

Louisa wore the half smile of someone who has made many con-
cessions. "No dear, you're not."

FOR HER PART, Regina threw herself into making Louisa feel welcome. Her guest, she surmised early on, was dazzled with grief, and
she was determined to bring her out the other side of it. In the first
weeks of Louisa's stay, Regina sat with her in the morning hours,
sewing, while Louisa just sat, all expression struck from her face.
Regina tried to chat about the family, but Louisa had nothing to add
to Regina's tidbits and just smiled her sweet smile, sometimes saying, "How strange! Life is so strange!"

That exhausted, Regina took to prattling about her current book
review, and Louisa, who had appeared to listen patiently but without interest, occasionally produced phrases for inclusion in the review, phrases that made Regina, perhaps in relief that her charge
had finally uttered something, howl with laughter. Then Louisa
would smile and release a few bars of her own laughter, but press on
her temples a moment later and wince.

Though she never complained, Regina recognized the temple
pressing as the symptom of piercing headaches and brought her
guest cold compresses. Louisa's eyes filled with tears of gratitude,
and she made an obvious effort to revive herself, an effort that
never lasted more than a few minutes. Sometimes she mentioned
the Ursuline convent in New Orleans and how she'd always
wanted to go to college there but had gotten married instead.
Regina never understood why. In the afternoons after dinner, when

her grief seemed to weigh on her the most, Louisa sat quietly on the porch and pretended to read cookbooks through her tears. Regina just let her be. Occasionally she saw Anna out there with her, chattering away, but thought there could be no harm in that.

In due time the portrait of Modesta Dumaine, Louisa's mother, was hung over the mantel in the library in place of Jackson and Lee, who were relegated to the unsealed room off the third floor, and Regina would later date the beginning of her friendship with Louisa to this hanging. Why the portrait had such an animating effect on her guest Regina couldn't guess, but she had no doubt that it was so: it was not the solicitations of the house that reawakened Louisa to life, it was the portrait. Though there were many rooms in the house in which the women, as friends, habitually carried on, it was in the presence of Modesta that they conceived the plan to save the house.

After it was hung, Regina noticed Louisa gravitating to the portrait of her mother. She paced underneath it, asked that they might take their morning coffee under it and, also under it, said yes to proposals—that they crank up the phonograph, play cards, attend Isabel's school recital—she would have declined previously. She never passed through the front door without first inclining her head toward Modesta and raising her eyes in silent salutation, as if taking strength from it for the journey outside, but at last she was willing to leave the house: to Mass, to the fish market, to the pictures. Sometimes she just hopped on the Dauphin streetcar and rode it around its circuit. She talked of learning to drive. The door from the hallway to the library was never closed now—Louisa saw to that—and Regina caught her in the hallway often enough, staring into the library at Modesta. "Why," Regina asked her one day when she found her on the front porch, looking through the French doors into the library, and hence at the portrait, "do you so adore that portrait?"

"Ach," Louisa said with a sheepish smile. "Don't ask me that. I don't know."

The portrait did not deserve its gold-leaf frame. It had been damaged in moving and Modesta's nose had a tiny T-shaped rip across its bridge. The famous Spanish portrait painter, who visited Mobile in 1860, had executed the three-by-six-foot portrait of Modesta as a child. The only way he managed to paint the portraits of twenty-five wealthy children in a two-week visit was by painting the bodies and backgrounds in advance. Then, in an hour's sitting, he painted the children's heads. Her visage a victim of haste, Modesta's five-year-old head round, her chin lumpy and large, her black hair parted in the middle and hanging in heavy plaits down the side of her head, as a result, was painted on the body of a breasted girl three times her age in a white satin dress and heeled boots, whose well-developed hand held some kind of bouquet. Modesta stands on a porch, its nondescript balustrade behind her, and behind that is foliage and a body of water over which grayish atmospheres hover with an unidentifiable portent.

Regina sat in an armchair upholstered with pink velvet and stared up at Modesta. She had also found herself drawn to the portrait, caught herself gazing at it in affection and discovered she had been praying for Modesta for some time. She had become fond of Modesta, though she had never met her and knew nothing about her life; Louisa herself knew little of Modesta, who had died when she was five. Regina's tenderness was all the more surprising because the portrait was a mediocre likeness of Modesta; in fact, the portrait didn't even look human in proportions. "Mother?"

Regina swung around in her chair. "Yes, dear?"

"I've been calling you for the last half hour," Isabel said, stomping into the room and stopping before Modesta, fists on her hips.

Regina looked at her daughter. "What do you need?"

She glanced from her mother to Modesta, pivoted on her heel and threw herself facedown onto the couch.

"What's wrong?" Regina asked, shifting to the edge of her chair, but she had turned her head into the back of the couch. "How are things with John?"

Isabel flipped her head around so that it pointed out toward her mother. "Fine," she said.

"Did you get your physics test back yet?"

"No."

Regina picked up her work and asked, "Did you get something to eat?"

Isabel sighed loudly in response. "No."

"Well, there's beaten biscuits and corned beef," said Regina, squinting at her crocheting.

Isabel said, loud and clear, "I need some new brassieres."

Regina continued to crochet. "All right," she said just as firmly, "I'll take you tomorrow afternoon."

"I want to go by myself."

"All right," Regina said, "I'll give you some money, then. How much do you need?"

Isabel breathed more deeply. "I don't know," she said. "Whatever you think." Regina didn't answer, and Isabel remained prone for several minutes before sitting up and saying, "Anna told me she wants to go to college at Ursuline in New Orleans."

Regina spoke impassively. "I know."

"Are you going to let her go?" prodded Isabel.

She squinted at the lace. "I don't know."

"That would cost a lot of money, wouldn't it?"

"I imagine so, Isabel," she said, testiness in her voice.

Isabel leaned forward. "Are you gonna sell more land? To pay for it?"

"We'll cross that bridge when we come to it, Isabel," she said with finality.

As LOUISA REVIVED, she and Regina fell into a comfortable routine. Their days began at seven-thirty when they met in the foyer and drove off to eight o'clock Mass in silence. They knelt side by side in the pew throughout the service and stayed behind for half an hour or so to say a rosary. On their way home, they stopped along the docks to pick up fish, selected a cut of meat from the butcher and stopped to purchase whatever freshest vegetables were being sold in Bienville Square. Back at home they changed their clothes and Regina joined Mr. Slay in the garden while Louisa went about some cleaning. "I would rather clean than cook," she had said at the beginning of her stay, "though I am something of an expert at making peppermint pull candy, if you've got a spare slab of marble." Their chores done, they lounged in the upstairs above the west wing, an attic that was once intended as a laboratory for her brother Louis. There they read and worked on the book review by the skylights. Afternoons they played cards in the parlor. They sat in the dining room after the midday meal sipping coffee and waiting for Isabel and Anna.

And through those first winter evenings the four ladies sat up in the radio room. Isabel and Anna made a show of doing their homework; Louisa thumbed through some volume or another—it might be a book on Alabama wildlife one day, a romance left by Aunt Naw the next, a history of Elizabethan England the next, advertisements for cleaning products the next; Regina read snatches of the paper aloud, which most of all just made them laugh. After washing up the supper dishes, Elmira, a bag of leftovers on her knee, joined them in front of the gas heater and chatted until she heard the streetcar bell. Then she ran down the driveway to catch it for home. Louisa, after she learned to drive, often drove her home. When she returned, it meant it was half past ten. Time for Isabel and Anna to head to bed and time for Regina or Louisa to put the coffee on—they alternated days—and turn the lights off and sip the black, boiling-hot coffee in silence but for the hiss of the gas heater. Then they retired to their rooms for prayer hour, which was from eleven to twelve.

Louisa took suggestions from Elmira and tackled a new chore every day until the house was spotless; then she began all over again from bottom to top. She swept out and mopped the dining room, swept the bedrooms, made the beds, Cloroxed the porcelain in the bathrooms, dusted furniture and ornaments, beat out the carpets and exacted the general "putting things where they belong," which she claimed was her talent. Everyone would ask her, chiming through the house, "Wheezie, have you seen my shawl?" "Yes, it's on the green rocker on the front porch." "Wheezie, have you seen my glasses?" "Yes, I saw them somewhere. Now, give me a minute; they're on the sink in the attic washroom." "Wheezie, have you seen my French book?" "Yes, it's either on the steps to the third floor or on top of the piano." She had that kind of visual memory for objects.

In spite of her modest demeanor and nearly complete silence, Louisa was capable of effecting quick changes in the house. While the sheets soaked, she single-handedly created new seating arrangements in almost all the rooms. Before long, all of Regina's brothers' things and Mother Riant's belongings were packed up and removed to the unsealed room off the third floor. Closets that had been cluttered were suddenly neat and bare. Rooms that no one ever slept in found themselves swept out, linen doilies on their dressers, bedspreads and throw pillows on their beds, flowers in vases on their nightstands, and chairs placed around coffee tables and under reading lamps to suggest conversation or repose. Louisa was constantly making gifts of material to Regina so that they might have new curtains in the library and in all the bedrooms. and new clothes. And she bagged up all the things she didn't like—knick-knacks, broken statues, worn-out bedspreads—and passed them on to Willie Slay and Elmira. Eventually, the house was ready for other guests.

Regina, in turn, concentrated on the garden and the food. With extra money from Louisa, she planted collard greens, potatoes, carrots and four different varieties of squash, including merliton, a Louisiana squash that didn't make it. She hired a man to repair the chicken coop and the barn and bought another milking cow and several chickens. She grew more relaxed about the use of sugar and butter and flour, and she continued with her reading, her reviews. Loving Louisa's presence, she became expansive. "There is no such thing as a bad book," she said one afternoon as she sat with Louisa in the attic, "and I believe I've read them all."

"I suppose not, as long as you don't have to finish it." They chuckled.

"No, you have to finish it to see how it's good. This one is annoying me no end, but that makes me want to finish it all the faster. I still hope it will have a turnaround."

"What is it?"

"*A Handful of Dust.*" Regina closed it and threw it on the floor. "I'm selling the orchard." Louisa looked up at her, startled. "Yes, my brothers need more money. I ignored their letters for so long that they finally telephoned. And that orchard. I've tried to make it fruitful, but it's just not. I'd have to hire twenty men."

"Why don't you?"

"No. It's better this way. It's like the book. When there's nothing left, they can't ask any more of me. The sooner it's all over with, the better."

"And you will take, what, a fifth of the money from the sale?"

"Mm," said Regina, "you know, I believe Isabel is falling for this fellow John."

"I did wonder," Louisa said, and closed the *Ladies' Home Journal* over her forefinger. "He's certainly handsome."

"Yes. He seems like a nice young man, nice family, handsome, a Catholic."

"Yes."

Regina hesitated. "But I don't think girls should get married so young. It didn't do me a bit of good."

"Nor I." They grimaced, each to her own. After a moment Louisa waxed on. "It's only in saying no—in the waiting—that a woman learns what powers she has."

Regina didn't like to hear such abstractions. "Yes, well," she said, "that brings its own trials I imagine. And Isabel isn't that kind of girl. I think she needs peace and the smallest amount of excitement."

"Perhaps she needs that now, but will she need that always?"

"It's too soon to tell," Regina said.

"It's so impossible to know whether you love someone or not, isn't it?" Louisa asked. "You almost have to force yourself to feel it. It doesn't come out of the blue as the romances would have us believe."

"At first it does."

"Yes, but that happens many times in one's life. And then you—ah, I can't explain it—you become somehow locked in before you know it, and love is something you serve for the rest of your life," Louisa mused.

Regina took up the thought. "That sounds terrible, yet that's what happens, and I was madly in love with the man I married."

"So was I," said Louisa. "But it didn't come out of the sky. It came from him, or he suggested it first, and it cropped up between us, and we decided to take it. But we never could study it well enough—I remember thinking that. It was ours but we couldn't compare it to anything. It was all we had. You can't turn away from it, though. There's nothing better than love, whatever kind."

"Yes, but then you're married." They laughed and fell silent.

# Honeymoon Bridge

AFTERNOONS STILL SITTING ON THE PORCH watching the sun cross one line, then another line: scissoring the water in the marble birdbath, slicing the bottom step, the tip of her boot, up her skirt, her neck cut with warmth. Louisa leaned her head back and closed her eyes. As the line moved onto her face she concentrated on the blanket of her closed eyelids, looked on while orange, red, yellow, brown, black spots carried on with their ceaselessly irregular dance, transposing themselves into a private theater, and the hair on her arms and on the back of her neck rose with the warmth that was suddenly chilly; the air around her stirred and she felt a turning in her stomach, a lightness at the source, a tightening of her anus. Beads of sweat formed on her upper lip; her mouth filled with saliva.

This threshold was familiar. She knew how to stop its coming on, open her eyes and stand up, clap her hands or make some other kind of noise, stomp her feet, move furniture, put her hands on her chest and take deep breaths. But then the headaches came. This time she let pass the chance to slip out from under the visions. The disks of sun tapped more frantically on her sockets, where the blood sought to copulate with the sun. Rivers of saliva spilled out of the corners of her mouth and down her chin, while a deep freeze took root at the base of her neck. The fire seeped from her hairline, spread and lit the skin of her forehead and temples and cheeks, and she thought her eyes would split from the pressure and then they did split, split to white.

Ladies, an endless line of them in hats, in traveling cloaks and sturdy boots, carrying suitcases and hatboxes and cosmetic cases, marched up the walkway, up the porch and into the house. Behind every fifth one was a rolling platform loaded with trunks, and after every sixth or seventh was a pause in the line long enough for the iron gate at the top of the walk to slam shut and be swung back, creaking, by the next lady. And as they climbed the front steps that used to be the back steps and proceeded through the front door, she saw their faces: skin crisscrossed with wrinkles, salt tracks through the powder on their cheeks, courageous smiles painted in red. She saw them, performers of the mourning rites for the entire land, as they flowed past valueless as water. The vast emptiness of their mysterious origin—nothing but a name—supplied pond after pond of pure grief, which they could pour on the lawn of the last house to which they were invited, to no fertile effect.

Louisa's body shook. A hot vise on her temples, a rain of flakes, a deep white blank, she came around all at once, shivering and clutching her head. Her skin was cold and damp and her hands felt, for a second, to be covered with slugs. She caught sight of Isabel and Anna coming up the walkway from school and went quickly inside to avoid them. She glared up at the portrait of Modesta as she passed the door to the library.

· · ·

SEVERAL YEARS HAD PASSED as they neared the end of a game of Honeymoon Bridge. Louisa nodded in the direction of a fictional west and said, "He would try to finesse the jack."

"Why?" Regina asked. "Dummy's got the nine, ten, ace. The queen's been played." The doorbell rang. They stopped talking, but neither moved. They heard Elmira opening the door and the sounds of someone approaching the library.

"It's her," Louisa said. They both glanced to Modesta, then to the door. "Hello ladies!" cooed a voice. The woman in the doorway was bent over, hands on her knees, peeking into the room from behind the doorframe. When she straightened up, Regina and Louisa flinched. She was the tallest woman either of them had ever seen, an effect that was accentuated by a pillow of red curls supporting a straw hat heavy with fruit, the balancing of which challenged her extremely long neck, and which she knocked against the doorframe as she advanced, making it even more lopsided. She wore a purple polka-dotted dress of an unfashionable length; long, skinny legs in white stockings protruded from it and called attention to heeled buckskin boots with fringe. "Which one of you is Regina?" she demanded.

"I am," said Regina on her feet, "and this is my cousin Louisa." Louisa also stood.

"Heavens," the woman said with a high-pitched titter, "two for the price of one." In one motion accompanied by the clash of the bangle bracelets that went up her arm, she grabbed each of their hands and kissed it. Then she threw herself on the couch next to Louisa, who edged away from her. "I'm Imogene," she breathed heavily, "Imogene Morgan. What are y'all playing? I'll have to teach you Bolivia. It's a new game I learned in Shreveport. There're a lot of rules, but you can just ignore most of them if you don't mind losing." Noticing the startled looks on their faces, her tone was suddenly solemn. "Weren't y'all expecting me?"

"Of course," said Regina quickly. "Won't you have some lemonade?"

"We were expecting you, but we don't know who you are," said Louisa. Regina shot her a curious look.

"I'd love some. Miss Regina, your cousin Beattie is a dear, dear friend of mine," she scolded. "She must have written to you five times of my coming, and I wrote another two times."

"That explains it," said Regina as she poured out three glasses of lemonade from the table in the corner. "We don't open our mail."

"Well, imagine that! I like that! I'm very opinionated when it comes to people, and I've learned to, as the psychiatrists say, trust my animal instinct. Not that I'm anything like an animal. You'll find me a very pleasant guest." Regina handed her a glass and Imogene drank thirstily.

"You're very welcome," said Regina after a sip. "How long do you intend to stay?"

Imogene was still drinking, and, tilting the glass up, she spilled some ice on her face, which she picked up from the carpet and tossed through the French doors and into a pot of geraniums on the porch. Then she rose and refilled. "As long as you'll have me. Well, let me explain myself. It's a sad little story, perfect accompaniment to the bitter little lemon." She sat back, cleared her throat and raised her chin. A glazed look came into her eyes as she clutched her lemonade.

"Wait!" Regina called from the doorway. "Let me get a piece of sewing," and she ran into the hallway. While she was gone Louisa reached under the couch for her basket of crocheting, and when

Regina returned they all settled back and Imogene began. "I grew up in New Orleans and have lived there my entire life, but I spent a summer here in Mobile when I was a girl of sixteen looking after my aged aunt E., who died the next winter, so I never had an excuse to return. Well, that summer I fell madly in love with a man named Frank de Valse. I'm sure you've heard the name?"

"I'm afraid not," said Regina.

Imogene's face fell. "Oh well. He worked at the paper mill—a manager of some kind he was, but rather unfortunate financially, though he had a generous heart." She sighed. "Not that the two were related. And he was bright and handsome, of course, though several years older than I, as you can imagine. I met him at the drugstore downtown—what's it called?"

"Antwerp's?" Louisa asked.

"Antwerp's, yes. In any case, he was eating a grilled cheese with pickles and coleslaw and I couldn't take my eyes off him, and he could tell. Later, when I knew more, I realized he must have been something of a womanizer. He had that sense, whatever it is, that knows just how far a woman will go, which in my case was far. And it came about that we met there for lunch every day. He had a car long before any of the young men in my set, and he took me for rides over the bay. . . ." She trailed off, maintaining in the silence such a breathless look that Regina and Louisa had time to form their own pictures of Frank de Valse. Regina's picture looked like Ahlong; Louisa's looked like a man named Reston Chevalier. The triple reverie was interrupted by Isabel and Anna, who came in and threw their bags on the floor.

"Girls, meet Imogene Morgan," Louisa said. "She's our new guest."

"Kiss me quickly, girls," said Imogene, "then take a seat and learn something from my tale of lost love." Presently they were seated, Anna on the arm of Isabel's chair, and all eyes returned to Imogene, who took another long drag of lemonade before beginning again.

"Naturally, all of our meetings were secret. I knew somehow that my family wouldn't approve, and he kept me from his acquaintances as well. We never talked about why—it was just so. We didn't have to talk about many things, yet we shared a complete understanding. Of course, that was one of the questions that plagued me later: if the understanding we enjoyed was based on the fact that we rarely spoke. I never could decide. . . ." Her head snapped back, and she smiled sadly at her listeners. "Needless to say, Aunt E. found out. I had been spotted with him at an oyster shack—imagine!—and it was then that I heard he had quite a reputation." She turned to Isabel and Anna—"Don't go to oyster shacks with strange men, girls; let that be lesson number one"—and then resumed her faraway look. "I never believed the things they said; all I believed in was our love. We were going to marry . . . we kissed as often as we could . . ." She paused again as a blush to match her hair crossed her face. "I loved him, I truly did."

All looked at their laps, afraid she might cry. Elmira, who had been listening from a chair near the doorway, finally whispered to Regina about the luggage, and it was decided in soft voices to put Imogene in the blue four-poster room. That done, Imogene flourished a handkerchief, sniffed violently and straightened her back. "So, let me finish my story! I'll make it quick so we can eat. It must be almost dinnertime. All right, well, after Aunt E.'s divulging of my affair—and I find it hard to believe she's in heaven today with such a heartless act as one of her last. No, I don't mean that. May she rest in peace, poor soul." She crossed herself rapidly. "As I say, she died the following November—but I was already gone, shipped back to

New Orleans at the beginning of August, and I never saw my true love again."

"How awful!" exclaimed Isabel.

Imogene looked at her with approval. "Exactly, my dear. Now it gets even more awful. I wrote to him—I managed his address, don't ask me how, we never got to say good-bye—swearing my heart to him, but I never heard a word. A girlfriend of mine said he must have moved, but I never believed it. He loved Mobile and his mother was here; he knew all these lovely spots. . . . I always felt that if I could get back here, destiny would throw us in each other's path and we would be reunited. Now, why didn't I return sooner? Well, I was young and foolish and didn't realize the value of what we'd had. Everyone said he wasn't good enough for me, even my friends, and I listened to them—or a part of me listened, though I never once stopped thinking all these years of my dear Mr. de Valse. Amazing, no? Twenty years?"

Suddenly she squealed with laughter, and covered her mouth with her hand as she shook. The hat, now entirely detached from one side of her head, edged dangerously toward a fall. They all stared at her with serious faces tinged with fear. She recovered. "And I had—everyone kept telling me how young I was"—she wiped the tears of laughter from the corner of her eyes—"what I had, which is the worst thing to have, girls—a sense of my own youth. I thought time would deliver me a sign in the way of a better man or of Mr. de Valse coming after me. Of course, I had no basis for judgment except the first stirring of love in my own heart. Those first stirrings are never matched, though I didn't know that at the time.

"Oh la, look at this one turning red!" she shrieked, and pointed at Isabel. Everyone glanced at Isabel and quickly away. Imogene covered her mouth again and giggled. "Oh forgive me, child, I didn't mean to embarrass you." She sighed loudly and recommenced: "So beaus and suitors and what have you came and went in the parlor of my parents' house on Prytania—as did the years. There was a Gilbert I was rather fond of at one time. . . . He made me laugh, but he was shorter than I was, and, well, I can't stand that. Of course, whenever it came to marriage, I thought about it being for life, and my Mr. de Valse would pass through my heart, and my feelings would curdle for whichever man it happened to be. Not that there were so many, mind you, but enough. There were enough."

She looked around and took several deep breaths. Then she spoke low and sober. "Lord, you all are sophisticated women, I can see that, and you don't want to hear the prattle of a lovesick old lady, but I'm almost finished so bear with me." She took another sip of lemonade. They all took sips of lemonade. Louisa looked up at Modesta and recocked her ear in Imogene's direction. She continued: "Well, it's often that you don't realize where you stand in the midst of life. It's hard to read one's own book. Look at me—I have no illusions as I say about my beauty, though I try to cultivate a certain fashionable flair, and I'm a great believer in lipstick. Look at me!" she yelled. They all turned. "I'm an old woman! I don't know how it happened!" She laughed. "I've had a ball on my own chosen course, understand me, and I'm thrilled to meet you ladies, and I hope it's not over by any means—it's life I'm speaking about—but I'm here on a mission, as I said. I know I talk too much, and y'all should just tell me to quiet if I go on too long."

"Oh no!" said Regina.

"All right, I intend to find Mr. de Valse, or at least discover what happened to him, or at least visit some of our old spots and conjure up some of the old sentiment—why do I call it sentiment? I mean *love*."

For the first time, Imogene lowered her defiant eyes to her lap, where she twisted her handkerchief around her ring finger. Regina and Louisa continued to sew. Anna and Isabel stayed focused on her, waiting for her to continue. Suddenly she burst out laughing, throwing her head back with a hilarity that made them all smile. "That's the end," she said. "Beattie Lamont, your fine cousin and a dear friend, said you were the ladies to see."

"Well," Regina said, recrossing her legs and smiling at her daughters.

"You know everyone in town, no?"

"I used to, but I'm not in society so much since . . ."

"Hard times," Imogene finished. "I know, honey."

"It's these girls who are out every night of the week," said Louisa.

"Oh, splendid! He loved to listen to music. Y'all must know some good jazz clubs."

"I don't think so," said Regina.

"Of course we do," said Anna.

Elmira stepped in. "Supper."

THE NEXT MORNING Imogene appeared at nine o'clock sharp in a becoming if uniquely bright shade of blue. Her head was wrapped in a turquoise turban, a style they had all seen in the magazines but never in person. Coffee and beignets were served in the parlor. The cool morning air of late April stirred through the French doors. Regina and Louisa had the peaceful attitude of people just returning from Mass and spoke little, while Isabel and Anna stole glances at the turban between sips of coffee and tried not to look at each other, for fear of laughing. But Imogene was oblivious. There was an overflowing bouquet of irises on the table, which she stared into as she chewed. She looked tired. "Explain to me the streetcar line," she said suddenly, though it was clear that her mind wandered during the explanation. Once she murmured, "What an idea! After twenty years!" but she wore a small smile on her face and went out of her way to thank Elmira for breakfast, saying, "I'll need the fortification." Then she rushed out.

"It's very romantic," said Isabel as they heard the front door close.

"I hope she finds him," said Anna.

Regina and Louisa said nothing. "I'm getting married to John," said Isabel. "You may as well know it, Mother." All looked at Isabel, their mouths hanging open.

Regina went cold. "What?"

Anna turned to her sister. "I told you not to tell her like this."

Louisa jumped to her feet and gestured to Anna. "Come on, dear, let's go see to the . . . something." They filed out, closing the door behind them.

Regina and Isabel were silent for several minutes. "I think you should wait," said Regina finally. Another several minutes of silence followed.

"My father killed himself, didn't he," said Isabel, brutal and quiet, her eyes on the coffee table.

"What?" But Regina had heard; they both knew she had heard. "It was an accident," she said. Isabel said nothing. "It was an accident, Isabel."

Isabel raised her head. "I know," she said, "and life is full of such accidents. And if my marrying John is one of them, then I'll know it eventually and I'll live with it, same as you lived with Father."

"I think you should wait," said Regina. The impetuous look in her daughter's eyes frightened her. "You are very young. It's hard to know what one wants in a man when one is so young, at the same time that your heart is crazy for love. It's a dangerous combination, darling. I worry for you."

Isabel scowled. "Wheezie told me all that yesterday. Why won't you just support me?"

"I do."

She shook her head, sadly. "Mother, I love John and I'm determined to marry him. I want to get out of this house of old women."

Regina drew back. "I see that well enough," she said, "and I'm sure you will have your way if you want it. But pure actions are the ones that aren't taken in reaction to something."

Isabel flicked her eyes to the chandelier. "God help me and save me from these women," she murmured.

"Be careful, Isabel," Regina shot back. "You're hurting my feelings and demonstrating your immaturity at the same time. I don't want these words to be ringing in our heads later on." She paused. "I try not to say things that will ring later on."

"All right, Mother," Isabel said wearily.

"Wait two months," Regina said. Isabel's frown deepened. "Wait two months, and we won't talk about it. You just keep the silence in yourself, pray, and think about it thoroughly. Then, whatever you decide, I'll support."

"All right, Mama," she said flatly.

"Don't imagine that I'm either for or against it," Regina went on. "Wheezie either. We just love you and want the best for you. You shouldn't do anything rash."

Isabel stood up and yawned. "All right, Mother," she said. With mouth turned down she left the room.

For the rest of the day, all kept to separate corners of the house, but when Imogene didn't return for dinner and didn't return for supper, Isabel and Anna were called up and sent looking for her. They found her at Antwerp's soda counter. Apparently she had been there since morning waiting for a sign of Frank de Valse. The girls brought her home, where Louisa insisted she have a plate of beef burgundy and a glass of sherry, ran a bath for her and put her to bed. She was up early the next day, however, and borrowed Regina's car to drive through neighborhoods to look for the car that matched her memory of Mr. de Valse's.

Over the next several weeks she prowled the neighborhoods. The color of his car alternated between sky blue and brick red in her memory, but that was the least of her difficulties. She parked and asked children and nurses if they had ever heard of him but had no luck. She grew bolder—knocking on front doors and poking around in backyards—until a policeman escorted her home with a warning. She was now barred from six out of the ten neighborhoods in Mobile, and though she threatened to ignore it and proclaimed herself "unstoppable," to the others it was obvious that her methods had to change.

Regina and Louisa consulted, decided that Isabel and Anna would accompany her on a search of jazz clubs, a task at which the girls persevered, though Imogene wasn't any fun. After scanning those present, she would sit at a table, her body rigid, eyes glued to the door. Isabel and Anna prevailed upon many a man to ask her to dance, but she didn't like to turn her back to the door for more than a minute and would abandon her partner midsong and return to her seat. She was not deterred by the absence of anyone her age or by a circular hole in the wall near her chair, which the neighboring table told them had been caused by a bullet the night before. The optimism of the girls sustained this pattern, night after night, for much longer than necessary. But even they ran out of gentleman friends to accompany them, grew exhausted from all the dancing, and when they appeared at breakfast with purple streaks under their eyes for the tenth day in a row, Regina put a stop to it.

By this time Imogene doubted the picture she had in her mind of Frank de Valse, and with her doubt the picture changed and changed again, sometimes adopting the features of Buster Keaton, her onetime beau Gilbert, Huey Long, or some blend of the three. She tried to imagine how his face would look after the twenty years but was not equal to it, and in fact didn't want to imagine it. With even more vigor she set out again, alone in the car, this time in search of the oyster shack, but as she scoured the docks on the fourth evening, she had her pocketbook stolen and returned to the house weeping. It took Regina and Louisa several hours to convince her to abandon this particular quest, which she finally agreed to do, though she had failed to sight a building that even resembled the fateful oyster shack.

Imogene spent the second half of May between the library and the courthouse, combing old newspapers, passenger and crew lists of the pleasure boats, log records of the shipping companies, lists of births, deaths, marriages and real estate sales—none had so much as a mention of the name de Valse. She would return home frazzled, sticky with a long day's worth of dried sweat, and drink off a few straight bourbons without talking, then retire. She had grown pale. Though she had more coats of red on her lips than ever, the clothes she wore were not clean. She had discontinued her reports to them on her daily activities, yet she borrowed the car almost every day without asking. Regina and Louisa didn't know what to do; Isabel and Anna, who suspected that Imogene was insane, began to avoid her. "Maybe you should take a break from the libraries," Louisa suggested tenderly one evening.

"I already have," snapped Imogene. Straightening to her full height, she walked stiffly from the room. None could guess where Imogene's search had taken her, but by then the heat had gotten to all of their heads. No behavior seemed out of the ordinary. That was the season, hotter and hotter, the season of blueberries, plums, thunderstorms, storm drains overflowing with the smell of swamp, shutters closed against the sun.

School was out and Isabel and Anna spent their days practicing their dance steps in the radio room with all the windows open, an electric fan blowing their skirts. At night they sat on the roofs of carriage houses with their men friends and drank from a sterling flask of shine, looking at the moon. Regina and Louisa switched to sprig muslin, took two cold baths a day and sat on the porch off the parlor, slapping mosquitoes. It was too hot to cook, and Elmira did all her boiling in the early morning. The rest of the day she stood in the open doorway of the kitchen, pursued a breeze and kept watch over the glaring yard and the ministrations of Willie Slay. When the thunderstorms started, they all gathered under the portrait of Modesta to read aloud from the book Regina was reviewing that week. Followed by a cold supper. Then Isabel, Anna and Imogene bathed and got dressed for the evening. They were rarely home by midnight, when Regina and Louisa switched off the radio and went to their rooms to pray. No matter what time they got to bed, all the women spent the nights in their underwear, tossing and turning in the thick air, wet washcloths on their foreheads. On the subject of John all were silent.

Imogene alone welcomed the heat as a chance to further prove her resolve. She went to all the barbershops, haberdasheries, and shoe stores in town, even the ones for Negroes, asking if any had an account in the name of de Valse. She went to the managers of the paper mill, the cotton mill and the shipyard to ask after him and could tell that they felt sorry for her, that the other workers stared at her, but she didn't care. No de Valse. She interrogated the newspapermen and visited old Mr. Antwerp on his deathbed. No de Valse. At last she sat on a bench in the noon glare of Bienville

Square and stared at all the sixty-year-old men she saw pass. Sometimes she even trailed them for as long as necessary to get a good look at their faces under their hats.

On the Friday before the Fourth of July, there were more men than usual in Bienville Square. They poured out of their offices early and stood in little groups smoking, talking about economic recovery and watching the decorations for the weekend's festivities go up. Imogene was in an ecstasy of possibility—surely he would be here, where all the men of Mobile were gathered. Overwhelmed, she could not take in so many men at once and became jittery on the bench. "Calm down, Imogene," she whispered to herself, "or you'll blow your chance." She forced her breath steady, then rose and bought a Coca-Cola. At once she spotted him on a ladder, attaching a string of flags to a light post. She approached slowly. He descended the ladder and looked up at his work. A small group of workmen stood near him at the base of the ladder. "Mr. de Valse?"

He whipped around. She straightened her hat, straightened her back and peered into his face. "Mr. de Valse?" He raised an eyebrow and looked behind him at the circle of men, none of whom was paying attention.

"I'm Imogene Morgan," she said.

"Pleased to meet you." Rather than take her hand, he turned to his friends, this time with a smirk that caught their attention. The chatter died down and they looked on curiously. She seized his sleeve. "Please don't smile! I'm Miss Imogene Morgan."

With a jerk of his arm he released her grasp. "Good for you." Again he turned to his friends, inciting a general chuckle in the group as he pointed to his head, indicating that she was crazy.

Her face flushed with heat but she forced herself to continue. "Don't you remember me?" He eyed her with a studied blankness, the cruelty of which infuriated her. She heaved, swung back and brought the palm of her hand toward his cheek, but he caught her wrist and held it, with a nod of his head calling over a policeman who had witnessed the entire scene. "I'm Miss Imogene Morgan," she said again, weakly, happy that he held her wrist, but he kept his eyes turned to the approaching officer.

"What's the problem, Frank?"

"I think the heat must have gotten to this lady," said Frank, "and she's forgotten who she is." She gasped just as he released her wrist, and lost her balance, toppling forward onto the officer.

"I see," she whispered from her slumped position over the crook of the officer's arm, her neck angled up so that she could see his face, her mouth gaping open as her eyes filled with hate. "I see. I see."

"Let's get you home, ma'am," said the officer.

"Don't touch me another instant," she said, and wheeled backward, disturbing a gathering of chickens near the tree. She turned, straightening her back, and ran a hand through her hair. Then she walked unsteadily out of the square. "You fell into my arms, lady!" the officer called after her amid general laughter, but she didn't turn around. Imagining Frank de Valse's eyes boring into the back of her head as she went, she forgot that she had driven and ignored the streetcar that paused to let her on. It thundered dimly as she began the long walk up Dauphin Street to the house.

Regina and Louisa sat in the library with all the lights off and the French doors open, timing the pickup of breezes and listening to the thunder. Their ears were tuned simultaneously to the front door, through which Isabel and Imogene were expected by turns. Anna had gone to bed early with a book and a slight cold, and only the pale face of Modesta was visible against her darkish surroundings. East dealt, and Regina began the bidding. "Pass."

"Two clubs."

"Double."

"Three clubs."

"Pass." They played silently until the rain intensified enough that it was spraying Regina's face. She rose and closed the half of the French door that was closest to her head. Through the pane she caught sight of Willie Slay hobbling as fast as he could toward the back porch. She watched from the window until he was out of sight.

Louisa lifted her head from the score sheet and said in response to their earlier discussion, "I agree that she's too young to be married. And that she doesn't know him well enough."

Regina hesitated before leaving the window to sit back down and sigh. "I don't know what to do but pray over it."

"I am praying over it, too, dear. I pray for them both." They fell back into silence. "It's gotten so dark!" exclaimed Louisa. "I feel as though we should make coffee, or turn the light on, but I don't feel like either."

"Neither do I." Regina paused. "I can't forbid her, you know." Nearby lightning double-illuminated the room. "Maybe if her father were alive . . ." A clap of thunder followed, then a series of lower rumblings, several minutes of nothing but rain.

Louisa adjusted her pillows. "Let's send Anna to college before she, too, gets swept into something."

Regina sighed again. "I don't see how I could possibly afford it."

Louisa didn't miss a beat. "I'd like to pay for it."

"Well, we'll talk about it later," Regina said, pursing her lips in consternation, standing up again with her hands on her hips and taking a few restless paces toward the window. "It's gotten so dark!" she said as she closed the rest of the French doors. She walked toward the center of the room. "I just wish"—but the end of her sentence was cut by the sound of the front door slamming shut, so that she had to repeat it—"we could send Isabel, too."

Heavy footsteps approached the library, and Imogene appeared in the doorway, hunched, every article of her clothing drenched. Rain dripped from every end of every hair on her head, from the tips of her fingers and lobes of her ears, running from the brim of her hat into her eyes. She ambled forward like an ape and sank to the floor. Regina rushed to her side; Louisa turned on a lamp. "What's wrong, Imogene, honey?" they asked.

She chose her words carefully. "When I began this search," she whispered, her head slackened to the side, "I still had a bit of dignity, just a bit. Now I am desperate, and I'm sure it's an unpleasant sight to witness. I pity you poor souls for having to put up with me."

They looked at each other at a loss for what to say. "Nonsense, Imogene!" managed Regina.

Louisa said, "I'll make some hot tea," and headed out the door, "and get you some dry clothes."

"If I give up, then this chance at love is over for my entire life," moaned Imogene, again and again, while Regina stroked her head until Louisa returned with a bottle of bourbon and dry clothes, which Louisa helped Imogene into while Regina put a light shawl around her shoulders. Louisa turned off the fan. They sat her in a comfortable chair in front of the window, moved chairs to each side of her and held a glass of bourbon up to her lips. She sipped quietly, her face exhausted, drained of all color, while tears ran continuously from her lifeless eyes.

"There are many different kinds of love," Louisa said quietly, but Imogene just stared at the rain on the black pane.

"Love is everywhere," offered Regina. "Maybe you just need to widen your gaze." Imogene held out her glass in silence, her dead look still on the window, and Regina filled it.

"To be alive is to have a broken heart," said Louisa after several minutes.

Imogene sobbed anew. "I want to live here with y'all!"

"You are," said Regina.

"You can," said Louisa.

Imogene took a deep breath and blew her nose. Again she held out her glass for a refill. "I don't know what happened," she said from a throat thickened by crying. "He lied to me, or he vanished, or maybe . . . he never existed." She yawned widely. "Maybe it was all a dream," she choked.

"A good dream," said Louisa.

"Maybe," said Imogene after a long silence.

"I'll have some of that," said Regina. Louisa nodded, and two more glasses were poured. They sipped for many minutes in silence. The rain slackened. "I'm about to die from the stuffiness in here," said Imogene. The fan was turned on. Louisa moved and opened the French doors. Then she put on the "Dance of the Seven Veils" from *Salome*. "You were going to teach us Bolivia," said Regina, "but you've been off chasing some ne'er-do-well since you came here. It's rather rude of you."

Imogene smiled thinly, but she was not one to stay down for long. By the time Isabel returned, they had forgotten they were waiting for her. They listened to *Salome* three times before unplugging the phonograph in favor of the lamp. They refilled their glasses and endeavored to learn Bolivia four or five times. They decided to turn the house into a boardinghouse for penniless relatives and had even made the beginnings of a guest list on the piece of paper they had been using to keep score. Louisa kept repeating the phrase "a business out of charity." Regina turned over the fact that they would have to start opening their mail, while Imogene assigned herself household duties with elaborate names like "Mistress of Galleries, Linens and Coffee" or "Madame Accommodation, Chief of Registry, History and Style." They were getting into the rules, terms and conditions when Isabel was suddenly in their midst, saying, "What's going on in here?" All three looked up at her.

"It's darling Isabel!" cried Imogene.

"It's been two months, Mother," she said with set face. "I've made my decision."

# Land of Marys

*NOTES FOR "ANYONE GOT A MATCH?"* Nick Anderson's sparsely written murder mystery, set in Marseilles at the beginning of the Spanish Civil War, criticizes high-brow Americans against the backdrop of four interwoven intrigues, all of which are hinged on a set of fingerprints left on the wrapper of a Cuban cigar. In a brilliant tour de force, striking just as the perpetrator is uncovered, the diligent reader gleans Anderson's thematic parallel: between so many Americans who treat Europe as a department store for culture and the indelible fingerprints. Lacking the pretensions of the Northeasterners here detailed, the Southerner will enjoy mocking the learned American along with Anderson . . . The sparsely written dialogue . . . Considering the economic straits of this country, one wonders if the impetus behind this book isn't a little outdated . . . We Southerners have no use for Europe, particularly Spain . . . The oft-repeated

phrase "Anyone got a match?" contributes a sublevel
refrain, beginning to strike terror in the hearts of the
reader and creating a metasymbolic patterning . . .

She wanted to say something about the suspense and was getting ready to cross out all the bits about Southerners when Isabel burst into the library and placed a picture of a wedding dress on top of her book-review notes. "Can you make it for me, Mother? In off-white lace?"

Regina handed the magazine over to Louisa and Imogene, who gasped, "Oh, it's gorgeous!" and passed it to Mary Lambert, who, clutching her cross, murmured, "So elegant . . ." and handed it to Tonadel Fry, who said, "Simply beautiful," and handed it to Merced Dumaine, who put her hand over her heart and said, "Ah!" and passed it back to Regina, who said simply, "I can make it."

"Can you really, Regina? Just from the picture?" Tonadel asked. Regina nodded.

Isabel took back the picture; she couldn't stand still. "Where's Anna?"

"Really, Regina, in the next three weeks?"

"I saw her reading on the back porch about an hour ago," one of the ladies said to Isabel as she dashed through the door.

"She certainly does seem happy," said Merced, turning over the queen of clubs. "Damn!"

Louisa watched Regina for a reaction, but Regina's placid smile revealed nothing to her guests. The chairs and couches under Modesta were now filled with eager listeners. "I think I can finish it in time," Regina said, "but I also have to write this book review and I haven't finished the book. If someone wants to read aloud to me, it will all go that much faster."

The ladies were delighted. "Of course," they chimed.

"Go order the material," Merced urged, sweeping up the volume, "and then we'll start." A few minutes later all were settled with their teacups. Isabel stood on the small ottoman so that Regina could measure her. Merced began to read.

WORD HAD SPREAD QUICKLY of the house on Dauphin Street, and the apartments were filled with middle-aged ladies, spinsters and widows who would not remarry. Traveling around in pairs, not more related to one another than third or fourth cousins, many times removed, these "aunts" were ubiquitous, moving through the limitless necks of their distant families, staying at each place for weeks, months, years. In some cases they were wasted, washed with tears, their faces smashed in, pained wrinkles covered with foundation. In others they were lively women who felt free in their poverty, felt fortunate to be liberated from the predictability of wife- and motherhood. In addition, living off charity restored their faith in God and made them, in turn, kind and loving women.

It was with this second type of Southern women that Regina, Louisa and Imogene endeavored to fill the house. Tonadel was the daughter of Captain Fry, the Cuban martyr, and Regina was proud to have her, as the Colonel had so admired her father. Merced Dumaine was Louisa's third cousin on her father's side, and the two had been close in childhood. The bishop at the cathedral had sent Mary Lambert to them when she'd shown up at his office and asked if he knew some nice ladies who ran a boardinghouse. Imogene had stayed on with the excuse that she couldn't leave before the wedding. And there were countless others who had come through— Belinda Lee, Prudence Dufosset, Miss Joan Román, Theresa de Lorenzo. Regina, Louisa and Imogene had to convert the parlor and part of its hallway, the west wing, the third floor and two rooms on the second floor into five separate apartments to accommodate them.

None of the ladies could pay even the most modest fees. Regina sold two acres on the east side to support them all, while the ladies tried to remunerate in ways other than money. Imogene saw to the menu and shopping. Among her specialties were hot stuffed okra, kidneys in brandy, the Jesuit bird (turkey), Helen's Tomato Mess, tripe eggs in mint sauce, tuna gougère, rum balls and apple ice cream. Meanwhile, Mary Lambert had joined Willie Slay in flower cultivation, and the two successfully lined the front walk with baby white gardenia trees and red rosebushes, which alternated in a candy-cane fashion. Merced took on the cleaning with Louisa, and Tonadel handled the enormous task of laundry.

No one was idle. Other visitors, passing through, filled various roles that suited their fancies. For instance, Belinda Lee took over houseplants, guest registration and pets. Prudence Dufosset organized a bridge tournament, Miss Román served as librarian and correspondent and Theresa de Lorenzo arranged their social calendar and planned outings.

As frugally as they lived, the house could not be made self-sufficient. Though the garden thrived, food was a large expense. Fish, meat, fruit and spices all came from outside the house. Then there was water, electricity and gas—the bills of which had increased dramatically with the extra guests—not to mention the mortgage payment, Anna's tuition and gasoline for the car that, no matter how many rules they made up, was always in use by one lady or another.

The money from the two acres would run out any day, but for the first time Regina wasn't worried in the slightest. She was happy, and happiness breeds faith. Something would work out. She communicated the financial predicament to the ladies and they enjoyed a good laugh over it. Merced said perhaps her uncle Julian would die in the knick of time. Imogene put her stock in Anna marrying a rich man. Prudence joked that a Hollywood talent scout would discover her and she would become rich playing grandmother roles. Belinda dreamed up the idea of launching an advertising campaign that would garner subscriptions to a fraudulent men's resort. No one quite understood her scheme but it didn't matter. Something would come through.

They were right. At the end of May, Regina learned that oil had been found on Charles's old land at Choctaw Bluff. She didn't understand what this meant until a lawyer from the drilling company explained it to her: though the land had been sold, Charles had retained the mineral rights. Regina would receive a regular check that would be more than enough to keep them afloat.

The windfall didn't change the ladies' routine, though they did rest easier and turned their attentive hearts to plans for Isabel's wedding, which they could now make more extravagant. Regina still tended to her vegetable garden, but most of her time was spent on the wedding dress. The date was set: June 1, 1938.

The upcoming event scared Regina and she sewed clumsily. After nicking the fabric when adjusting the darts to the bodice, she had to order another two yards of material. Then she set to work on the skirt but had to redo the casing in the middle of the garment to control fullness. Before beginning work on the tunic again, she set herself to some of the by-hand tasks: hemming the skirt, adding inner hooks and clasps to the back. Regina felt strongly that Isabel shouldn't go through with the wedding and even sensed her daughter's hesitation, but she knew enough not to push her in one direction or another. Other times she caught Isabel looking beautiful and was hopeful. John did make her happy.

As the wedding approached, Isabel and Anna went out more than ordinarily, so much that all the ladies mildly disapproved. Merced and Tonadel commented on how they ought to stay home and help their mother sew that dress instead of frolicking around. "You all have a social calendar as busy as the queen of England," commented Louisa. "And," she said, "if y'all continue to clack about in your heels, you're likely to vanish—taken up by the spirits into an endless party. My mother used to tell me about such spirits," she remarked. She raised her eyes to the portrait and continued. "The girl too in love with her own youth and freedom gets taken up by the spirits of carnival and has to dance and look pretty in an uncomfortable dress and pinching heels and smile at gentlemen she doesn't like who never get serious. For all eternity. One day she just disappears, leaving nothing but the scent of champagne in the air. All that's left of her is a faint trace of her perfume."

"That doesn't sound like such a bad place," laughed Anna. "Who wants the men to get serious?"

"John is serious," Isabel stated.

"Actually"—Louisa bowed to Anna—"that's the worst of it, and that they never change. It's the same handsome young men for all eternity—long enough to make you thoroughly sick of them, I would guess." Anna had moved to the window, parted the curtain and waved to the car outside. "And of course the agony of the shoes," Louisa went on.

"But do the women get to change their dresses?" Anna wondered.

"Oh constantly! Too constantly, though. It's almost a new, beautiful dress in the latest style every second, but they all come to look the same. The styles begin to repeat themselves, but you can't wear anything twice—not even jewelry or pocketbooks, and there's few things more exhausting in this life than chasing the latest fashions."

A horn sounded from outside. "Don't men ring doorbells these days?"

"It's only John," said Isabel sourly.

"And who's the other gentleman?"

Anna smiled sheepishly. "No need to be such a goose, Wheezie. You've already met them many times. Of course, we love that you're a goose, but to pile it on just now, when we're late . . ."

"Come on and kiss us," said Imogene, who had been silent.

"This isn't the prom," said Isabel as she doled out her kisses. Then, to Anna, "Let's go."

SHE WAITED UNTIL THE RECEPTION had properly ended and Isabel and John had driven off before she walked out on the back lawn that was now the front lawn in search of Willie Slay. Dusk had just come down and shapes were hard to make out, but she found him trimming dead sections off a bed of amaryllis. She gave him a glass of champagne; they moved along and sat down in the two iron chairs by the stone swimming pool and he drank it off in the ever-darkening light. "Thank you for all your help with the reception," she said over the crickets.

"You're welcome, Miss Regina. You're such a nice person."

"You are, too, Mr. Slay."

After a minute she got up, told Mr. Slay good night and returned to the house. The other ladies had gone to bed, but she was able to join Louisa, Imogene and Anna in the dining room. Louisa and Anna had taken their shoes off and lounged on each side of the pale pink couch, gulping cold ginger ale. Imogene slumped in a green leather armchair, which she had moved away from the table. Regina sat down near them, in a spot near the head. The table was still cluttered with glasses. She sipped on the glass of someone she didn't know and slipped off her shoes.

"Let's all have a cigarette," Anna said. Taking one for herself, she gave the pack to her mother. Regina and Imogene put one in their lips. "Come on, Wheezie!" Anna cajoled, "Mother's having one." Louisa acquiesced, and the cigarettes were lit. Anna and Imogene puffed away happily, but Regina and Louisa tended to neglect theirs in the ashtray.

"I was kind of embarrassed at Merced's bawling during the entire ceremony," Regina said suddenly.

"Yes, it was pitiful," giggled Louisa.

"I know," said Anna, exhaling.

Imogene turned to her. "Darling, are you going to be terribly lonely without your sister?"

"I'll be all right," she said. "It's not as if she's going to be far!"

"That's true," said Regina.

Louisa struck up after a time, "What are you reading these days, Anna?"

"Balzac," she said without enthusiasm as she put out her cigarette. "I'd better get to bed." She kissed all three women on the cheek and headed out. In the doorway she turned. "It all went off very well, don't you think, Mother?" she asked.

"Yes," said Regina. "Good night, dear."

Regina put her feet up on the chair opposite hers and reached for a different glass. Louisa rose and took one herself, then curled her feet under her on the couch, drinking timidly. Imogene rolled down her stockings. Regina unhooked the onyx beads that had been weighing on her neck and put them on the table. "I don't know, the wedding made me think of Charles so strongly. The day we got married. How good he was." She shook her head. "I miss him, I suppose," she said, then shrugged off her abstraction. "It's not that

I don't love it here with you all. In fact, I feel I'm finally doing what God wants me to do. . . ."

"I've never felt that in my life!" burst out Imogene, bolting her champagne and standing up. "I'm going to start praying to you!" Regina and Louisa laughed heartily. "I'm sorry, but I'm too happy for serious talk. Good night, ladies," Imogene said as she kissed them on the tops of their heads. Then she exited, and Regina and Louisa were left in the dining room among the remains of the party—spills, ghosts, glasses, ashes.

"I keep thinking about the oil money from Choctaw Bluff," Regina began. "I don't want it. If Charles had to die in order to pay me back in this strange way from the afterlife . . . well, it wasn't worth it."

Louisa knew Charles only from the few comments Regina had made over the years. "Regina," she said firmly, "he didn't die for money, you know that, but he was obviously thinking of you before he died."

"I guess I don't understand why he died," Regina said.

"He died. That's it," said Louisa. "There are a lot of reasons why."

Just then Regina couldn't think of a single one. "Like what?" she asked.

Louisa took her time responding. "Well, he was too sensitive for this world, as you've said. He was closer to God than any of us, probably."

"I want to be with him," Regina said.

"Well, you'll die sure enough and be with him then. There's no reason to rush it."

"I know," she said. "I can't believe I'm behaving like this." She felt for the placement of her hair, looked toward the ceiling. "It's one little thing that sends me ten years back in grief."

"It's not little, honey. Oil money is a lot."

"It is?"

Louisa nodded knowingly. They sipped their champagne. Louisa stretched her legs out on the couch in front of her.

"All in all, it went pretty well, right?" asked Regina in a voice that revealed her exhaustive thinking on the topic.

"I think so," Louisa answered with assertion. "Isabel looked beautiful. And so did John, for that matter. The two of them are going to have beautiful children. You should be proud, Regina."

"I know."

"What's wrong, then?"

"Are we just repeating ourselves?"

"As long as time moves forward, things are bound to change," Louisa said.

"Maybe we should just burn it all down," Regina said flatly. Louisa looked up at her friend to see if she were serious. She was. "Anyone got a match?" Regina asked, and reached for the pack of cigarettes.

Louisa tossed her the matchbook. Regina struck a match and dropped it to the floor. It caught a section from the newspaper and a dinner napkin that had been left under the table. They hastened to stomp it out, then roared with laughter. Louisa clutched her stomach in glee as Regina struck a match once again, again dropped it to the floor. This time the fire caught the other half of the napkin, more of the newspaper and Regina's notes for her book review. Both women stared at it growing. Regina lit a cigarette off it and Louisa followed suit, though she singed her eyelashes on the small conflagration. They stomped it out again, their eyes smiling. "It's eleven o'clock," Louisa said. They gathered their shawls. Regina went around the table with the candlesnuffer, and Louisa followed behind her to trim the wicks. Saying not a word more, they went upstairs for prayer hour.

## Acknowledgments

THE AUTHOR WOULD LIKE TO THANK the many family members and friends who helped, one way or another, in the preparation of the manuscript, especially Adelaide Trigg, Eleanor Benz, Regina Scully, Peter Lupini, Sarah Brockett, Calliope, Francis Scully, Jill Samuels, Kathleen Amshoff, Ariel Boles, Angela Trigg, Denise Bonis, Andrea Young, Eleanor Trigg and Frank and Mary Scully. Thanks also to Mark Souther, C. D. Wright, Jane Unrue and John Biguenet. Very special thanks to Jim Rutman and Meredith Blum. Without their support and vision this book would not have been possible.

*About the Author*

HELEN SCULLY was born in Norfolk, Virginia, in 1977 and gradu-
ated from Brown University. She worked in publishing in New
York City before moving to Barcelona in 2001, where she wrote
columns for the magazine *Barcelona Metropolitan*. She now lives in
New Orleans, Louisiana.